Forbidden Desires

DANI COLLINS
LINDSAY ARMSTRONG
MARION LENNOX

First Published in Great Britain 2017
By Mills & Boon, an imprint of HarperCollins*Publishers*
1 London Bridge Street, London, SE1 9GF

FORBIDDEN DESIRES © 2017 Harlequin Books S. A.

A Debt Paid in Passion, *An Exception to His Rule* and *Waves of Temptation* were first published in Great Britain by Harlequin (UK) Limited.

A Debt Paid in Passion © 2014 Dani Collins
An Exception to His Rule © 2014 Lindsay Armstrong
Waves of Temptation © 2014 Marion Lennox

ISBN: 978-0-26392-981-2

05-0917

Our policy is to use papers that are natural, renewable and recyclable products and made from wood grown in sustainable forests.The logging and manufacturing processes conform to the legal environmental regulations of the country of origin.

Printed and bound in Spain
by CPI, Barcelona

A DEBT PAID
IN PASSION

BY
DANI COLLINS

Dani Collins discovered romance novels in high school and immediately wondered how a person trained and qualified for *that* amazing job. She married her high school sweetheart, which was a start, then spent two decades trying to find her fit in the wide world of romance writing, always coming back to Mills & Boon.

Two children later, and with the first entering high school, she placed in Harlequin's *Instant Seduction* contest. It was the beginning of a fabulous journey towards finally getting that dream job.

When she's not in her Fortress of Literature, as her family calls her writing office, she works, chauffeurs children to extra-curricular activities and gardens with more optimism than skill. Dani can be reached through her website at www.danicollins.com.

Generous readers, you're my Valentines.

Thank you for making all those hours in my
stuffy attic writing room worth it.

CHAPTER ONE

LOOK AT ME, Raoul Zesiger willed Sirena Abbott.

He had to lean back in his chair to see her past the three men between them. He should have been looking at the judge, but he couldn't take his eyes off Sirena.

She sat very still, face forward, her profile somber. Her absurdly long gypsy lashes had stayed downswept as his lawyer had risen to speak. She didn't even flick a glance in his direction when her own lawyer stood to plead that jail time was counterproductive, since she needed to work to pay back the stolen funds.

Raoul's lawyers had warned him this wouldn't result in incarceration, but Raoul had pressed hard for it. He would see this treacherously innocent-looking woman, with her mouth pouted in grave tension and her thick brunette locks pulled into a deceptively respectful knot, go to jail for betraying him. For stealing.

His stepfather had been a thief. He had never expected to be taken advantage of again, especially by his reliable PA, a woman he'd come to trust to be there, always. But she had dipped her fingers into his personal account.

Then she had tried to manipulate him into going easy by *being* easy.

He didn't want the flash of memory to strike. His ears were waiting for the judge to state that this would progress to a sentence, but his body prickled with heat as he

recalled the feel of those plump lips softening under his.
Her breasts, a lush handful, had smelled of summer. Her
nipples were sun-warmed berries against his tongue, suc-
culent and sweet. The heart-shaped backside he'd watched
too often as it retreated from his office had been both taut
and smooth as he had lifted her skirt and peeled lace down.
Thighs like powdered sugar, an enticing musky perfume
between that pulled him to hard attention as he remembered how tight—almost virginal—she'd been. But so hot
and welcoming.

Because she'd known her criminal act was about to
come to light.

His gut clenched in a mixture of fury and unparalleled
carnal hunger. For two years he'd managed to keep his
desire contained, but now that he'd had her, all he could
think about was having her again. He hated her for having such power over him. He could swear under oath that
he'd never hurt a woman, but he wanted to crush Sirena
Abbott. Eradicate her. Destroy her.

The clap of a gavel snapped him back to the courtroom.
It was empty save for the five of them behind two tables,
both facing the judge. His lawyer gave Raoul a resigned
tilt of his head and Raoul realized with sick disgust that
the decision had gone in Sirena's favor.

At the other table, partly obscured by her lawyer, Sirena's spine softened in relief. Her wide eyes lifted to the
heavens, shining with gratitude. Her lawyer thanked the
judge and set a hand under Sirena's elbow to help her rise,
leaning in to say something to her.

Raoul felt a clench of possessiveness as he watched
the solicitous middle-aged lawyer hover over her. He told
himself it was anger, nothing else. He loathed being a vic-
tim again. She shouldn't get away with a repayment plan
of six hundred pounds a month. That wasn't reparation.
That was a joke.

Why wouldn't she look at him? It was the least she could do: look him in the eye and acknowledge they both knew she was getting away with a crime. But she murmured something to her lawyer and left the man packing his briefcase as she circled to the aisle. Her sexy curves were downplayed by her sleek jacket and pencil skirt, but she was still alluring as hell. Her step slowed as she came to the gate into the gallery.

Look at me, Raoul silently commanded again, holding his breath as she hesitated, sensing she was about to swing her gaze to his.

Her lips drained of color and her hand trembled as she reached out, trying to find the gate. She stared straight ahead, eyes blinking and blinking—

"She's fainting!" He shoved past his two lawyers and toppled chairs to reach her even as her own lawyer turned and reacted. They caught her together.

Raoul hated the man anew for touching her as they both eased her to the floor. She was dead weight. He had to catch her head as it lolled. She hadn't been this insubstantial the last time he'd held her. She hadn't been *fragile.*

Raoul barked for first aid.

Someone appeared with oxygen in blessedly short time. He let himself be pushed back a half step, but he couldn't take his eyes off the way Sirena's cheeks had gone hollow, her skin gray. Everything in him, breath, blood, thought, ground to a halt as he waited for a new verdict: that she would be okay.

It was his father all over again. The lack of response, the wild panic rising in him as he fought against helplessness and brutal reality. Was she breathing? She couldn't be dead. *Open your eyes, Sirena.*

Distantly he heard the attendant asking after precxisting conditions and Raoul racked his brain. She wasn't diabetic, had never taken medication that he'd seen. He reached for the phone he'd turned off while court was in session, intent on accessing her personnel file, when he heard her lawyer answer in a low murmur.

"She's pregnant."

The words burst like shattered glass in his ears.

Sirena became aware of something pressed to her face. Clammy sweat coated her skin and a swirl of her ever-present nausea turned mercilessly inside her.

She lifted a heavy hand to dislodge whatever was smothering her and a voice said, "You fainted, Sirena. Take it easy for a minute."

Opening her eyes, she saw John, the highly recommended lawyer who'd been perfunctory until she'd almost vomited in his wastebasket. She'd told him the father's identity was irrelevant, but Raoul was glaring from beyond John's shoulder with all the relevance of an unforgiving sun on a lost soul in the desert—and he appeared about as sympathetic.

She had tried hard not to look at Raoul, former boss, brief lover, unsuspecting father. He was too…everything. Tall, dark, unabashedly urbane and sophisticated. Severe. Judgmental.

But of their own accord, her hungry eyes took in his appearance—her first opportunity to do so in weeks. She cataloged his razor-sharp charcoal suit, the solid black tie. His jaw was freshly shaved for his morning appointment, his dark hair recently cut into the sternly simple style of a successful businessman.

And there were his eyes, the gray irises stormy and full of condemnation as they snared hers in an unbreakable stare.

John asked, "Is there any pain? We've called an ambulance."

Sirena flashed a terrified glance back at Raoul. It was

a mistake. She realized immediately that he'd read it for what it was: an admission of guilt. A betrayal of truth.

Clenching her perfidious eyes closed, she willed him not to pick up on what had been revealed, but he was the most acutely intelligent person she'd ever met. He missed nothing.

If he knew she was carrying his baby, there'd be another fight. Considering what this current contest had taken out of her, she wasn't ready for another. She wouldn't, *couldn't*, let him think he had a right to custody of her child.

"Sirena," Raoul said in that dark chocolate voice of his.

Her skin rippled in a pleasurable shiver of recognition. Two years of hearing every intonation in that voice left her with the knowledge that her name on his lips right now was an implacable warning.

"Look at me," he commanded.

Sirena reached blindly for John's hand, clenching her icy fingers on his warm, dry ones. Beneath the oxygen mask, her voice was hollow and whisper thin.

"Tell him to leave me alone or I'll take out a restraining order."

CHAPTER TWO

THE FIRST VOLLEY of the second war was waiting when she got home from the hospital. More tests had been scheduled, but for the moment her doctor was putting her faint down to stress and low blood sugar resulting from her unrelenting nausea.

Sirena thought nothing could be more stressful than facing prison while dealing with an unplanned pregnancy, but Raoul knew no bounds when it came to psychological torture. She read the email John had forwarded:

My client has every reason to believe your client carries his baby. He insists on full involvement in the care through pregnancy and will take sole custody at birth.

Her blood congealed, even though this was no surprise. Raoul was possessive. She'd learned *that*. This reaction was fully expected, but having anyone try to take this baby from her was unthinkable.

Blinking the sting of desperation from her eyes, she typed, It's not his, saying aloud, "And tell him to go to hell."

She didn't let herself dwell on the fact that Raoul wanted his baby. It would make her weaken toward a man she needed to believe was a monster—even though she'd spent two years falling into deep infatuation with not just a dynamic tycoon, but a man who was a caring son and protective older stepbrother. In some ways he was her mirror image, she'd often thought fancifully. They'd both lost a parent and both wanted the best for their younger siblings. She had come to believe him to be an admirable person with a dry wit and standards that put her learned habits of perfectionism to shame.

No, she reminded herself as she prepared a slice of toast she would force herself to eat. He was a cruel, angry, small person who felt nothing. For her, at least. He'd proven it when he'd made passionate love to her one day, then had her arrested the next.

A black hole of despair threatened to open beneath her feet, but she was safe now. That part was over. She'd made a horrible mistake and the judge had accepted her remorse, even if Raoul hadn't. She had no idea how she would come up with six hundred pounds a month, but that was a minor worry against convincing Raoul the baby wasn't his.

There was no way she could live with having another loved one wrenched from her life. The fear of her baby growing up without its mother, the way she had, had given her the strength to fight tooth and nail against Raoul's determination to put her in jail. Somehow she would rally the strength to oust him from her life for good.

Which left her feeling incredibly bereft, but she ignored it.

Taking tea, toast and a tablet for nausea to the sofa, she scanned her laptop to see if any transcription jobs had come in. The legal bills were appalling and being fired three months ago had decimated her very modest savings.

If only she could take back that one awful moment when she had thought, *Raoul will understand.* She rubbed her brow where it crinkled in lament. Borrowing from him had seemed the most simple and obvious thing to do when her sister had been in tears, saying, *I guess I'm not meant to be a teacher.* Their father was expecting payment from a big customer any day. Ali had struggled so hard to get her marks up and be accepted into the specialized program. The tuition was due, but the cash was not in hand.

I can cover it, Sirena had assured her, confident the balance would move out and come back into Raoul's account on the same statement. He probably wouldn't even notice, let alone care. He paid *her* to worry about little details like that.

Then her father's customer had gone insolvent.

Not overnight, of course. It started with a delay of a few more days. A week. Sirena had begun chasing it herself, right up to the monthly cutoff date, not wanting to mention her self-approved loan to her boss until she had the funds to repay it.

The money hadn't appeared and the opportunity to explain hadn't arisen, not before other events.

And since she didn't want to involve her father when his livelihood was nose-diving, she had shouldered the fallout herself, keeping her motives from Raoul and not revealing to her family what she'd done or that she was facing jail time for it.

This had been the most crushingly lonely and frightening time of her life.

A muted beep announced an incoming email. From Raoul. Her heart leaped in misplaced anticipation. It was one word.

Liar.

He wasn't buying that the baby wasn't his.

Gritting her teeth against an ache that crushed her chest, she added Raoul to her email block list and sent a missive to John.

Tell him that contacting me directly is out of line. If the
baby was his, I would sue for support. I would have asked
for leniency when he was trying to put me in jail. This baby
is not his and he must LEAVE ME ALONE.

Hitting send was like poking herself in the throat. She
drew a pained breath, fighting the sense of loss. But life
hit you with sudden changes and you had to roll with them.
She had learned that when her mother had died, and again
when her stepmother had whisked her father and half sister
to Australia with brutal speed as soon as Sirena graduated
and enrolled in business school.

People *left,* was what she'd learned. They disappeared
from your life whether you wanted them to or not. Sometimes they even fired you and tried to lock you away in
prison so they'd never have to see you again.

Making a disgusted noise at herself for indulging in
what amounted to emotional self-harm, she turned her
thoughts to the little being who wouldn't leave her. With
a gentle hand on her unsettled abdomen, she focused on
the one person she'd do everything in her power to keep
in her life forever. She didn't intend to smother the poor
thing, just be his or her mother. She couldn't countenance
anyone taking that role from her. And Raoul would try.
He was that angry and ruthless.

She shivered as she recalled seeing that side of him for
the first time, after making bail. The only thing that had
gotten her through the humiliating process of being arrested, fingerprinted and charged was the certainty that
Raoul didn't know what was happening to her. Some ac-
countant had done this. A bank official. They didn't understand that Raoul might be gruff on the outside, but she was
his best PA ever. His right hand. They'd become intimate.
He would be furious that she was being treated this way.

She had believed with all her heart that as soon as she told him what had happened, he'd make it right.

He hadn't. He'd made her wait in the rain at the gate of his mansion outside London, eventually striding out with hard-hearted purpose, his severe expression chilly with distaste as he surveyed her.

"I've been trying to reach you," Sirena had said through the rungs of the security gate, frightened by how unreachable he seemed. "I was arrested today."

"I know," Raoul replied without a shred of concern. "I filed the complaint."

Her shock and stunned anguish must have been obvious, but his mouth had barely twitched in reaction. Cruel dislike had been the only emotion in his scathing expression. Sirena's stepmother had been small and critical, but she hadn't outright hated Sirena. In that second, she realized Raoul reviled her, and that was more painful than anything.

Guilt and remorse had made her want to shrivel up and die, but she couldn't—wouldn't—believe she'd ruined her career and her budding relationship with the man of her dreams over one tiny misstep.

"But…" Everything she wanted to say backed up in her throat. They'd developed friendship, reliance and respect over two years of working together and just yesterday they'd taken that relationship to a new level. He'd been tender and teasing and…

God, she had believed he'd been *loving.*

"But what?" he challenged. "You thought sleeping with me would make a difference to how I'd react when I found out you had stolen from me? I was bored. You were there. That's all yesterday was. You ought to know better than to think it would make me go easy on someone who was cheating me. Get a lawyer. You need one."

Swallowing the rock that her crust of toast had become,

Sirena pushed the betrayal firmly away. Raoul was in her past and somehow she had to make a future for herself and her baby. She turned her attention to putting out more feelers for work.

But over the next several weeks, the attacks from Raoul kept coming. Settlement offers that increased in size. Demands for paternity tests. Time limits.

Pacing John's office, she bit back a rebuke at him for revealing her pregnancy that day in the courtroom. She hadn't admitted to anyone that Raoul was the father and she was determined she never would.

"Here's what I would like to know, John. How am I supposed to pay more legal bills I can't afford when it's not even my wish to be talking to you about this?"

"Your wish may be coming true, Sirena. He's stated clearly that this is his final offer and you're to accept it by Monday or forever go empty-handed."

She stopped and stilled. Loss again. Like watching the final sands drifting through the neck of an hourglass, unable to stop them. Pain in her lip made her aware she was biting it to keep from crying out in protest. Rubbing her brow with a shaking hand, Sirena told herself it was what she wanted: Raoul gone from her life.

"Look, Sirena, I've told you several times this isn't my area of expertise. So far that hasn't mattered because you've refused to admit the baby is his—"

"It's not," she interjected, keeping her back to him. She wasn't a great liar and didn't like doing it, but she justified it because this baby was *hers*. Full stop.

"He obviously thinks it's possible. You and he must have been involved."

"Involvement comes in different levels, doesn't it?" she snapped, then closed her mouth, fearful she was saying too much.

"So you're punishing him for bringing less to the relationship than you did?"

"His mistresses spend more on an evening gown and he tried to send me to prison for it!" she swung around to blurt. "What kind of relationship is that?"

"You're punishing him for his legal action, then? Or not buying you a dress?"

"I'm not punishing him," Sirena muttered, turning back to the window overlooking a wet day in Hyde Park.

"No, you're punishing your child by keeping its father out of the picture—whether that father is Raoul Zesiger or some other nameless man you've failed to bring forward. I'm a father, so even though I don't practice family law, I know the best interests of the child are not served by denying a parent access just because you're angry with him. Do you have reason to believe he'd be an unfit parent?"

Completely the opposite, she silently admitted as a tendril of longing curled around her heart. She had seen how Raoul's stepsister adored him and how he indulged the young woman with doting affection while setting firm boundaries. Raoul would be a supportive, protective, exceptional father.

Her brows flinched and her throat tightened. She *was* angry with him. And secretly terrified that her child would ultimately pick its father over its mother, but that didn't justify keeping the baby from knowing both its parents.

"Have you thought about your child's future?" John prodded. "There are certain entitlements, like a good education, inheritances…"

She had to get this baby delivered first. That's where her focus had really been these last several weeks.

Sirena's fists tightened under her elbows as she hunched herself into a comfortless hug. Her mother had died trying to give birth to the baby who would have been Sirena's little brother. Sirena's blood pressure was under constant monitoring. Between that and the lawyer meetings, she was barely working, barely making the bills. The stress was making the test results all the more concerning.

She tried not to think of all the bad things that could happen, but for the first time she let herself consider what her child would need if she couldn't provide it. Her father and sister were all the way in Australia. It would be days before they could get here—if her stepmother let either of them come at all. Right now Faye was taking the high ground, sniffing with disapproval over Sirena's unplanned, unwed pregnancy. No one would be as emotionally invested as the baby's father...

"Sirena, I'm not trying to—"

"Be my conscience?" she interjected. He was still acting as one. "I have a specialist appointment on Monday. I don't know how long it will take. Tell him I will give his offer my full attention after that and will be in touch by the end of next week."

John's demeanor shifted. "So he is the father."

"That will be determined by the paternity test once the baby is born, won't it?" Sirena retorted, scrambling to hold onto as many cards as she could because she was running out of them, fast.

Raoul's mind had been going around in circles for weeks, driving him mad. If Sirena was pregnant with his child, she would have used that to keep him from trying to incarcerate her. Since she hadn't, it must not be his. But she could have used her condition for leniency during the proceedings and hadn't. Which meant she wanted to keep the pregnancy from him. Which led him to believe the baby was his.

Most troubling, if he wasn't the father, who was?

Raoul sent baleful glances around his various offices as he traveled his circuit of major cities, aware there were a

plethora of men in his numerous office towers with whom
Sirena, with her voluptuous body and warm smile, could
easily have hooked up.

The thought grated with deep repugnance. He'd never
heard the merest whisper of promiscuity about his PA, but
she'd obviously led a secretive life. It wasn't as if she'd
been a virgin when he'd made love to her.

She'd been the next thing to it, though, with her shy
hesitancy that had turned to startled pleasure.

Biting back a groan, he tried not to think of that afternoon in a house he'd toured as a potential real estate
investment. Every day he fought the recollection of their
passionate encounter and every night she revisited him, her
silky hair whispering against his skin, her soft giggle of
self-consciousness turning to a gasp of awe as she stroked
him. The hum of surrender in her throat as he found the
center of her pleasure nearly had him losing it in his sleep.

Every morning he reminded himself he'd used a con-
dom.

One that had been in his wallet so long he couldn't remember when or for whom he'd placed it there. He'd only
been grateful to find it when a downpour had turned Sirena from the open front door into his arms. A stumbling
bump of her pivoting into him, a gentlemanly attempt to
keep her on her feet, a collision of soft curves against a
body already charged with sexual hunger.

When she'd looked up at him with wonder as her abdomen took the impression of his erection, when she'd parted
her lips and looked at his mouth as though she'd been waiting her whole life to feel it cover her own...

Swearing, Raoul rose to pace his Paris office. It was as
far as he was willing to get from London after trying to
settle with Sirena once and for all. The remembered vision
of her passion-glazed eyes became overlaid with a more

recent one: when her lawyer had mentioned her pregnancy and she had shot that petrified look at Raoul.

The baby was his. He knew it in his gut and if he'd been ruthless with her for stealing money, she had no idea the lengths he'd go for his child.

Doubt niggled, though. If the baby was his, and she was the type to embezzle, then try to sleep her way out of it, why wasn't she trying to squeeze a settlement out of him?

None of it added up and he was losing his mind trying to make sense of it. If she'd only *talk* to him. They used to communicate with incredible fluidity, finishing each other's sentences, filling in gaps with a look…

Lies, he reminded himself. All an act to trick him into trusting her, and it had worked. That's what grated so badly. He'd failed to see that she was unreliable, despite his history with shameless charlatans.

And how the hell had he turned into his father? Was it genetic that he should wind up sexually infatuated with his secretary? He'd successfully ignored such attractions for years. His father had killed himself over an interoffice affair, so he'd made it a personal rule to avoid such things at all costs. It was a matter of basic survival.

His surge of interest in Sirena had been intense right from the beginning, though. He'd hired her in spite of it, partly because he'd been sure he was a stronger man than his father. Maybe he'd even been trying to prove it.

It galled him that he'd fallen into a tryst despite his better intentions. But he might have come to terms with that failing if she hadn't betrayed him. Suddenly he'd been not just his father, but his mother, naively watching the bank account drain while being fed sweet, reassuring words to excuse it.

I was going to pay it back before you found out.

He tried to close out the echo of Sirena's clear voice, claiming exactly what any dupe would expect to hear once she realized her caught hands were covered in red. That he'd seen her as steadfast until that moment left him questioning his own judgment, which was a huge kick to his confidence. People relied on him all over the world. His weakness for her made him feel as though he was misrepresenting himself, and more than anything he hated being let down. It galled him. Mere repayment wasn't good enough to compensate for that. People like her needed to be taught a lesson.

Staring at his desktop full of work, he cursed the concentration he'd lost because of all this, the time wasted on legal meetings that could have been spent on work.

And the worst loss of production was because he was trying to replace the best PA he'd ever had!

Seemingly the best. His only comfort was that he hadn't given her the executive title he'd been considering. The damage she could have done in a position like that was beyond thinking. She was doing enough harm to his bottom line no longer employed by him at all.

It couldn't go on. He'd finally, reluctantly, sent her a strongly worded ultimatum and his palms were sweating that she would reject this one, too. She knew him well enough to believe that when he said final, he meant final, but he'd never had anything so valuable as his flesh and blood on the table. If she refused again...

She wouldn't. Sirena Abbott was more avaricious than he'd given her credit for, but she was innately practical. She would recognize he'd hit his limit and would cash in.

As if to prove it, his email blipped with a message from his lawyer.

Sirena Abbott had an appointment on Monday and wanted the rest of the week to think things through.

Raoul leaned on hands that curled into tight fists. His inner being swelled with triumph. Silly woman. When he said Monday, he meant *Monday*.

* * *

As Sirena entered the alcove that housed the front of her building, she was still preoccupied by the lecture from the obstetrician about taking time to relax. She needed to read up on side effects of the medication he'd prescribed, too.

Distracted, she didn't notice anyone until a lean, masculine body stepped out of the shadows. Her pulse leaped in excited recognition even as she jerked in alarm.

Her keys dropped with a clatter. Pressing herself into the glass door, she pulled her collar tighter to her throat. His familiar scent overwhelmed her, spicy and masculine beneath a layer of rain. The late-afternoon gloom threw forbidding shadows into the angles of his features and turned his short, spiky lashes into sharp blades above turbulent eyes. He was compelling as ever and she was as susceptible as always.

"Hello, Sirena."

That voice.

"What are you doing here?" Her knuckles dug into her neck where her pulse raced with dangerous speed. She was supposed to be avoiding this sort of elevation of her heart rate, but Raoul had always done this to her. Thank God she'd spent two years perfecting how to hide her girlish flushes of awareness and awestruck admiration. With a tilt of her chin she conveyed that he didn't intimidate her—even though she was in danger of cracking the glass at her back, she was pressed so hard against it.

"You didn't really think I'd wait until Friday," he said, uncompromising and flinty.

"I didn't think you'd be waiting at my door," she protested, adding with admirable civility, "I'll review the documents tomorrow, I promise."

Raoul shook his head in condescension. "Today, Sirena."

"It's been a long day, Raoul. Don't make it longer." Her

voice was weighted with more tiredness than she meant to reveal.

His eyes narrowed. "What sort of appointment did you have? Doctor?"

A little shiver of premonition went through her. Something told her not to let him see how unsettling the news had been, but the reality of all those tests and personal history forms had taken a toll. If she had thought she could avoid signing a shared custody agreement with Raoul, today she'd learned it was imperative she do so.

"Is the baby all right?" Raoul demanded gruffly. The edgy concern in his tone affected her, making her soften and stiffen at the same time.

"The baby is fine," she said firmly. If the mother could keep herself healthy enough to deliver—and ensure there was at least one parent left to rear it—the baby was in a great position for a long and happy life.

"You?" he questioned with sharp acuity. Damned man never missed a thing.

"I'm tired," she prevaricated. "And I have to use the loo. It's only five o'clock. That gives me seven hours. Come back at eleven fifty-nine."

Raoul's jaw hardened. "No." Leaning down, brushing entirely too close to her legs, he picked up her keys and straightened. "No more games, no more lawyers. You and I are hammering this out. Now."

Sirena tried to take her keys, but Raoul only closed his hand over them, leaving her fingers brushing the hard strength of his knuckles.

The contact sent an electric zing through her nervous system, leaving her entire body quivering over what was a ridiculously innocuous touch.

She'd been too stressed and nauseous to have sexual feelings these last months, but suddenly every vessel in her body came alive to the presence of *this* man, the avenging god who had never had any genuine respect for her in the first place.

Tamping down on the rush of hurt and disappointment that welled in her chest, Sirena found her spine, standing up to him as well as a woman in flats could to a man who was head and shoulders taller than she was.

"Let's get something clear," she said, voice trembling a bit. She hoped he put it down to anger, not weak, stupid longing for something that had never existed. "Whatever agreement we come to is contingent on paternity tests proving you're the father."

Raoul rocked back on his heels. His negotiation face slid into place over his shock. In the shadowed alcove, Sirena wasn't sure if his pupils really contracted to pinpoints, but she felt his gaze like a lance that held her in place. It made her nervous, but she was proud of herself for taking him aback. She couldn't afford to be a pushover.

"Who else is in the running?" he gritted out.

"I have a life beyond your exalted presence." The lies went up like umbrellas, but she had so few advantages.

He stood unflinching and austere, but there was something in his bearing that made her heart pang. She knew he was the father, but by keeping him guessing she was performing a type of torture on him, keeping him in a state of anxious inability to act. It was cruel and made her feel ashamed.

Don't be a wimp, Sirena. He could take care of himself. The only thing she needed to worry about was her baby.

"Let's get this done," she said.

CHAPTER THREE

RAOUL HAD NEVER been in Sirena's flat. When he entered he was surprised to immediately feel as though he was returning to a place both familiar and comfortable. It was so *her*.

She was a tidy person with simple taste, but her innate sensuality came through in textures and easy blends of color. The open-plan lounge-kitchen was tiny, but everything had a place, houseplants were lush and well tended. Family snapshots smiled from walls and shelves. He had time while she was in the powder room to take in the miniscule bedroom kept as scrupulously neat as the rest, the bed notably a single.

Sirena cast him a harried glance as she emerged and shrugged from her coat, draping it over the back of a dining chair.

Her figure, voluptuous as ever, had a new curve that made him draw in a searing breath. Until this moment, *pregnant* had been a word bandied through hostile emails and legal paperwork. As he cataloged the snug fit of leggings and a stretchy top over a body that hadn't filled out much except in the one place, he felt his scalp tighten.

Sirena was carrying a baby.

Her pale, slender hand opened over the small bump. Too small? He had no idea about these things.

Yanking his gaze to her face, he saw defensive wariness

and something else, something incredibly vulnerable that triggered his deepest protective instincts.

Thankfully she glanced away, thick hair falling across her cheek to hide her expression. Raoul regrouped, reminding himself not to let her get to him, but he couldn't take his eyes off that firm swelling. He'd spent two years fighting the urge to touch this woman, had given in to a moment of weakness once, and it took all his self-discipline not to reach for her now. His hands itched to start at that mysterious bump then explore the rest of her luscious shape. He shoved his fists into his overcoat pockets and glared with resentment.

"I'm having ice water and an orange. Do you want coffee?" she asked.

"Nothing," he bit out. No more foot dragging. He was still reeling from her coy remark about paternity, played out so well he was entertaining a shred of uncertainty. He couldn't begin to consider what he'd do if he wasn't the father.

The not knowing made him restless, especially because he couldn't understand why she was tormenting him. Yes, his position would be strengthened if she admitted he was the father, but so would hers. He would do anything for his child. One glimpse of a pregnant belly shouldn't affect him this deeply, but all he could think was that his entire life had changed. Every decision from now on would be weighed against its effect on that tiny being in Sirena's center.

She took her frosted glass and plate of sectioned orange to the table, opening a file as she sat down. One glance invited him to take the chair across from her. They didn't stand on ceremony. He didn't hold her chair; this wasn't a date. It was reminiscent of the times they'd planted themselves on either side of a boardroom table and worked through projects and tasks until he'd cleared his plate and loaded hers full, confident it would all be completed to his exacting specifications.

He tightened his mouth against a blurted demand for answers. *Why?* If she had needed money, why hadn't she asked him for a loan? A raise? The salary he'd been paying her was generous, but he'd seen she was ready for more responsibility and the compensation that went with it. Had *this* been her plan all along? Pregnancy and a custody settlement?

The thought occurred as she opened the file and he glimpsed a copy of a contract filled with notations and scribbles.

"You *have* read it," he said with tight disgust.

"I do my homework, same as you," she retorted, ice clinking as she sipped. Her skin, fine grained as a baby's, was pale. Weren't pregnant women supposed to glow? Sirena didn't look unhealthy, but there were shadows under her eyes and in them. She touched her brow where she used to complain of tension headaches. He could see the pulse in her throat pounding as if her heart would explode.

The precariousness of his position struck him. He wanted to be ruthless, but not only was he facing a woman in a weakened condition, her condition affected a baby. As he absorbed the raised stakes, his tension increased. The scent of the fresh orange seemed overly strong and pungent.

"I want medical reports," he said with more harsh demand than he would typically use at the opening of a negotiation.

Sirena flinched and laced her fingers together. Without looking at him, she said, "I don't have a problem sharing the baby's health checkups. So far it's been textbook. I have a scan on my laptop I can email you once we've signed off." Now her eyes came up, but her gaze was veiled. She was hiding something.

"Who are you?" he muttered. "You're not the Sirena I knew." His PA had been approachable and cheerful, quick to smile, quick to see the humor in things. This woman was locked down, serious and more secretive than he'd ever imagined.

Like him, which was a disturbing thought.

"What makes you think you ever knew me, Raoul?" The elegant arches of her dark brows lifted while bitter amusement twisted her doll-perfect lips. "Did you ever ask about my life? My plans? My likes or dislikes? All I remember is demands that revolved around your needs. Your intention to work late. Your bad mood because you hadn't eaten. You once snapped your fingers at me because you wanted the name of the woman you'd taken to dinner, maybe even bed, the night before. She needed flowers as a kiss-off. On that note, as your former PA I'm compelled to point out that your new one dropped the ball. I didn't get my lilies."

Her audacity tested Raoul's already dicey mood. His inner compass swung from contempt to self-disgust that he'd slept with her at all to a guilty acknowledgment that no, he hadn't spent much time getting to know her on a personal level. He'd wanted too badly to take things to an intimate level, so he'd kept her at a distance.

Not that he had any intention of explaining when she was coming out swinging with two full buckets of scathing judgment and brutal sarcasm.

"That ice water seems to have gone directly into your veins," he remarked with the smoothness of a panther batting a bird from the air.

"Yes, I'm a kettle and so much blacker than you." She pivoted the file and pushed it toward him. "You might as well read my notes and we'll go from there."

Cold. Distant. Unreachable. She wasn't saying those words, but he'd heard them from enough women to know that's what she was implying.

Oddly, he hadn't thought Sirena saw him that way, and it bothered him that she did. Which made no sense, because he hadn't cared much when those other women said it and he hadn't once put Sirena in the same category as his former lovers. She was never intended to be his lover at all. When he took women to his bed, it was without any sort of expectation beyond an affair that would allow him to release sexual tension. Sirena had already been too integral a part of his working life to blur those lines.

Yet he had. And she seemed to be holding him to account for his callous treatment of her—when she had only slept with him for her own gain! Possibly for the very baby they were fighting over.

Drawing the papers closer, he began taking in her notations. The first was a refusal to submit to paternity tests until after the birth, at which point this contract would come into effect if he was proven to be the father.

He didn't like it, but in the interest of moving forward he initialed it.

Things quickly became more confusing and audacious. Distantly he noted that she'd circled a formatting error— one more eagle-eyed skill he regretted losing from his business life.

"Why the hell is everything to be held in trust for the baby?"

"I don't want your money," she said with such flatness he almost believed her.

Don't get sidetracked, he warned himself. Obviously she had wanted his money or she wouldn't have stolen from him, but arguing that point was moot. Right now all that mattered was getting paternity resolved and his right to involvement irrevocable.

He lowered his gaze to the pages in front of him, trying to make sense of her changes when they all favored the baby's financial future and left her taking nothing from him. Raoul cut her a suspicious glance. No one gave up this much…

"Ah," he snorted with understanding as he came to the codicil. *"No."*

"Think about it. You can't breast-feed. It makes sense that I have full custody."

"For *five* years? Nice try. Five days, maybe."

"Five days," she repeated through her teeth, flashing an angry emotion he'd never seen in her. Her eyes glazed with a level of hatred that pierced through his shell with unexpected toxicity, leaving a fiery sting.

And was that fear? Her generous mouth trembled before she pressed it into a firm line. "If you're not going to be reasonable, leave now. You're not the father anyway."

She rose and so did he, catching her by the arms as she tried to skirt past him. The little swell at her belly nudged into him, foreign and disconcerting, making his hands tighten with a possessive desire to keep her close. Keep *it* close, he corrected silently.

"Don't touch me." Fine trembles cascaded through her so he felt it as if he grasped an electric wire that pulsed in warning.

"Sure you don't want to try persuading me into clemency again?" he prodded, recognizing that deep down he was still weakly enthralled by her. If she offered herself right now, he would be receptive. It would change things.

"I didn't sue you for sexual harassment before, but I had every right to."

Her words slapped him. Hard.

Dropping his hold, he reared back, offended to his core. "You wanted me every bit as much as I wanted you," he seethed. His memories exploded daily with the way her expression had shone with excitement. The way she'd molded herself into him and arched for more contact and cried out with joy as the shudders of culmination racked them both.

"No, you were *bored*," she shot back with vicious fury that carried a ring of hurt.

It shouldn't singe him with guilt, but it did. He'd been saving face when he'd said that, full of whiskey and brimming with betrayal. The news that she had been released had been roiling in him like poison. Having her show up at the end of his drive had nearly undone him.

Now he teetered between a dangerous admission of attraction and delivering his brutal set-down for a second time.

"Get out, Raoul," Sirena said with a pained lack of heat. She sounded defeated. Heartbroken. "I'm sorry I ever met you."

The retort that the feeling was mutual hovered on his tongue, but stayed locked behind teeth clenched against a surprising lash of…hell, why would he suffer regret?

Pinching the bridge of his nose, he reminded himself the woman he'd thought he'd known had never existed. He threw himself back into his chair. "We'll hire a panel of experts to work out the schedule of the baby's first five years based on his or her personal needs. At four years we'll begin negotiating the school years."

"A panel of experts," she repeated on a choking laugh. "Yes, I've got your deep pockets. Let's do that."

"If you're worried about money, why are you refusing a settlement?"

Her response was quiet and somber, disturbingly sincere. "Because I don't want money. I want my baby." She moved to the window. It was covered in drizzle that the wind had tossed against the glass. Her hand rested on her belly. Her profile was grave.

Raoul dragged his eyes off her, disturbed by how much her earnest simplicity wrenched his gut. It made him twitch with the impulse to reassure her, and not just verbally. For some reason, he wanted to hold her so badly his whole body ached.

That wasn't like him. He had his moments of being a softy when it came to his mother or stepsister. They were beloved and very much his responsibility even though they weren't as helpless these days as they'd once been. He still flinched with guilt when he remembered how he'd been living it up his first year of college, drinking and chasing girls, completely oblivious to what was happening at home. Then, despite how brutal and thoughtless his stepfather's gambling had been, the man's death had shattered the hearts of two people he cared for deeply. Faced with abject poverty, it had been easy for Raoul to feel nothing but animosity toward the dead man, but the unmitigated grief his mother and Miranda had suffered had been very real. He'd hated seeing them in pain. It had been sharply reminiscent of his agony after his father's suicide.

But as supportive as he'd tried to be while he took control and recovered their finances, he'd never been the touchy-feely sort who hugged and cuddled away their pain.

Why he craved to offer Sirena that sort of comfort boggled him.

Forcing himself to ignore the desire, he scanned the changes she'd made to the agreement, thinking that perhaps he was more self-involved than he'd realized since he had been focused this entire time on what the child meant to him, how his life would change, how he'd make room for it and provide for *his* progeny. What *he* wanted.

Suddenly he was seeing and hearing what Sirena wanted and it wasn't to hurt him. She had ample ways to do that, but her changes to this document were more about keeping the baby with her than keeping it from him.

"Did you think about termination at all?" he asked with sudden curiosity.

"Yes."

The word struck him like a bullet, utterly unexpected and so lethal it stopped his heart. Until his mind caught up. Obviously she'd decided to have the baby or they wouldn't be here.

He rubbed feeling back into his face, but his ears felt filled with water. He had to strain to hear her as she quietly continued.

"I was only a few weeks along when I found out. There's a pill you can take that early. You don't have to go into hospital, there are fewer complications... There seemed to be a lot of good reasons not to go through with the pregnancy." Her profile grew distressed and her fingertips grazed the pulse in her throat.

Reasons like the threat of prison and having a man she didn't want in her life demanding access to her baby. Raoul's sharp mind pinned up the drawbacks as quickly as her own must have. His blood ran cold at how close he'd come to not knowing about this baby at all.

"I couldn't bring myself to...expel it from my life like that. I want this baby, Raoul." She turned with her hand protectively on her middle again, her eyes glittering with quiet ferocity. "I know it's foolish to let you see how badly I want it. You'll find a way to use it against me. But I need you to believe me. I will *never* let anyone take my baby from me."

His scalp tightened with preternatural wariness and pride and awe. Sirena was revealing the sort of primal mother instinct their caveman ancestors would have prized in a mate. The alpha male in him exalted in seeing that quality emanating from the mother of his child.

While the cutthroat negotiator in him recognized a tough adversary.

"You're trying to convince me I can't buy you off," he summed up, trying not to let himself become too entranced by her seeming to possess redeeming qualities. She had fooled him once already.

"You can't. The only reason I'm speaking to you at all is to give my baby the same advantages its father might provide its future siblings, whether that's monetary or social standing or emotional support. Consider what those things might be as you work through the rest of that." She nodded at the contract and slipped into the powder room again.

Future siblings? Raoul's mind became an empty whiteboard as he bit back a remark that he hadn't expected *this* child; he certainly wasn't ready to contemplate more.

Three months later, Raoul was taking steps to ensure he was prepared for the birth, looking ahead to clear his calendar in six weeks. He rarely took time off and found even Christmas with his mother an endurance test of agitation to get back to work. Anticipation energized him for this vacation, though.

Because it was a new challenge? Or because he would see Sirena?

He shut down the thought. The baby was his sole interest. He was eager to find out the sex, know it was healthy and have final confirmation it was *his*.

Not that he had many doubts on any of that. True to their agreement, Sirena had sent him updates on the baby's progress. Nothing concerning her own, he had noted with vague dissatisfaction, but he expected he would be informed if there were problems. The second scan later in the pregnancy had not revealed an obvious male, so he'd assumed the baby was female and found himself taken with the vision of a daughter possessing dark curls and beguiling green eyes.

As for paternity, to his mind, the fact Sirena had signed made the baby his. The final test after the birth was a formality that would activate the arrangements, that was all.

But that was a month and a half from now and he had people to organize. People who were abuzz with the news that the driven head of their multinational software corporation was taking an extended absence.

Only a handful of his closest and most trusted subordinates knew the reason, and even they didn't know the mother's identity. The scandalous circumstances of his father's infidelity and suicide had made Raoul a circumspect man. Nothing about his involvement with Sirena, their affair, her being fired for embezzlement or her pregnancy was public knowledge. When people asked—and she'd made enough of an impression on associates and colleagues that many did—he only said she was no longer with the company.

Part of him continued to resent that loss, especially when the assistants he kept trying out turned out to be so *trying*. The highly recommended Ms. Poole entered the meeting with a worried pucker in her magic-marker brows.

"I said life or death, Ms. Poole," he reminded, clinging to patience.

"She's very insistent," the spindly woman said, bringing a mobile phone to him.

"Who?" He tamped down on asking, *Sirena?* Her tenacity was something he'd come to respect, if not always appreciate.

"Molly. About your agreement with Ms. Abbott."

He didn't know any Molly, but something preternatural set an unexpected boot heel on his chest, sharp and compressing, causing pressure to balloon out in radiant waves. Odd. There was no reason to believe this was bad news. Sirena hadn't contacted him directly since he'd left her looking wrung out and cross at her flat that day, neither of them particularly satisfied with the outcome of their negotiations, but possessing a binding document between them.

"Yes?" He took the phone in a hand that became nerveless and clumsy. As he stood and moved from the table, he was aware of the ripple of curiosity behind him. At the same time, despite everything that had passed between them, he experienced a flick of excitement. His mind conjured an image of Sirena in one of those knitted skirt-and-sweater sets she used to wear.

"Mr. Zesiger? I'm Sirena Abbott's midwife. She asked me to inform you that the baby is on its way."

"It's early," he protested.

"Yes, they had to induce—" She cut herself off.

He heard muffled words and held his breath as he strained to hear what was said.

She came back. "I've just been informed it will be an emergency cesarean."

"Where is she?" he demanded while apprehension wrapped around him like sandpaper, leaving him abraded and raw.

"I understood you were only to be informed and that a paternity test be ordered, not that you would attend—"

"Save me the phone calls to find her so I can come directly," he bit out.

A brief pause before she told him. "But the results won't be known for days."

"Tell her I'm on my way," he said, but she was already gone.

CHAPTER FOUR

A WOMAN MET him in the hospital reception area. She wore red glasses and a homespun pullover. Her ditch-water hair was in one thick plait, her expression grave.

"Raoul? Molly." She held out a hand and offered a tight smile. "Sirena told me I'd know you when I saw you. The baby is a girl. They've taken the samples and should have the results in a few days." Her manner was disconcertingly strained.

Because she didn't want to get his hopes up? The baby was here, the moment of truth at hand. He shouldn't be so stunned given the nature of the call or the time it had taken to fight traffic to get here, but the swiftness of the procedure surprised him. At the same time, he was aware of a gripping need to see the infant and *know* she was his.

A girl. He hadn't realized how much he wanted one. And safely delivered. The abruptness of the call and lack of details had unsettled him, but they were fine. Everything was fine.

"Good," he heard himself say, finally able to breathe. "I'm pleased to hear they came through all right." He gestured for her to lead the way, assuming she'd show him to their room.

Molly didn't move. "Premature babies always have certain hurdles, but the pediatrician is confident she'll progress as well as the best of them." She seemed to ponder whether to say more.

"And Sirena?" he prompted. Some unknown source of telepathy made him brace even as the question left him. A kind of dread that was distant but gut-churningly familiar seeped into his bloodstream like poison, unwanted and tensing him with refusal and denial before he even knew what she would say.

Molly's eyes became liquid. "They're doing all they can."

For a long moment nothing happened. No movement, no sound, nothing. Then, from far off, he heard a torn inhale, like a last gasp of life.

No. Her words didn't even make sense. He suddenly found himself bumping into a wall and put out a hand to steady himself. "What *happened?*"

"I wondered if she had told you about her condition." Molly moved closer. Her touch was a biting grasp on his upper arm, surprisingly strong and necessary as he wondered if he'd stay on his feet. "It's been a risky pregnancy from the start. High blood pressure, then early-onset pre-eclampsia. She's been managing that condition these last few weeks, trying to buy the baby more time. Today they couldn't wait any longer without risking both their lives, so the doctors induced. After she had a seizure, they stopped the labor and took her for surgery. Now she's lost a lot of blood. I'm sorry. I can see this is hard for you to hear."

Hard? All his strength was draining away, leaving him cold and empty. Clammy with fear. Her life was about to snap free of his and she *hadn't even told him.* She might as well have swallowed a bottle of pills and left herself for him to find when he got home from school. Suddenly he was nine again, barely comprehending what he was seeing, unable to get a response out of the heavy body he was

shaking with all his might. Not there soon enough. Helpless to make this right.

"Why the hell didn't she *say something?*" he burst out,
furious that she'd given him no indication, no warning, just
left him tied to the tracks to be hit with a train.

Molly shook her head in bafflement. "Sirena didn't talk
about the custody agreement, but it's been my impression
things have been hostile."

So hostile she kept from him that her life was on the
line?

"I don't want her to *die!*" The word was foul and jagged
in his throat. He spoke from the very center of himself,
flashing a look at Molly that made her flinch. He couldn't
imagine what he looked like, but his world was screech-
ing to a halt and everything in it was whirling past him.

"No one does," she assured him in the guarded tone developed by people who dealt with victims. It was the same
prudent nonengagement with explosive emotions that the
social worker had used as she had steered his young self
from his father's body.

"Take me to her," he gritted out. A horrible avalanche
of fear like he'd never known crushed him. He wanted to
run shouting for her until he found her. This wasn't real.
It couldn't be.

"I can't. But—" She seemed to think twice, then gave
him a poignant smile. "Maybe they'll let us into the nursery."

He forced one foot in front of the other, walking as if
through a wall of thick, suffocating gelatin as he followed
Molly to the preemie clinic, ambivalence writhing like
a two-headed snake inside him. Was it his fault Sirena
hovered on the brink? Or another man's? He adamantly
wanted his child, but the idea that one life could cost another appalled him.

He came up to the tiny, nearly naked being in the incubator, her bottom covered in an oversized nappy, her hair hidden by a cap. Wires extended from her bare fragile body and her miniature Sirena mouth briefly pursed in a kiss.

He couldn't see anything of himself in her, but a startlingly deep need to gather and guard the infant welled in him. Pressing his icy hands to the warm glass, he silently begged the little girl to *hang on*. If this was all that would be left of Sirena...

He brutally refused to entertain such a thought, turning his mind to sending a deep imperative through the walls of the hospital to the unknown location of this baby's mother. *Hang on, Sirena. Hang on.*

Sirena had the worst hangover of her life. Her whole body hurt, her mouth was dry and nausea roiled in her stomach. In her daze, she moved her hand to her middle, where the solid shape of her baby was gone, replaced with bandages and a soft waistline.

A whimper of distress escaped her.

"Lucy is fine, Sirena." His voice was unsweetened cocoa, warm and comforting despite the bitter taint.

"Lucy?" she managed, blinking gritty eyes. The stark ceiling above her was white, the day painfully bright. Slowly the steel-gray of Raoul's gaze came into focus.

"Isn't that what you told Molly? That you wanted your daughter named for your mother, Lucille?"

You don't mind? she almost said, but wasn't sure where the paternity test was. When she had signed the consent forms, they'd told her the kind of proof he'd requested, the kind admissible in court, was a more complex test that would take several days. She wondered if waiting on that had been the only thing keeping him from whisking Lucy from this hospital before she woke.

She didn't ask. She could barely form words with what felt like a cotton-filled mouth. It took all her concentration to remain impassive. Seeing him gave her such a bizarre sense of relief she wanted to burst into tears. She reminded herself not to read anything into the shadow of stubble on his jaw or the bruises of tiredness under his eyes. The man was a machine when it came to work; he could have been at the office late and dropped by on his way to his penthouse.

Still, that scruff of light beard gave her a thrill. She'd seen him like this many times and always experienced this same ripple of attraction. The same desire to smooth a hand over his rough cheek. He would be overworked yet energized by whatever had piqued his ambition, his shirt collar open, his sleeves rolled back and soon, a smile of weary satisfaction.

But not today. Today he was sexily rumpled, but his demeanor was antagonistic, making a shiver of apprehension sidle through her as he spoke in a rough growl. "You should have told me you weren't well."

The harsh accusation in his tone was so sharp she flinched. All she could think about were those harrowing moments when they'd told her the baby had to come out. Not for Lucy's sake, but her own. The fear in her had been so great, she'd been on the verge of begging Raoul to come to her. The Raoul she had once imagined him to be anyway. He was so strong and capable and she'd instinctively known she'd feel safe if he was near.

He hated her, though. He wouldn't care. Like always, she'd been on her own.

She'd gone through the induction and the beginning of pains without anyone at her side, only calling Molly when the nurse confirmed that yes, labor was properly started. That was when she'd been required to notify Raoul. She had been explaining that to Molly when something went wrong.

She didn't even know what had happened. Having a

huge blank like that was frightening. His blaming her for not advising him it was a possibility added insult to injury, putting her on the defensive.

"Why would I tell you anything?" she challenged from her disadvantaged position, flat on the bed, tied down with wires, voice like a flake of yellowed onionskin. "You can't be happy I pulled through."

"You haven't yet," he said, snapping forward in a way that made her heart jump. He set his big hands on either side of her and leaned over her, promising reprisal despite her pathetic condition. "And don't ever accuse me of anything so ugly again."

Sirena tried to swallow and couldn't even feel her dry tongue against her arid lips. "Can I have some water?" she begged in a whispered plea. "Please? I'm so thirsty."

"I don't know if you're allowed to have anything," he said with a scowl, something avid and desperate flickering through his eyes before he bent with the sudden swoop of a hawk going for a kill.

His mouth covered hers for the briefest second. His damp tongue licked into the parched cavern of her mouth to moisten the dry membranes. The relief was incredible, the act surprising and intimate beyond measure.

"I'll tell the nurse you're awake." He walked out, leaving her speechless and tingling with the return of life to her entire body, mind dazed and wondering if she was still unconscious and hallucinating.

Sirena had thought nothing could make her melt so thoroughly as the vulnerable sight of her premature daughter. Then she began hearing the stories of Raoul learning to diaper and feed her. Raoul, who didn't even know for sure he was the father, had paced a path between Lucy and Sirena, talking unceasingly to Sirena when they had feared she would slip into a coma. He'd only gone home for a shower and sleep now that Sirena had woken, nearly seventy-two hours after the birth.

She told herself not to read it as a sign of caring. If Raoul was tending to Lucy, he was only stamping a claim while trying to prove Sirena was dispensable. To some extent she was. She quickly learned she could hold her baby, but she was too sick and weak for anything else. She was pumping her breasts, but only to keep her thin milk supply going while she waited for the cocktail of medications to leave her system. She couldn't feed Lucy or do anything else a mother ought to do.

Dejected, she was fretting over how useless she was as she headed back to bed the next morning, wiped out by the tiny act of brushing her teeth.

Raoul walked in on her attempt to scale the bed, finding her with one hip hitched on the edge, bare legs akimbo as she quickly tried to stay decent under her hospital gown.

Aside from faint shadows under his heavy eyes, he looked fantastic in casual pants and a striped shirt. He brought a wonderfully familiar scent with him, too. For a second she was back in the office welcoming her freshly shaved boss, sharing coffee with him as they discussed how they'd tackle the day.

He eyed her balefully, but that might have been a reaction to the ferocious scowl she threw at him. She hadn't been allowed coffee since early in the pregnancy and he was sipping from a travel mug tagged with a ProZess Software logo. He was a picture of everything she couldn't have.

"Why are you here?" she asked, struggling to use her severed stomach muscles to heft herself onto the bed.

He smoothly moved to her side, set down his coffee and helped her.

"I don't—" She stiffened in rejection, but he bundled her into his crisp shirt anyway. The press of his body heat through the fabric burned into her as he used a gentle embrace to lift her. His free hand caressed her bare, dangling leg, sliding it neatly under the sheet as he slid her into bed as if she weighed no more than a kitten.

Shaken, she drew the sheet up to her neck and glared at him.

He picked up his coffee and sipped, staring back with his poker face. "Your doctor said he'd have the paternity results when he did his rounds this morning."

Her heart left her body and ran down the hall to bar the door of the nursery.

She wasn't ready to face this. Last night had been full of sudden jerks to wakefulness that had left her panting and unable to calm herself from the nightmare that Raoul would disappear with their daughter.

That *he* would disappear from her life again.

Why did it matter whether he was in her life? She felt nothing but hatred and mistrust toward him, she reminded herself. But the weeks of not seeing him while she waited out her pregnancy had been the bleakest of her life, worse even than when her family had left for Australia.

Logic told her he wasn't worth these yearning feelings she still had, but she felt a rush of delight that he kept showing up. When he was in the room, the longing that gripped her during his absences eased and the dark shadows inside her receded.

She couldn't forget he was the enemy, though. And she was running out of defenses.

He must have seen her apprehension, because he drawled, "Scared? Why?" The question was like a throwing star, pointed on all sides and sticking deep. "Because I might be the father? Or because you know I am?"

The stealthy challenge circled her heart like a Spanish inquisitor, the knife blade out and audibly scraping the strop.

She noticed her hands were pleating the edge of the sheet into an accordion. What was the use in prevaricating? She licked her numb lips.

"Are you going to try to take her from me if you are?" she asked in a thin voice.

If? You bitch, he thought as the tension of not knowing stayed dialed high inside him. The last three days had been hellish as he'd grown more and more attached to that tiny tree frog of a girl while cautioning himself that she might belong to another man.

Just like her mother.

"I could have taken her a dozen times by now," he bit out. "I should have."

It wasn't completely true. The hospital had accommodated his visiting the baby, but only because he was the kind of man who didn't let up until he got what he wanted. They wouldn't have let him leave with her, though.

If Sirena believed he could have, however, great. He wanted to punish her for the limbo she'd kept him in.

Her hands went still and pale. All of her seemed to drain of color until she was practically translucent, her already wan face ashen. Fainting again? He shot out a hand to press her into the pillows against the raised head of the bed.

She tried to bat away his touch, but in slow motion, her tortured expression lifting long enough to let him glimpse the storm of emotions behind her tangled lashes and white lips: frustration at her weakness, a flinch of physical pain in her brow, defensiveness that he had the audacity to touch her and terror. Raw terror in the glimmering green of her eyes.

Rolling her head away, she swallowed, her fear so palpable the hair rose on the back of his neck.

Advantage to me, he thought, trying to shrug off the prickling feeling, but guilty self-disgust weighed in the pit of his stomach. All he could think about was the hours he'd spent right here, telling her how unfair it was for a child to grow up missing a parent. The questions Lucy would have, the empty wedge in the wholeness of her life, would affect the child forever.

Blood ties hadn't mattered at that point. He and Lucy had been linked by the prospect that she would suffer his pain—an unthinkable cruelty for an infant just starting her life. The whole time he'd been urging Sirena to pull through, he'd been mentally cataloging everything he knew about her, wanting to be Lucy's depository of information on her mother.

While all he'd heard in the back of his mind had been Sirena's scathing, *What makes you think you ever knew me, Raoul?*

His heart dipped. She wanted her baby. He knew that much. As he'd gleaned all the details of this pregnancy that had nearly killed her, he'd wondered about her feelings for the father. Did the lucky man even know how stalwartly determined she'd been to have his child?

If that man was him… His abdomen tensed around a ripple of something deep and moving, something he didn't want to acknowledge because it put him in her debt.

The specialist swept in, taking in the charged tension with a somber look. "Good morning. I know you've been waiting, Raoul. Let me put you at ease. You are Lucy's biological father."

Relief poured into him like blood returning after a constriction, filling him with confidence and pride in his daughter, the little scrap with such a determined life force.

No reaction from Sirena. She kept her face averted as though he and the doctor weren't even in the room.

"I don't have plans to take her from you," Raoul blurted. The impatient words left him before he realized they were on his tongue, leaving him irritated by how she weakened him with nothing but terrified silence.

She gave him a teary, disbelieving look that got his back up.

The physician distracted her, asking after her incision and leaving Raoul to face a cold, stony truth: he couldn't separate mother from daughter.

Her accusation when she'd woken yesterday that he would have wished her dead had made him so sick he hadn't had words. His own father's absence had been self-inflicted—he'd *left* Raoul and his mother—but it didn't make the idea of Sirena's baby accidentally being motherless any less horrific. Raoul wouldn't be able to live with himself if he was the instrument that divided a parent from a child.

"When can I take her home?" he heard Sirena ask the doctor.

An image flashed into Raoul's mind of her collapsing the way she had at the courthouse, but without anyone to catch her or the baby in her arms.

"You're not taking her to your flat," he stated bluntly, speaking on instinct from the appalled place that was very much aware of how ill and weak she was.

Sirena's gaze swung to his, persecuted and wild. "You just said—"

"I said I wasn't so low I'd steal your baby from you. But you're more than prepared to keep Lucy from me, aren't you?" That reality was very raw. "You're the one who steals, Sirena, not me."

A humiliated blush rolled into her aghast face.

The physician broke in with, "Let's get you and Lucy well first, then we'll talk about where she's going." It was a blatant effort to defuse their belligerent standoff.

The doctor departed a few minutes later, leaving Sirena trying to decide which was worse: having Raoul in the room, where his presence ratcheted her tension beyond bearing, or out of the room, where she didn't know what he was up to.

"The contract is in effect now," she reminded him in a mutter. "I'll adhere to it."

"Will you? Because you've done everything possible to keep me from even knowing she's mine." His temper snapped. "How could you do that? I lost my father, Sirena. I know how it feels to grow up without one."

"And I lost my mother," she cried, then cringed as the force of such harsh speech sliced pain across her abdomen. "Why do you think I stood up to the most pitiless man in the world?" she asked in a thick voice, clenching her eyes shut as she fought for control, so emotional from everything that she verged on breaking down. "You really know how to put a woman through hell, Raoul. I can't even get myself down the hall to her and you're playing stupid mind games. *I won't take her, but you can't have her.* Maybe you would deserve a place in her life if you just once showed an ounce of compassion."

Silence.

She threw her heavy arm over her closed eyes, pressing back weak tears, concentrating on her breathing to pull herself together. The worst part was, she felt horrible about trying to keep him from Lucy. He had a right to be angry about that—along with the stealing—but she couldn't undo any of it. Her life was a giant mess and she had no idea how she was going to fix it and carry on.

"Let's go," Raoul said in a gruff tone that was too close to the bed.

Sirena lowered her arm to eye him, startled to see he'd brought the wheelchair to her side.

"I'll take you to see Lucy. We'll both calm down and maybe start communicating like adults."

"Don't be nice," she groaned. "It makes me feel awful."

"You should feel awful." He braced her as she slid off the bed and into the chair.

She slumped into it and dropped her face into her hands. "I love her more than you can know, Raoul. And you've been horrid, trying to take her from me the instant you heard I was pregnant. What else could I do except lie about paternity?"

The chair moved and she lifted her head, glad she didn't have to face him, especially when he said with quiet sincerity, "You're wrong. I do know how much you love her. I feel the same way. That's why I've been so tough about it. I didn't know about your mother. I thought this was all payback for the court case."

"No," she breathed, shoulders slumping. "I'm angry about that, but—" her voice hitched with yearning "—I just want to be her mum."

"What happened to yours?" His voice sounded deeper and quieter than she'd ever heard it, making her feel small for trying to cut him from his daughter's life. She didn't know how he'd lost his father, but that nascent connection she'd always felt toward him over their shared grief extended from within herself, like a strand of spiderweb drifting behind her, searching to anchor itself to him.

"This." She waved a trembling hand at her pathetic physical state. "Her complications were different so this wasn't hereditary, but it was always in my mind that having a baby isn't as simple for some as it is for others. I was only six when she died, so I don't have a lot of memories, but that's why losing her hurt so much. I can't bear the idea of Lucy going through all her life markers of puberty and boyfriends and childbirth without her mother there for her."

He stayed silent behind her, giving no indication whether her words had any impact. She wasn't able to twist around and look and didn't want to anyway. He might be interpreting her confession as a plea for sympathy when it was the kind of opening of her heart that left her feeling so raw and exposed she could hardly bear it.

She was grateful they entered the quiet warmth of the nursery at that point. Seconds later, as she cuddled Lucy into her chest, her world righted, becoming achingly perfect, even with Raoul's commanding presence hovering over them. Maybe because he was here. Much as she resented him, she wanted Lucy to have her father.

After feeding and changing and getting an update on Lucy's progress, Raoul returned Sirena to her room. She was quiet, visibly exhausted, their silence no longer hostile. When he helped her into bed, she only murmured, "Thank you," before plummeting into sleep.

Such a ferocious scrapper and now he understood why. The way she'd talked about missing her mother had made something lurch in his chest. It was a renewed snag of guilt at not really knowing her. His resentful *I never dreamed she was capable of stealing* was shifting into *still waters run deep.*

The way his father had quit on him made him highly susceptible to exalting a woman who had fought so hard to give her child life and to be in it.

He didn't like this shift in him. It made him wonder about her motives for stealing, and he didn't want to develop compassion and forgiveness for that. Opportunists took advantage of weak emotions like affection and trust. Next thing you knew, you were on the streets with two dependents—a social pariah—and your path forward was a broken cliff into an abyss.

He couldn't doubt Sirena's love for their daughter, though. While in the nursery, the old Sirena had returned, all warm smiles and soft laughter, her expression open and her wit quick, making the nurses laugh. He'd had to bite back his own chuckle more than once, fighting a desire to let go of his defenses and fall under her spell again.

Scowling, he tried to imagine how this impossible situation would play out. A foolish idea was taking hold in the back of his mind, one that looked ridiculous as a thought bubble. It would be outrageous in real life. He needed distance, not more exposure to her, but they were both coming from the same place with regard to Lucy. He couldn't ignore that. In fact, as the days passed, it was *all* he could think about.

Their truce lasted through the week as Raoul spent most of the day with them. Sirena stopped using the chair and started breast-feeding, even brought Lucy into her room with her overnight, which was a struggle she tried not to reveal, fearful of winding up in a fight with Raoul that she didn't have the energy to win. The rapport between them might be guarded and impersonal, but it was safe. As long as she didn't give him anything to criticize, they got along fine.

Meanwhile, the reality of taking a baby back to her flat when she couldn't even properly care for herself ate at her. When her doctor cleared her for discharge, she should have been elated, but she was so overwhelmed she hardly contained her tears.

Of course Raoul arrived at that exact moment. He was wearing a suit and tie, the shoulders of his jacket speckled with damp spots of late-spring rain. No time to worry how she'd cope when she had bigger concerns confronting her from the foot of her hospital bed. Dark, handsome, vengeful concerns.

"I told you a week ago you I won't let you take her to your flat," he said unemotionally.

It was the fight she'd been dreading, but she still wasn't prepared for it.

"And I'm pretty sure we signed an agreement that said I could," she replied, trying not to let him stir her temper. "I have nights with Lucy. You can visit during the day, exactly as we're doing here. Are we ignoring the panel of experts you hired?" Her quick sarcasm was a show of strength she didn't have. She had just gotten back from walking down the hall and that snappy reply was the extent of the spunk in her.

"You have the stamina of a trampled daisy. What if something happened? No. You're coming home with me," Raoul pronounced.

For a few seconds, she couldn't even blink. A tiny voice deep in her soul asked, *Me? Not just Lucy?* Her pulse tripped into a gallop and tingling excitement raced all the way to her nerve endings.

Get a grip, Sirena!

"I have staples, Raoul. It's not nice to make me laugh," she retorted, trying to gather thoughts that had scattered like shards of glass from a broken window. Stay in his house? With him? She already felt too vulnerable seeing him during the day. Living off him would decimate her pride and put her in his debt.

"You do," Raoul agreed with edgy derision. "Staples and tubes and a unit of someone else's blood. You're on medications that make you light-headed and have appointments for follow-up and a baby to care for. You can't do it alone."

In her heart of hearts she'd been counting on a miracle with her sister, but of course that hadn't panned out. Her father wasn't working, so he couldn't foot the bill for plane fare and God knew she couldn't afford it. Besides, Ali was in her first semester at uni—that had been the whole point of Sirena sending the money so many months ago.

Sirena had friends she could call for the odd thing, but

not the sort of steady help she needed these first weeks at home. Frustration made her voice strident.

"Why would you even suggest it? You don't want anything to do with me," she accused, voicing the fear that was a dark plague inside her.

He tilted his arrogant head to a condescending angle. "You may not be my ideal choice as the mother of my child, but I can't overlook the fact that you are, or that you love her as much as I do. We both want to be with her and you need looking after. Bringing you into my home is clearly the most practical solution."

That uncouched *not be my ideal* stung like mad. She knew she looked awful, hair flat and dull, no makeup. Her figure would remain a disaster until she could start on the treadmill again.

Was he seeing anyone, she wondered suddenly? It was the sort of thing she hadn't been able to avoid knowing when she'd been working for him—and bizarrely, after being fired she'd found the not knowing even worse. How would she feel to learn he was with another woman while she was sleeping under his roof?

She broke their locked gazes, deeply repelled by the idea of him in bed with other women. "We don't even like each other. It would be a disaster."

"We're going to have to get past that for Lucy's sake, aren't we?" he countered.

"And my being dependent on you will foster goodwill? I doubt it," she argued, even as she mentally leaped to the pro of still being able to do her transcription jobs if he was on hand to care for Lucy for an hour here and there. That would mean she could keep her flat. The prospect of losing her home had become a genuine concern.

Raoul folded his arms as he put his sharp mind to work finding the argument that would clinch what he wanted.

Not that he *wanted* her in his home, he reminded himself. It was his daughter he was after.

"If I were to have another child, I would look after the health of that child's mother. Didn't you tell me you expect me to offer Lucy the same considerations I would offer all my children?"

He was pleased to recall the demand she'd thrown at him weeks ago. It justified taking her into his home. He didn't need a volatile mix of leftover attraction and betrayal confronting him with his eggs every morning, but Lucy's needs trumped his.

Sirena heard the logic, but couldn't bring herself to acknowledge it. His dispassionate reasoning was exactly that: lacking in feeling, practical. Cold.

It was also a perfect out, allowing her to accept a crazy arrangement for sensible reasons, but she feared she was only giving in to temptation. She knew why, too. Deep down, a grossly foolish part of herself believed that if she could just have his attention long enough, she could explain and earn his forgiveness.

The loss of his good opinion crushed her, not abating despite the months that had passed since the lawsuit. Experience with her stepmother told her that imagining she could earn Raoul's admiration was pure self-delusion, but that didn't alter the fact that she desperately wanted him to stop hating her.

While he wanted unfettered access to his daughter. That's all that motivated him and he was trying to make it happen with his typical brook-no-arguments leadership and infinite resources, standing there casually impeccable and vaguely bored, certain he had the entire thing sewn up.

"Did I ever tell you how annoyingly bigheaded you can be when you think you've had the last word?" she muttered while casting for a suitable reason to refuse.

"I don't *think* I've had it, I know it. The doctor won't release you unless you have a care plan in place. I'm it."

"You're my get-out-of-jail card? When you put it like that…"

Every muscle in his body seemed to harden. "Be careful, Sirena. I'm taking into account you're still only half-alive. Once you're back to full strength, I won't be nearly so charitable. I've forgotten nothing."

A futile yearning swelled in her chest and burned in the back of her throat. He had every right to be angry, but to have her arrested when she'd been like an appendage for him for two years, then had given herself to him without hesitation…?

"You know I can't have sex for another five weeks, right?" she threw at him. "If you're thinking to have a convenient outlet on hand, it won't happen."

He swept her with one pithy glance that reminded her she was far beneath her best. She hated both of them in that second. Why did she care whether he was attracted to her or ever had been? He hadn't. He'd been horny and she'd been handy. He'd told her so. Apparently having her underfoot wouldn't be handy enough to tempt him again. That should be a comfort, not a knife in the heart.

"Just until the doctor clears me to live alone," she muttered, bolstering her humiliated blush with a level glance into his implacable face. "I'm only staying until I'm back to full strength. Then Lucy comes to my flat with me."

"We'll burn that bridge when we get to it."

Despite the welcome of blooming gardens at the house in Ascot, Sirena was icy cold as they drove past the gates where she'd stood waiting for Raoul in the rain, begging him over the intercom to speak to her.

Finding him here that day had been a matter of calling in a favor with an out-of-the-know workmate. After that she'd been shut out completely, her personal items from her desk returned and her keys, company ID, equipment and expense cards taken back.

Unable to look at him, she set a light hand on the warm shape of the baby between them and rocked numbly with the car when the chauffeur halted under the portico. As she reached to unclip the child seat, Raoul's adept fingers brushed hers away.

"I'll bring her." He relayed the diaper bag to his chauffeur and lifted Lucy out the opposite door, coming around to meet Sirena where the chauffeur had opened her door.

She tried to climb from the low-slung car and was more resentful than grateful when Raoul reached to help, offering his arm so she could cling to it with a shaky grip. Her muscles burned at the strain of pulling up and steadying herself on her weak legs. Pain sliced across her middle where her incision was healing.

As they went up the steps, he slipped his arm around her and half carried her.

She made a noise of protest, but couldn't help leaning into his support, both bolstered and weakened by his lean hardness. She finally gave in to the pull of attraction and let her head loll into his shoulder for just a second before he spoke, his tone flatly shoving her back to reality.

"You shouldn't have been discharged."

"I don't want to be this feeble," she grumbled, pulling away as they crossed the threshold. The loss of his touch made her feel weak and sorry for herself. "Even that time in Peru I managed to keep going. I'll get better. I have to." She sank down on the velvet-upholstered bench in the foyer and cupped her swimming head in her hands.

"When were you sick in Peru? That time half the conference came down with food poisoning? You didn't get it."

"I did! But someone had to take charge, extend the arrangements with the hotel and rebook the flights. I didn't hear you volunteering."

He grew an inch in height and his mouth opened, but she waved a hand against whatever scathing response he was on the verge of making.

"It was my job. I'm not complaining, just saying that's the most wretched and useless I've ever felt, but this is worse. I hate being like this."

"You should have told me. This time *and* then."

"It was my job," she repeated, ignoring his admonition in favor of reminding him her work ethic had been rock solid. She looked up at him and he met her gaze with an inscrutable frown and a tic in his cheek.

"I expect you to tell me what your needs are, Sirena. I'm not a mind reader. We'll go to your room now so you can rest. Can you manage these stairs with me or shall I have a room prepared down here?"

"Upstairs is fine, but Lucy will need a feed before I lie down." She deliberately kept her gaze on the baby and not on these beloved surroundings. Silly, naive fool that she was, she used to host fantasies about one day being mistress here. She loved everything about its eclectic style.

The lounge where she moved to nurse was one of her favorite rooms, with its Mediterranean colors, contemporary furniture and view to the English garden. Raoul had a lot of worldly influences in his life, from his Spanish mother's ancestry of warmth and sensuality to his father's Swiss precision. He had been educated in America, so he brought those modern, pop-culture elements into his world with contemporary art and futuristic electronics. All of his homes were classy, comfortable and convenient.

And all contained the one ingredient to which she was drawn inexorably: him.

He stood in profile to her, lean and pantherish, thumb sweeping across the screen of his mobile as he dealt with all the things she used to do for him. Her heart panged. She had loved working for him, loved the job that challenged her. Transcribing had put her through business school and kept her fed these last months, so she couldn't knock it, but it didn't take her off her steno chair, let alone around the world.

"Are you going in to the office this afternoon?" she asked, of two minds whether she wanted him to leave. Being on guard against him drained her, but another secret part of her drank up his nearness like a cactus in a rare rain.

"They're asking the same. Things are in disarray. When you delivered, I had only starting to put things in place for an absence I thought would happen next month."

"I'm sorry," she said, feeling the habitual words leave her lips and thinking, *Why are you apologizing? It's not your fault!*

"A warning that premature delivery was a possibility would have been helpful."

The supercilious remark got her back up. "I didn't need the extra stress of you hanging over me telling me what to do," she said with acerbity. "I followed doctor's orders and tried to go to term, which is all I *could* do. If you're inconvenienced by the early birth, well, welcome to parenthood. I believe we're both in for adjustments."

"A little communication goes a long way, is what I'm saying. Keeping things to yourself is a theme that keeps getting you into trouble." His deceptively silky tone rang with danger.

"Oh, and you gave me ample opportunity to communicate after informing me *through the arrest charges* that you knew money had gone missing?"

"Before that," he snapped. His jaw was like iron, his gray eyes metallic and locked down, but he did darken a shade with something that might have been culpability.

"You could have told me you were having financial troubles and we could have worked something out. Stealing from me was unacceptable."

"I agree. That's why I only borrowed."

"So you've said," he ground through his teeth. "But if you—"

Lucy made a little sputter. Sirena quickly sat her up, glancing at Raoul to finish his sentence, but he had stopped speaking to stare openly at her nude breast. She'd come to the demoralizing realization that there was no dignity in childbirth and there wasn't much more afterward. You needed two hands on a newborn, leaving none for tucking yourself back into a bra that had more jibs and sails than a yacht.

"You burp her," she ordered out of self-conscious embarrassment, screening herself with an elbow and quickly covering up once he'd taken the baby. It was an awkward moment on the heels of a deeper fight that promised her stay here would be a dark corner of hell.

When he helped her up the stairs a few minutes later, draped a coverlet over her and set a baby monitor on the nightstand, tears nearly overwhelmed her. A confusion of gratitude and relief with a hefty dose of frustration and fear of the unknown filled her. This wasn't the way she'd expected her life would turn out and she didn't know which way it would bend next. She couldn't trust Raoul, but she had to, at least for an hour while her body recovered enough to take him on next round.

Struggling to keep her heavy eyelids open, she said, "I didn't look to see which room you're putting her in. I won't know where to go if I hear her."

With a sardonic quirk of his mouth, he said, "The monitor is so I can hear you. I have a cot in my office for Lucy."

She really did want to cry then. He was the capable one and she would never measure up. She closed her eyes against the sting and clamped her trembling lips together, praying he couldn't tell how vulnerable she was.

Sirena fell asleep like a blanket had been dropped over her.

Raoul frowned, wanting to set a hand alongside her face to check for temperature, but he didn't want to disturb her. She needed the rest too badly.

Yet she insisted on wearing herself out by fighting him at every turn. What would she be like full strength? He kept seeing glimpses of the old Sirena in her sharp wit, but the hostility and challenges were new and disconcerting. How much of her real personality had she repressed while she had worked for him because he was the boss and she the employee?

And because she had wanted to lull him into not missing stolen money?

He scowled. That act didn't fit with the woman who had pushed herself to work when she was sick. Or pushed herself through a difficult pregnancy to give the best start in life to a baby whose birth could have killed her.

The sight of Sirena unconscious and white, tubes and wires keeping her alive, would never leave him. For that act alone, he owed her consideration. A chance to recover, at least.

Her obvious love for their daughter played on him too. Her worry after each medical checkup. The way she looked to him for his interpretation and reassurance. A cynical part of him warned against being taken in again, but her connection to their baby was too real to be manufactured.

Then there was the sexual attraction that was as bad as ever, despite how pale and weak she was. He hadn't been able to stop himself ogling her naked breast. Her ass was gorgeously round and begging to be fondled. Every time he got near enough to catch her scent, he wanted to pull her close and kiss the hell out of her plump, smart mouth.

He rubbed his face, more preoccupied than ever by a woman he never should have touched. Work was what he needed. Studying had been his escape from the struggle to understand his father's suicide. From age twenty, once his stepfather's perfidy came to light, he'd been immersed in recovering their finances. The urgency of that task had been a type of salvation from emotional angst as well.

Thankfully, despite having to drop out of university, he'd had a basic version of a software program more than halfway through development. Taking it to completion and selling it had staved off his sense of failure over not realizing what his stepfather had been doing. Piling up dollars and assets like points on a screen ever since had become enormously satisfying. It always reassured him to know he was creating not just a financial umbrella, but a giant, inflated mattress of protection for his family.

A family that now included a helpless infant. That gave him more motivation than ever.

And that baby's mother?

He took his seat at his desk and angled the baby monitor, staring hard at it until he heard her whispery breath, wondering where Sirena would fit into his life long-term.

CHAPTER FIVE

IN SOME WAYS, living with Raoul was too easy. The subliminal communication they had developed working together laid the groundwork. She knew his moods, picked up the small cues that meant his call would be a long one and already knew his boundaries when it came to making a space for her within his. Plus, he was such a work hound she was able to sneak away to quiet corners until he took a breather and came looking for his daughter.

But being out of his sight didn't mean he was out of her mind. Why, oh, why did she have to track him with internal radar, her entire being called by his dynamic presence? No matter how many times she told herself to get over him, knowing how close he was made her mind trail back to a rainy afternoon's passionate coming together. So stupid! Daydreams like that made her a pushover for what had been an impersonal coupling on his part. It's what had gotten her into this mess.

She should move back to her flat, but that circumstance was being influenced by other ones, putting a pleat in her brow.

"Was that the doctor?" he asked, startling her with a jolt of unexpected excitement because she had been certain he was in his office down the hall.

Trying to downplay the way she exploded with joy-

ful awareness, she walked the cordless phone across the
lounge to return it to its cradle.

"Indra. My neighbor." Her skin tingled despite her internal willing of the heat to leave her cheeks. These en-
counters in lounges and dining rooms were unbearable.

"Did something happen? You're frowning."

Don't study me, she wanted to cry. Never had she imagined she would long to go back to when she'd been one
more piece of equipment in his high-tech office, but his
aloof attitude had been a lot easier to deal with. Nowadays
he watched her every move as though trying to read between her lines and catch her in a lie.

"Everything is fine," she said with false nonchalance.
"She was asking how long I'd be out of my flat. We always had an arrangement when I was traveling that if she
had family staying, they could use my place. Her niece is
arriving with her new husband and, not surprisingly, they
would love the privacy."

Awkward sexual awareness poured through her in an in-
furiating blush. She hadn't been cleared for sex and Raoul
had made it plain he wasn't interested. Talking about intimacy shouldn't cause her to simmer with responsiveness,
but she became enormously conscious of his masculine
silhouette—so wide across the shoulders and narrowing
down to those powerful thighs. She desperately wished she
could swallow back her reference to the intimate things
that happened between a man and a woman.

While Raoul flicked a glance down the T-shirt and yoga
pants that were snug on her still-plump body. "What did
you tell her?" he asked, his voice so devoid of any hint as
to his thoughts she only felt more ill at ease and anxious
to disappear.

"That I wished I could help her, but I'll need it sooner
rather than later." There. She'd drawn the line.

He met her stare with one equally as steady. "What has the doctor said?"

"Stay out of the pool for another week but short walks are fine. Sleep." She gave him a dry look. "Apparently he's unaware that babies are night creatures."

He frowned. "Why didn't you say? I can get up with Lucy."

"What's the point? You don't have functioning breasts." Again with the dirty talk. Now all she could think of was his naked, very masculine chest, layered with muscle and sprinkled with fine, springy hairs. *Stop!* She turned to hide her flaming face.

"I can change her and settle her back to sleep as well as you can," he pointed out.

She tensed. He was proving himself to be the generous, involved parent she had known he would be, but after so many years without any sort of support, it was ingrained in her to do things by herself.

"I need to manage on my own," she dismissed. "Soon I'll have no choice. And you're working. You need your sleep."

"What do you call transcribing?" he asked with the irritated tone he'd taken the first time he'd found her at it. "You're courting a setback, pushing yourself like that." He spoke in the lofty way that made him a confident company president and a completely annoying adversary.

"I'm not overdoing it. My recovery is my priority. I know my freedom with Lucy hinges on it." She flashed a meaningless smile. "Don't worry. I won't be underfoot any longer than necessary."

That didn't seem to reassure him. His frown deepened. Fortunately Lucy woke and Sirena had a reason to escape the intensity of his inscrutable presence.

Raoul's perfectly functioning libido watched Sirena's curvy behind zip from the room. He was highly attuned to the meaning behind sudden blushes and flustered dis-appearing acts. They were the kind of signals that pro-voked any man's interest and he was already interested. Way too interested.

Back when he'd first hired Sirena, he'd seen the same little betrayals of attraction. It hadn't meant anything to him, since women always reacted to him. He had money, worked out, dressed well and groomed daily. Sirena's sup-pressed awareness had been routine.

He'd ignored it and his own sexual curiosity right up until That Day. Since then, she'd been spitting and hissing and so washed-out he'd felt like a lecher for any less than pure thoughts. Today, however, her nervously smoothing her hair and standing straighter while seeming ultraper-turbed by her aroused senses was insanely seductive.

Emphasis on *insane*. So what if her body was recovered enough to feel a flash of chemistry? He couldn't act on it. They were barely capable of civility. Sex would make an already complicated relationship completely unworkable.

It would be easier on his libido if she left, he acknowl-edged grudgingly. Her involuntary reaction had pulsed male arousal through him so strongly he was drawn taut, his erection thrusting against the confines of his pants, throbbing with imperative to hunt down the woman who had incited him and find relief in the wet depths that had welcomed him deliciously almost a year ago.

There was the problem. It had been a year, he dismissed, trying to forget the whole thing.

He remained edgy into the late hours, though, even after he had accounted for his long spell of abstinence with time spent at work and with lawyers. He'd been too busy to date. It wasn't that he was so bewitched by one particular woman that only she would do.

Hell. He should visit the city and exercise his urges.

Yes, that was the solution. He loathed the idea of Lucy moving out, so—

He paused in dousing his bedroom light, hearing Lucy start crying again. Sirena kept telling him the nights were hers, but this was silly. They shared parenting well enough through the daylight hours. She was being stubborn to prove a point that was totally lost on him.

By the time he moved down the darkened hall, Lucy was quiet again and Sirena was gently closing the nursery door. She jumped as his shadow joined hers on the wall, gasping as she swung around to confront him.

Clutching her heart, she scolded in a whisper, "You scared me to death!"

"I live here," he drawled, not the least bit scared even though his heart began to pound. She stood eye level to his naked chest, her bewildered expression burnished gold by the night-light. She was braless under a sleeveless tank and a pair of loose shorts that looked like men's boxers, her nipples sharply peaked against light cotton.

Damn. This was the wrong kind of night sharing, but he couldn't stop the bombardment of erotic signals that plowed into his sexual receptors. Her hair was loose and wavy. She was lightly scented from the bubble bath she'd taken earlier. Her breath hitched behind invitingly parted lips while her hungry gaze swept across his pecs, stinging him like licks from a velvet whip.

He wore loose pajama pants that drew a relaxed line across his flat abdomen, but they began to tent—

She yanked her gaze to his, embarrassed and deeply apprehensive.

And, if he wasn't mistaken, as dazed with repressed sexual need as he was.

"It didn't sound like she was settling," he managed gruffly, recalling why he was here. "I was coming to take over so you could go back to bed." *Bed.* It was all he could think about. They'd used a sofa that other time and for less than an hour. He wanted more. Hours. Days.

Raoul's voice made the hairs stand up all over her body. His scent was charged and aggressive, as though he hadn't quite made it to bed yet, while she was sleepy and befuddled. She became screamingly aware that her hair was everywhere and her thin tank and loose shorts weren't exactly sexy lingerie. That was probably a good thing, but she secretly wished she looked attractive.

Idiot.

"She's sleeping now," she mumbled and sidestepped at the same time he did, almost coming up against him as he loomed before her.

It was the foyer in Oxshott again. Her startled gaze came up in time to see his focus drop to her mouth. Her heart soared and her mind blanked, just like last time.

Not again, she thought, but couldn't move, paralyzed by attraction and wonder.

His hand came up and hesitated. The bare skin of her shoulder waited, nerve endings reaching out in anticipation. Raoul started to bend his head.

Don't let it happen, she warned herself with anxious intensity, but her self-preservation instincts were flash-firing so rapidly she couldn't figure out if she should retreat the wrong way down the hall, barrel through him or exit into Lucy's room.

His big hand cradled the side of her face, tilting her mouth up to his as his mouth crashed down on hers on an aggrieved groan.

Don't— Oh, do...

Everything about him was strong and the way his mouth covered hers, so confident and hungry, overcame her willpower. The shape of his lips fit hers perfectly. When the tip of his tongue parted her lips, she shuddered in renewal. *Oh, please.* She melted into him. She couldn't help it. She knew how good it could be between them. Her body remembered the virile feel of his muscles gathering, the fullness of him inside her...

His forearm angled across her back with proprietary strength, tugging her into a soft collision that made her release a throaty cry that he swallowed. Their nightclothes were no shield. She felt *everything*. The hot roughness of his chest, the flat muscles of his waist under confused hands that didn't know where to land and the fierce shape of his supremely eager erection.

Her hands splayed on his smooth waist while her thoughts receded behind a kiss that began to consume her. Sweet, deep arousal, a sensation she hadn't felt in months, twined through her, coiling deliciously. It felt so good to be held. The way his breath hissed and he plundered her mouth as though he was slaking a lifetime of need caught her as nothing else could, making her strain to match his voracious desire.

As his hands slid over her shape, she wriggled and pressed into his touch, reveling in the way he shifted her into the hard plane of the door so he could sandwich her with his weight. When his hot hand rode up her bare thigh under the leg of her shorts and found no underpants, he groaned and nipped a line down her neck while his flat hand shaped the globe of her bottom, squeezed gently, massaged and claimed.

She arched her breasts into his chest and her hands went to where his rampant stiffness was nearly piercing a hole through the light silk of his pants.

"Yes, touch me," he said raggedly and bared himself, wrapping his hand over hers with a crushing grip. His mouth came back to catch her cry of surprise while his own hand went up the front of her thigh, fingertips unerringly finding her plump, aching center and drawing a line into the wet slickness. The circling touch of his fingertip against the tight knot of nerves struck bolts of need into her core, driving her to push against his touch, squeeze him tight, kiss him with complete abandon.

He bared her breast and bent his head. She thought, *I'm nursing*.

The reality of what they were doing crashed into her. She shoved him back a step, dislodging his touch, making him stagger and lift his head.

There were so many reasons to be aghast. Her appalled fear must have shown on her face. His glazed eyes met hers and he drew in a breath of shock.

Maybe he was equally horrified to see whom he'd accidentally fallen into kissing.

Just the nearest woman. The one who was *handy*.

Hurt knifed into her abdomen, twisting painfully. Freshly humiliated, Sirena elbowed past him and fled to her room.

She slept late. That beastly man had sneaked into her room after she fell asleep and stolen the baby monitor. He was at the breakfast table when he should have been in his office. Why he wasn't going into the city to work escaped her. It had been nearly a month since he'd had a full day there.

"Lucy?" she prompted, looking past him.

"I gave her a bottle, but she didn't take much. She's down, but probably not for long."

At least that gave her an excuse to avoid him while she disappeared to pump the ache out of her swollen breasts. He was still at the table when she returned. He wore his I've-got-all-day-so-don't-bother-stalling face.

"I don't want to talk about it," she said flatly, veering her gaze from the way his muscled shoulders filled his ice-blue shirt. If only she wasn't so hungry. She folded a leg under her as she took a seat and reached for a piece of cold, buttered toast, biting into it mutinously.

He set aside his tablet and leaned his forearms where his place setting had been cleared.

"I know you can't make love yet. I wouldn't have taken it that far. I didn't have protection either and I sure as hell don't want to get you pregnant again."

The bite of toast in her mouth turned coarse and bitter. All the hurt she'd been bottling and ignoring rose in the back of her throat to make swallowing difficult. She rose up from her chair with what she hoped was enough indignation to cover her wounded core.

"Do you think I don't wish every day that Lucy's father was anyone but you?" She heard the cut of his breath and knew she'd scored a direct hit, but there was no satisfaction in it. She had zero desire to stick around and gloat.

She was almost to the door when he said with sharp force, "Because I don't want to risk your life again. Given how dangerous I've learned childbirth can be, I don't intend to put any woman through that ever again."

The statement was shocking enough to make her hesitate. She glanced back, certain he couldn't be as serious as he sounded. His still posture and set jaw told her he was incontrovertibly sincere.

"Millions of women sail through pregnancy and deliver without any trouble," she pointed out. "You don't know how you'll feel in future, with a different woman."

He only gave her that shuttered look that told her any sort of discussion on the matter was firmly closed. She was wasting her breath if she thought she could reason with him. His rigid expression was so familiar, his certainty that he was right so ingrained and obvious, she felt her lips twitch in amusement.

It was the last reaction she expected. Her body was still humming with unsatisfied arousal, which only increased her aggravation and trampled self-worth. Her heart had shriveled overnight into a self-protective ball, but for some reason his misplaced, oddly gallant statement uncurled it a bit. He was showing the protectiveness she so admired in him, and it was directed at her. Well, all women, maybe, but it still felt kind and yes, there was even a weak part of her that took comfort in knowing he wasn't likely to fill his life with children by other women. The thought of him making babies with someone he actually loved had been quietly torturing her.

"What's funny?" he demanded.

"Nothing," she assured him, pressing a hand to her hollow stomach as it growled.

He rose with impatience to hold her chair. "Sit. Eat. You need the calories."

She returned to slide into her chair as his housekeeper brought a plate of eggs and tomato.

To her consternation, Raoul sat down again.

The memory of last night blistered her as the housekeeper left them alone. She had tossed and turned after their rendezvous, trying to figure out how it had happened. For her it was simple: she still reacted to him. For him... convenience? It had to be. He wasn't going into the city to work *or* to work out his kinks.

Blushing with anger and remembered excitement, she stared at her plate, picking at her food with the tines of her fork. That wild moment was going to sit between them like the wall of resentment over the missing money, filling all of their interactions with undercurrents. She needed her own space.

"I should be able to move into my flat after my next appointment," she said.

He made a noise of negation.

She set her chin to disguise the leap in her heart. She was still processing that he hadn't actually insulted the hell out of her a few minutes ago. Was he resisting her leaving because he wanted her here?

Pressing her knotted fists into her lap, she asked, "Sooner, then?"

"Never. I want Lucy full-time. That means you have to stay, too."

The words went through her like a bomb blast, practically lifting the hair off her head and leaving her ears ringing. Unexpected yearning clenched in her and last night's excitement flared like stirred coals reaching toward a conflagration. Warning bells in her head clanged *danger, danger.*

"There you go testing my incision again," she said, and scooped eggs into her mouth as though the matter was closed. It was. "No," she added in case he needed further clarification.

"Why not?" His challenge was almost like idle curiosity. Pithy and confident he'd eventually get his way.

She goggled at him. "That train wreck last night for starters," she blurted, face seared with a mask of humiliated embarrassment. If he'd made a pass and she'd rejected him, that would be one thing, but the way she'd responded had been horribly revealing. She dropped her gaze, wishing she could take back her reaction, especially when it occurred to her he might use it to get what he wanted.

"So the chemistry between us is alive and well. We've successfully ignored it in the past. Maybe we'll even look at resuming that side of our relationship once you're fully recovered. It's got nothing to do with my desire to raise my daughter."

Sirena choked. "What relationship? What chemistry?" Incredulous, she leaped to her feet without being aware of it. Her entire being rejected everything he was saying. It was so cruel she couldn't bear it. "I'm moving back to my flat as soon as the doctor clears me." She threw her napkin on the table and started to walk out again.

"You're going alone," he said in an implacable tone that chilled her to her marrow. "Lucy is staying here."

Slam. Here it was. The brick wall she had always known he would push between her and her child. Had she actually felt herself softening toward him? He was a bastard, through and through. And it hurt! He was hurting her by treating her this way and he was hurting her by not being the man she wanted him to be.

"That is not what our *legally binding* agreement says," she whirled to state.

"Keep your lawyer on retainer, sweetheart. We're going to rewrite it."

He wasn't bluffing. Her heart twisted while the rest of her, the part that had lost to a bully once before, put up her dukes. She had never wanted to physically harm anyone in her life, but at this moment a swelling wave of injustice pushed her toward him in aggressive confrontation, muscles twitching with the desire to claw him apart because he was striking at her very foundation.

He rose swiftly as she approached, surprised and instantly guarded, taking on a ready stance, his size the only thing that stopped her from lashing out with everything in her.

"Well, isn't that like you," she said with the only weapon available: a tongue coated with enough resentful hatred it wielded itself. *"I want you, Sirena,"* she mocked. *"Touch me, Sirena.* And the next morning it's, take everything that matters to her and kick her to the curb. Go ahead. Send me into John's office for another pile of legal bills I can't afford. I'll raise the stakes and take this to the court of public opinion. I'll hurt you in every way I can find. I'll take your daughter, because I will *not* let her be raised by someone who treats people the way you do."

She wiped the back of her wrist across her lips, her incensed emotions deflating to despair as she heard her own words and knew that she was bravado against his arsenal of money, position and power. What did she have? Charges against her for theft.

She couldn't continue to face him without breaking down.

"Where do you get the nerve to judge *me?*" she managed as a parting shot before she decamped to higher ground.

Raoul stood in astonished silence as he listened to Sirena's retreat. He felt as though he'd just surprised a wounded lioness and barely escaped still clutching his vital organs. Adrenaline stung his arteries and he had to consciously tell his muscles to relax.

None of that closed what felt like a giant chasm in his chest. *Touch me, Sirena. Kick her to the curb.* Shame snaked through him, keeping his jaw clenched even though he wanted to shout back at her in defense. *He* was the one with the right to trust issues. Where did she get off accusing *him* of manipulation?

His housekeeper came through, startling him. "More coffee?" she asked, obviously surprised to see the table deserted.

"No," he barked, then pulled himself together. "No, thank you," he said with more control, rubbing his face then disheveling his hair. "Please make up some sandwiches for Sirena, since she didn't finish her breakfast. I'll be in my office."

He went there for privacy, to work through their confrontation, not to make a dent in the work that piled up every minute he was distracted by this new family of his.

Just a daughter, he reminded himself. Not a partner.

Touch me. His gut tightened in remembered ecstasy as he felt again her light fingers encircling him. Desire had exploded in him last night. For her. Despite all his attempts to make excuses, the sad truth was no other woman tempted him. Even before conceiving Lucy, he'd been taking women to dinner without taking anything else.

He didn't want Sirena to be the only one he wanted. He ought to have more control over himself. As he'd eschewed sleep this morning in favor of forming arguments to keep Sirena and Lucy living with him, he'd convinced himself it was a convenient solution to their custody battle, nothing to do with sexual attraction.

While he'd relived her soft mewling noises and passionate response to his kiss in the hallway, her body incapable of lying.

Sirena didn't want anything to do with him, though. Maybe she was physically attracted, but her ferocity this morning warned him that she would rather smother him in his sleep than share his bed for lovemaking.

He stared blindly at the colorful gardens beyond his office window, his mind's eye seeing her savaged expression the day at the gate, then again this morning. A hard hand closed around his heart, squeezing uncomfortably. A million times he'd told himself she was as jaded and detached as all the rest of his lovers, but today something admonished him. He feared he'd hurt her in a way he hadn't realized he could. But how was his treatment of her any different than hers of him? She had gotten him depending on her, then backhanded him with theft. She'd ruined him for other women and was completely wrong for him at the same time.

Movement caught his eye. Sirena had brought Lucy into the garden. She wore a summer dress and bare feet. Her hair hung in a damp curtain down her back, its curls weighted into subtle waves that would spring up as the sun dried it. Folding one leg under herself the way she often did, she sat on the covered swing and kicked it into a gentle rock, head tilting back as she inhaled deeply.

She was pure woman in that moment, sensual yet maternal. Beautiful.

The want in him took on a new, disconcerting depth. It wasn't just sexual. He remembered her efficiency, her smooth handling of difficult people, her quick smiles.

He wanted the Sirena he'd believed her to be before his dented bank balance had proved she wasn't.

Damn it, he didn't *do* complex relationships. Motherson. Simple. Protective big brother. Easy. Boss and employee. Black-and-white.

With one noted exception.

His father's suicide over what had seemed to be a sordid yet standard affair was earning some of his empathy. If his father had struggled with things like overstepping boundaries in the workplace and a lust that battled strength with his love for his child, Raoul could see where he'd felt torn in too many directions. Raoul wasn't anywhere near killing himself over it, but he wasn't getting much sleep.

But if he was about to be exposed for his perfidy, he might start thinking drastic thoughts. Sirena had threatened a publicity backlash and he believed her. He was learning there was a no-holds-barred quality when her basic rights were threatened and part of him respected her for it.

And if there was one thing he prided himself on, it was upholding his end of a bargain.

Cursing, he opened the French doors onto the patio and strolled across to Sirena, footsteps whispering across the grass. Her eyes opened, but only to slits.

"I'm floating down the river of denial. Don't kill the mood," she warned with a chilly edge to her soft tone.

The corner of his mouth quirked. She had always caught him off guard with her colorful expressions. There was a hidden poet in her, he suspected. A romantic.

He frowned, unable to fit that with the calculating vamp he knew her to be.

"Look," he said, sweeping her multiple facets aside to work at keeping things simple. He'd been angry when he'd thrown his ultimatum at her, grumpily aware that he wanted her rather desperately while she thought he was trying to manipulate her. The manipulating factor was this infernal chemistry!

"I was wrong to say I'd go back on our agreement. You're right. You negotiated in good faith and things between us will only get ugly if we don't talk these things through without using Lucy as leverage."

"Are you on drugs? I thought you said I was right." Her eyes stayed shut, not revealing any of the willingness to compromise he was looking for.

"Where is all this sass coming from?" he demanded. "You never used to say things like that to me."

"Sure I did. In my head. Now that you've fired me, I can use my outside voice."

He accepted that with a disgruntled press of his lips, pushing his hands into his pockets as he rocked on his heels. The sun on his back was so hot he could feel the burn through his shirt. Sirena and the baby were in the shade, though, so he didn't insist they go back into the house yet.

"Will you stay? You know what my workload is like. I have to travel and I don't want to be half a globe from Lucy, not for weeks at a time."

"So when you say stay, you mean follow you around like nomads?" Her eyes opened, lashes screening her thoughts, but the indignant lift of her brows said plenty.

"Why not? You liked the travel when you worked for me, didn't you?"

Sirena pursed her lips. "When I got out of the hotels to see the sights."

He frowned, sensing criticism when he was well aware

she'd enjoyed visiting foreign cultures, welcoming new people and perspectives with excited curiosity, always ready with small talk full of well-researched questions about museums or local wonders, always craning her head at markets when they passed. She made good use of all she learned too, providing tidbits that informed his negotiations through foreign bureaucracy, but he wondered suddenly if he'd kept her too busy to actually experience all she'd wanted to.

They'd been there to work, though. That's what he did and who he was.

He scowled as he contemplated how little of those countries *he'd* seen.

"It doesn't matter what I want," she sighed. "Lucy will have school—"

"Years down the road," he argued, not letting her finish. "I'll make allowances for that, but you know as well as I do it will take time to put things in place. For the next few years, as long as she has us, she'll be happy anywhere. I'm not talking about leaving tomorrow. I realize you have medical checkups. We'll stay here as long as you need, but later in the year I don't see why we can't take a few weeks in Milan. My mother is already asking when I'll bring her to New York."

"I can't live with you permanently. How would we explain it to people? Your future bedmates sure wouldn't like it, and what if one of us wants to get married?"

Irritated by the mention of bedmates and life mates, he dismissed both. "I've never been interested in marriage and see even less point now. As for bedmates, for Lucy's sake, we should keep that in-house."

Sirena suddenly stopped the swing. Raoul sensed refusal so tangibly he bristled.

"Wow. For Lucy's sake I ought to have sex with you?

That's the kind of reasoning even someone with my damaged morals has trouble following."

"If we sleep together, it'll be because we both want to," he snapped, aware he was handling this badly, but she was frustrating the hell out of him. "That train wreck last night was a head-on crash from both sides. You want me and when you get cleared by the doctor, you'll be cleared for sex. Think about *that*."

CHAPTER SIX

SIRENA DIDN'T HAVE much choice about whether to think on it. Her body was enamored with the idea of falling into bed with her old boss. Her mind drifted in that direction at the least bit of encouragement. Asleep, awake... He was always nearby, smelling like manly aftershave or endearingly like baby powder, telling family secrets to Lucy or speaking in some sexy foreign language on the phone, the syllables drifting teasingly into her ears...

She got so she conjured reasons not to trust him in order to counter the attraction, which wasn't healthy. *I've never been interested in marriage and see even less point now.* That certainly told her where his interest in her as a *bedmate* started and stopped.

They wound up having abbreviated conversations punctuated by glances of awareness and stubborn avoidances. She *had* to move back into her own flat.

The trouble was, her neighbor's niece was still begging to take it over. Sirena began thinking that if she could find a decent job in a less-expensive part of London, she might be able to keep renting out her existing flat and take something smaller for herself. Her flat was an asset she didn't want to lose and without a better income soon, she would. Even at that, she wasn't sure how she'd pay for day care so she could work.

Which was the sort of worn path of worry that made her

circle back to what Raoul was offering. But it would be so *wrong*. He had wronged her and continued to feel wronged *by* her. She might have drunk herself into oblivion out of frustration if she didn't have a baby to think of. At least she could meet a friend for a small one.

Raoul didn't know what to make of her announcement that she was going out for the evening. His brows almost went through his hairline, but she didn't let that deter her.

"Amber is a friend who moved to Canada years ago. She's coming into London tonight. It's her only free time, so I'd like to join her for tapas and a drink and leave Lucy with you."

"Are you sure you're up for it?" he asked with one of those sweeping glances that lit fires all over her.

"Of course," she said more stridently than she intended, but the way she tingled every time he so much as turned his head in her direction was driving her crazy. She couldn't wait to get Amber's objective view of this situation.

With a shrug, Raoul said, "Pack a bag and we'll stay at the penthouse. That way you won't be so late getting in and I can go into the office in the morning. We'll test-drive one aspect of this arrangement I've suggested."

One aspect. Part of her wanted to refuse on principle, but she liked the idea of a shorter trip home. Her doctor was pleased with her progress, but between Lucy's needs and her body's wants, she wasn't sleeping enough.

And by the time she'd packed, driven in, unpacked and settled the baby, she was ready for bed, not a night on the town. She put on a black skirt and ruffled green top anyway. Both were a bit tight. At least her hair was an asset. She'd been clipping it up for months and hadn't realized how much it had grown. She rather liked it clouding around her shoulders, drawing attention from her still-thick waist. Wearing heels and makeup for the first time in ages, she looked pretty good.

Echoes of her stepmother's critical voice swept through her, cataloging her flaws and bringing Sirena down a smidge, but she had been practicing how to block that painful denigration for years. She stood straight and ignored the whispers of insecurity, jumping when Raoul appeared in her bedroom doorway.

"*Who* is this Amber?" he asked in a dark growl.

"A friend from school." Sirena turned from the mirror, a wicked slide of excitement careening through her as she took him in.

He wore jeans and a button-down shirt open at his throat, cuffs rolled up to his forearms. He was the man who always made butterflies invade her middle.

"You dress like this for a woman?" His gaze made a slow, thorough study of her from collarbone to ankles.

"This is all that fits. I can't show up in my sweats and trainers. Or do you mean I look like a pile of socks pushed into a leg of tights? Should I change?" Her hand went to the zip of her skirt.

His expression was dumbfounded. "Yes. *No*," he insisted. "You look fine. Excellent. Beautiful. You're not meeting a man?"

"Because my dating profile of 'unemployed new mum with custody issues' is so irresistible? No. I'm meeting a *girl*friend. I wish you would quit calling me a liar."

"I called you beautiful," he said with a raking glance of masculine hunger, his frown both askance and…not critical, but not pleased.

She curled her toes in her shoes, disconcerted by how admiring and possessive he seemed. "I wasn't fishing for flattery."

He barred the door with his arm.

An uncomfortable silence stretched as her stepmother's voice did a number on her again, cataloging the extra pounds and shadows under her eyes and lack of a manicure, but as Raoul skimmed his gaze down her figure once more, and his expression reflected nothing but male approval, she felt quite beautiful.

The swirling sensation in her abdomen redoubled and little sensors in her body began reaching out toward him, tugging her with magnetic power toward him.

She forced herself to stand still, but he dropped his arm and stepped forward until he was standing right in front of her, towering despite her heels. His gray eyes shone with a startlingly warm regard as he scanned her face and hair. Strong hands came up to frame her face with disconcerting tenderness.

Her breath stalled in her lungs as he started to bend his head, his gaze on her mouth.

"What are you doing?" she managed, pressing against his chest.

He paused, gaze smoky with intent. "Reminding you that if a man comes on to you tonight, you have one right here willing to satisfy your needs."

He began to lower his head again but she leaned away.

"Don't smudge my lipstick," she argued shakily, the best protest she could rouse when her whole body wanted to let his take over. Her breasts ached for contact with the hardness of his chest and heat pooled between her thighs. A fine trembling invaded her limbs, making her weak. Her arms longed to reach out and cling to him.

At the last second, he veered to bury his lips against her neck. His light stubble abraded her skin while his open mouth found a sensitive spot on her nape that took out her knees.

"What are you doing?" she cried, melting into the arms that caught her. Her nipples sharpened into hard points as he applied delicate suction, marking her.

She should have stopped him, but she was held not just by his strength, but by a paralysis of physical joy. Her mouth ached for the press of his while her mind became a turmoil of unconscious thoughts, processing only the sensations of knowing hands skimming her curves as he laid claim to her hips and bottom. He was hard, ready, so tempting—

"You make me lose my mind," he growled, steadying her before he released her. "Do not start anything with anyone tonight. The car is waiting. That's what I came to tell you." He walked out.

Raoul didn't resent Sirena taking a night out, but he didn't like having no right to question her comings and goings and suspected the reason was old-fashioned jealousy. *Not* an emotion he'd ever experienced, and definitely unwelcome, but she was so hot. As sexy as a year ago, but less buttoned-down and professional. With her hair loose and her full breasts brimming her top, he'd seen what every man in London would see: a beautiful woman.

And he wouldn't be there to warn them off with a don't-even-try-it stare.

He shouldn't have kissed her, but he hadn't been able to resist imprinting her with the knowledge he wanted her. She'd been skittishly avoiding him since their kiss outside Lucy's bedroom and he'd been trying to ignore how badly he craved her, but his hunger grew exponentially every day.

It was frustrating as hell, but no matter how uncomfortable they both were with each other, they were equally devoted to Lucy. He couldn't countenance anything more than a few hours of separation from his child, so he kept coming back to sharing his house with her mother.

Disgruntled, still smelling of her perfume, he waited in the foyer to watch her leave, arms folded.

Sirena appeared, checked her step and flushed. Ducking her head, she opened her pocketbook. "I have my phone if Lucy needs me."

"We'll be fine. Do you have David's number?" he asked, mentioning his London driver.

"Yes, it's programmed—" She swept her thumb across the screen and frowned. "Oh, I missed this from Amber. She's sick. That's disappointing."

More like devastating, if her body language was anything to go by. Raoul was disgustingly relieved, but as he watched her shoulders fall and the pretty glow of excitement extinguish from her expression, he couldn't help feeling sorry for her.

She tempered her sad pout into a resigned quirk. "All dressed up and no place to go," she said wryly. "Sorry to drag you all the way to London for nothing. I guess it'll be sweats and trainers after all. I'll just let her know I got the message..." She ducked her head to text a reply.

"You were really looking forward to this," he commented as she finished.

She shrugged. "We chat online, but it's like with my sister. Sometimes I want to see her and it's frustrating when I can't." She blinked and he thought he glimpsed tears, but she started back to her room.

"Sirena."

She stiffened, not turning. "Yes?"

He'd surely regret this, but there was something about the brave face she was putting on and hell, she looked amazing. He couldn't let this butterfly crawl back into her shapeless cocoon.

"Come have a drink with me." He jerked his head toward the unlit lounge.

"What? No. Why? I'll be feeding Lucy later. I can't."

How many shades of refusal was that, he wondered with a twinge between amusement and exasperation.

"We'll stick to the plan," he countered. "Have the glass of wine you were planning to have with your friend and

I'll feed Lucy a bottle when she needs it. Going out was obviously something you were anticipating."

"It wasn't the wine." She rolled her eyes. "I wanted to see my friend."

"So come tell me why she's so special to you." He herded her toward the lounge and suspected she only let him because she was trying to pull away from contact with his palm against the small of her back.

"I don't understand why you'd want me to." She scuffed her spiky heels as he crowded her into the room with the sunken conversation area and the wet bar in the corner. He gave up trying to steer her and walked ahead of her, turning on a lamp on the end table before he brought the track lighting over the bar up to half power, keeping the mood soothing and intimate.

"You keep accusing me of not taking time to ask about your life. And…" He gestured at where her leg peeked from the slit in her skirt to the ruffles that framed her cleavage. "I can't stand the idea of this going to waste. I'd take you out, but unlike you I haven't arranged a sitter. Here. Have a seat and tell the bartender about your day."

He held one of the high stools and she hesitated before warily scooting her hip onto it. He let his gaze linger on the curve of her pert backside as it flowed into the slope of her lower back. Damn, but he wanted to stroke and claim.

Thief, he reminded himself, but it didn't do much to quell his hunger. Rounding the bar, he looked for a suitably light white wine in the small cooler.

"I should tell David he's off for the night," she said in a tone that put him back a year. Efficient, forward with responsibility and attention to detail, lilting just enough to invite a correction if she was off course. She rarely ever had been, except—

As she placed the call, he gestured for the phone.

She handed it across, brows lifted with inquiry.

He enlightened her as he made his request of David. "We've had a change of plans. Can you run to Angelo's and ask them to make us a couple of plates? Whatever they have on special, but no mushrooms for Sirena. You can go home after that."

"Are we working late?" she mused facetiously.

"I don't feel like cooking. Do you?"

"*Can* you cook? I've never seen you try."

"I can grill a steak." He was currently polishing glasses like a pro, having picked up both skills working in restaurants for much-needed cash a long time ago.

"But a man in your position never *has* to do anything, does he?" Her lips curved in a deprecating smile, niggling him into a serious response.

"I'm always irritated by the suggestion I haven't worked for what I have. I might have been born into a life of privilege, but that bottomed out thanks to my stepfather. Everything I have I built myself, and it comes with obligations and responsibilities that take up time. If I can delegate the small things, like cooking a steak, so I can negotiate a union contract to keep myself and a few hundred people working and fed, I will." He poured two glasses and pushed one toward her.

She looked at her wine, then gave him a glance of re-assessment. Lifting her glass, she awaited the soft clink of his.

"To pleasant conversations between old friends," she said with gentle mockery.

He leaned back on the far side of the space behind the bar, eyeing her through slitted lids. "I can't get used to this."

"Used to what?" She set down her glass and rotated her knees forward so she faced him, elbows braced on the bar's marble top.

"This woman full of backchat and sarcasm. The one with secrets and a double life. The real you."

She might have flinched, but her chin quickly came forward to a defiant angle. Her gaze stayed low, showing him a rainbow of subtle shadows on her eyelids. "You're attributing me with more mystery than I possess. Yes, I'm being more frank with you than I was, but you can't tell your boss he's being an arrogant jerk, can you?" She lifted her lashes to level a hard stare at him. "Not if you want to pay the bills."

He thought about letting this devolve into something serious, but opted to keep things friendly. "I wouldn't have fired you for saying that," he assured her, waiting a beat before adding, "I would have said you were wrong."

Her mouth twitched, then she let the laugh happen and he experienced a sensation like settling into your own sofa or bed. *Definitely a bed,* he thought as a tingle of pure, masculine craving rose inside him. He let himself admire her painted lips and graceful throat and the exposed alabaster skin on her chest to the swells of her breasts. Why had he never taken her to dinner before?

Oh, right. She had been working for him.

It was freeing not to have that obstacle between them anymore.

Slow down, he reminded himself as she sobered and flicked a glance in his direction. The sexual undercurrents might be acknowledged, finally, but just because he wanted to bed her didn't mean he should.

Sirena couldn't take the intense way Raoul was staring at her. Every single day of working for him, she'd longed for him to show some sign of interest in her. Now that he had, it scared the hell out of her. But then, she knew better than to trust he was genuinely interested.

Accosted by harsh memories, she slid off the bar stool and took her wine to the expansive glass windows where the London Eye and the rest of the waterfront stained the river with neon rainbows.

"So is this how you start all your flashy dates? Or do they end here?"

"Flashy?" His image, only partially visible in the dim reflection on the glass, came around the bar to stand like a specter behind her.

"Women line up for the privilege, so I assume a date with you is pretty fantastic. Are they impressed when you bring them back here for a nightcap?" And a thorough seeing to? *Don't think about it.*

"I don't go out of my way to impress, if that's what you're implying. Dinner. A show. Does that differ hugely from one of your dates?"

She cut him a pithy look over her shoulder. "Since when do I have time to date?"

He absorbed that with a swallow of wine. "You've suggested a few times that I overworked you, but you also want me to believe your private life included a man who could have fathered Lucy. Which is the truth?"

"I was saving face when I said that," she admitted to the window.

"So I was an ogre who demanded too much? You could have said something."

Sirena hitched a shoulder, bothered that she felt guilty for not standing up for herself. "I didn't want to let you down or make you think I couldn't handle it." There was her stepmother walking into the room again, tsking with dissatisfaction, setting the bar another notch higher so Sirena would never, ever reach it, no matter how hard she tried. But oh, how she tried, hating to fail and draw criticism. "Some of that's my own baggage. I'm a workaholic. You can relate, I'm sure."

He moved to stand beside her. "I thought you were

happy with the workload. It didn't occur to me I was killing your social life. You must have felt a lot of resentment."

He was jumping to the conclusion that that's why she'd
stolen from him.

"No." Annoyed, she walked to the far end of the windows. "I never had a social life, so there was nothing to
kill."

"You weren't a virgin. There was at least one man in
your life," he shot back.

"One," she agreed, staring into the stemmed glass. "His
name was Stephan. We lived together for almost two years,
but we were both starving students, so date night was microwave popcorn and whatever movie was on the telly."
Stephan had had about a thousand allergies, including alcohol, so even a cheap wine or beer had been out of the
question. "Sometimes we went crazy and rented a new
release, but my hand-me-down player said 'bad disc' half
the time, so it wasn't worth the hassle."

"You *lived* with him?" Raoul's brows went up in
askance reaction.

"It's not the same as dating," she hurried to argue. "It
was—" Convenient. A desperate act in a lonely time. A
mistake.

"Serious?" he supplied in a honed voice. He moved a
few steps closer, seeming confrontational, which disconcerted her.

"Why are you judging me?" She rounded the conversation area, circling back to the bar, where she took a big
gulp of wine before she set down her glass. "All I'm saying is that I never dated. This is turning into a long conversation about nothing."

"You lived with a man for two years. That's not nothing, Sirena. Did you talk about marriage?"

"I—" She didn't want to go there, still feeling awful
about it. Crossing her arms, she admitted, "He proposed.

It didn't work out." There, that was vague enough to keep her from looking as bad as she felt.

"You were *engaged*—"

"Shh! You're going to wake Lucy," she hissed. "Why are you yelling? I'm sorry I said anything." She looked for her watch, but she'd removed it because it didn't go with this outfit. "David should be here with the meals soon, shouldn't he?"

Raoul could barely compute what he was hearing. Another man had been that close to locking Sirena into marriage forever. How could he not have known?

"Did working for me cause the breakup?" he asked with a swift need to know.

"No." She sounded annoyed.

"What then?" For some reason this was important. He needed to know she'd severed all ties with this other man, irrevocably. "Do you still have feelings for him?"

"I'll always love him," she said with a self-conscious shrug.

The words rocked him onto his heels, like the back draft from a semitruck that nearly flattened him.

"In a friend way. That's all it ever was. A friend thing. Do you really need all the gory details?"

"I do, yes," he said through lips that felt stiff and cold. He wondered how he'd kept his wine from spilling, because he'd forgotten he held the glass. He moved to set it on an end table before giving Sirena his full attention, still reeling with shock when really, it wasn't as if people living together was a scandal. He just hadn't realized she had been so deeply involved with anyone. Ever.

When he lifted his gaze to prompt her into continuing, a shadow of persecution clouded her expression.

"It was a lonely time in my life. Amber was in Canada, my family had left for Australia. Stephan was the first boy who'd ever noticed me—"

"I find that hard to believe," Raoul interjected.

"The first boy I'd ever noticed had noticed me, then. Maybe there were crushes before that, but I wasn't allowed to go out when I was living at home—not even to spend the night at Amber's, in case we snuck out to a party. My stepmother wasn't having a pregnant teenager on her watch, so there were chores and a curfew and a little sister to babysit. When I enrolled at college, Stephan was the first boy I had the opportunity to spend time with. He was nice and I was romantic enough to spin it into more than it was." She shrugged again, looking as though she wanted to end there.

"It was obviously more if he proposed."

"That was impulse on his part. I decided to quit my degree and go with the business certificate so I could start earning proper money, rather than temping and doing transcription around my courses. He was afraid I'd meet someone else and I realized I wanted to, so we broke up."

Raoul felt a shred of pity for the man's desperate measure that hadn't paid off. At the same time, he was relieved, which unsettled him. He saw nothing but misery and remorse in her, though. "A puppy love relationship isn't anything to be ashamed of. Why do you feel guilty?" he asked.

"Because I hurt him. Part of me wonders if I wasn't using him because I was broke and didn't have anywhere else to turn. I didn't mean to lead him on, but I did."

The buzzer announced David with their meals.

Raoul turned to let him up, but all he could think was, *You used me. Do you feel bad about that?*

CHAPTER SEVEN

TYPICAL OF ANGELO'S welcoming charm as a restaurateur, he had sent along a single white rose with a silk ribbon tied to the stem. *We've missed you,* the tag read.

Sirena stifled a pang of wistfulness as she picked up the budding flower from where it sat next to her plate and searched for a hint of scent in the tightly closed petals.

David had brought the basket of chinaware and scrumptious smells to the table beside the pool, setting it out in a way she imagined he'd done for countless of Raoul's paramours. Everything glittered, from the silver to the candles flames to the stars and city lights winking in the warm night air. Raoul set relaxing acoustic guitar music to come through the outdoor speakers and arrived with their glasses.

His brows went up with silent inquiry.

"Fast asleep," Sirena answered. She had known Lucy would be, but checking on her had been a timely excuse to leave Raoul's intense presence. She wasn't sure she was ready to face him again.

A distant beep sounded, signaling that David had left the apartment. They were alone again. *Round two,* she thought and reached for the wine Raoul set above her knife tip. He had topped up her glass, bringing the temperature of the pinot grigio down a degree so it soothed her throat as she drank.

She hesitated to start eating, even though the food was Angelo's typical appetizing fare of creamy pasta, bright peppers and fragrant basil. This wasn't like all those other times when she and Raoul had a tablet or laptop between them and she had chewed between typing and answering calls. They'd never stood on ceremony while working, but this was anything but casual. More than ever, she was aware of Raoul's potent masculinity, his quiet habits of sharp observation, his undeniable air of command.

And she was hyperaware of her dolled-up attire, the way even Angelo seemed to know this was different and had added the extra touch of silver and china.

This felt like a date.

"Problem?" Raoul asked.

She shook her head, chastising herself for falling into old fantasies of romance. "Just thinking I should put this in water," she said, gesturing to the rose.

"It can wait until we've eaten," he said.

He seemed to be waiting for her to start and that made her nervous. She searched for a neutral topic to break what felt like a tense silence. He spoke first.

"Why didn't you go to Australia with your family?"

Oh, hell, they were going there, were they? It wasn't enough to pry open the oyster, making her feel as though her protective shell was snapped in half and left with jagged edges. No, he wanted to poke a finger into her vulnerable center and see if there was a pearl in there, one glossed over for years, but gritty as obsidian at its heart.

She licked sauce from the corner of her mouth, stating plainly, "I wasn't invited."

He lowered his fork as his brilliant mind absorbed what was a logical and sensible answer, yet didn't make sense at all. He frowned. "Why weren't you invited?"

She held back a rude snort at a question she'd never been able to answer. Picking up the napkin off her lap, she dried her lips, wondering if she'd be able to get through this plate of food when her appetite was fading so quickly.

"I had just started school," she said, offering the excuse Faye, her stepmother, had used. "My father had given me some money toward tuition, about the same amount as airfare. It didn't make sense to throw it away."

"So you were given a choice between school and going with them?"

"No." She couldn't help the bluster of resentment that hardened the word. Old, angry tension started clenching up her insides and she had to make a conscious effort not to let it take her over. Picking up her fork, she deflected the subject a little.

"This is why I was looking forward to dinner with Amber. She knows my history with my stepmother and lets me vent about whatever is bothering me, without my having to lay the groundwork and examine how much is my fault and whether I'm being paranoid. Amber takes my side, which is refreshing, whereas if I try to explain it all to you—" she waved a hand toward him, feeling herself getting worked up, but unable to stop it "—you'll be like Stephan and say maybe Faye didn't mean it that way, that I'm being oversensitive and her reasons make sense and I'm misinterpreting. Her reasons *always* make sense, Raoul. That's the beauty of her dictatorship."

Oh, God, shut up, Sirena.

She clenched her teeth, intending to drop the subject, but she couldn't hide the way her hand trembled as she tried to twirl noodles onto the tines of her fork.

"Why don't you give me an example," he suggested in a tone that echoed with reasonability, as though he were trying to talk a crazy person off a window ledge.

Sirena crammed too big a bite into her mouth, but he waited her out, saying nothing as she chewed and swallowed. The pasta went down like a lump of coal, acrid and coarse.

"For instance," she said tightly, "when I was so pregnant and swollen I could hardly get myself out of bed, worried I would *die,* I asked if my sister could come and was told that my father's plumbing business had fallen off and Ali had exams and the doctors were keeping an eye on Faye's thyroid so the timing really didn't work."

She glanced up to see a frozen expression on his face. "You should have called *me.*"

A pang of anguish struck. She'd been tempted a million times, but replied, "The people who were supposed to love and care about me wouldn't come. What was the point in asking you?"

He jerked back as if she'd thrown her pasta in his face.

She looked away, trying to hide the fact she was growing teary over old conflicts that would never be resolved. Her stepmother cared nothing for her while she, Sirena, loved her father and sister. There was nothing that could be done except manage the situation.

After a few seconds, he inquired in a stiff tone, "What about Amber? Why didn't you call her, if you're such good friends?"

"She's in a wheelchair." She cleared the huskiness from her throat. "Which isn't to say she wouldn't have been a help, but my flat is a walk-up and she has other health problems. That's what brought her to London. She's seeing a specialist then heading straight home."

His silence rang with pointed surprise. "I really don't know anything about you."

She wasn't touching that with a ten-foot pole.

They ate in silence for a few minutes until he asked, "Your father wasn't worried about you?"

"Of course, but he remarried because he didn't know

what to do with a little girl. He wasn't about to play mid-wife to a grown woman."

"And your sister? She can't make her own decisions?"

Sirena let out a poignant sigh, bristling at his judgment because if he didn't understand Ali's vulnerability and how much she needed support, he'd never understand why she'd taken his money for the young woman.

"Ali's young for her age. She struggles in school, so exams are a real issue for her. Pitting her against her mother has never seemed right, no matter how much I've wanted to. I adore her like I can't even tell you and I miss her terribly. I practically raised her. Faye wouldn't change a nappy if I was around to do it. Homework was me, running flash cards and spelling lists. The questions about puberty and sex and buying her first bra all came to me. But they left nearly eight years ago and I haven't seen her since. Faye had been cooking up the move the whole time I was applying to school, never mentioning it until my plans were sealed. Tell me that's not small-minded and hurtful."

"You could have gone to see them."

"Oh, with all my spare time working two jobs while studying? Or do you mean after you hired me? Go all the way to Australia for one of those generous single weeks you'd allow me? Every time I asked for more than five days you'd get an expression on your face like you were passing a kidney stone. I tried taking a stretch after that trade fair in Tokyo, but the database melted down in Brussels, remember? I had to cancel."

A muscle ticked in his cheek. "You might have explained the circumstances."

"To what end, Raoul? You never once showed the least bit of interest in my private life. You wanted an extension of your laptop, not a living, breathing woman."

"Because you were my employee," he bit out, pushing away from the table in a minor explosion.

She'd seen him reach the limit of his patience, but usually within the context of a business deal going south. To have that aggressive male energy aimed at her made her sit very still, but he wasn't throwing his anger at her. He paced to the edge of the pool, where he shoved his hands into his pockets and scowled into the eerie glow of the blue-green depths.

"You have no idea what it's like to lust after your co-worker, knowing that's the one person off-limits."

I beg to differ, she thought, but swallowed it back because... She shook her head. "How can you say something like that when you made it quite clear "

"I know what I said that day. Stop throwing it in my face," he growled. "Why do you think I let it go so far so fast in Oxshott? I'd been thinking about it for two solid years. And the next day—" he gestured in frustration "—the very next day, I found you'd been stealing. You betrayed my trust and you used me. What the hell was I supposed to say? Admit you'd hurt me? It was too humiliating."

She'd *hurt* him?

No. She didn't let herself believe it, not after all these months of scouring the joy and tenderness from her memories, reframing it as a meaningless one-afternoon stand. Maybe in her mind their day in Oxshott had been special, but all he was saying was that he'd had sexual feelings for her while she'd been employed by him. That was only a fraction more personal than being *handy.* His ego had been damaged, not his heart.

"I was trying to behave like a professional as well," she said thinly. "Not dragging my personal life into the office. I don't see the point in sharing it now." She plucked her napkin from her lap and dropped it beside her plate. "You still don't care and I still can't see my family."

"What makes you think I don't care?" he swung around to challenge.

His naked look of strong emotion was a spear straight into her heart. She averted her gaze, tempted to dissect what sort of feelings underpinned his intense question, but refusing to. That way lay madness.

"Don't," she said through a tight throat. "You hate me and I'm fine with that because I hate you, too." *Liar,* a voice whispered in her head, but she ignored it along with the hiss of his sharp inhale. "Let's just keep things as honest as possible. For Lucy's sake."

It was hard to look at him, but she made herself do it. Made herself look him in the eye and face his hatred with stillness and calm while she wrapped tight inner arms around her writhing soul.

"I wish it was that simple." He surged forward to grip the back of his chair. "I want to hate you, but now I understand why you felt you couldn't come to me. You didn't know I was acting uninterested to curb my attraction, but it was there all along."

She recoiled, swinging from disbelief to heart-pounding excitement to intense hurt that he had treated her the way he had regardless of having feelings for her. They weren't very strong if he could behave like that, were they?

Speaking very carefully, crushing her icy fingers together in her lap, she stated the obvious. "Lust is not caring, Raoul."

He straightened to an arrogant height.

"No, listen," she rushed on, fearing he thought she was begging for affection. "I didn't think one hookup meant we were getting married and living happily ever after. I'm just saying I thought you had some respect and regard for me. But even a dismissal slip would have been better than having me arrested without speaking to me. That was…"

She faltered. He was staring at her with an expression

that had gone stony. Steeling herself, she forced herself to continue, even though her voice thinned.

"Discovering I was pregnant, knowing they'd take the baby from me in prison—" She stood in a shaken need to retreat, very afraid she was going to start to cry as the memories closed in. "Even my stepmother didn't go that far to hurt me."

"I didn't know you were pregnant," he reminded her ferociously.

"Exactly! And if you did, you would have gone easy for the baby's sake, not mine. You didn't care about *me*. Not one bit."

CHAPTER EIGHT

RAOUL FELT AS though he was pacing in London's infamous fog. The walls of his penthouse were clear enough, the sky beyond the windows dull with a high ceiling, but his mind wouldn't grasp a lucid concept. He kept replaying everything Sirena had said last night, which had him writhing in a miasma of regret and agitation.

Lucy squirmed in his hold.

He paused to look at her, certain she must be picking up his tension. That's why she was so unsettled. He was pacing one end of his home to the other trying to soothe her, but neither of them was finding any peace.

How peaceful would Sirena have felt pacing a twelve-by-twelve cell?

His stomach churned.

He hadn't let himself dwell on that picture when he'd been trying to put her away, but now he couldn't get it out of his head. Vibrant Sirena who craned her neck with excited curiosity from the airport to the business center in every city they visited, locked in a cage of gray brick and cold bars.

You hate me and I'm fine with that because I hate you, too.

"What are you doing in here?"

Her voice startled him, causing a ripple of pleasure-pain down his spine. He blinked, becoming aware he'd wandered into the small flat off the main one. It was meant for a housekeeper or nanny, but stood empty because his maid service came daily to his city residence.

"Just something different for her to look at." He stopped rubbing Lucy's back and changed her position so she could see her mother. "She's fussy."

Sirena's brow crinkled as she took in the rumpled clothes he'd been wearing since their unfinished dinner by the pool.

His neutral expression felt too heavy on his cheekbones, but he balked at letting her see the more complex emotions writhing in him—uncertainty and yearning that went beyond the simply sexual. Pain. There was a searing throb inside him he couldn't seem to identify or ease.

"Have you been up all night? You should have brought her to me." She came forward to take the baby and was greeted with rooting kisses all over her face. She laughed with tender surprise, a sound that his angry attempt to jail her would have silenced forever. His heart shriveled in his chest.

"Did Daddy forget to feed you?" she murmured as she moved to the sofa.

"I tried a few minutes ago. She wasn't interested." His voice rasped.

She flinched at his rough tone, and flicked him an uncertain glance. "Giving him a hard time, are you?" She shrugged out of one side of her robe and dropped the strap of her tank top down her arm to expose her breast.

He had walked in on her feeding so many times she was no longer self-conscious about it. He didn't think of it as sexual, but seeing her feed their daughter affected him. It was the softness that overcame Sirena. Her fingers gently swirled Lucy's dark hair into whorls as the baby relaxed and made greedy noises. Her expression brimmed with such maternal love his breastbone ached.

He hadn't known she was pregnant when he'd pushed for jail time, but she had. She must have been terrified. While he, the first person she should have been able to rely on, had been the last person she would ever consider calling.

She glanced up. Her smile faded. Last night's enmity crept back like cold smoke, suffocating and dark. "I've got her," she said, dropping her lashes to hide her eyes. "You can get some sleep or go in to the office like you planned."

"No. I can't."

He ran a hand through his hair, becoming aware of a persistent headache and a general bruised feeling all over his body. His breath felt thick and insufficient. He spoke in a voice that very reluctantly delivered what he had to say.

"Sirena, you know I lost my father. What I never tell people...I found him. I came home from school and there he was, overdosed. Deliberately. He'd been having an affair with his secretary." He paused. "I called an ambulance, tried to revive him, but I was only nine years old. And it was too late."

Sirena's eyes fixated on him, the green orbs wide with shock. "I had no idea."

"I hate talking about it. My mother doesn't speak of it either."

"No, the few times she mentioned your father she sounded as if..."

"She loved him? She did. I only know about the affair because I found the note in the safe when we moved. It was full of assurances that he loved us both, but he still chose death because he couldn't live without this woman. I can't help blaming her." He knew it wasn't logical, but nothing about his father's death made sense to him.

"The note was the only thing left in the safe," he continued. "My stepfather had emptied it of everything else. My mother loved him, too, and he appeared to love her back.

I thought she'd found some comfort with him after our loss, but my stepfather was using her. He gambled away every cent we had. I came home from university because he'd had a heart attack and that's when I found the phones were about to be cut off and the electricity was overdue. We lost him and the house in the same month. My mother was a mess, grief stricken, but also feeling guilty for having trusted him and giving me no indication things were sliding downhill so fast."

He pushed his hands into his pockets, seeing again his mother's remorseful weeping and hearing her broken litany of, *He said he would turn it around.*

"You mentioned last night he was the reason you started over. I didn't realize it was that grim. What did you do?" Her voice was all softness and compassion, her bared shoulder enhancing the picture of her as vulnerable and incapable of causing harm.

"I developed a deep animosity toward anyone who tries to rob me," he admitted with quiet brutality.

She paled. Her gaze fell and her expression grew bleak.

"Maybe it doesn't excuse my having you arrested without speaking to you first, but I felt justified when it happened. I was... Damn it, Sirena, it was a perfect storm of my worst nightmares, falling for my secretary the way my father had, then being betrayed by someone I had come to rely on. I lashed out hard and fast."

She gave a little nod as she drew the sleepy infant off her breast and shrugged her robe into place. "I understand."

How many times had he seen that look on her face, he wondered, taking in the lowered lashes and stoic expression. He was tough to work for, he knew that. He pushed himself hard and was so overcommitted he didn't have time for mistakes. She'd always been the first to hear about any he found.

The phrase *long-suffering* came to mind as he saw past

her impassive expression to the self-protective tension in her body language. For the first time he heard the stark despondency in her voice. It had the same underlying incomprehension he felt when he talked about his father's suicide. She didn't understand. She was merely accepting what she couldn't change.

His heart lurched. He prided himself on supporting his family and living up to his responsibilities, but he had leaned heavily on Sirena when she worked for him. Where was her pillar of support, though? Her talk last night of being scared and ill and forsaken by her family had terrified and angered him anew. He wondered why she had needed the money. She had never said, but he was damned sure it wasn't for gambling debts or high fashion or drugs.

"Why did you steal from me, Sirena?"

She flinched at the word *steal,* then a kind of defeat washed over her, shutting her eyes and making her shoulders slump. "My sister needed money to pay her tuition fees."

The words left a bang of silence like a balloon popping into jagged pieces. He hadn't expected it, but it seemed oddly predictable after the fact.

She rushed on. "She was so upset after working so hard to get accepted to her degree program. They have a huge waiting list. She couldn't just wait a semester and apply again. And she'll make an amazing teacher, because she understands what it's like to struggle. I honestly thought it would only be for a few days until Dad got payment from his customer— Please don't go after him for repayment," she said with sudden stark alarm. "Things happened with his business. He doesn't have it and he's really struggling. It would kill him to know how much trouble I got myself into."

Her misery was real, her regret so palpable he could taste it. There was no struggle over whether to believe her.

The explanation fit perfectly with her revelations last night about her love for her sister. He'd always seen her as loyal. It was why he'd been so blindsided by and furious about her dishonesty. It was exactly like the woman he knew to step up and fix things as expediently as possible.

None of that excused her behavior, but at least he understood it.

"I think she'll go down for a while now." She rose, pale and not meeting his eyes.

He should have let her leave him to his thoughts, but put out his hand to stop her.

She halted, eyes downcast. Subtle waves of tension rolled off her. He could tell she wanted to be away from him, but she wasn't willing to allow contact with his outstretched arm even to brush it aside so she could leave the room.

Her refusal to touch him spread an ache of dismay through him. They'd torn the curtains back and exposed their motives for treating each other the way they had, but it didn't change the fact that she'd stolen and he'd wanted her jailed for it. Those sorts of injuries took a long time to heal.

But they had to ignore the pain and make this work in spite of it.

"The simplest, most advantageous solution for Lucy would be for us to live together permanently," he began.

Her shoulders sagged. "I know, Raoul. But it wouldn't work. We don't trust each other."

She seemed genuinely distressed. He felt the same, but he couldn't give up. It wasn't in his nature.

"We can start over. We've cleared the air. Damn it, Sirena," he rushed on when she shook her head. "I want to be with my daughter and you feel the same. You can't tell me you'd rather put her in day care for most of the time you'd have her. And when she's with me, I'm hiring a nanny to watch her so I can work? It makes no sense."

"But—"

"We put this behind us," he insisted, overriding her. "You just have to be honest from now on. Swear to me you'll never steal from me again. I want that promise," he stated firmly. More of an ultimatum, really.

Her eyes welled. He was coming at her from so many angles and she was still muddled from a rough sleep. She'd been deeply hurt last night. She'd tossed and turned, convinced that telling him anything about how badly he'd wounded her had been a mistake. What would he care? He would find a way to use it against her.

When she'd risen, she'd been determined to start the move back to her flat.

Then she'd found him looking like a pile of forgotten laundry, hair rumpled, sexy stubble on his cheeks and tortured shadows under his eyes. Her heart had been knocked out of place and was still sitting crooked in her chest. Everything he'd said had put her determination to leave him into disarray.

Falling for my secretary...

That barely there hint of regard shouldn't make her blood race, but it did.

"We've managed until now and we were furious with each other," he cajoled.

"I'm still furious," she interjected with more exasperation than heat. A lot of her bitter loathing was dissolving. She couldn't help it. Getting that peek into his past explained so much, not least his single-minded determination to succeed.

And it did nothing to dissipate the attraction she felt toward him. If anything, it was worse now. The thick walls she'd built against him were thinning and little fantasies of somehow finding a future with him, earning his trust and maybe his love, sparkled like fairy dust in the edges of her vision.

So dumb.

Given what he'd just told her, it was time to accept that he would never, ever love her. The best she could hope for was this, a truce and a fresh start.

Injustice sawed behind her breastbone like an abrasive file.

Lucy grew heavy in her arms. She started to change her position, then let Raoul take her, watching as the limp infant was tucked lovingly into her father's chest.

Folding her empty arms, she tried telling herself she could manage alone, but she couldn't ignore his point about day care.

"My mother wants to see her," Raoul added in quiet insistence. "You know how hard travel is on her. Lucy obviously hates the bottle. We could force the issue—"

"No!" she blurted, hating thinking of Lucy being distressed about anything. If she preferred to breast-feed, well, this was a finite time in both their lives.

"You'll come to New York with us, then."

"Don't start with your pushy tactics! I know how you work, getting a small concession and turning it into a major one," she said with mild disgust. "I'll *think* about New York. And if I go, it won't be as your—"

Lover? Mistress? Girlfriend? The words all sounded so superficial and temporary, paring her self-worth down to nothing.

"Nanny?" he prompted, mouth quirking briefly, then he sobered. "I'd have to hire one if you don't go. I'd prefer to pay you. You could quit the transcription."

"Don't make it sound easy. It's not."

One long masculine finger touched her jaw, turning her face to his. "What's hard? Making the promise about not stealing? Or keeping it?"

His challenge pinned her so she felt like an insect squirming in place, unable to escape even though she wanted to scamper away. Dying by increments, she felt the spasm of hurt reflect in her face before she was able to mask it, but a pierce of pain stayed lodged in her heart like an iron spike.

Looking him straight in the eye, she defiantly said, "I will never take anything from you. Ever."

He held her gaze for so long she almost couldn't stand it. Tightness gripped her chest and her skin felt too small for her body.

He nodded once.

As he walked away, she hung back, trembling. Had she lost or won?

Raoul's mother cried when she held Lucy for the first time.

"I never imagined he'd give me a grandchild. He's such a workaholic." Beatrisa was a tall, slender woman who dressed well and bound her silver hair into a figure eight behind her head. Her subtle makeup enhanced her aristocratic features and she wore elegant jewelry that Sirena suspected were gifts from her son.

Beatrisa had always seemed to lack a real spark of life and now Sirena understood why. She felt a tremendous need to be kind to the older woman, and was glad she'd conceded to the trip, even though everything about staying in this house was awkward.

"She thinks we're a couple," she hissed when they were given a room to share.

"What a crazy assumption, with the baby and all," he drawled.

"You should explain to her."

"How?" he countered with exasperation.

Oh, that attitude of his grated. Especially since she could see how it would go. Beatrisa was being incredibly polite, plainly trying not to pry as she accepted their "modern" relationship with a murmur about admiring independent women. Any attempt to clarify would crack open the marriage question and Raoul *didn't see any point in that*.

Not that she wanted to marry him. No, they might have found a truce and a crooked understanding with their revelations about their past, but it wasn't as though he'd magically fallen in love with her. For her part, she was too aware of how easily she could tip back into crazy infatuation with him, making her vulnerable to his dominant personality. He'd broken her heart once already. She couldn't let him do it again.

"I'll use the bed in Lucy's room," she said.

His sigh rang with male frustration. "The doctor cleared you for more than travel, didn't he?"

"So I'm supposed to fall into bed with you?" She swung around to glare at him across the foot of the enormous, inviting bed with its plump pillows and slippery satin cover. "I realize you think I slept with you to hide my crime, but sex isn't that mindless for me. I need feelings on both sides."

A chill washed over her as her words rang in her ears. Nausea threatened, the kind that came from deep mortification. She was an independent woman, all right, one whose only solace against her obsession with her boss was that he'd never known how deep it went, but she'd just snapped her way into humiliation. Her clothes might as well be on the floor around her ankles, she felt so naked and exposed.

He stood arrested, but the wheels were spinning fast behind his inscrutable stare.

Trying to stay ahead of any conclusions he might draw, she gathered her toothbrush and pajamas from her bag, aware she was shaking but unable to control it.

"Of course, I'm given to self-deception," she stammered. "And thank God, or we wouldn't have Lucy, would we? But we both know how we feel about each other now and I make enough fresh mistakes without having to repeat old ones, so…"

She practically ran from the room before locking herself into Lucy's, where she threw herself facedown on the bed and quietly screamed into a pillow.

CHAPTER NINE

RAOUL HAD GROWN up in New York, but he didn't care for it. Too many dark memories. The climate didn't help, always socked in with rain or buried in snow or suffocatingly humid with summer heat. The place forced on him a heavy feeling of a weight inside him that he couldn't shift.

He was already struggling with that when he paused on his way into a meeting and instructed the receptionist to interrupt him if Sirena called.

"Ms. Abbott? I thought she'd left the company! How is she?" The woman's warmth and interest were sincere.

His blunt "Fine" was rude. And a lie. He'd left the house before he'd seen her this morning, but he knew from the way Sirena had blanched last night that she was not fine. He almost suspected she was injured in a way he hadn't considered.

Brooding while he half listened to his engineers develop a workback schedule, he did some math. He hadn't added everything together since their talk over drinks that night by the pool because he'd been distracted by other revelations, but if it was true she hadn't dated after that boy in college, she'd had exactly one lover since her first, ill-fated relationship.

Him.

...sex isn't that mindless for me. I need feelings on both sides.

The way she'd practically grabbed the voice bubble from the air and gobbled it back indicated pretty clearly that she'd never meant to admit that to him. Which made it disturbingly sincere.

Of course, I'm given to self-deception, she'd added to cover up, but that only made him grind his teeth, wondering if he was as well. Despite her motives for stealing unfolding into a picture of a woman who hadn't believed he'd help if she asked, he'd never wavered from believing she'd slept with him to cover up what she'd done.

He needed to believe it. Anything else was too uncomfortable. He wasn't a womanizer. He didn't take advantage of the vulnerable. He didn't lead women on.

She hadn't expected one hookup to be a marriage proposal, she'd said, but had expected to be treated with respect.

At the time of their affair, he'd been way past respect into genuine liking. Affection. Something deeper he'd never contemplated letting himself feel.

God, when he thought back to how those twenty-four hours had gone, it was like another lifetime. The sweetness of her, the relief of finally giving in to touching her, the powerful release that had shaken him to the core...

The doors opening inside him, a sensation like footsteps invading the well-guarded depths of his soul. Even as their damp, half-clothed bodies had been trembling in ecstasy, he'd crashed back to the reality of what they'd just done. Whom he'd done it with. How vulnerable he felt.

His inner panels had lit up with alarm signals. While Sirena's plump lips had grazed his throat, he'd been withdrawing, deeply aware of a sense of jeopardy. His father hadn't killed himself because he'd fallen for his secretary. He'd killed himself because he'd *fallen.* In love. Deep emotions drove men to desperate acts.

What he'd felt for Sirena in those loaded minutes of sensual closeness had scared the hell out of him.

He'd pulled away, said something about the rain having stopped. By the time he'd dropped her at her building and returned to his own, he'd been primed for a reason, any reason, to knock her so far away from him she'd never reach him again.

And he had.

...Even my stepmother didn't go that far to hurt me.

Rather than killing himself, he'd destroyed what had been growing between them.

It was a sickening, horrid vision of himself. He lurched to his feet, needing to escape his own pathetic weakness, but only drew the attention of the room.

"Problem, sir?" The group stood back to look between him and the Smart Board where the schedule could have been written in Sanskrit for all the sense it made.

"I have to make a call," he lied, and strode through the maze of cubicles clattering with keyboard strikes into his office. It contained two desks, one that was a bold, masculine statement and the other a stylish work space that, for a time, had been the first place he glanced. Now it stood as a monument to his colossal overreaction.

He rubbed his face, hating to feel this tortured, this *guilty.* The fact remained, she had stolen from him, he reminded himself.

But he hadn't lashed out at her for that. She'd angered him, yes, but her real crime had been moving him in the first place. Sirena had dared to penetrate walls nobody else had dared breach.

Lust isn't caring.

No, it wasn't, but what he felt wasn't mere lust.

Sirena was grateful that Raoul had left for the office before she rose. Of course, she was also hypocrite enough to miss him despite her chagrin over her revelation last night. There was also envy and disgruntlement that he still worked in one of the many dynamic, ever-changing offices she had loved so much. Who had taken her place? She hated her usurper on principle.

Chatting with Beatrisa, hearing stories of Raoul's childhood became a nice distraction from her muddled emotions.

When he returned unexpectedly at lunch, it was with a surprise: tickets to a matinee. "Musicals aren't my speed. I'll stay with Lucy. You ladies have fun."

It was an incredible treat, the sort of thing Sirena used to wish for every time they visited New York, but had never found time or funds for. Afterward they had tea and scones in a glitzy café until Raoul texted that his daughter had inherited his stubborn streak.

Giggling over his self-deprecating assessment, they rushed back so Sirena could feed their starving baby. Full of excitement about their afternoon, she was disappointed when Raoul said, "I'm glad you enjoyed it. Start dinner without me. I have a call to make."

When he found his way to the table, he was wearing his cloak of remoteness. His mother didn't pick up the signals of his distraction, but Sirena did. While Beatrisa talked about their day, the feeling of being left out of his world struck Sirena afresh, but she supposed his turning aloof was better than another clash like last night's.

As Beatrisa wound down over coffee, Raoul finally said, "I'm afraid we've had a change of plans, Mother. We won't be able to stay the week. The company has been nominated for an award in L.A. I have to fly out to pick it up."

"You hate those things!" Sirena blurted. It had always been her job to figure out who could show up in his place, make the arrangements and prepare a speech.

"Surely you could do that without dragging Sirena and the baby across the country? They can stay here with me," his mother said.

Sirena shrugged. Lucy was out of sorts enough with the time change from London. She didn't need another one.

Raoul only gave his coffee cup a quarter turn and said, "They've specifically asked if Sirena would attend. It's that bunch we worked with for the special-effects software," he told her. "You always made an impression with my associates. You've been sorely missed by a lot of them."

Sirena flushed hot and cold, not sure how to respond. She missed everything about her job, but she couldn't go back to it, so she tried not to think of it.

As she considered all those beautiful women he'd taken to galas and cocktail parties, she also felt too inadequate to be his date. "I never attended that sort of thing with you before—" she started to dismiss.

"Things are different now, aren't they?"

How? She lifted a swift glance and collided with his unrelenting stare, like he was pushing his will upon her. She instinctively bristled while the fault line in her chest gaped and widened. "There's no one to watch Lucy."

"Miranda's agreed to fly in and sit with her."

"You want to fly your stepsister to L.A. to babysit?" It was ludicrous—and the way he briefly glanced away, as though he wasn't being honest with her, put her on guard.

"She flies all the time doing those trade shows. We'll need to leave early, but we'll come back here for a day or two on our way back to London." He rose, putting an end to the discussion in a completely familiar way.

Old habits of accommodating his needs collided with the newer ones of taking care of her baby's needs and her own. "Raoul."

"This is important to me, Sirena. Please don't argue."

Wow. Had he just said *please?* Shock struck her dumb long enough he was able to escape without her raising another argument.

By morning, it was too late. When he said early, he meant early, coming into her room to begin packing Lucy's things while shooing Sirena's sleepy head into the shower. Being naked and knowing he was just beyond the door made her senses flare, but he was completely indifferent. They were on the plane within the hour.

Lucy didn't enjoy the altitude climb, so they were well in the air before Sirena caught her breath. She gratefully embraced a cup of coffee while Raoul swept and tapped his way across a tablet screen.

"I liked that crew from the film, too, but I can't believe you shook us out of bed for them. What's really going on?" she asked.

"Use the stateroom if you want more sleep." He didn't even look up.

"No, I've had coffee now. You'll have to entertain me," she volleyed back.

His gaze came up with pupils so big his eyes were almost black. After a checking glance to their sleeping infant, he swung a loaded *"Okay"* to her.

In a blink, he'd transformed from the distracted man intent on his work that she'd seen a million times to a predatory male thinking of nothing but sex.

Her skin tightened and a flush of excitement flooded her with heat. Most betraying of all, tingles pooled in a swirl of sharp desire deep between her thighs.

His tense mouth eased into a smile of approval while he took a slow visual tour to her breasts, where her nipples stung with need. He didn't move, but suddenly he felt very close. He knew exactly what was happening to her.

She yanked her gaze away, but the picture of his masculine beauty stayed with her. The man had a chest to absolutely die for and she ached to see it again, run her hands over his smooth shoulders and taut abs.

Embarrassed by her shortened breath and prickling arousal, she swallowed and said a strangled, "I think we've covered that. It's not on."

Silence. And when she risked a glance at him, his jaw was clenched.

"Because you think I don't have feelings for you," he growled.

"I don't expect you to," she stated stiffly, then had to dip her face to stare into her empty mug, hiding that she was going red with indignity. "Obviously you've been very decent, taking me in when I was sick, but that was more to do with Lucy, wasn't it? And yesterday was nice, but it was a treat for your mother. Shows like that aren't your thing, you said. So you sent me, which isn't to say I didn't enjoy it, just that I realize it wasn't about me."

"You have a stellar opinion of me and my motives, don't you?"

"I'm not trying to insult you."

"You're doing a helluva job of it anyway. Let's hope this trip redeems me in your eyes." He went back to his tablet, shutting her out, which was probably a good thing.

He'd disconcerted her, sounding almost injured. A tiny worm of ambiguity niggled in her. Was she working so hard to protect herself she was failing to see the softer feelings she'd once been convinced were there? Or was that delusion a short trip to another painful tumble?

Despite the caffeine in her system, she wound up dozing and before she knew it, they were in California. They didn't stay in the suite they'd used two years ago, when he'd been working with the special-effects company. This was a new, ultrachic building designed on a curve, like a giant glass-and-bronze half cylinder with its back to the ocean.

Inside the penthouse, the floor-to-ceiling windows were framed in gray-and-white geometric squares. The tiles and carpet marked severe paths through the open plan of lounge, kitchen and dining area. All of the furniture was angular and modern, but luxury softened the hard edges. Jewel-colored pillows and billowy curtains gave it a sexy, romantic feel and the stunning three-sixty views to mountains and ocean and cityscape were breathtaking. Sirena's first thought was of the bath she'd take after dark, surrounded by the twinkling lights of the city.

As was her habit, she ran a brisk inventory as she explored, ensuring all the standard arrangements for Raoul were made.

"No Chivas and no cord for the secure internet connection." She adjusted the drapes in the main room to let in more of the brilliant sunshine and view of the ocean. "I'll call down. Did you want extra of that rain forest coffee you like to take home?"

He didn't answer, so she turned to see him watching her with a bemused expression. "I would love that, thank you."

His appreciation poured sunlight directly into her soul. A huge smile tried to take over her face and she had to turn away to hide how easily he flipped her inside out. What the hell was she doing? No way was she begging for a shred of affection. She needed to nip this craziness in the bud.

Fortunately their daughter woke and demanded attention, then a stylist showed up with a measuring tape and color swatches.

"What? Why?" Sirena argued as Raoul took the baby so she could lift her arms.

"We have that red carpet thing in a few nights," he reminded.

"You didn't say red carpet! I thought it was a cocktail party." She hadn't gained a ton of baby weight, she'd been too sick, but even though she'd started back on the treadmill, she was soft and had bags under her eyes. She'd never clean up like the stunners who usually hung off his arm.

Muddled and anxious, she got through the rest of the day and took some air on the balcony after her bath. A clean breeze off the water had swept away the pollution and the air smelled sultry, helping ease her unsettled mind.

Raoul joined her, making her stomach quiver in awareness. She ignored it.

"What do you think? Should I buy this unit?" he asked her.

"They're treating you to entice you?" she guessed, then rejected the luxurious surroundings with a haughty shake of her head. "I came out here to see the fireworks over the happiest place on earth and I don't, so it's no good. A major disappointment."

"I'll make the purchase contingent on their moving the building to the next county," he drawled.

"Ha!" She laughed at herself. "I guess I should look at a map. It's just always been on my bucket list to come to L.A., visit the theme parks, wear the ears…I thought I'd at least see the castle and fireworks while I'm here."

"You can. We'll be here a week. Take—" He cut himself off.

"Lucy isn't old enough to appreciate it," she scoffed, predicting what he had almost said. "No, I can wait for another time." To avoid his casually rumpled masculine appearance, she looked to the glowing blue of the pool jutting off to the right on their patio, a few steps down. It was surrounded by orange trees in oversized planter pots and twined with pinpoints of white lights. "If we come here again."

She pursed her lips, wondering if this would become her life. She suspected so and took a second to self-examine.

"Honestly, Raoul? I don't know if I would have enjoyed the travel half so much if we'd been staying at cheap motels and taking shuttle buses through dodgy back alleys. You live very well. It makes me very tempted to stay with you indefinitely."

"That's the only thing that tempts you?" he asked with mild disgust.

"Oh, please! You're not that insecure." She was glad it was dark and he couldn't see how she took in his physique with a swift glance and a hard blush. "You could drive shuttle buses for back-alley hotels and still be appealing. But I've been in a relationship for practical reasons. They aren't as great as they look. I knew from the outset I wouldn't be with Stephan forever and it made me feel trapped. I don't want to start something unless I know we can both live with it for a very long time."

"I hate hearing you talk about him." He gave her a pointed look that landed like a spear in her heart, sticking and vibrating. "This is the least practical or convenient relationship I've ever been in, but I still want it. I want *you*."

"You mean you—"

"Don't," he interrupted, stepping so close she pressed back into the rail.

She gripped it, heart zooming into flight as his potent masculinity clouded around her like a spell. "Don't what?"

"Don't say I only want my daughter. I do, but that's not why I'm out here. I saw you walk by with this robe clinging to your damp skin…" His nostrils flared as he seared his glance down her front. One hand came out to hook into her belt, tugging lightly.

She should have let him draw her forward, but she resisted and the belt gave way.

Something flared in his silver eyes.

"Raoul." She meant it as a protest, but it was more an enticing whisper.

"Let me," he growled, and with slow deliberation parted

the edges of her robe. She was naked beneath and he swore softly before murmuring, "You're so beautiful."

She desperately needed to hear that. No one ever complimented her and seeing the way he ate up her figure was intensely gratifying, filling up a hollow part of her soul.

The cool night air made her skin pimple, knotting her nipples into tight buds and swirling to the warm places on her abdomen and thighs. A suffusion of heat followed, one incited by the hunger and admiration in his long study of her nude body.

"Raoul," she moaned again, this time on a helpless whimper.

He groaned and stepped closer, shod feet bracketing her bare ones. His hot hands sought her waist and circled to her back, pulling her into contact with his clothed body.

She let her head fall back and met his open mouth with her own, moaning at how wrong this was, but she wanted it so badly. Her hands eased their death grip on the rail and rose to stroke over his shoulders, following the rippling flex of his shoulder blades as he swooped his hands over the small of her back, cupped her naked bottom and pressed her aching pelvis into firm contact with the ridge of his erection.

There was no buildup, no mental debate as she wondered if her desire would catch. Everything about this man turned her switches on. All he had to do was touch her. Her hips tilted, seeking more intimate contact with his hardness.

He thrust his tongue into her mouth in a bold claim, cupping the side of her face to hold her for his devastating kiss. She pulled him into her, wanting more, loving the stroke of his restless hands, the way he clasped her breast and gently crushed and massaged and softly bit her lips before he lifted his head.

"Bedroom," he said, starting to pull her with him.

She came to her senses and pressed a hand to his chest. "We can't."

"Why not?"

For the life of her, she couldn't think of anything but feeling him inside her, but that's all it would be. Physical feelings. For him. As much as she wanted the release, she knew she'd never be able to keep it that dispassionate.

As he read her rejection, his expression shuttered. With a feral noise, he lurched away and grasped the rail to the lower balcony and vaulted to the pool deck below.

"What—?"

He landed between a pair of loungers, took three long strides and dove straight into the pool.

Sirena slapped a hand over her mouth, astonished as she watched his blurred image move with surprising speed down the length of the pool, all underwater. He was halfway back before he rose to gasp for air.

"What on earth are you doing?" she cried.

"What the hell are you doing?" he shot back, kicking himself to the far edge and hefting himself onto the ledge. Yanking at his wet shirt, he struggled out of it and dropped it beside his hip with a splat. "Get inside or I'm coming after you and this time I'm not stopping."

She spun and ran to her room, where she hugged a pillow and told herself she'd made the right decision.

Even though it felt like the stupidest choice in the world.

"Sirena!"

It was about time. Odious man. First he made her so crazy she spent the night hating herself for not sleeping with him when she would have hated herself more if she *had.* Then he left without writing a note, giving no indication of where he was going or when to expect him back—although he had prepared the coffee machine so all she had to do was push the button. But that didn't excuse barging in here, yelling her name when she was trying to settle their daughter.

"Sirena, where—? Oh, here you are."

She glared at him. "She was almost asleep." She lightly bounced the baby to ease her drowsy eyes closed again.

"I'll take her," he said, moving forward in that battleship way of his.

"Fine, take her. Maybe she'll sleep for you," she muttered, grouchy because she needed a nap as badly as the baby. Maybe going to bed with him *now....*

Shut up, Sirena.

"I don't want you to drop her," he said, "when you see who I brought with me."

She sidestepped to see a young woman in the doorway. She was blonde, slender, achingly sweet-looking in her innocent way, yet tall and curvy without a hint of the preadolescent she'd been the last time Sirena had seen her.

Allison's soft brown eyes pooled with giant tears while a great, mischievous grin widened her mouth. She thrust out her arms. "Me," she burst out. "Surprise!"

A scream built in Sirena's throat and locked it, making pressure expand so hard her eyes filled. She choked, trying to gasp a breath, and began to shake. She wanted to move forward, but her knees started to sag.

Raoul caught her, swearing under his breath. "I should have warned you, but I didn't want to build expectations if anything went wrong—"

"It's okay, it's okay," she babbled, wanting to lean into him, but forcing her legs to take her weight. She passed through a thick mist that was pure sparkle and magic. As she reached the familiar yet very grown-up sister she hadn't seen in the flesh for so long, she realized her cheeks hurt because she was smiling bigger than she ever had in her life.

"You don't look this tall when we talk on my tablet,"

she managed to joke even as a sobbing laugh rattled her voice. Her arms wrapped around her baby sister.

Ali's wiry embrace crushed her. The physical contact was so deeply moving, Sirena thought she'd break into pieces.

The women held on to each other a long time, making Raoul's throat close. Ali, as she had said she liked to be called, had chattered excitedly in the limo, her gestures and tone oddly Sirena-like despite the faint accent and fair coloring. She had a measure of Sirena's steely core, too. When he'd asked why her parents hadn't come, she'd only said, "Mum can be funny sometimes," and lifted her chin. He had the impression this trip was a bit of rebellion and wondered if it would have repercussions for Sirena.

He'd found Faye oddly obstructive, considering he was offering an all-expenses-paid trip to America. It had been hard to sidestep her demand to speak to Sirena, which he suspected might have called off Ali's visit.

Navigating future altercations with Sirena's family was a concern for another time, he decided. This moment, seeing how happy he'd made Sirena, was worth any trouble down the road.

The women pulled back to stare at one another, glowing in an aura of happiness.

Ali's gaze dragged toward him. "Can I meet Lucy? I've been dying to hold her." She took her niece and sighed with adoration. "Oh, Sin, she's beautiful."

Sin, he silently repeated, liking the nickname immediately.

"Isn't she?" she agreed shamelessly. Eyes damp and lips trembling, she cupped her flushed cheeks in her hands.

She looked so taken aback and overwhelmed Raoul couldn't help moving toward her, but he was almost afraid to touch her. She seemed to be struggling to contain her emotions. Gently he smoothed her hair back from the side of her face. "I didn't realize this would be such a shock. Are you all right?"

She flashed him one glimpse of the naked emotions brimming in her, then threw herself at him.

He took the hit of her soft weight with a surprised "Oof," then closed his arms around her.

She buried her face in the middle of his chest, clinging tightly, barely audible as she said, "You have no idea what this means to me. I can't ever thank you enough."

All the sexual heat of last night's embrace came back as he felt the press of her breasts and was surrounded in her feminine scent of green tea and pineapple. An incredible wash of tenderness accompanied it. He had wanted to do something nice, but had never suspected such a small thing would have such magnificent impact.

Governed by instinct, he enfolded her and stroked her hair. His chin caressed her silky locks and he had to swallow the emotion from his throat. He'd forgotten this perk in letting yourself feel for another person. When they were happy, you were happy. He should have done this sooner. He'd healed a crack in her heart, filled it with joy, and it had taken nothing. A couple of phone calls and a plane ticket. What did that say about how lonely she'd been?

"You two," Ali trilled. "You're so cute."

Sirena realized she was all over Raoul like a coat of paint. After last night she didn't know where they stood. She always felt this pull around him and at this moment felt positively anchored to him, heart to heart. Misreading their connection had gotten her where she was today, though.

Pulling away, she swiped her fingertips under her eyes, trying to get a grip. Her overwhelmed emotions weren't just shock and joy over seeing her sister. There was a huge part shaken to the core that Raoul had done this for her. She tried to remind herself that the cost was nothing to him, but to think of it and make it happen…

Did he feel something for her after all?

She was afraid to look at him, fearful of seeing nothing and being disappointed. She was also terrified that her shields were so far gone he'd see right into her soul and the special place she reserved for him beside it.

"This is like Christmas," she said, clearing her throat and searching for a stronger voice. "It really puts to shame that tie I haven't even bought Raoul."

They all laughed and the day became a celebration, California-style. Raoul ordered brunch and mimosas and joined them on and off as they sat by the pool, taking turns holding Lucy and catching up.

By evening, the excitement and time change had caught up to all of them and they had an early night. The next morning, she met Raoul in the kitchen.

"Can't sleep?" she said with an attack of nerves, feeling defenseless without Lucy or Ali to still the sexual vibrations that immediately flared between them. "Me, either."

"I have a heavy morning before everyone in Europe goes home, but I wanted to give you these." He showed her some tickets. "I almost spilled the beans about Ali when you were talking about this the other night. I came this close to suggesting you take her."

Sirena gasped as she caught sight of the iconic fairy circling the castle with dust. "Raoul!"

"For the record, these are not for her, although I hope she enjoys the day as much as you do. These aren't for Lucy either." The bright tickets came alongside her jaw as he crooked his finger under her chin, making her lift her eyes to his. "These are for you, because it's something you've always wanted."

He kissed her. The gesture was so sweet she couldn't help clinging to his lips with her own. His taste made goose bumps lift all over her body.

She swallowed and tried to hide how touched she was

by joking, "I really don't know what to think of all this."
Her heart rate picked up, daring to conjecture there might
be a hint of tenderness or affection driving him after all.
"You're going to a lot of trouble just to keep things *in-house*."

"Sirena—" His quick, defensive blurt of her name made
her wave a quick hand.

"I'm sorry. I'm being cheeky because I don't know what
else to say, not because I think you have ulterior motives,"
she hurried to excuse.

He sighed. "I realize I'm not demonstrative." Leaning
near the sink, he studied her, his body language heavy. A
range of emotions ran across his usually stoic face. They
were intimate and, she suspected, indicative of deep scar-
ring.

She instantly wanted to reach out with reassurance, but
felt too shy and uncertain so she wound up standing there
with her hands wringing, the silence thick and awkward.
What could she say anyway? That a couple of kisses and
nice gestures had won her over? They hadn't. She had
tons of misgivings.

He ran a hand over his face. "After my father, I pushed
everyone to a safe distance. What he'd done was too cruel.
He was a good man, a good father. We played catch, went
fishing. It was a perfect childhood. I'll never understand
why he killed himself or how anyone could say they love
someone and hurt them that badly. Letting down my guard
with anyone since then…it's not something that's comfortable for me."

Outwardly she handled what he was saying, taking it on
the chin without flinching, even though she was screaming inside. Even though she was pretty sure she paled and
her bones turned to powder. Somehow she stayed there,
nodding circumspectly, saying, "I understand."

Her words seemed to hurt him. He winced.

"No, I do," she assured, being as honest as he was. "I have my own baggage that makes me worry you'll pull up stakes without a moment's notice. It makes me scared to let things move to…" She swallowed, trying to find a description that wouldn't reveal too much. "To a level of deeper dependence."

"I'm not going anywhere. This is everything I want, right here." He pointed to the floor between them, suggesting the domesticity of waking every morning with her and their little family, which was nice, but it wasn't the fairy tale on the tickets.

She had to let go of that. Better to keep her expectations realistic even if it hurt. And it hurt so much to know he would never love her. Not the way she loved him.

Oh. The knowledge of how deep her feelings had become went through her like a sweet, potent potion. This wasn't infatuation with the boss. It wasn't hormones raging for the wrong man. It was the evolution of feelings and attraction she'd always felt toward him. They had tumbled into deep devotion and longing to make a life with him.

Swallowing the lump that came into her throat, she hid her angst with a smile. "Even though you seem to do everything and I haven't done one thing for you? How about breakfast, at least?" She turned her back on him as she peered into the refrigerator, defusing the charged moment.

The spoiling didn't stop, however. After their day at the park, he appalled the upscale clientele of a rooftop restaurant by daring to bring a baby, of all things, into their exclusive establishment. They saw the fireworks from their table, of course. A trip to the beach was arranged the next day and a drive along the coastline the following. They lunched on fresh seafood and local wines and scouted art studios for bargains.

Then the preparations for the technology awards started.

Raoul escorted them into a design house on Rodeo Drive and handed over his credit card to a stylist.

"Ali, find some things for yourself and if you see something your mother would like, put that on there too. I'm having a prototype of my new gadget flown in for your father. You can take that back for him, but if you see something for him…" He leaned to kiss Sirena's cheek, trailing off as he prepared to take his leave.

"Dad's tastes are pretty simple," she said blankly, startled by his casual affection. He'd been so solicitous these last few days, a hand often finding its way to the middle of her back or resting at her waist, but she still wasn't used to it.

"Whatever you think is best. I'll be at Armani, having my tux fitted. Because I need another one." He rolled his eyes. "I'll come back for Lucy when I'm done."

They seated Ali in an overstuffed armchair and offered her champagne. Sirena leaned down to give her Lucy so she could have her fitting and Ali whispered, "It's like we're living *Pretty Woman*. You're going to marry him, right?"

"Sweetie, I keep telling you, it's not like that. We just had a moment that got us into a situation and we're trying to make the best of it." She didn't know how else to explain her circumstances without revealing details that were far from romantic.

Back when she'd been pregnant and under suspicion, she'd kept the arrest from her family. It hadn't been her father's fault, but he would have felt responsible. She certainly didn't want her sister feeling guilty about pursuing her teaching dream.

Now, well, she didn't want to tell Ali everything for fear she'd think badly of Raoul. The things Raoul had shared with her were deeply personal and without being able to balance his actions against his motives, he would look like a cold, unforgiving monster. Which was miles from the truth.

Sighing a little, she had to admit he was actually what she'd always admired him for being: a strong, ambitious man with a deep streak of responsibility and loyalty to his family. He was gallant after growing up around women, innately desiring to protect and provide for his own. Even if he had been toothless, dirt-poor and overweight, he'd still open doors and show incredible patience for women who couldn't decide which shoes or lipstick to wear. He'd still walk a baby all night and start the coffee for her mother.

And she'd still love him.

"Oh, Sin, you're gorgeous," Ali murmured as Sirena walked back to her.

With a pinch in her heart, she studied the emerald gown and thought about how she was the complete opposite of Raoul. She could dress up in world-class finery, have her teeth whitened, love their baby and he'd still only see her as a thief.

CHAPTER TEN

RAOUL WENT IN search of Sirena, hearing Ali saying with exasperation, "She'll be fine. We both will. I swear."

"But call if you need to. Or text. You have Raoul's number if I don't hear mine?"

Suppressing a grin, he stepped into the doorway of the room operating as their nursery. Vaguely aware of Ali efficiently changing his daughter's nappy, he caught an eyeful of Sin and felt as though his breath had been punched out of him.

She had her back to him, but he was transfixed. He took in the curls pulled away from one ear to cascade like a waterfall over her opposite shoulder. Her off-the-shoulder gown in gypsy-green dipped to reveal one shoulder blade. A cutout on the other side offered a peek of her waist and spine. The skirt draped gracefully over her rounded hips to puddle sumptuously behind her. Distantly, he realized he wasn't getting any air, and that she hadn't even turned around, but she'd stolen his breath.

"Your date is here. Quite a dish, too," Ali said, cocking her chin in his direction.

He barely noticed the girl as the woman turned. Her plump bottom lip was caught in her teeth while her mossy eyes were pools of uncertainty. Always beautiful, Sirena didn't need makeup and the stylist had known it, only enhancing her stunning bone structure and opulent lashes with a streak of frosted jade and shimmering gold.

A wink of emeralds dangled from her ears and encircled her wrist. They were loaners, but he decided to buy them. They matched her eyes too perfectly to allow them to go to any other woman.

"I'm sorry," she said faintly. "Have you, um, been waiting for me?"

All my life.

"Get her out of here," Ali said with a nudge into Sirena's back. "She's being a nervous Nellie even though I keep telling her I babysat all of Sydney until I finally got a proper job at the real estate office."

Raoul held out his arm, not trusting his voice to tell her how beautiful she looked, then winced as she got there first, saying, "You look nice."

Her light touch curled into the curve of his elbow and a subtle mix of aromas filled his senses with floral and berry notes underscored with tangy citrus and a mysterious anise.

He waited until they were in the elevator, where he let the doors close without choosing a floor, before he gave in to temptation and reached to adjust the drape of her gown, revealing her leg and a shoe with a dominatrix heel.

"What are you doing?" She started to step her foot back inside the skirt, but he set a hand on the bared skin of her waist.

"Don't move, *Sin.*"

She gasped, cocking her hip to escape his touch as though it burned, but the flush of color that flooded under her skin and the spark that invaded her glistening eyes told him it was a more erotic reaction.

"You look amazing," he murmured as he removed his phone from his breast pocket.

Her eyes widened in surprise and her wicked mouth

twitched before she screened her thoughts behind a tangled line of mink. "Really?" She settled into a pose with the confidence of a woman who knew she looked her best and was having fun with it. Her shoulders went back, her breasts came up, her hips slanted and her feet parted just far enough to be provocative. "Men are so predictable."

She tossed her hair and offered a screen-legend smile.

"It's true," he agreed, snapping the photo. "We're simple creatures. Now take it off."

She laughed and hit the button for the lobby. "I'm keeping it on at least as long as it took me to get into it. Let me see." Her cool fingers grazed his in a soft caress as she urged him to slant the screen of his phone.

As he studied the photo with her, he saw what he hadn't meant to reveal. He'd liked the way the mirror showed the back of the gown and had angled the frame to catch it, but he hadn't noticed his own expression was caught in the reflection. Lust tightened his face. He wasn't ashamed of it, but his expression held something else.

He tucked the phone away, not wanting to examine the naked emotion on his face.

Discomfited, Sirena told herself she ought to be used to Raoul's mercurial moods, switching from warm familiarity to all business in the space of a heartbeat. With a pang near her heart, she tried to calm her racing pulse and quit building this into something it wasn't. But Ali's romantic nature was contagious. *He's going to propose. Why else does a man go to all this trouble?*

Ali didn't realize this level of luxury wasn't trouble for Raoul. It was completely normal and he probably took photos of all his dates, inserting them into his iLittleBlackBook so he could keep track of who was who.

The biting thought was wiped clear by another and she cringed inwardly. She really was the most misguidedly devoted ex-PA if she had to bite back remarking to him, *You know what might be a cool idea for an app?*

She was trying so hard to ground out her electric excitement she didn't realize the elevator doors had opened onto the opulent lobby.

"What's wrong?" he prompted.

Idiot. Trying to make light of her distraction, she quoted Julia Roberts under her breath. "If I forget to tell you later, I had a nice time tonight."

He didn't get it. In his typically classy fashion, he said very sincerely, "So did I."

Oh.

Her bones went soft as she took the hand he offered and let him lead her to the limo. It was like sitting down to an IMAX film where scenery rushing by became more intense and colorful, pulling her into a surreal world she had seen from a distance before, but that now drew her in three dimensionally.

Bulbs went off as they walked the red carpet. Action stars were everywhere and this wasn't even a big awards show. *Just Hollywood indulging itself,* Raoul had said. Still she could hardly keep her jaw from dropping.

The show was a pageantry of talent, one woman's singing almost bringing Sirena to tears. During a break, Raoul said, "You're really enjoying this."

"How could I not? I don't have any natural talents of my own, so I'm in complete awe of those that do."

"You're an excellent mother, Sirena."

"Oh, please," she deflected, uncomfortable with flattery. "Having a baby nearly killed me and I'm bumbling my way through colic and feeding. I'm hardly gifted."

"Don't joke about that," he said with gravity. "Ever."

Like all criticisms, deserved or not, she took his remark to heart and hid her abraded soul by sitting straight, chin level. His category was called next anyway, putting an end to the short conversation.

He won, of course, which was well deserved. As he rose, he clasped her hand and tried to bring her up with him.

"No!" she said, horrified. Her emotions were right there under the surface, barely contained. She wasn't standing under massive lights when she was this close to tears.

Setting his mouth into a displeased line, he went to the podium and waited for the applause to die down.

"This innovative software came out of a need for a specific effect. It wouldn't have been developed if not for the people who demanded it. But I think the entire team will agree that we wouldn't have delivered on time, on budget without the support of my exceptional assistant at the time, Sirena Abbott. She refused to come on stage with me because she's more comfortable in a supporting role than in the spotlight. I've come to realize that about you, Sin."

The nickname was a tiny endearment, but the intensity of his gaze picking her out across the crowded auditorium was monumental. Later she would realize heads and cameras had turned her way, but in this moment, all she saw and felt was Raoul's undivided attention.

"You recently did the hard work on a very special project in which I played a very small role. I won't take credit for the beautiful baby girl you made us. If we were giving golden statues for that tonight, this would be yours."

Now her makeup was going to run, vexing man! She blinked, trying to hold back the tears.

He was escorted offstage by handlers for photos. He'd warned her that would happen and she gratefully grasped the chance to slip into the ladies' room to collect herself. No one had ever made such a production of appreciating her. She didn't know how to cope with it. Criticism was hurtful, but she was comfortable with it. She knew what to do after receiving it. The path to Better was right there and she always took it.

Arriving at Well Done made her look around in confusion. Part of her wanted to dismiss what Raoul had said as empty flattery, but she knew that wasn't healthy and she loved their daughter too much to reduce the sweet things he'd just said about her, even if that meant accepting praise for her own contribution.

She *did* try to be a good mother and a good person. Was it so far-fetched that he might have noticed and come to value those things about her?

With her breath still hitching, she left the ladies' room and ran straight into Raoul. He was clutching his award in one fist as he paced. He stopped when he saw her.

"I was about to come in there looking for you."

"Shoes and a dress like this are challenging," she joked to hide her discomfiture.

Someone else came into the short hallway and he nudged her farther into the moderate privacy of an area where a bank of outdated pay telephones still hung. That was the millionth time he'd stroked his fingers over the bare skin at her waist and it was totally short-circuiting her brain.

"Are you upset with me?" he asked.

"For what?" She ducked her head to the snap on her pocketbook, not wanting him to see how gauche she felt, unable to take one little compliment.

"For telling the world we have a baby together."

"Oh. That." She pressed her freshly painted lips together, mouth quirking wryly. "It's not the way I would have done it, but I'm not going to pretend she doesn't exist."

"It's not the way I meant to reveal her either. I was fielding some awkward questions backstage about whether we're getting married. It made me realize we should. Then you wouldn't worry about whether you could depend on me."

Stunned, Sirena could only stare at his bow tie, eyes burning as she reflected that it was even less sentimental than Stephan's awkward "Maybe we should get married."

"And before you accuse me of saying it purely for practicality's sake—" He clunked his heavy award onto a shelf and crowded her into a corner. "Let me remind you there's a reason we wound up with an unplanned pregnancy."

There went that hand again, possessively sliding to the small of her back, fingers dipping behind silk as he curved her into him, bumping her thighs into his.

She automatically caught at his sleeve for balance, but her other hand braced her pocketbook into his shoulder. Her head fell back a little, lips parting on a shocked gasp as her entire front lit up with seeking tingles, wanting contact with his.

"Fresh lipstick," she managed as his mouth neared hers.

"I don't care." He pressed hard lips over her trembling ones, both soothing and inciting the ache spreading through her body. Heat rose like a circle of flames around them, burning her alive as they pressed together, spinning and hurtling directly into the sun.

She groaned and met his tongue with hers, lifting on tiptoes to increase the pressure and even diving her fingers into his short hair to pull him down, urging him to kiss her harder. He did, rocking his mouth on hers with feral hunger. Hard fingers dug into her buttock and spine as he crushed her to him.

His erection imprinted her through the fabric of his pants, making the ethereal layer of silk gown seem nonexistent. She didn't want it between them. She wanted to feel nothing but satin skin over hard flesh, flexing muscle and the slam of his heartbeat against hers. She whimpered, almost sobbing in her need for him.

Drawing back a fraction, he muttered, "This is crazy." He had a hand tangled in her hair, clenching a handful in a way that kept her immobile. It would have been too cave-man and primitive if he wasn't also holding her as if he was saving her from a shipwreck and dropping hot kisses down the side of her face to her nape.

She trembled, mortified by how close she was to losing it in public. It was no consolation that he had her buried in a corner. People were coming and going behind him. They had to be glancing this way. Her hands had burrowed beneath his jacket, but they were flexing on his shirt, try-ing to pull it from his waistband so she could stroke the indent of his spine.

"Raoul, we have to stop."

"I know. I'm about to drag you into a janitor's closet." He straightened and pulled his snowy handkerchief from his pocket. He swiped it across his mouth, then asked her with a look if he'd gotten all the color off.

She thumbed a tiny smudge from the corner of his mouth and stole the cloth for herself, thinking to take it into the ladies' room, but he caught her hand and his award and started for the exit.

"What—?"

"Don't make me pick you up, Sin."

"I have a feeling you just did," she mumbled and heard him chuckle as he snapped for a limo.

"That one's not ours," she said.

"Ours will find us when we're ready," he assured her and had them driven about four blocks to the palatial entrance of a hotel. Throwing his platinum card on the counter, he got them a key in record time and seconds later they were walking into the decadence of the honeymoon suite.

Sirena stopped a few steps in, wondering what she was doing. It was one thing to be swept away, quite another to book a room and take off her clothes with deliberation.

Raoul unbuttoned his tuxedo jacket, shrugging out of it and throwing it across the arm of a wingback chair. "Second thoughts? I've had a vasectomy, if that's what you're worried about."

"What?" Her pocketbook hit the floor before she realized her fingers had released it. She quickly crouched to retrieve it, but couldn't take her eyes off the man with his hands pushed into tight fists in his trouser pockets. "When?"

"About a week after we fought about it. You asked if I'd pulled a hamstring on the treadmill and I said, 'something like that.'"

"You should have said—" She was floored, unable to process it. "Why would you do that? I'm a fluke. Other women—"

"I don't think about having sex with other women. Only you."

Her heart stumbled and she had a hard time rising to stand on her weak knees.

"I have condoms, too." He extracted a length of conjoined foil squares from his pocket. "In case you're worried about anything else. I've been tested and have never, ever not used one of these. Which frankly makes me nervous of my performance without one, given it's been so long since we were together."

Her mouth opened. Her lips and tongue wanted to form words, but no air moved from her throat. Her voice had left the building. He hadn't been with anyone else?

"We're good together, Sin." He crossed to her with a laconic scuff of his shoes on the tiles. "Even without taking this to the bedroom. We always were."

"Because I did as I was told," she managed to counter.

He took her chin, forcing her to look into his eyes. Her hair practically lifted off her scalp at his touch. His nearness and the way he studied her mouth caused her breath to stutter.

"I can't stand being around idiots or sycophants or

women who act helpless. You're bright and funny and incredibly competent. I've always been as attracted to that as the knockout body and gypsy looks."

Her lips began to quiver. "I still feel like anything could happen and it would all fall apart and you'd hate me again."

A sharp spasm seemed to take him. "You know what I hate? Not having you in my life at all. Oh, hell, don't cry. There's a lot to build on here, Sin."

"I know," she murmured, fingering the tail of his bow tie, wishing she had the courage to boldly yank it free. "Not to mention how much it would mean to me that Lucy would never wind up with a stepmother like my own."

His bearing hardened before her eyes, taking umbrage.

"Oh, please, you don't really need to hear that's not my only motive. I've been insanely attracted to you for years."

"I do need to hear that," he said with a tight white line around his mouth. "I need to hear it, see it, *feel* it…"

When he covered her mouth with his, the passion behind his kiss was cataclysmic. If she had wanted to be swept away, the tsunami of desire was here, lifting her so she found herself clutched to his chest and carried to the bed. But there an odd, intent stillness took him over. Everything slowed.

He sat beside her to run light fingers from her bare shoulder to her wrist, lifting her hand to his mouth. Hot, damp lips pressed into the thin skin of her inner arm, following the faint blue line to the crease of her elbow.

She compulsively wove her fingers into his silky hair, enjoying the play of the short strands on the sensitive spaces between her fingers. He smelled faintly of aftershave and firmly of himself. The compelling scent overwhelmed her as he nuzzled the hollow of her shoulder, then grazed his lips over the upper swell of her breast.

His shirt was a crisp annoyance as she sought the heat

beneath his collar, restricted by the tight buttons and bow tie and his refusal to crush her under his weight.

"I want to feel you," she complained, restively scraping her fingers up from his waistband to free his shirt, crumpling the fine silk.

He sat up. His narrow eyes glittered with something smug and arrogant, but his movements were urgent as he pulled at his clothing.

He does need to hear it, she thought, even as she rose on an elbow and picked at his buttons, trying to hurry him. As he threw off the shirt, she stroked across the twitching muscles of his chest, lightly scratching with her nails as she stroked from his collarbone to his abs.

"You're so hot," she breathed, thinking, *figuratively and literally.* He epitomized an underwear model's fine physique, but radiated heat from his swarthy, flush-darkened torso. His pure male sexuality weakened her. She was glad she was lying down, but a distant part of her was flinching in alarm. She'd done this once, stroked and satisfied her curiosity and his libido, and the next day her world had been devastated.

"Every time you clip up your hair, I want to let it down," he said in a sensuous rumble, gently seeking pins to release the hair pulled back from her temple. As he finger-combed, he bent to let his hot breath tease the delicate whorls of her ear. "I think of you doing very erotic things to me with this hair," he said, words and lips sensitizing her to screaming pitch before he took her to a new level of shivering excitement, dabbing his tongue and lightly biting and sucking her lobe. By the time he moved to the flesh at her nape, she was head-to-toe goose bumps, forehead pleated in an agony of delicious excitement. He further paralyzed her with soft bites into the incredibly responsive tendons of her neck, making her moan and arch to offer herself.

"What are you doing to me?" she gasped, making no

protest as he slid her wrists upward and clasped them in one of his hands.

"I haven't even got your dress off," he husked, seeking and finding the zip at her side. Slowly he released it, watching her pant as she waited, completely absorbed, wanting nothing except to belong to this man.

"You're like a goddess. A fantasy coming true, making me insane. I can't think of anything but having you." He released his grip on her to peel the one shoulder down her arm, exposing her breasts and avidly looking at them.

"Raoul." She brought her elbows down and forward, forearms wanting to shield herself, but his undisguised desire was a type of seduction. A deep part of her wanted to please him and if the thrust of her breasts excited him, she wanted to give him that.

He clasped the full globes in splayed hands and anointed them with reverent kisses. "So beautiful. So perfect." His hands slid to push the fabric down further and she lifted her hips, letting him take the gown off her legs, leaving her naked but for her slutty shoes and a nude thong that wasn't any kind of cover.

She'd been waxed, plucked, exfoliated and moisturized today, but she still held her breath, fearful he'd make note of her imperfections.

He chuckled with gruff pleasure and drew a wickedly teasing fingertip over the silk covering her hot and pulsing mound. His sure hands skimmed away that defense and suddenly she was painfully aware of wearing only shoes on a broad bed while she writhed in arousal before a half-dressed man.

"Raoul."

She didn't know what she wanted to say, but he said, "Shh," with quiet command.

His brows lowered in concentration as he cupped her hip in one hand, stilling her. His other hand moved to smooth a testing fingertip over her C-section scar. It was the starkest mark left by childbearing, even more pronounced than the faint stretch marks and the fading brown line descending from her belly button.

"Don't," she said, wriggling self-consciously and trying to brush his hand away.

"Tender?"

The scar was oddly both oversensitive and numb, but mostly his touch felt too personal. He bent to touch a kiss there and she gasped, shocked and moved and flooded with embarrassed excitement.

Then he shifted to blow softly over her mound. He'd been seducing her so gently, she'd overlooked how powerful and forceful he really was. Her contracting thighs smoothly parted for his superior strength as he made room for his wide shoulders, settling low to press licking kisses high on the insides of her legs.

"You don't have to…"

"Oh, sweet, hot Sin, I do. I really, really do."

She clenched her eyes shut as knowing fingers caressed. This was the sort of intimacy she'd never been able to relax for, knowing he was looking at her— *Oh, God.* Her muscles clenched on the finger that slid in to test her slippery depths.

"Tell me when I get it right," he said, taking a soft bite of her flesh. At the same time he withdrew his touch, then filled her with the span of two thick fingers. His tongue flicked and she couldn't bite back her keening moan. Everything in her gathered to this one bundle of pure sensation, paradise beckoning with each languid caress that he lazily bestowed on her, as if they had all the time in the world.

It was pure torture and so good she was dying, losing herself, growing wanton, inviting more with a tilt of her hips, encouraging him in gasps of sobbing murmurs.

"I can't take it," she cried, pulling mercilessly at his hair.

He reared back onto his knees with a near-primal growl, making her wail with loss even though she'd forced the issue.

Jerking at his trousers, he freed himself, shoving them off and away before he crawled over her. Her legs instinctively twined up to hitch her ankles behind his waist, trying to draw him down as he clasped the sides of her face and kissed her, hard.

His weight settled, crushing her pelvis before he lifted to allow her seeking hand to clasp his sleek shaft and guide him into her.

He slid home with a delicious plunge that turned his whole body to granite. For a few seconds he was a blistering, immovable cage around her, mouth locked to her lips, his heart the only movement as it pounded the wall of his chest, trying to reach hers.

A sigh of pure bliss left her. It felt so good to have him in her, filling the hollow ache she'd thought would be with her the rest of her life.

Then he eased back, pulling at her nerve endings as though they were harp strings, drawing her taut with ecstatic tension before he thrust again. Joy expanded within her.

The crescendo built, both of them clasping to be closer even as they fought to make the strokes harder, deeper, more irrevocable. This wasn't just her, she knew distantly. He was as lost to need as she was, clawing for satisfaction as if their lives depended on it. It did. She needed this, him, the raw hunger and the sweet struggle and the fight to hold on, hold back, to never let this end, to give and take...

The pinnacle arrived, holding them balanced on its tip, breath caught as they swayed between anguish and joy.

Elation won, tumbling them into the maw. He crushed

her as he throbbed with his final thrusts making deep contractions pulse rapture from her center to the tips of her fingers. Deaf, dumb, blind, she could only feel. She was in heaven.

CHAPTER ELEVEN

RAOUL HAD NEVER feared for his life during sex, but tonight came pretty close. His heart still felt as though it was under enormous pressure. Taxed. Too full.

Sitting on the foot of the bed, he wanted to believe a trip to the cardiologist would fix him, but it wasn't the answer. The woman avoiding his gaze as she pulled the green gown over her head and let it fall into place was the shard of glass piercing his chest.

"Are you all right?" he asked, voice burning like whiskey in his throat.

"Of course." She flipped her hair free of the gown and bent her attention to the narrow zipper along her side.

She'd been the one to hear the chime announcing a text from her sister while he'd been brain-dead from the most powerful orgasm in history. His legs wouldn't hold him, his skin wanted nothing but the silken brush of Sirena's smooth nudity and all his libido could think was *more*.

This sort of dependence scared the hell out of him, making him want to retreat, maybe do some work for a few hours. Definitely remove himself from her presence until he'd recovered his equilibrium.

At the same time, he was disturbed by Sirena's emotional withdrawal. She'd been as caught up as he, it had been incredible, but now she was subtly tense, offering to text the limo driver to pick them up.

He did it, then said what was top of mind before he thought better of it. "I'm not ready to share you. Maybe if we stayed in here a week—"

Like magic, her force field of aloofness fell away and a sweet smile appeared. "If these breasts were detachable, I'd send them ahead and have the driver collect the rest of me tomorrow."

The medieval clamp on his heart eased. Her humor made it easy to amble across to smooth her hair off her shoulder and admit, "That was incredible. Thank you."

"I thought so, too." Her tiny voice tightened the follicles all over his body.

But the way she shyly ducked her head made this all feel too fleeting. He wanted this new circumstance locked into place. Couldn't she see how simply right this was?

"We're getting married," he said with quiet assertion.

Sirena felt something in her ease. She'd been quietly fighting terror that paradise would swing one-eighty into hell again, but his arrogant order let her know he wasn't planning to dump her as quickly as he'd seduced her. Still, she didn't hear anything about love and that tightened her heartstrings to a point near breaking.

Reminding herself they'd come a long way and she shouldn't expect too much, she said lightly, "Let me guess. I have two choices? Say yes now or say yes later?"

He blinked, not revealing what was going on in his quicksilver brain.

"Do you want to say no?" His instant air of detachment pushed her heart to the edge of a plank, but she supposed he could be having as much difficulty dropping his defense mechanisms as she was.

"No." The word came out a bit forlorn. Never had she imagined marrying a man who didn't love her, but if he couldn't see himself having sex with anyone else, she couldn't see herself marrying anyone else. There were enough bonuses to balance the limitations, she promised herself.

"Then it's settled," he said.

She bit lips that wouldn't stop trembling.

They reached the penthouse and Ali eagerly perched across from her in the lounge, practically bouncing with excitement as Sirena sat down to feed Lucy.

"Well?" Ali demanded.

"Well, what?" Sirena asked, inwardly tracking Raoul to the bar.

"Oh, you're hopeless. Raoul, did you propose or didn't you?"

He paused with his glass half raised to his lips, gaze flicking to Sirena's.

"We decided to marry, yes," Sirena said with as little inflection as she could manage.

"I *told* you a man doesn't go all out like this without a ring in his pocket. Let's see it." Ali clapped her hands then held them out, wiggling her fingers to coax Sirena to show her own.

"I—"

To her right, she heard the bottom of a glass hit the bar top with a firm *clunk,* but she refused to look in his direction.

"Sweetie, we have a baby," she said to Ali. "Getting married is a formality. I don't need an engagement ring for the few days it will take to get a license and sign some papers."

"You're not having a real wedding? But you always planned the full dress and fancy cake and Dad walking you down the aisle—"

"I was a kid when I talked like that! No, listen." She hurried to forestall her sister beating this particular dead horse. "Dad and Faye have made it plain they're not up to traveling and Raoul has lost a lot of time with Lucy coming early. It was very sweet of him to arrange for us to have this visit—" she made a point to let him see she was utterly sincere in her appreciation of that, but his inscrutable expression and unmoving stature cowed her "—but we don't need any more disruptions," she finished.

Ali didn't want to let it go, that was her nature. She might be nineteen, but she was still a little girl in some respects. Sirena had grown up enough to realize you had to move past childish dreams and be realistic. She got Ali to drop it and Raoul left the room.

It was Ali's last night, so Sirena wasn't entirely sorry they'd been called back early. She settled Lucy, took off her makeup, then she and Ali had tea and talked about the stars Sirena had rubbed elbows with. Deep inside, she hugged close the secret of all that had happened with Raoul. Ali would never understand if she told her how far they'd come, but the closeness they'd achieved was huge. No brilliantly cut chunk of stone or fancy frock would ever mean as much to her as the way he'd held her as if he didn't want to let her go.

It was late when they finally said good-night and sought their beds.

Sirena came up short as she found hers occupied.

Raoul set aside his tablet as she stopped inside her door. The lamps slanted golden light across his bare chest, making a relief map of his muscled shoulders and abdomen. She couldn't decipher everything in his austere expression, but there was no mistaking the possessiveness of his quick glance from her lapels to her naked legs.

Tremendous self-consciousness struck. Playing with the tie of her kimono, she tried for nonchalance as she said, "I didn't know you were waiting for me."

"I was trying to fix that situation in Milan." His scowl

told her he was still trying. "I'll give my schedule a hard
look and figure out when we can get to Australia. Do you
want to put off the wedding until then?"

"No," she said firmly, hurrying to the bathroom to brush
her teeth, hoping he'd take it as a signal to end the subject,
but he didn't. When she returned to the bedroom, he continued as if she hadn't left.

"I've booked a jeweler to bring some engagement rings
before we have to drop Ali at the airport."

"I won't wear one." The words came out with more ve-
hemence than she meant, but the sort of wedding she'd always dreamed of had been a celebration of love and this
relationship wasn't that soul mate connection. Yes, she
loved him and he'd come a long way toward showing more
than lust for her, but going through all the hoops and bar-
rels of a big wedding would feel fake. It was vitally important they keep things as honest as possible considering
their rough start.

He had one knee crooked beneath the sheet and one
strong wrist braced on its point. "Do you intend to wear
a wedding band?" His tone held a stealthy note of danger
that made her tummy flutter.

She was shocked by how defenseless yet wonderful the
idea of wearing his wedding band made her feel. An engagement ring was a romantic gesture; a wedding band
was a lifetime commitment. Her throat thickened and she
grew warm all over as she murmured, "Of course."

Trying to cloak how disturbed she was, she clicked off
the lamp and gestured toward the one on his side.

He didn't move. "Why won't you wear an engagement
ring, then?"

"Jewelry with stones isn't practical around babies.
And—" She hugged herself. A tiny part of her still hated
for him to think she was avaricious, but it was more than

that. "I'm not interested in being a bride. I just want us to be a family."

His unapproachable vibes dissipated. He reached to flick the sheet back, motioning her into the bed beside him. She hesitated, unable to be casual despite how intimate they'd been a few hours ago. He was naked and despite her exhaustion, she was dying to feel him against her, but shedding her robe as if they'd always been sleeping like this was impossible.

Amusement curled his masculine lips into a sardonic smile. "Really?" He turned away to click off the light.

"Don't laugh," she grumbled as the darkness made it safe to drop her robe and slide into bed.

Warm hands pulled her into contact with his hot, ready body. "I have better things to do than laugh, Sin."

They married in Las Vegas on the way back to New York. Sirena made all the arrangements over the internet and this time, when they were given a shared room at his mother's, she didn't hesitate. Despite the perfunctory ceremony, the state of being married felt surprisingly natural.

They fell easily into old patterns. Within days of returning to London, Raoul had talked her into giving up her transcription customers and taking charge of his personal calendar instead. It came with an allowance similar to her old salary, which was rather generous considering her flat was paying for itself in rent and she didn't have any other living expenses. Still, taking his money needled her. It would probably be healthier for them if she remained financially independent, but she accepted because she loved being part of his day-to-day life.

"And hire me a decent PA, would you?" he added as they finished up breakfast one of their first mornings back.

"Perhaps they have a two-for-one special at the nanny agency," she mused, flicking the screen on her tablet, not looking up even though she was aware of him pausing after rising from the table.

"Do you think you're funny?" he asked above her in the ominous tone that used to make her quake, but now made her grin.

"You just handed me a list that includes booking you a play date—" for squash, but she overlooked that "—and buying your mother a birthday gift. Throw in a nappy change and I'm spot-on."

He was silent, then said, "This is the sort of thing you used to say in your head when you were afraid I would fire you if you said it aloud?"

She kept her chin tucked and lifted only her lashes. "I'm just having fun, Raoul."

"Are you?" She knew him well enough to recognize when he was completely serious, but she was distracted by the way his stern natural handsomeness gave him an air of commanding masculine authority. Her nerve endings came alive in tingling pulses and the rest of her wanted to melt into a puddle of undying adoration.

"Yes," she croaked, and tried to clear the huskiness from her throat, not quite remembering what they were talking about.

"Because there was a time when I planned to offer you a position on my executive. If you'd rather pursue your career, you can have a job with me and it won't be nepotism. You're qualified. Or look for something else that appeals. I would hate trying to navigate the two schedules," he said with a significant pause to let the downside sink in, "but we could make it work if this isn't challenging enough for you."

She warmed, wistful about the reasons her promotion had never come about, but she wasn't sure she would have taken it even if he had offered it. With her nose wrinkled in self-deprecation, she admitted, "I like working directly with you, being part of the action without having to take the lead. It makes me feel needed. Is that bad?"

"You are needed." He nodded at their daughter in her bouncy chair. "By both of us. If I took you for granted before she came along, well, rest assured I came to realize what I'd lost and very much appreciate all you do for me now."

She softened all over. Her smile wouldn't stay pinned. "Thank you for that."

He bent to steal a swift kiss that turned into a lingering one, sweet as molasses. As he straightened and gathered his things, he added, "And you should know by now that my fantasies run to sexy secretaries over naughty nannies."

She was so in love it was hard to remember he didn't feel the same.

Working for him, she had been one of many distant moons in his dynamic orbit. Now she was a part of his world in a way she hadn't expected could happen. Raoul didn't try to cram her into a corner of his busy life. He made a space for her and Lucy that gave them priority over everything else. When work demanded his time outside the office, he made every effort to include her, keeping her firmly at his side, not the least awkward about the fact she used to be his PA.

Tonight's cocktail party was different from an award ceremony or the meet and greet he'd had with his new clients last week, though. No one there had known she used to be his employee. Here, the hosts would likely remember her as the girl with the quick-draw tablet and Bluetooth earplug who had brought them coffee and arranged their lunch.

Sirena braced herself when Paolo Donatelli, an international banker, and his wife, Lauren, welcomed them into the luxurious foyer of their Milan penthouse. They were a stunning couple, Paolo casually elegant in a gorgeously Italian way, his wife tall and warmly glowing in the family way.

"Congratulations on your happy news! You took everyone by surprise. Even Paolo," Lauren said, kissing both Sirena's cheeks.

"You're misquoting me, *bella*," Paolo said, copying his wife's affectionate gesture toward Sirena. "I said if you two were involved, no one would know unless Raoul wanted it known. He's the most discreet man I've ever met."

Sirena blushed, throat going dry as she felt their curiosity for more details on how their marriage and baby had slid under the radar the way they had.

"We surprised ourselves," Raoul said, drawing her closer as he looked into her eyes. The reassurance in his gaze warmed her, easing her past the discomfiting moment. "And discretion is what you pay for, Paolo," he added, neatly halting further prying.

"This is true," the Italian said wryly. "On that note…"

The men disappeared into Paolo's study. Before Lauren drew Sirena into the gaggle of guests, she clasped her arm. "Did we put you on the spot? I'm sorry. The truth is, I'm thrilled. I don't always feel a connection to the spouses of Paolo's associates, but you've always been so nice. I'm glad I'll be seeing more of you."

"Don't think I won't cash in on that," Sirena said, relaxing as she sensed a genuine offer of friendship. "I'm dying to shop with you. You always look amazing and here I am in Milan, but I don't speak Italian."

Lauren's eyes widened in excitement. "I would love that!"

It was the boost of acceptance she needed. Lauren also helped her find her own style, so Sirena's confidence grew as she spent more time on Raoul's arm. Their days were busy and their nights incredible, building tiny bridges of connection she began to trust were sturdy and reliable.

That developing sense of closeness and familiarity brought her into his London office tower one afternoon simply because she was missing him.

"Hello," she said, using her weight to press the door shut behind her while she took in the familiar sight of him at his massive desk against the wall of windows, London's skyline behind him.

"This is an unexpected pleasure." He leaned back.

"Lucy had her photo shoot this morning. I wanted to show you the proofs. It could have waited, but since I was only a few blocks away..." She dug the flash drive from her coat pocket as she came around to the side of the desk where the outlets were mounted. "And I wanted to see your face when you see them rather than—oh!"

Tumbled into his lap, she took a breathless second to figure out how she'd wound up here. As if there was any mystery, when her husband was looking at her as though he wanted to eat her alive. An appreciative smirk twitched his mouth while an intriguing tension made his cheekbones taut.

"Where's Lucy?" He drew the chopsticks from her hair so her waves tumbled free.

Grinning, she toyed with the knot of his tie. "Watching her new nanny try to flirt with your new PA, completely oblivious to the fact she's barking up the wrongly oriented tree."

"Lucy or the nanny?" He released the zip on her calf-length boot and slipped his hand inside. His warm touch cupped her calf then circled to fondle her knee.

She purred, losing track of the conversation. Settling into him a little more, she felt the press of his growing arousal. His light caress climbed to the side of her thigh beneath her suede skirt. When she pressed her lips into his throat, she felt him swallow.

"Did you lock the door?" His hand was well under her skirt now, moving insistently beneath the tight, unforgiving cut, delving to the top of her leg.

"A detail-oriented girl like me? What do you think?"

"I think I'm about to lose all ambition for the rest of the day." He bent his head to kiss her and the phone rang. The heat flaring in his eyes sparked to frustration. "Only you and my mother have that line."

"I might be pocket-dialing you, if that's my phone digging into my hip."

He chuckled, "Smart-ass," and leaned to tap the button for speakerphone. "Mother?" he prompted.

"Yes, it's me."

"Good timing. Sirena is here." The ironic face he made had her catching back laughter with a hand against her mouth.

They exchanged pleasantries before his mother got to the reason for her call: a misplaced bracelet.

"I know it's silly to ask if you remember seeing where I left it, but I've been up and down through the house and it hasn't turned up."

Raoul flashed a glance to Sirena. It was a quick, unexpected slide of a knife between her ribs, barbed with *Again?*

He recovered quickly, even showed a hint of culpability in the way his gaze wavered and flicked away. "I remember you wearing it to dinner," he said to his mother.

"Sirena?" she prompted.

Her ears rang with all that had just gone unsaid. Her skin chilled and the heart that had been flowering open shriveled to a poisoned husk. The bleak world she had inhabited for so many months crept toward her like dark clouds closing in from the horizon.

"Same," she said through a tight throat, all too aware she'd admired the tennis bracelet openly, listening intently to Beatrisa's story of how touched she'd been to receive it from her son for her sixtieth birthday.

It was all going to start happening again and this time it would hurt even more.

Raoul was aware of his wife turning to marble as he finished with his mother—which he hurried because Sirena's growing tension needed to be addressed. She tried several times to climb off his lap, but he held her in place until he'd ended the call.

"Let me up," she said icily.

"I don't suspect you of taking that bracelet," he growled. Doubt might have flickered through his mind, but he was entitled, wasn't he?

She dug her elbow into the middle of his chest. Her legs determinedly tried to find the floor. "Get your hands off me," she snarled.

He lifted his grip, angry that she was angry. He didn't help her rise, just protected his genitals as she scrambled to her feet and zipped her boot. Flushed, with her hair loose and disheveled, she located her purse and would have walked out without another word.

Leaping up, he met her at the door. "You're not walking out like this."

"Oh, you expect me to stay here and put out so you can accuse me of using my body for leniency again?"

The muscles in his abdomen were so tight there shouldn't have been room for his stomach to compress under a blow, but his gut knotted as though she'd kicked him.

He clenched his fist where he'd braced his arm across the closed door, aware that his wife was incredibly passionate, but the lack of inhibition she showed him was the result of weeks of building on their connection out of bed as much as in it. She still had morning-after blushes and charming as they were, they reminded him that physical intimacy was still new to her. She wasn't capable of using sex for any kind of manipulation. It was purely joy and pleasure for both of them.

"No," he bit out, shamed anew that he'd ever reduced her generous giving of herself to such a low transaction. He knew how much damage his accusation had done to her acceptance of his desire and need for her. Bringing it up again only pushed them farther apart than they already were and he felt a cold, anxious sweat break over him, not wanting to be here in this uncertain place. "I do expect you to talk this out like an adult, though. Not storm off in a fit," he insisted.

"I'm the one reacting badly? Your first thought was that I'd stolen again! I knew you didn't trust me when you set up my account without giving me access to any of yours, but to look at me like that, so blatantly accusing me—"

"You did it once before, damn it. Is it so surprising—"

"Once," she cried, holding up a single finger. "One time I thought I'd lean on someone else's resources instead of trying to do everything myself. It was wrong, I know that, but it was *one time*. Have I taken anything from you before or since? Not even a few bob for nappies from the change on your night table. But you can't wait to find fault! Does it feel good? Does it justify the way you hold back your heart and don't trust me? God, I knew it would be a mistake to get this involved with you!"

She turned away, so she didn't see the way he was knocked back, as if her outburst had been a spray of bullets. He couldn't even defend himself, aware that subconsciously he *was* waiting for a sign that his growing feelings for her were misplaced. She was coming to mean far too much to him. Every time he thought the level of emotion between them was as much as he could handle, his attachment grew. The more you cared, the more you risked and he was getting in so deep there was no self-protection left. He didn't like it, he couldn't deny that.

But to hear her call their relationship a mistake was a brutal blow. He hated seeing her shoulders buckle, hated knowing that she was only standing here in this room with him because he was barring the door.

"Look, the thing with the account I set up for you—"

"I don't want to hear it, I really don't. Would you let me take Lucy home? She needs her nap."

"I'll come home with you." He moved to fetch his laptop. As he did, she walked out. Beyond the door, Lucy let out a sudden cry.

"I'm sorry," the nanny said anxiously as he emerged to find Sirena trying to comfort the baby. "She scratched herself."

An urgent call came in at that second and Sirena wound up leaving without him. When he managed to fight traffic and get home, he was relieved to find them there, even though Sirena was pale and frazzled. Mother and baby were both out of sorts. He was beginning to think Lucy had Sirena's sensitive nature for undercurrents, because she was obviously unsettled by her mother's tension.

He took over soothing the fussy infant and, despite his urgent need to sort things out between them, suggested Sirena take a bath. It was late when they sat down to a quiet dinner, just the two of them. Sirena picked at her food.

The silence built.

"Sin—"

"I don't want to talk about it."

"I called her back," he said, overriding her hostility. "Her housekeeper is sure she saw it on her dresser top after we left. It's fallen behind some furniture or something."

"So it's not that you believe me. You believe the house-keeper."

He drew patience into his lungs with a long inhale. "You barely wear the jewelry I give you and don't spend half the money in the account I opened for you. I have no reason to believe you'd want or need that bracelet."

Her mouth stayed pinched while she rearranged her food.

"I've put what happened behind us. Today was a slipup on my part, that's all."

"Fine," she said in the way women did when they meant, *Like hell,* but he took her at her word, determined to get them back on the comfortable footing they'd been enjoying. When they went to bed, he reached for her as he did every night.

She didn't melt her body into his the way he'd come to expect.

He wanted her. Badly. This break in their connection needed to be reestablished with the physical joining that brought him a kind of pleasure and sense of accord he couldn't even articulate. But while she didn't outright push him away, she didn't open to his kiss and heat to his touch the way she usually did.

With urgency riding him, he slowed his touch, trying to reassure her and himself that nothing had changed. He knew all her trigger points and lightly stimulated them: the dimples at the small of her back that made her shiver, the tendon in her neck that turned her to pudding when he scraped his teeth against it, the underside of her arm that was ticklish, but also made her turn into him and twine her leg around his waist.

When she moaned softly and combed her fingers into his hair, he shuddered with relief, but kept the pace gradual and thorough, wanting her to know how much he revered this bond between them. He didn't know how else to express his feelings for her. They were too deep and disturbing to even try to voice. Surely when they were like this, she felt it and understood?

Her hand moved restlessly on his shoulder and he kissed his way down the inside of her arm. Her wrist was sweetly feminine, the fine pulse beating frantically against his tongue, her fingers trembling against his mouth. He lightly sucked one, then another, anointing all her sensitive places, biting into the mound below her thumb until he'd imprinted himself on her lifeline.

She arched, the seeking signal enough to blast through his control, but he was determined to have every inch of her before she had one inch of him. He rolled her onto her stomach and used his leg to pin hers, then stroked her body with his. Her skin was soft and smooth, her form lovely with its curves and nectarine-scented skin. He kissed his way down her spine as he stroked her legs and buttocks, intensely turned on as she gasped and lifted into his touch and moaned his name.

Pushing the mane of her hair away from her neck, he settled on her, letting her feel how aroused he was. The slam of his heartbeat was like a piston trying to stamp into her. He slid a hand beneath her, cupping her breast then moving lower to the wet heat that was all his.

"I can't get enough of you," he admitted in a hot whisper against her bared ear. "I think about this all the time, giving you pleasure, feeling you melt for me." She was close to shattering, straining beneath him, making gorgeous noises that had the hairs all over his body standing up as he fought losing it without even entering her.

Easing away, he rolled her to face him.

She was trembling, her arms shaking as she tried to draw him over her. Her thighs fell open, but he only kissed down her breastbone to her navel.

"Raoul, I'm dying," she moaned, trying to draw him back up to her.

He was hanging by a thread, but took his time settling on her. Easing into her was like immersing himself in heaven. He went slowly, savoring every heartbeat while fighting the threatening eruption. Catching her inciting hands in his own, he held them still and let her feel him in complete possession of her.

"I will never be careless with you," he told her, deeply aware of the effect he was having on her, the twitch of her thighs scissoring his waist, the clasp of her sheath, the shaken breaths sawing between her lips. "This is too important to me."

He swallowed her gasp as he covered her trembling lips with his, wanting to crush her with all the passionate hunger in him, but venerating her instead, doing everything in his power to transmit that she was pure sweetness, utter joy to him. Perfect.

But he wasn't superhuman. The connection so vital to him was also his lifeblood and he needed to stoke it. The withdrawal and thrust sent a wave of intense pleasure down his back, pulling him tighter and harder, making the need to drive himself into her unbearable. He basked in the sheer magnificence of her, moving with gentle deliberation as he savored the effect she had on him, the way she responded to his strokes.

Their struggle was long and slow and deep. Impossible to give up and impossible to prolong. When the high keening noise came into her throat and her teeth closed on his earlobe, when her climax was only a breath away, he let himself fall, his wife clutched firmly in his arms.

CHAPTER TWELVE

As Raoul knotted his tie, he wasn't sure if he should feel smug or sorry. Over his reflected shoulder, Sirena was motionless on their ravaged bed, deeply asleep.

Last night had been intense. Even after he'd fetched Lucy for a feed a couple of hours ago and come back fully expecting they'd both finally catch a few winks, Sirena had reached for him as though they hadn't been colliding all night. They'd nearly killed each other with the force of their most recent release.

Then they had finally passed out. When his body had woken him out of habit at six, he'd considered canceling today's meetings, but two very in-demand people had flown in on his request. He had to make time for them.

He didn't like leaving Sirena without saying goodbye, but he was loath to wake her when he was the reason she needed her rest. Shrugging on his suit jacket, he moved closer to gauge how deep into REM she was.

Her face was contorted with agony and her limbs gave a twitch of sleep-paralyzed struggle. Alarmed, he sat to grasp her shoulder, sharply saying, "Sin!" to snap her awake.

"Nooo!" she cried and her hand came up so fast it caught him in the mouth before he knew it.

"What the hell?" He dabbed a finger against his lip, expecting she'd split it.

Her wild eyes came to rest on him, terror slowly receding as she curled her offending hand into her chest. "Did I hit you? Oh, my God, I'm so sorry." Her horror was as real as the remnants of panic still whitening her lips.

"You were having a nightmare. What was it?"

Shadows of memory crept into her eyes before she shielded them with her lashes. Without enlightening him, she drew the blankets up to her neck, shivering and looking to the clock. "What time is it? I didn't realize it was so late. Did your alarm go off?"

"Sin?" He smoothed her hair away from her sweaty temple. "Tell me."

"I don't want to think of it. Will you check Lucy while I have a quick shower?"

"You should sleep in."

"I don't want to try in case it comes back." She slid from the far side of the bed, leaving him uneasy.

Despite the passion that remained acute as ever between them, Sirena couldn't shake the sense of an ax about to fall. She brushed aside her worries by day, telling herself to trust that Raoul really had put his suspicions away, but her subconscious tortured her at night. He woke her from horrible nightmares at least once a night, bleak, frightening dreams where he wrenched Lucy from her arms and condemned Sirena to utter abandonment. Sometimes she was in prison, sometimes she was outside his gates, rain soaking her to the skin, cold metal numbing her fingers, his feelings for her completely beyond her reach.

He'd reassure her and be considerate and affectionate and would make love to her so sweetly she thought she would die, but she still wound up alone and rejected when she closed her eyes.

"I don't know what else I can say," he bit out over a

week later after a sullen dinner when he had remarked on the dark circles under her eyes.

They were in Paris, the city of lovers, sharing after-dinner coffee in the lounge. The nanny had taken an evening off with friends. The housekeeper had tidied up the dishes before leaving for the night. Outside the rain-specked window, the ink-black path of the Seine wound in gilded streaks past the purple and red and yellow lights of the buildings on the far shore.

"Tell me the bracelet has turned up," she said with a melancholy shrug, trying to be dismissive but actually feeling quite desperate.

Thick silence. He'd made her tell him what the dreams were about, but it hadn't helped either of them cope. His lack of response almost sounded accusatory to her.

"It's not like I want to be like this," she pointed out defensively.

Her phone rang in the depths of her purse. She stood to find it, hoping to avoid another dead-end conversation about something she couldn't control.

"You could try trusting me. That's what this comes down to."

She caught back a snort and insisted, "I do," but her heart twisted as though it knew she was lying. What could she do about that? If he loved her, she might be able to believe that he wasn't on the verge of rejecting her. But what he felt for her was passion—and that wasn't a forever type of feeling, was it?

"You don't even trust me enough to talk about this without seizing any excuse to walk away," he said pointedly.

"What is there to say?" She dropped her purse onto the sofa and folded her arms. "I'm supposed to ignore the fact there's no one else it could be? Is your mother losing her memory? Not a bit that I've noticed. Could it be the housekeeper? The one who's been with her for ten years?

Oh, I know, it's Miranda, who gets paid a fortune on top of that trust you set up for her."

A flash of something moved in his eyes. She didn't try to interpret it, too busy rushing on with the facts piled up against her.

"Did a thief break in and steal one bracelet in a house-ful of electronics and art? No! Unless *you* took it, the only other person it could be is *me*." She pointed to her chest. "I'm ready to confess just to get the breakup and court proceedings over with."

A cloak of such tangible chill fell over him, he virtu-ally turned gray and breathed fog. "A divorce? Is that the kind of court proceedings you're referring to?"

Her fingernails clawed into her upper arms. It wasn't, but if he reached for the D-word that quickly, it must be something he was considering. The pain that crept into her then didn't even have a name, it was too all encom-passing and deadly.

Into their staring contest, his phone rang. He didn't move, but it broke the spell. She looked away, body puls-ing with anguish.

"Is it?" he demanded through his teeth, ignoring his phone.

"How else will you react when it never turns up?" she said in a strained voice.

When she dared to look at him, he was so far inside himself there was no reaching him. It was as if the man who had been her protector and sounding board and part-ner had checked out and left the brute from the end of his driveway.

Her heart retracted into a core of ice, cracking from its own cold density.

His phone went silent and her tablet burbled.

"Oh, for God's sake!" she cried, rounding to the coffee table and glancing at the screen to see it was her sister. A different chill moved into her chest. The timing was wrong for a friendly visit—

She swiped at the screen. "Ali?" she asked before the vision of her sister came into focus, crying.

"It's Dad. He's had a heart attack. Mum's in the ambulance. I'm going to meet them at the hospital."

Sirena wasn't aware of swaying, only felt herself steady as firm hands grasped her and eased her onto the sofa. Raoul caught the tablet as it tumbled from her numb fingers.

"She'll be there as soon as I can make arrangements," he said in a rasping voice, ending the call. He tried to take her hands, but Sirena jerked from his touch, practically leaping to her feet.

"I have to pack."

"You're in shock."

"I need to do something."

"Fine. I'll order the flight." He ran a hand over his face, looking surprisingly awful. Maybe it was memories of losing his own father.

That thought made her stomach bottom out. Not dwelling on it, she went through the motions of packing, counting nappies for Lucy, fretting about the time it would take to circle half the globe. Would she reach her father in time?

Calling back the nanny didn't make sense. As nice as she was, she wasn't family. Sirena just wanted Raoul. For all their horrid conflict, he was a pillar. She couldn't dismiss how supportive he was as he booked a private jet, bundled them into a limo and buckled Lucy securely beside her in the plane's cabin.

"Text when you land so I know you arrived safely," he said.

"You're not coming?" Her barely there control shredded to near nothing.

"There's something I have to do."

Divorce. The ugly word came back, more noxious than ever. This was it, the expulsion from his life she had feared. Or rather, expected. Bile rose to the back of her throat, sitting in a hot burn despite her convulsive swallow. At least she had Lucy.

Without saying a word, she set her hand on their daughter and looked straight ahead. Funny how after all this time of aching for forgiveness, she didn't care what he believed. She only wanted him to be with her, but he walked away.

As she watched him depart, everything in her was mute and bereft. Minutes later the plane was climbing and the delicate silken ropes binding her to him stretched, thinned and finally snapped.

Forty-eight hours later, the only good news in her life was that her father's surgery had gone well and he would recover in time.

On the other hand, she had a baby who cried if she so much as thought about putting her down. As if the awkwardness of reacquainting with Faye wasn't hard enough without the buffer of her father to smooth the way, her sister insisted on returning to school on the other side of Sydney to be with—*don't tell Mum*—her boyfriend.

"This way you can use my bed," Ali insisted in front of her mother, putting Sirena on the spot. It was Ali's way of being helpful. She was oblivious to the undercurrents.

A cot for Lucy had already been borrowed from the neighbor and Sirena didn't want to appear churlish, but it only took one remark from her stepmother to put Sirena squarely back into her broadly criticized childhood.

"I imagine she'd be sitting up if she wasn't so fat."

Lucy was going to have a figure like her mother's. Not everyone thought that was a problem, Sirena bit back retorting. *Ask my husband.*

Her chest burned as she wondered how long she'd be able to refer to him that way.

He stunned her by contacting her at that moment, through her smartphone.

Highly conscious of her stepmother listening in, she bounced the baby on her hip and tried not to reveal how put out she was that the Wi-Fi she'd scrimped to pay for all those unemployed months, so she could contact her father and sister as often as she liked, had been canceled. *Ali's gone to school. What do we need it for?*

The phone screen was a poor substitute for her tablet and this conversation would cost her a fortune. She felt her scowl and Raoul gave her a forbidding look right back, killing any remote hopes she entertained that they weren't on the skids.

He was in his New York office, the dull sky behind him. His queries about her father and hope for his quick recovery were delivered in a strained rumble that was barely audible over her stepmother bashing dishes.

Sirena could only swallow, such deep emotions were accosting her, and she didn't know what to say with prying, critical ears a few steps away.

"You'll be there until he's released?" Raoul presumed.

"Yes, I—" She was aware of the temperature dropping to arctic levels as Faye absorbed the notion of unwanted houseguests for the indefinite future. "I have a lot to figure out. I'll call you once I know what I'm doing."

"Very well." He sounded about as friendly as Faye.

Ending the call, she endured an oppressive evening where it took everything in her not to reveal her misery and sense of failure to a woman who would dance a jig over her suffering. She barely slept, but when she woke, it was with a fresh sense of purpose.

She was not the unwanted stepchild any longer. Maybe her marriage was a disaster, but she was still a woman with resources and skills. After popping by the hospital to photograph her weak but proud father holding his grand-daughter, she called a real estate agent.

It would be a fresh start in a place that wouldn't remind her of Raoul. An hour later, she was shown into a building under redevelopment.

"This is available immediately?" she asked, thinking that trading on her husband's name had its perks.

"As soon as your credit is approved, hopefully later today," the agent told her.

Money would be tight. She doubted Raoul would con-tinue her allowance if they separated, but she hadn't let on to the agent that a breakup was in the cards. She was using her London flat, which was solely in her name, as leverage. She'd have to rely on transcription to make her payments until she found a decent job, but Raoul had said she had executive potential. She wouldn't sell herself short. None of this would be easy, but living with Faye and her father was not an option and neither was returning to her husband.

She needed her own space. Her heart was breaking into little pieces to match her marriage. She'd always known it wouldn't last, but she still needed solitude to come to terms with it.

After her and Lucy's first night in the quiet of their new flat, they woke early for their morning visit to the hospi-tal. They picked up groceries on the way back and, as a distraction from her misery, invited Faye to see the place. Sirena had concocted a story about Raoul wanting them to have a condo for their visits here, unwilling to confess to her imminent divorce. Unfortunately, that gave Faye carte blanche to show up with paint chips and a pile of unsolicited decorating advice.

"It's just been painted," Sirena argued.

"This oxblood is far too loud for a baby. Look at this eggshell. It will keep her calm. Book the painters to come in after you go back to London. It'll be finished and the fumes gone before your next visit."

She wasn't going back to London.

A knock at the door relieved Sirena from having to explain. She expected the building manager. He had promised to take care of some finishing items today.

As she reached the door, she hoped she could use this excuse to encourage Faye on her way—

"Oh!" Her heart leaped into her throat as she found Raoul outside her door.

He narrowed bleary eyes on her. Bleak lines were carved into his face, barely disguised by a cantankerous expression. When he raked his avaricious gaze down her simple blue capris and collared top, her pulse reacted with a dancing skip, but he looked so forbidding she could only stare dumbly at him.

"I didn't expect you," she said stiltedly.

"No?" He shouldered his way into the tiny flat, taking in the bare walls, the clean but dated furniture and the woman trying to tease a pacifier into his daughter's jabbering mouth.

Faye left off as Raoul approached, coming to attention in the instinctual way most did when confronted with his authoritative presence.

He nodded at her before he set a wide hand on his daughter's tummy. "How are you, kitten?"

Lucy kicked in excitement, grinning toothlessly with recognition and joy, arms flailing.

"I missed you, too," he said, hand staying on her while he took a better look around the flat. Disapproval blazed off him, like sharp, aggressive, glinting knives. No tender welcome or affectionate nickname for her, Sirena noted with a hollow ache.

"You must be the father?" Faye said haughtily when his gaze came back to her.

"My husband, yes," Sirena hurried to interject, pulling herself out of her shock. "Raoul, my stepmother, Faye."

"Nice to meet you," he said without inflection. "Would you be kind enough to watch Lucy while Sirena and I have a private conversation?"

Sirena's stomach hardened into a knot. She could practically hear Faye's, *I told you men expect to make these decisions themselves,* but Faye's opinion was the least of her problems. She hadn't really thought Raoul would give her Lucy, had she?

No, she might have hoped in her heart of hearts that their daughter would be a connection that brought him to her, but this didn't feel as though they were bridging differences. A huge chasm separated them, full of mist and frost.

"I can't walk her in this heat," Faye began, but Raoul negated the suggestion with a flick of his hand.

"We'll be upstairs, viewing the penthouse." His tone was so much that of a confident tycoon, even Faye didn't argue.

Sirena took a moment to set her phone to dial his so Faye could reach them, then accompanied him into the elevator, watching nervously as he punched the P.

"I don't understand—"

"Your agent called to clear your finances and within five minutes was trying to sell me the top floor. It seemed the most expedient way to get into this building if you refused to let me up, so I took the codes and said I'd look at it."

The elevator stopped and her knees weakened. She steeled her spine, but her voice was wobbly. "Of course I'd let you up. We're on perfectly friendly terms."

"Are we?" he rasped, holding the door while she exited, then moving to tap a code into the penthouse's security panel. The half-renovated space was empty of workmen, the concrete floor bare but for a few paint spatters, the walls down to timber frame and the plumbing extracted.

"I can't live with Faye," she blurted, arms flailing defensively. "I've tried to explain how she and I—"

"I understand that," he said with an inscrutable stare. "But you could have gone to a hotel."

She looked away. "That would have been expensive."

"And you weren't about to ask me to cover it, were you?"

Her throat tightened as she tried to swallow, unable to look at him because that topic was just too raw.

"And it would be too temporary," he said in a tone that made her feel wobbly inside. "Because you're staying here. Not coming back to me." It wasn't a question and the graveled way he said it made her flinch.

"There's no point, is there? I realize this seems like I've chosen the farthest place I could get from London, but my family is here, Raoul. Surely you understand why I'd prefer it?" She needed something, someone. They'd never take his place in her heart. The hole was too big, but she couldn't live with this ashen emptiness.

"Oh, I understand." His harsh laugh cut through the tense air. "Run as far from London as you want. I'll follow. If you're adamant about living in that flat you just bought, I'll be in this one."

The words struck like a burst of hot, dusty wind, choking and dry, making her eyes blink. *I'll follow,* but he was following Lucy.

She resisted the desire to rub where her breastbone rang in disappointment. It should be an enormous comfort to her that he hadn't arrived with threats to rend their child from her arms, but all she could think was how jealous she was of her daughter's ability to draw this man's eternal, all-encompassing love.

She might be selfish enough to take their daughter from her father, but he wouldn't separate mother and child.

She touched her brow where it was crinkled, aware of him pacing to the space under the floating staircase near the balcony doors. His footsteps were hollow, everything about this place echoing with the same emptiness she felt. His intention to live here was both pleasure and pain, but she'd had a baby with this man. Their lives would be linked forever. She'd never be given a chance for distance and space and getting over him. They would circle each other for eternity, two planets in the same solar system that never touched.

"Every working cell in my brain is telling me I have no right to keep you from leaving me, but the thought of letting you go makes me sick."

Her heart took a stumbling leap in her chest. She caught back any jumps of joy. It was Lucy he was worrying about losing. Lucy, and maybe a passionate bedmate and a scrupulously organized life.

"I..." She trailed off, realizing she'd been so focused on how anguished she felt, she hadn't noticed how broken he looked. If he'd slept since they'd been in Paris, it hadn't been much. He looked as if he'd aged and his shadow of stubble gave her that same old desire to smooth her hand on his rough cheek.

"Miranda had the bracelet," he spit out, as though the words were so bitter he could hardly keep them in his mouth. "I went to New York to confront her. When you threw her name at me in Paris, I realized immediately it was something she would do. She borrowed it for a night out and forgot to return it." He added in a mutter that his stepsister was a "bloody scatterbrain."

Sirena winced, glad to have the question answered, but in the big scheme of things, what did it matter? He had said he didn't think she'd taken it, but he'd had to go all the way to New York to have it confirmed. That hurt. Blinking, she fought back the burn of head-to-toe agony, willing her mouth to stay steady and the constriction in her chest to ease, but she didn't know what to say.

"No more nightmares, all right?" he said gruffly. "It's resolved. You're not in danger of going to prison. I'm never going to try putting you there and I won't let anyone else do it. Do you understand that, Sirena? That threat is gone. Forever."

His implacable tone and the way he tried to impose his will on her was so endearingly familiar she wanted to cry. She shrugged a fake acceptance, because what did he know about it? She woke up crying because the bed was empty beside her. He wanted to live apart. Her life was missing a giant, ornery, wonderful piece and she could barely stand here absorbing his closeness, knowing they'd never again be *close*.

"I've caused you so much pain, haven't I? And why? Because I was afraid to feel any!" He knocked his fist into his chest with self-disgusted violence, making her start. His ragged voice held her very still, frightened, but not of him. Of how angry he was with himself. He was deeply agonized and it both startled and shook her.

"You were right when you said I was looking for every reason to keep you from affecting me. Your nightmares are my punishment. Tell me they're over now, Sin, because they're beyond anything I can stand. Every night I'm confronted by what a thoughtless, cruel bastard I was to you. How I let you down so grossly. When I think of what I tried to do when you were so fragile, killing yourself to keep our child—"

"Don't," she urged, rushing forward a few steps, anguished by how tormented he was. His remorse was too intense to witness.

"It was worse being away from you, not there to wake

you," he said with a dazed affliction. His voice was like someone whose spirit was dead. "I only left because I wanted the mystery solved once and for all, so you'd finally sleep peacefully again. I was arranging the flight, anxious to get here and ease your mind, when your damned agent called and I learned you never intended to let me share your bed again."

"The dreams weren't that bad—"

"Don't downplay what I did to you!" His near shout made her jump again and he ran a hand over his face, visibly trying to bring himself back under control. "Damn it, do you ever think of yourself? That generosity of yours is exactly what gets to me and makes you necessary in my life every second of every day." His hand came out in a plea. "I've always been aware of it, but I never valued it the way I should have. It's why you risked your job to help your sister. I should have seen you'd never do something like that for personal gain. I didn't need protecting from you. It was the other way around." His face twisted with agony. "Don't let your soft heart forgive me. I don't deserve it. Make me live six floors apart from you and suffer like a soul in hell."

For all the jagged pain in his voice, there was a shred of hope in his eyes. He was looking at her as though she were a lifeline just beyond his reach.

She began to tremble, so confused and shaken she could only blurt, "I *can't*. I want to live with you. You're the one who brought up divorce. You're the one who put me on a plane and sent me away! The nightmares are about you not loving me and I love you so much I can't bear it!" She had to bury her face in her hands then because she was revealing too much. This swell of emotions was too much to hold inside.

Hard hands bit into her arms and she was crushed into his chest. His ragged groan vibrated through her as he held her so hard she thought he'd splice them into hybrid branches on a single trunk. A moan of relief from pain escaped her and she let her hands close on his back in pinching handfuls that had to hurt, but she was ravaged by such deep emotions she needed this embrace to keep from splintering into pieces.

"I love you, Sin. I've been sick without you and all I could think about was my father feeling this way and how deep his pain must have been at not having the woman he loved. It's even worse when I had her and ruined everything…"

"No, you didn't," she moaned and cradled his stubbled face to bring his mouth to hers, cutting off his self-recrimination with a tender kiss, wanting to taste that glorious word he'd used.

He opened his mouth on hers with a groan of greed. Their chemistry flared, but it was so much more. They kissed with aching hunger, shuffling to press tighter, thighs weaving, hips rubbing with shiver-inducing friction.

Cupping her head, he drew his own back, hissing a breath at the ceiling. "I'm not taking you on a damned concrete floor where anyone could walk in."

The landing at the top of the stairs caught his gaze and for a second he considered… When he glanced at his wife, she was bringing her sultry gaze back from the same direction. Her body leaned with heart-swelling pliancy against his.

Tempted nearly to breaking point, he hugged her close and reminded himself how incredibly lucky he was to have this second chance. No way was he screwing it up.

Pressing a kiss to her temple, he said, "I don't deserve you. Let me try to do something right, rather than repeat Oxshott."

Her gaze fell and he feared she took it as rejection, even

though he wasn't able to quit stroking her, filling his hands with the reality of her when he'd been sure they were over.

"I liked Oxshott," she murmured, pouted lips nearly touching his breastbone.

"I loved Oxshott," he said softly, stroking her hair back from her face and looking into her eyes, so moved, so bewildered she could love him, he could barely find words.

"I love you," he repeated, even though it was an inadequate description of the depth of regard and adoration he felt toward her.

A misty look came over her face, but a specter moved behind the gaze she lowered. "You don't have to say it if it's not true. I still want to live with you."

"It's not a conscious choice, Sin," he snorted softly. Looking back on how hard he'd fought against feeling this way put a chill in his blood.

"But you're not happy." Her bottom lip moved unsteadily until she caught it in her teeth.

"It hasn't been a comfortable journey, but right now I couldn't be happier."

Her mouth twitched and she nudged against the erection imprinting her abdomen. Her brow cocked as though to ask, *are you sure about that?*

On the verge of becoming distracted, he cupped her jaw, urging her with a caress of her peach-flushed cheek to look into his eyes. This was too important. He saw the hesitancy and vulnerability she was trying to hide behind her flirty smile. His heart lurched.

"I want to make love to you so much I can hardly breathe." A pleasant shiver chased over him at the mere thought of burying himself in her. "Holding you and touching you is the most incredible experience of my life." He caressed her almost convulsively, reassuring himself that he was touching this beautiful woman who meant so much to him. "I was really scared, Sin. I didn't know how I was going to convince you to give me another shot."

Something stark flashed in her eyes before she ducked her head. "I've loved you from practically the minute we met. You're the only man I'll ever want to be with."

Loyal to a fault and so emotionally brave. He would be a lonely coward if he didn't emulate her.

"And you're the only woman I can imagine spending my life with. You believe that, don't you?" he prompted, rather desperate to know her subconscious wouldn't put her through the wringer ever again.

"Of course," she said, adding cheekily, "I have Lucy."

"Don't joke." He leaned back a fraction, waiting for her chastised gaze to come up to his. "I mean it. I want to spend my life with you. I want to marry you. A proper wedding this time. Your dad can give you away…"

She shook her head, trying to forestall him.

"Why not?" he demanded. "You don't want to be the center of attention?" It was the only excuse he could accept. He wouldn't force her into something that made her uncomfortable.

"Those romantic dreams were a young girl's rescue fantasy." She waved them away as she disentangled herself from his embrace. "I've grown up, got my head on straight. I don't need some empty gesture because you feel guilty. I'm fine. We're fine." Her smile was soft and lovely and tried hard to disguise a deep insecurity.

He stared at her, aware he only had himself to blame. "You still don't trust me," he accused gently.

"Of course I do."

"You don't believe my feelings for you are as strong as yours are for me." He was insulted to the core by that, but this wasn't about him. It was about the fragile self-worth he'd damaged too many times.

"I—" What could she say? It was true. "I'm not trying

to start a fight. I know things will only get better from now on."

He allowed the conversation to end there and they returned to Lucy, then went to the hospital for an introduction to her father. By the time they crawled into bed, she truly felt they were on their way to a stronger relationship than ever. He made love to her with the same sweet power as always and held her all night long.

And then he took over in that mildly annoying way of his, throwing Faye for a loop, checking to see if their house needed modifications for when her father came home. He had a man-to-man chat with her father about his finances, too.

"Don't hurt his pride," she urged before he left for the hospital, and got a pithy look.

"I want him to know he has a fallback if he doesn't get on his feet right away. I take care of my family," Raoul said.

For the first time in a very long time, she began to feel she had a cohesive family. With her confidence renewed in her position as a mother and his wife, she tried to let go of her baggage and enjoy her time with her father and sister. Faye became someone she shook her head over, rather than taking her words to heart, especially after her father remarked on their relationship.

"After your mother died, I saw you growing up so fast, trying to take on all her responsibilities. I married the first woman who looked like she'd have me, hoping to give you back your childhood, but it didn't work. You two never connected. You were so independent. Faye didn't know what to make of you. Moving here, I honestly didn't think you'd miss us or that it would be so long until I saw you again. You sounded happy with your job and traveling..."

Startled by this view of herself, she asked Raoul later, "Do I take charge of everything?"

"You've taken over the renovations of the penthouse."

"You told me to— oh!" She caught a glimpse of the grin he was suppressing and gave him a little shove.

He snagged his arm around her and warmed her with an admiring look. "You're smart and confident and good at anything you chose to do. Which might threaten some men, but I need that sort of inner strength in my wife. It's reassuring to me that you won't give up and drop out on me."

"No, never," she promised.

In fact she felt more integral and necessary to him all the time. He changed the access on all his accounts so they were joint holdings and made it her job to keep everything balanced. She reeled under the depth of responsibility and trust he was showing in her.

Perhaps they were going to make it after all.

By the end of the following week her father was well into his recovery and they were winding up their visit. They were keeping the penthouse for future visits, planning two a year at least, but Raoul really did work best out of London. Everything was returning to a steady, reliable keel and if she felt a little wistful each time he said he loved her, she told herself to be grateful he was able to say the words, even if he didn't mean them the way she did.

The day before they were to leave, Sirena woke late. Raoul had pulled his favorite trick of stealing both baby and monitor, but since he'd been rather passionate last night, not seeming able to get enough of her, she appreciated the extra sleep. Her body was a teensy bit achy in the best possible way, making her feel sensual and well loved even as she was disturbed by the memory of his near-frenetic hunger for physical connection.

Was something wrong? She went looking for him, and reassurance, as soon as she rose.

The flat was small, so it was easy to find him in the lounge, where a muted instrumental was playing, giving the sunny room a lazy Sunday feel. He'd bought her flowers yesterday, enough for three vases, filling the room with splashes of color.

He was closing the main door and had a royal-blue garment bag in his hand. As he moved to drape it over the back of the sofa, he saw her. "Good morning."

Did he sound extra serious? Her tummy gave a flutter of apprehension.

"Good morning. Where's Lucy?" she asked, bending her brow at the fancy logo on the bag. What was it?

"Ali just took her upstairs."

"To the penthouse? Why? I thought we were all having lunch—"

The way he approached, all serious looking in his crisp white shirt and perfectly creased pants, gave her another hitch of anxiety. He was so damned good-looking, freshly shaved and with his new haircut—something he'd sought out himself yesterday without asking her to book it. Very out of character.

In fact, lots of odd details were adding up in her mind to something going on that was being kept from her.

He took her hands and she almost pulled them away, suddenly quite worried, but not sure of what. All her inner signals of conspiracies and loss were firing.

Don't, she told herself, forcing herself to trust him by letting her fingers relax in the firm grasp of his.

He frowned at how chilly her hands were. Emotion seemed to catch at him in a way he couldn't control, causing a flinch across his features. The line of his closed lips wasn't entirely steady and for a second he seemed to struggle to meet her eyes. When he did, her heart bottomed out.

This was big. Whatever it was, it was big and scary.

"What's wrong?" she whispered.

"You're so beautiful," he said, as if it hurt him.

She shook her head. Not right now she wasn't, wearing

only a robe that had taken a splash of coffee yesterday, eyes still smudged with last night's makeup, hair tousled from their extensive lovemaking. Her lips were chapped, her—

Stop it, she told herself. If he said she was beautiful, she had to believe that to him she was. It was just so hard when he looked so uncharacteristically hesitant.

"Raoul?" she prompted.

"I'm not trying to be mysterious, Sin. I'm nervous as hell. I—well, there's nothing to say except…" He released her and took a half step back.

She closed her hands into fists, drawing them tight into her stomach, where serpents seemed to be writhing.

To her eternal shock, he drew something from his pocket and lowered to one knee. Holding out a ring pinched between his finger and thumb, he said, "Will you marry me?"

Sunlight glanced off the diamond, throwing rainbow sparkles into her vision. The moment was imprinted for all time: the delicate notes of music behind the question, the perfume of freesias and roses, the way her heart began to pound with sheer joy, the naked feelings in Raoul's beloved face as he looked up at her: desire, regard, admiration.

She realized she couldn't speak because she'd clapped her hands over her mouth. "We're already married," she reminded him from behind them.

"I want to marry you properly. Everyone is upstairs waiting for us."

Her eyes grew wet as she goggled at him.

"I know you didn't want this," he continued. His voice seemed to come from very deep in his chest. "But I need to know you want to be married to me as much as I love being married to you. I've spoken to your father, told him everything, asked him for your hand…"

"You what?" she gasped. Her heart tried to jump from

her chest. She was both touched and alarmed, unable to process it.

"He took his time thinking about it, and I don't blame him." His shoulders took on a weighted slant. "If I could go back and change things...but I can't. I know why you think I married you. I know you think I'm only trying to assuage guilt. I'm not. Although it would certainly reassure me if you said yes in spite of everything I've done."

The regret in his eyes was too painful to face.

"Don't," she murmured, moving forward to graze her hands over his ears, startled when he locked his arm around her and pressed his face into her middle.

"You will make even the most impossible relationships work so you can stay in the lives of the people you love. I know that about you, Sin." Anguish seemed to hold him in a paroxysm that nearly suffocated her, but she only held him tighter. "You'll be tempted to say yes to me today simply because you hate letting me down. But I can't bear you thinking my love for you is impossible, that what I feel for you isn't real."

"I—" Her arms involuntarily loosened and he surged to his feet, grasping her by the shoulders and compelling her with the force of his personality to take heed.

"I *love* you. This isn't pandering to your romantic side—even though I love the idea of making your dreams come true. It's me asking you to marry me properly. Not for Lucy's sake, but because we love each other. If you don't want that, if you don't believe we're equally invested in this relationship, then don't do it."

He was right, she couldn't imagine hurting or humiliating him with refusal.

He seemed to read her mind as he straightened to look down his nose at her. "Don't marry me out of pity or a sense of obligation. I'd rather a hit of revenge. But, Sin, think about it. Why would I set myself up for this kind of drubbing unless I wanted to prove something to you? Something really important."

Like what?

The truth revealed itself like a specter condensing from something she had tried too hard to see.

"You shouldn't have to prove anything to me. I should just believe you. Trust you," she said, smothered by growing compunction. "That's what I always wanted from you, faith in my feelings and intentions toward you..." She pressed her lips together so hard her chin crinkled. Why hadn't she put it together before this? "I'm so sorry."

"We're not holding grudges, Sin." He stroked a tender hand down her cheek. "This is our fresh start."

She nodded agreement, letting him draw her into his embrace. With her head on his chest, she said, "I love you so much. It's hard to believe you could feel this same way for me. It's so big and endless and you are so incredible. You deserve to be loved like that, but I'm just me."

"If you could see yourself the way I do. The way we all do. You're such an amazing woman, Sin. So strong, but so kind. I'm proud that you're my wife. I want the world to know how much you mean to me."

For such a naturally circumspect man, this was quite an act. She couldn't think of any reason he would do such a public thing, take such a risk, except that he loved her.

She was so overwhelmed and touched she could only wrap her arms around him and hold on, trying to keep the bursting sensations from breaking her skin.

"Will you?" he asked, kissing her hair. "Marry me?"

She nodded through happy tears. "Of course. I'd love to. I love you, Raoul."

"And wear my ring this time," he grumbled, easing back to thread it onto her finger. It was a band of baguette diamonds, smooth enough that the claws wouldn't catch on baby clothes or skin, stunning enough to make her gasp as she really took it in.

"I might have been overcompensating," he commented sheepishly.

"You think?" She laughed, then looked up at him. "I don't know how to handle being this happy." Her cheeks ached from her huge smile. "It means so much to me."

It wasn't the proposal; it was knowing he loved her that made her misty with emotion. She felt his lips touch hers as she blinked fast, trying to keep her eyes from overflowing.

"Ali helped me set it up. I hope our day is everything you imagined your wedding day would be."

It was already better than she'd ever dared hope, but she was still awed by the small touches that made her wedding ceremony utterly perfect. As she was too curvy for ruffles or a full skirt, Ali had found her a gown of lace over silk with a modest train. She did her own hair and makeup, only calling in Ali at the last minute to help her with the veil. Faye loaned her the blue cameo pendant that had been in her family for ages and her father met her at the elevator, still unsteady, but so proud to walk with her. Her heart soared.

When she saw her daughter in a confection of a flower-girl dress sitting on Amber's knee, she almost tripped. Then Raoul's mother and stepsister came into focus and some of their longtime work associates...

He had really laid himself on the line with this arrangement.

Now in a morning suit that took her breath, he turned to her with such unashamed adoration in his eyes, she couldn't speak. Unbelievably moved by their vows, feeling the sincerity deep in her heart as they spoke them, she knew he loved her. *Her*.

And they had a lifetime ahead of them.

He lifted her veil and she kept her eyes open, wanting him to see the same devotion in her gaze as she found reflected in his. They sealed their promises to each other with a tender kiss.

* * * * *

AN EXCEPTION
TO HIS RULE

BY
LINDSAY ARMSTRONG

Lindsay Armstrong was born in South Africa, but now lives in Australia with her New Zealand-born husband and their five children. They have lived in nearly every state of Australia, and have tried their hand at some unusual—for them—occupations, such as farming and horse-training: all grist to the mill for a writer! Lindsay started writing romances when their youngest child began school and she was left feeling at a loose end. She is still doing it and loving it.

For my family, Dave, Susie, Matt, Sally, Anabel and
David for all their patience.
And my editor, Megan Haslam, for all *her* patience!

CHAPTER ONE

DAMIEN WYATT WAS lounging in an upstairs study.

He wore jeans, a khaki bush shirt and desert boots, all visible since his feet were up on the desk. His dark hair was ruffled and there were blue shadows on his jaw.

The windows were open and the roses in the garden below were in bloom. So was the star jasmine creeper clinging to the house. Beyond the garden wall a beach curved around a blue, inviting bay. You could hear the sound of the waves on the beach and there was a tang of salt in the air.

'Hang on,' he said with a sudden frown. 'Is it remotely possible that this Ms *Livingstone* we're talking about is actually *Harriet* Livingstone? Because, if so, forget it, Arthur.'

Arthur Tindall, art connoisseur and colourful dresser—he wore jeans and a yellow waistcoat patterned with black elephants over a maroon shirt—looked confused. 'You've met her?' he asked from the other side of the desk.

'I don't know. Unless there are two Harriet Livingstones, I may have,' Damien said dryly.

'There could well be. Two, I mean,' Arthur replied. 'After all, it's not the wilds of Africa where it was highly unlikely there'd be more than one *Doctor* Livingstone popping up out of nowhere.'

Damien grinned fleetingly. 'I take your point.' He sobered. 'What's your Harriet like? Tall, thin girl with wild hair and an unusual taste in clothing?' He raised an enquiring eyebrow.

Arthur looked blank for a moment. 'Tall, yes,' he said slowly. 'Otherwise, well, certainly not fat and her clothes are—I don't seem to remember much about her clothes.'

'Have you actually met her?' Damien enquired with some irony.

'Of course.' Arthur looked offended then brightened. 'I can tell you one thing: she has very long legs!'

'So does a stork,' Damien observed. 'I couldn't tell with my Ms Livingstone,' he added. 'I mean for someone that tall she obviously had long legs but whether they were—shapely—I couldn't say because they were all covered up in some kind of wraparound batik skirt.'

Arthur stared narrowly into the distance as if trying to conjure up a batik wraparound skirt then he blinked again and said triumphantly, 'Glasses! Large, round, red-rimmed glasses. Also...' he frowned and concentrated '...a rather vague air, although that may be due to being short-sighted, but as if her mind is on higher things.' He grimaced.

Damien Wyatt smiled unpleasantly. 'If it is the same girl, she ran into me about two months ago. At the same time she was wearing large, round, red-rimmed glasses,' he added significantly.

'Oh, dear! Not the Aston? Oh, *dear*,' Arthur repeated.

Damien looked at him ironically. 'That's putting it mildly. She had no insurance other than compulsory third party and the...*tank* she was driving survived virtually unscathed.'

'Tank?'

Damien shrugged. 'It might as well have been: a solid old four-wheel drive with bull bars.'

This time Arthur winced visibly. 'How did it happen?'

'She swerved to avoid a dog then froze and couldn't correct things until it was too late.' Damien Wyatt drummed his fingers on his desk.

'Was anyone hurt?'

Damien looked at him, his expression sardonic. 'The dog was retrieved by its owner *completely* unscathed. All she broke were her glasses.'

He paused as he recalled the melee after the accident and the curious fact—curious from the point of view that it should have stuck in his mind—that Harriet Livingstone had possessed a pair of rather stunning blue eyes.

'That's not *too* bad,' Arthur murmured.

'That's not all,' Damien remarked acidly. 'I broke my collarbone and the damage to my car was, well—' he shrugged '—the whole exercise cost me a small fortune.'

Arthur forbore to make the obvious comment that a

small fortune would hardly make the slightest dent in the very large fortune Damien Wyatt owned.

But Damien continued with palpable sarcasm, 'Therefore, dear Arthur, if there's any possibility it's one and the same girl, you do see there's no way I could let her loose here.' He removed his feet from the desk and sat up.

Arthur Tindall discovered he could certainly see something cool, determined and even quite grim in Damien's dark eyes but he also found he wasn't prepared to give up without a fight.

Whether it was the same girl or not, it did sound like it, he had to admit, but the thing was he'd promised Penny, his young and delicious yet surprisingly manipulative wife, that he would get the Wyatt job for her friend Harriet Livingstone.

He sat forward. 'Damien, even if she's the same girl—although we don't absolutely know that!—she's good,' he said intently. 'She's damn good. So's her provenance. Your mother's collection couldn't be in better hands, believe me! She's worked in one of the most prestigious art auction houses in the country.' Arthur emphasised this with rolling eyes and a wave of his hand. 'Her father was a noted conservator and restorer of paintings and her references are impeccable.'

'All the same, you've just told me she's vague and distracted,' Damien said impatiently. 'And *I've* had the woman literally run into me!'

Arthur said intensely, 'She may be vague over other things but not about her work. I've found her knowledgeable on not only paintings but porcelain, ceramics, carpets, miniatures—all sorts of things. And she's experienced in cataloguing.'

'She sounds like a one woman antiques roadshow,' Damien observed caustically.

'No, but she's the one person I could recommend who would have some familiarity with most of the odds and ends your mother collected. She's the one person who would have some idea of their value or who to get a valuation from, some idea of whether they need restoring, whether they *could* be restored, who could do it if it was possible, who—'

Damien held up his hand. 'Arthur, I get your point. But—'

'Of course,' Arthur interrupted, sitting back and looking magisterial, 'if it is the same girl, there's the distinct possibility nothing on earth would induce her to work for you.'

'Why the hell not?'

Arthur shrugged and folded his arms over his black and yellow waistcoat. 'I have no doubt you would have been quite scathing towards her at the time of the accident.'

Damien rubbed his jaw. 'I did ask her,' he said reminiscently, 'whether she'd got her driver's licence out of a cornflakes packet.'

Arthur whistled but said, 'I've heard worse. Was that all?'

Damien shrugged. 'I may have said a few other…less than complimentary things. In the heat of the moment, of course. My car *was* smashed. So was my collarbone.'

'Women don't necessarily see things like that in the

same way. About cars, I mean.' Arthur waved his hands again. 'Pure excellence, pure *fineness* in a motor vehicle and then to see it all smashed up may not affect them as deeply as a man.'

Damien chewed his lip then shrugged and picked up his phone as it buzzed discreetly.

Arthur got up and wandered over to the windows. It was a lovely view, he mused, but then Heathcote, home to the Wyatt dynasty, was a magnificent property. They ran cattle and grew macadamias with equal success in the Northern Rivers district of New South Wales but it was machinery—farm machinery, and lately mining machinery—that was the backbone of their fortune.

Damien's grandfather had started it all with a tractor he'd designed and manufactured but, so it was said, Damien had tripled it by investing in mining machinery. And all sorts of mining was happening all over Australia, Arthur thought rather ruefully.

His own connection with the Wyatts had started with Damien's father and his interest in art. Together they'd built up a collection to be proud of. Then, seven years ago, both his parents had been lost at sea when their yacht had capsized. Consequently Damien had inherited the collection.

It was the upheaval after this that had brought to light the full extent of his *mother's* collection of objets d'art—something the rest of the family had tended to overlook. In fact it wouldn't be unfair to say that Heathcote was stuffed to the rafters with them. But it had taken several more years for this decision to do something about them to be made, and hence to his advice being sought.

His first inclination had been to suggest that it should all be crated up and sent to an appropriate firm for assessing. Damien, however, supported by his aunt, had been disinclined to allow any of his mother's treasures to leave Heathcote and it had been their suggestion that he look for someone to do the job in situ.

No easy task since Lennox Head, Heathcote's nearest town, was a long way from Sydney and a fair way from Brisbane or the Gold Coast, the nearest large cities.

Therefore, when Penny had presented him with Harriet Livingstone he'd more or less looked upon it as a godsend...

Arthur turned from the view and studied Damien Wyatt, who'd swung his chair so he was partially facing the other way and was still talking on the phone. At thirty-one, Damien was loose-limbed, lean and deceptively powerful. He was well over six feet tall, broad-shouldered and he had the facility to look at ease in any milieu. Yet there was something about him that let you know that whilst he'd be good outdoors, good at battling the elements, good at managing vast properties, good with mechanical things, he'd also be good with women.

He certainly possessed a pair of fine dark eyes that often had a glint in them indicative of a mercurial personality and a lively intelligence.

Not to put too fine a point on it, Arthur ruminated, as his wife Penny had once remarked: you couldn't call Damien exactly handsome but he was devastatingly attractive and masculine.

He also had thick dark hair and he did possess a powerful intellect. Not only that, but he had an affection for getting his own way and a *cutting,* irritable way it was with him at times, as Harriet Livingstone had apparently encountered, poor girl.

So why, Arthur wondered suddenly, if she was the same girl—and he was pretty sure she was—had she been happy for him to go ahead and sound Damien Wyatt out on this job? She must have recognised the name. She must have some very unpleasant memories of the incident.

She must, above all, find it extremely hard to believe he would ever offer her a job after smashing his beloved Aston Martin with a vehicle not unlike a tank and breaking his collarbone.

So what was behind it, this willingness even to meet Damien Wyatt again? Did she have designs on him? Did she, he swallowed at the mere thought, plan to, if she got the job, fleece him of some of his mother's treasures?

'Hello!'

Arthur came back to the present with a start to see that Damien had finished his call and was looking at him enquiringly.

'Sorry,' he said hastily, and sat down again.

'How's Penny?'

Arthur hesitated. Despite the fact that Damien was always unfailingly polite to Penny, it was hard to escape the feeling that he didn't really approve of her.

Or, if not that, Arthur mused further, did Damien view his belated tumble into matrimony after years of bachelorhood with some cynicism? He was now approaching fifty and was twenty years older than Penny.

Probably, he conceded to himself. Not that Damien Wyatt had anything to be superior about on that score. He might not have been twenty years older than his wife but he did have a failed marriage behind him—a very failed marriage.

'Arthur, what's on your mind?'

Once again Arthur came back to the present with a start. 'Nothing!' he asserted.

'You seem to be miles away,' Damien commented. 'Is Penny all right or not?'

'She's fine. She's fine,' Arthur repeated, and came to another sudden decision, although with an inward grimace. 'Look, Damien, I've changed my mind about Harriet Livingstone. I don't think she's the right one after all. So give me a few days and I'll find someone else.'

It was a penetratingly narrowed dark gaze Damien bestowed on Arthur Tindall. 'That's a rather sudden change of heart,' he drawled.

'Yes, well, a blind man could see you two are unlikely to get along so...' Arthur left his sentence up in the air.

Damien settled more comfortably in his chair. 'Where are you going to find a paragon to equal Ms Livingstone? Or was that a slight exaggeration on your part?' he asked casually enough, although with a load of implied satire.

'No it was not!' Arthur denied. 'And I have no idea where I'm going to find one—be that as it may, I will.'

Damien Wyatt rubbed his jaw. 'I'll have a look at her.'

Arthur sat up indignantly. 'Now look here; you can't change your mind just like that!'

'Not many minutes ago you were hoping to goad me into doing *just* that.'

'*When*?'

'When you told me I'd be the last person on earth she'd work for. You were hoping that would annoy me or simply arouse my contrary streak to the extent I'd change my mind.' Damien's lips twisted. 'Well, I have.'

'Which streak prompted that, do you think? A rather large ego?' Arthur enquired heavily after a moment's thought.

Damien grinned. 'No idea. Bring her here for an interview tomorrow afternoon.'

'Damien—' Arthur rose '—I have to say I can't guarantee the girl.'

'You mean everything you told me about her provenance et cetera—' Damien raised his eyebrows sardonically '—was a lot of bull dust?'

'No,' Arthur denied. 'I followed up every reference she gave me and they all checked out, I've talked to her and sounded her out on a range of art work, as I mentioned, but—'

'Just bring her, Arthur,' Damien interrupted wearily. 'Just bring her.'

Despite this repeated command, Damien Wyatt stayed where he was for a few minutes after Arthur had gone, as he asked himself why he'd done what he'd just done.

No sensible answer presented itself other than that he *had* somehow felt goaded into it, although not because of anything Arthur had said.

So—curiosity, perhaps? Why would Harriet Livingstone want to have anything to do with him after, he had to admit, he'd been pretty unpleasant to her? Some quirky form of revenge?

More likely a quirky form of attaching herself to him, he thought cynically. All the more reason to have stuck to his guns and refused to see the girl.

What else could have been at work behind the scenes of his mental processes then? he asked himself rather dryly. Boredom?

Surely not. He had enough on his plate at the moment to keep six men busy. He had an overseas trip coming up in a couple of days, and yet…

He stared into the distance with a frown. Of course the possibility remained that it *wasn't* the same girl…

At three o'clock the next afternoon, Harriet Livingstone and Arthur Tindall were shown into the lounge at Heathcote by a tall angular woman with iron-grey hair cut in a short cap. Arthur addressed the woman as Isabel and kissed her on the cheek but didn't introduce her. Arthur was looking worried and distracted.

Damien Wyatt came in from outside through another door, accompanied by a large dog.

He threw his sunglasses onto a side table and said something to the dog, a young, highly bred and powerful Scottish wolfhound, that sat down obligingly although looking keenly alert.

'Ah,' Damien Wyatt said to Arthur after a brief but comprehensive study of Harriet, 'same girl.' He turned back to Harriet. 'We meet again, Miss Livingstone. I'd almost convinced myself you wouldn't be the same person or, if you were, that you wouldn't come.'

Harriet cleared her throat. 'Good afternoon, Mr Wyatt,' she said almost inaudibly.

Damien narrowed his eyes and cast Arthur an interrogative glance but Arthur only looked blank.

Damien returned his attention to Harriet Livingstone.

No batik wraparound skirt today, he noted: an unexceptional navy linen dress instead. Not too long, not too short, not too tight, although it did make her blue eyes even bluer. In fact her outfit was very discreetly elegant and so were her shoes, polished navy leather with little heels. This caused a faint fleeting smile to twist his lips as it crossed his mind that this girl probably rarely, if ever, wore higher heels. And he wondered what it must be like for a girl to be as tall, if not taller, than many of the men she met. Not that she was taller than he was...

Then there was her hair. Shoulder-length, fair and with a tendency to curl, it no longer looked as if she'd been pulled through a bush backwards. It was neatly tied up instead with a black ribbon. Her make-up was minimal. In fact it was all so...what? he asked himself. Well-bred, classic, timeless, discreet—he had no difficulty imagining her in the hallowed halls of some revered antique and art auction company or a museum.

But, and this caused him to frown rather than smile, the main difference between this Harriet Livingstone and the girl who'd run into him was that she was no longer thin. Very slender, perhaps, but no, not exactly skinny.

Despite being slender rather than skinny and despite her more composed outward presentation, it was, however, plain to see that she was strung as taut as a piano wire.

It was also plain to see—and his eyes widened slightly as his gaze travelled down her figure—that her legs were little short of sensational…

'Well,' he said, 'you were right, Arthur, but let's get down to brass tacks. We've organised a few of my mother's things in the dining room. Please come through and give me your opinion of them, Ms Livingstone.'

He moved forward and the dog rose and came with him but stopped to look at Harriet with almost human curiosity. And, as Harriet returned the dog's gaze, just a little of her tension seemed to leave her.

Damien noticed this with a slight narrowing of his eyes. And he said, somewhat to his surprise, 'I'm sorry, I forgot to introduce you—this is Tottie, Miss Livingstone. Her proper name is much more complicated. Something tells me you like dogs?'

Harriet put out a hand for Tottie to inspect. 'Yes. It's one of the reasons I ran into you,' she murmured. 'I thought I'd killed the dog and I—just froze.'

Arthur tut-tutted.

Damien Wyatt blinked, twice. 'Much worse in your estimation than killing me, I gather?'

Harriet Livingstone allowed Tottie to lick her hand then said quietly, 'Of course not. I didn't—I'm sorry but I didn't have time to think about you or anything else. It all happened so fast.'

'I'm suitably damned,' he replied. 'All right, let's get this show on the road.'

'If you're having second thoughts I'd quite under-stand,' Harriet said politely, with a less than polite glint in her eye, however.

She really doesn't like him, Arthur thought and rubbed his face distractedly. So why is she doing this?

But what Damien said took him even further by sur-prise. 'On the contrary, after what Arthur has told me about you I'm positively agog to see you in action. Shall I lead on?'

He didn't wait for her response but strode out with Tottie following regally.

Harriet put the exquisite little jade peach tree down on the table with a sigh of pleasure. And her gaze swept over the rest of the treasures spread out on the dining room table. 'They're all lovely—she had marvellous taste, your mother. And judgement.' She took off her red-rimmed glasses.

Damien was leaning his broad shoulders against the mantelpiece with his arms crossed. He did not respond to her admiration of his mother's collection but said, 'Is that a new pair or did you get them fixed?' He nodded towards her glasses resting on the table.

Harriet looked confused for a moment, then, 'Oh, it was only a lens that got broken so I was able to get a new one.'

'Red glasses.' He looked her up and down. 'Not quite

in keeping with the restrained elegance of the rest of you—today, that is.'

A fleeting smile twisted Harriet's lips. 'Ah, but it makes them a lot easier to find.' And, for a moment, she thought he was going to smile too but he continued to look unamused.

Harriet looked away.

'How would you catalogue them?' he asked after a moment. 'This is not even one tenth of them, by the way.'

'I'd photograph them in the sequence I came upon them and I'd write an initial summary of them. Then, when they were all itemised—' Harriet laced her fingers '—I'd probably sort them into categories, mainly to make it easier to locate them and I'd write a much more comprehensive description of them, their condition, any research I'd done on them, any work required on them et cetera. I'd also, if your mother kept any receipts or paperwork on them, try to marry it all up.'

'How long do you think that would take?'

Harriet shrugged. 'Hard to say without seeing the full extent of the collection.'

'Months,' Arthur supplied with gloomy conviction.

'Were you aware it was a live-in position, Miss Livingstone?' Damien queried. 'Because we're out in the country here, whoever does the job will spend an awful lot of time travelling otherwise.'

'Yes, Arthur did explain that. I believe there's an old stable block that's been converted to a studio and it has a flat above it. But—' Harriet paused '—weekends would be free, wouldn't they?'

Damien raised an eyebrow. 'Didn't Arthur tell you that?'

'He did,' Harriet agreed, 'but I needed to double- check.'

'A boyfriend you're eager to get back to?' Damien didn't wait for her response. 'If that's going to be a problem and you're forever wanting time off to be with him—'

'Not at all,' Harriet cut across him quite decisively.

'Not at all, you wouldn't be wanting time off all the time or not at all, there is no boyfriend?' Damien enquired.

Arthur coughed. 'Damien, I don't think—' he began but Harriet interrupted him this time.

'It's quite all right, Arthur.' She turned back to Damien. 'Allow me to set your mind at rest, Mr Wyatt. There is no fiancé, no husband, no lovers, in short, no one in my life to distract me in that direction.'

'Well, well,' Damien drawled, 'not only a paragon in your profession but also your private life.'

Harriet Livingstone merely allowed her deep blue gaze to rest on him thoughtfully for a moment or two before she turned away with the tiniest shrug, as if to say he was some kind of rare organism she didn't understand.

Bloody hell, Damien Wyatt found himself thinking as he straightened abruptly, who does she think she is? Not content with smashing my car and causing me considerable discomfort for weeks, she's—

He didn't get to finish this set of thoughts as the woman called Isabel popped her head around the door and offered them afternoon tea.

Arthur looked at his watch. 'Thank you so much, Isabel, but I'm afraid I won't have time. Penny wants me home by four.' He paused. 'What about you, Harriet? We did come in separate cars,' he explained to Damien.

Harriet hesitated and glanced at Damien. And because most of his mental sensors seemed to be honed in on this tall, slender girl, he saw the tension creep back as she picked up her purse and her knuckles whitened.

And he heard himself say something he hadn't expected to say. 'If you'd like a cup of tea, stay by all means, Miss Livingstone. We haven't finished the interview anyway.'

She hesitated again then thanked him quietly.

Isabel retreated and Arthur, looking visibly harassed, subjected them to an involved explanation of why he needed to be home. Plus he was obviously reluctant to miss any of the verbal duel he was witnessing. But he finally left. And the tea tray arrived but this time Damien introduced the bearer as his aunt Isabel, and invited her to join them.

'Sorry,' Isabel said as she put the tea tray down on the coffee table set in front of the settee in a corner of the dining room, 'but I'm popping into Lennox to pick up our dry-cleaning. Please excuse me, Miss Livingstone,' she added.

Harriet nodded somewhat dazedly and once again the door closed, this time on his aunt.

'I don't think there's anyone else who could interrupt us,' Damien Wyatt said with some irony. 'Do sit down and pour the tea.'

Harriet sank down onto the settee and her hand hovered over the tea tray. 'Uh—there's only one cup.'

'I never drink the stuff,' he said dismissively, 'so pour yours and let's get *on* with things.'

Harriet lifted the heavy silver teapot and spilt some tea on the pristine white tray cloth.

Damien swore beneath his breath, and came over to sit down beside her. 'Put it down and tell me something, Harriet Livingstone—why are you doing this? No, wait.'

He picked up the pot Harriet had relinquished and poured a cup of tea without spilling a drop. Then he indicated the milk and sugar but she shook her head. 'Th-that's fine, just as it comes, thank you.'

He moved the cup and saucer in front of her and offered her a biscuit that looked like homemade shortbread.

She shook her head.

'I can guarantee them. The cook makes them himself,' he said.

'Thank you but no. I—I don't have a sweet tooth.'

He pushed the porcelain biscuit barrel away. 'You look—you don't look as sk— as thin as you did that day,' he amended.

A flicker of amusement touched her mouth. 'Skinny you were going to say? I guess I did. I lost a bit of weight for a time. I've probably always been thin, though.'

'Sorry,' he murmured. 'But look, why *are* you doing this?'

Harriet hesitated and watched the steam rising gently from her tea.

'You obviously haven't forgiven me for the things

I said that day,' he continued. 'Most of the time since you've been here you've been a nervous wreck or, if not that, beaming pure hostility my way. The only thing that seems to relax you is contact with my dog or my mother's odds and ends.'

He broke off and looked rueful as Tottie rose, came over and arranged herself at Harriet's feet.

Harriet glanced at him briefly. In jeans, boots and a khaki bush shirt, with his thick hair ruffled and blue shadows on his jaw, he looked the epitome of a man of the land whereas, when she'd bumped into him, in a grey suit, he'd definitely been more of a high-flying businessman.

She shivered involuntarily. He'd been so angry in a quiet but deadly sort of way.

'Talk to me, Harriet,' he said firmly.

She took a sip of tea and then a deep breath. 'I need a job, quite urgently.'

'You—according to Arthur, anyway—are highly, if not to say über-qualified. Why would you want my job?' He frowned. 'It's stuck out in the country even if you don't have an army of lovers to worry about.'

'It...' Harriet paused '...suits me.'

'Why?'

A short silence developed between them and lengthened until he said impatiently, 'Oh, come on Harriet! I—'

'I just want to get this job,' she said with sudden intensity, 'on my merits.'

'Well, your merits are fine but I need to know more,' he said flatly.

'This kind of job doesn't grow on trees,' Harriet said

after a long moment. 'And it so happens it's the right district for me.'

'Why?'

Harriet sighed. 'My brother was badly injured in a surfing accident. He's now in a rehabilitation centre at—' she named a facility '—that's handy to Lennox Head and Heathcote. He has to learn to walk again. That's why—' she looked up at last and smiled with considerable irony '—when this job came up, it seemed like an answer to all my prayers. Until, that was—' She stopped abruptly.

'You found out whose job it was,' Damien supplied.

She didn't answer but looked away.

'You decided to proceed, however.' It was a statement, not a question.

'Yes.'

'And I suppose that's why you wanted to make sure the weekends were free? So you could see your brother. Talk about coals of fire,' he murmured wryly. He added impatiently, 'Why couldn't you have just told me all this in the first place?'

Harriet shrugged. 'Ever since I found out about the job, I've been...I have been a nervous wreck,' she conceded. She gestured. 'It would be so perfect but...' She shrugged again. 'To be perfectly honest, you're the last person I would want to accept a favour from.'

He grimaced. 'Needs must when the devil drives. You need the money?'

'I need the money,' she agreed rather dryly. 'This is a private hospital and it's not covered by my brother's medical insurance but it has a terrific reputation. And to be able to be close to Brett at the same time is an obvious bonus.'

'I see. Has it—' he paused and raised an eyebrow at her '—occurred to you that I was simply driving along minding my own business that day when all hell erupted, in a manner of speaking?'

She cast him a dark little look from beneath her lashes. 'Accidents happen.'

'Yes, but I thought you might be able to cut me a little slack—no, I see not,' he murmured as her lips set.

And, he continued, but to himself, you not only have amazingly long eyelashes, Harriet Livingstone, but a rather gorgeous mouth, severely sculptured yet somehow incredibly inviting. Plus—he allowed his dark gaze to roam over her—satiny-smooth skin, slender delicate wrists and lovely hands that I quite failed to notice the last time we met.

So that's it, Damien Wyatt, he castigated himself inwardly. Even with all the things you didn't notice then, this damn girl made an impression on you two months ago and that's why you felt goaded into seeing her again. What's more, she's making even more of an impression on you today, which is not going to lead *anywhere*, he told himself grimly.

But how to knock her back for the job?

In all decency you can't, he decided. So what to do if she keeps on making an impression on you?

A dry smile briefly twisted his lips—think of your poor car before it got fixed...

'Well, you've got the job if you want it,' he said

abruptly. 'Would you like to see the studio and flat before you make up your mind?'

Harriet clenched her hands in her lap. 'You don't have to feel sorry for me,' she said carefully. 'When one door closes another usually opens.'

'Harriet,' he warned, 'I don't appreciate being told what I should or should not feel but, if you want to get it right, I don't only feel sorry for you—most people would in the circumstances—but I feel as guilty as hell for the things I said over what was, you're right, an accident.'

'Oh...'

'Now, could we get *on* with it? You've barely had a drop of your tea,' he added with sudden frustration.

Harriet grabbed her purse. 'I'll leave it.'

She got up so precipitously, she tripped over Tottie and would have fallen to the floor if Damien hadn't lunged forward and caught her.

The next moments were confused as he untangled her from the dog, the coffee table and she ended up standing in the middle of the room in his arms.

'You wouldn't be accident-prone, would you?' he asked incredulously.

Harriet tried to free herself but, although he held her quite loosely, he made it plain he was not about to let her go. 'I...I suffer from a left-handed syndrome,' she said a little raggedly.

'What the hell's that?'

'My father's invention to explain the fact that I'm a bit uncoordinated at times.'

'So, yes—' he raised his eyebrows '—accident prone?'

She shrugged. 'Maybe. Would you mind letting me go?'

Damien Wyatt still had a spark of amusement in his eyes as he said wryly, 'Yes I would, heaven alone knows why. Well, for one thing I've never held a girl as tall as you but it feels good.'

'I...' Harriet opened her mouth to protest but he lowered his head and started to kiss her.

Shock seemed to take away all her powers of resistance and when he lifted his head she could only stare up at him with her eyes wide, her lips still parted and her heart beating heavily.

'Mmm...' He ran his hands up and down her back and hugged her. 'I must have been mad ever to think you were skinny, Ms Livingstone!'

Harriet gathered herself. 'This is...this is,' she started to say.

'Insane?' he supplied.

'*Yes,*' she agreed, almost biting her tongue in her frustration.

'You're not wrong. On the other hand, we've experienced quite a range of emotions—'

'That's—what's that got to do with it?' Harriet broke in desperately.

'We've been angry with each other,' he went on.

'You murderously,' she pointed out darkly.

'Well, not quite, but you've hated my guts,' he responded. 'I reckon we're destined to run through the whole spectrum—you know, your eyes are stunning.'

'I...they...'

'And there's your skin.' He transferred his hands to her arms and ran his palms down them. 'Smooth and satiny. As for your legs—by the way, I wouldn't ever wear that wraparound skirt again...' He paused as she moved convulsively and waited for her to quieten before he went on. 'Only because it's criminal to hide your legs.'

'Mr Wyatt,' Harriet said through her teeth, 'please don't go on and will you let me go!'

'In a minute. The other thing Arthur was right about; you have a slightly superior edge at times.'

Harriet, about to make a concerted effort to free herself, stopped dead and stared at him, completely mystified. 'What do you mean?'

'Well, for example, in the lounge earlier,' he elucidated, 'you looked at me as if I'd crawled out from under a rock.'

'I did not!' she denied.

'You probably don't realise you're doing it. Actually, what Arthur said was that you sometimes look as if your mind is on higher things.'

Harriet blinked. 'What does that mean?'

He dropped his arms and moved back half a pace but Harriet stayed where she was. 'That you think you're above this "mortal coil"?' he mused, and shrugged. 'Perhaps way above the sweaty realities of life and love, not to mention men? You did say there was no one. One has to wonder why.' He stopped and shrugged.

Harriet Livingstone very rarely lost her temper but when she did the consequences were often disastrous, mainly because she was tall enough to be effective about it. She advanced the half step towards Damien Wyatt and slapped his face. She did more.

'Oh, how I've wanted to do that,' she gasped but with great passion. 'Talk about being above the mortal coil—*you* obviously see yourself as the bee's knees!'

His lips twisted as he fingered his cheek. 'Bee's knees—haven't heard that one for a while. All the same, Stretch,' he responded, 'I—'

'*Don't* call me that,' she warned.

'Whatever.' He shrugged and took her in his arms and proceeded to kiss her again but this time there was a definite purpose to it. This time it was a battle, not a shocked passive response on her part and a more light-hearted exploration on his.

Until he lifted his head and said abruptly, 'No, no more anger and hate, Harriet.'

'What do you mean?'

'It's time to move on. No, don't do a thing, I'm not going to hurt you, it's just that fate seems to have intervened.' He shook his head. 'It certainly has for me.'

And this time, before he kissed her again, he drew her into his body and ran his hands over her in a way that made her go still and her eyes widen in a different kind of shock because it was as if he was imparting an electric current through her, a tide of sensuality she couldn't resist.

Then he released her and cupped her face in his hands and they looked into each other's eyes for a long, long moment. And as she breathed in the essence of Damien Wyatt it had a powerful effect on her. Not only did he bring the outdoors into the dining room—there were sweat stains on his shirt, his hair was ruffled—but a physical force and the aroma of pure man.

Then, as she searched his dark eyes and saw the way they were focused on her and felt the way his hands moved down to her hips and were gentle but skilful on her body, she got a different sense of him.

As if she was viewing the man behind the man. As if, underneath that prickly, easily prone to irritation exterior, there was a man who knew how to make love to a woman in a way that thrilled her and drove her to excesses she hadn't known she could reach...

And when he started to kiss her again, because of that sense of him, because of the rapturous tingling of all her senses, something she'd been denied for a long time, because of the feel of the hard planes of his body against her, because he was actually taller than she was and because there was something terribly, awe-inspiringly masculine about him unless you were a block of wood, she found herself kissing him back.

They drew apart briefly once. They were both breathing raggedly. He pulled the ribbon out of her hair and ran his fingers through it. She spread her fingers on his back and felt the sleek strength of it beneath his shirt.

Then he was kissing her again and her breasts were crushed against him as he held her hard.

It was the dining room door opening and a spontaneous whistle that brought Harriet Livingstone and Damien Wyatt back to earth.

Not that Damien betrayed any sign of discomfort, at first.

He released her in a leisurely way and tidied the collar of her dress before he said over her shoulder, 'Charlie, this is Harriet Livingstone. Harriet—' he put his hands on her shoulders '—it's OK. Meet my brother, Charles Walker Wyatt. He's renowned for rushing in where angels fear to tread.'

Harriet swallowed and put her hands up to try to tidy her hair before she forced herself to turn around.

Charles Walker Wyatt wasn't as tall as his brother Damien and he looked to be several years younger. He also bore an arrested expression on his face, as of one who had received a smack on the head when least expecting it.

'Holy...Mackerel, Damien!' he exclaimed then. 'The last thing I expected to find in the *dining room* of all places was you kissing a girl I've never laid eyes on! That's hardly *fools rushing in* material—wouldn't you agree, ma'am?' he appealed to Harriet as he advanced towards them.

'By the way, please forgive me,' he went on, 'for labelling you "a girl"—not that you're *not* but it sounds sort of generic and I don't mean to classify you like that. Not at all! But—'

'Charlie.' There was a definite warning note in Damien's voice.

'Damien?' Charlie replied, looking innocent. 'Just tell me what I'm allowed to say and do and I'll try not to put a foot wrong!'

'What anyone with a grain of courtesy or good sense would have done in the first place,' his brother replied evenly. 'Retreated and shut the flaming door!'

The last bit was said a little less than evenly and it

struck Harriet that Damien Wyatt was not completely unaffected by his brother's intrusion.

'Ah.' Charlie rubbed his chin. 'OK—but actually, I've had a better idea. What's wrong with me getting to know Miss Harriet Livingstone?' And he looked admiringly at Harriet.

'Everything,' Damien snapped. 'Just go away, Charlie!' he added, his irritation and rising impatience plain to be seen.

Something Charles Walker Wyatt obviously saw for himself because he sketched a salute, did a military about-turn and said, 'Just going, sir.' He marched out smartly.

Damien waited until the door closed before turning back to Harriet. 'Do you know something?' he said bitterly. 'Every time we get within cooee of each other, you and I, it turns out to be a shambles!'

Harriet swallowed. 'I think I should just go. It could never work.'

'*Go*?' he said through his teeth, 'How the hell can you kiss a guy like that and just go?'

CHAPTER TWO

'YOU STARTED IT,' Harriet said and immediately despised herself for sounding incredibly lame and childish. 'I mean...' But she found it impossible to sort out her thoughts let alone her emotions.

'If you hadn't tripped over the damn dog, I might not have started it,' he replied irritably. 'Anyway! How come Tottie is so taken with you?'

'I don't know.' Harriet shrugged helplessly. 'Dogs do just seem to take to me.'

'Look—' he studied her '—sit down and have another cup of tea—no, I'll pour it—hang on, I've got a better idea.' He guided her to a chair at the dining table and pulled it out for her. 'Sit down and study some of my mother's incomparable collection; it might calm you. While I pour us a drink.'

He turned away towards a cocktail cabinet.

Harriet drew a deep breath and combed her hair with her fingers but she couldn't find her ribbon so she had to leave it loose. She took a hanky out of her purse and patted her face. Then her attention was drawn to an exquisite cameo in an old-fashioned rose-gold and pin-point diamond setting and she forgot about the wreck she might look as she stared at it rapturously. And Damien Wyatt put a glass of brandy down beside her and pulled out a chair opposite to sit down with his own drink.

'Cheers,' he said.

Harriet hesitated.

'Don't think about it; just drink it,' he advised.

So she took a couple of sips and felt the brandy slip down and a warm glow of—what was it? Some confidence?—rise in its place.

But, before she could formulate anything sensible to say, he spoke. 'How well do you know Arthur?'

'Hardly at all. I know Penny better. We were at college together for a while, although she's a few years older. Then we lost track of each other until I came up to Ballina. It was quite an amazing coincidence. I literally bumped into her—no,' she said with her lips quirking suddenly as his eyebrows flew up, 'not the way I bumped into you. This was on the pavement as we were walking along.'

A gleam of amusement lit his eyes. 'I'm relieved to hear you say so. Go on.'

She looked rueful. 'So we had coffee and compared notes. She told me about Arthur and how they'd moved from Sydney to Ballina to get out of the rat race. She told me she'd started a picture-framing business and a small art gallery and how Arthur still dealt in art—he was born up here apparently.'

'Yes. He was a friend of my father's; more than that, he helped Dad establish his collection.'

'So I told her I'd also decided to get away from the rat

race and I was looking for a job. That's when she grew thoughtful and finally dragged me off to meet Arthur.'

'I see.' Damien swirled the liquid in his glass. 'So they didn't know—' he lifted his dark gaze to her '—about your brother?'

'No.' Harriet traced the rim of her glass with her forefinger then took another sip. 'I know it seems a bit deceitful, but I find it hard to deal with people feeling sorry for us.'

He was silent for a time, then, 'What were you doing up here two months ago, when you bumped into me?'

'I was checking out this rehabilitation centre. It was the first time I'd been to this area—another reason I was a bit dithery, I guess; I didn't know my way around.'

'It's not exactly a metropolis,' he said wryly then gestured as if to delete the comment. 'But you're living up here now? Your brother's in the rehab centre?'

Harriet nodded.

'Where are you living?'

She hesitated then took a sip of the brandy and shrugged. 'In a rented caravan in the caravan park. I do have a job—it's waitressing, so it keeps the wolf from the door, but—' She broke off.

'Only just?' he suggested.

She didn't respond but stared a bit blindly down at her glass.

'OK,' he said quietly, 'no more interrogations. The job is yours if you want it but what are we going to do?'

'Do?' she repeated.

He set his teeth. 'Yes, do! About the rest of it?'

Her deep blue eyes widened. 'The rest of it?'

He grimaced. 'You must have a short memory span as well as being accident-prone. Or do you often go around kissing guys like that?'

The confidence she'd got from a few sips of brandy ebbed a little at the same time as her eyes widened as the full memory of their passionate encounter hit her.

She took a larger mouthful of brandy.

'You had forgotten,' he marvelled.

'No. But we did get interrupted,' she responded tartly. 'I don't know about you, but I found it extremely embarrassing. Enough to make the rest of it, well…' She broke off as she searched for the right words.

'Pale into insignificance?' he suggested dryly.

'Not exactly,' Harriet denied and took another sip of her drink. 'But it did—move it back a bit if you know what I mean.' She paused and shrugged. 'It probably put it into its right perspective.'

'What would that be?'

She glinted him an assessing look from beneath her lashes, then thought—why should I try to spare his feelings? 'It was just something that happened in the heat of the moment, wasn't it?'

'Go on.'

Harriet hesitated, unable to read his expression but feeling a prickle of apprehension run through her. 'Well, you insulted me, I responded—'

'With a blow, allow me to remind you.' He looked sardonically amused.

Harriet compressed her lips. 'I'm sorry. I believe I had cause, however. Look—' she paused '—I wouldn't be surprised if you weren't still furious with me over your car.'

'Not to mention my collarbone. There are still some things I can't do. I'm not still furious, however.' Damien Wyatt crossed his arms and leant back with a frown growing in his dark eyes. 'Well, I may have been a bit annoyed but I have to say I'm mostly confused now. In fact I'm beginning to wonder if I'm hallucinating. Did you or did you not kiss me back almost like a woman starved for— that kind of thing?'

Harriet stared at the cameo for a long moment then looked at him squarely. 'Maybe. But it's best forgotten.'

'Why?'

Harriet pushed her glass away and stood up. 'Because I have no intention of getting involved with you, Mr Wyatt. Please don't take that personally. I'm…I'm… happy to be fancy-free, that's all.'

He stared at her and she was suddenly conscious that not only was she completely unable to read his thoughts but, more than that, it troubled her.

Why? Why should she care one way or another about what he thought of her? The sensual response he'd managed to draw from her had come about because he was experienced and worldly—she had little doubt of that— so why should she invest it with any special meaning or depth?

Well, she amended her thoughts, she had to take some responsibility for her reaction, surely? Starved? Perhaps—but she didn't even want to think about that…

'Would you mind if I went now? I'm sorry if I've

wasted your time but I honestly don't think it could work.'

Damien stayed absolutely still for a moment longer then he straightened and stood up, leaning his fists on the table. 'Yes, I would mind,' he said dryly, 'and I'll tell you why. I don't propose to have you on my conscience for a moment longer, whether I realise it or not, Harriet Livingstone.'

'You don't have to have me on your conscience!' she objected.

'Believe me, I'd rather not but—'

'What do you mean—whether you realise it or not?' Harriet broke in to ask with a frown.

He shrugged. 'I can't work out why else I agreed to see you again.'

Harriet linked her fingers together and told herself not to pursue this but some demon prompted her, rather than simply getting up and walking out, to say, 'If you think I could ever work for you, you must be mad, Mr Wyatt.'

Their gazes clashed.

'The job is yours, Miss Livingstone,' he replied deliberately. 'You can move in the day after tomorrow— I'll be gone then. I'm going overseas for some weeks, at least a month. Of course Isabel, who runs the house and the rest of it when I'm not here, will be in residence. So will Charlie, for a while anyway. Did Arthur get around to mentioning the remuneration package we thought was suitable?'

Harriet blinked. '…Yes.'

'You can add a twenty per cent commission on any items I decide to sell. Will that do?'

'I...I...' She hesitated.

'Don't go all dithery on me again, Harriet,' he warned. 'Finish your brandy,' he ordered.

She stared at him, deep hostility written into her expression. 'No. I've got to drive.'

'All right, but I need to know if you're going to take it or not.'

Harriet would have given the world to answer in the negative but if he was going to be away...and surely she could finish the job in a month if she worked day and night...?

'I'll take it,' she said barely audibly.

'Do you want to see the studio and the flat?'

'No.' She shook her head. 'I'm sure they'll be fine.'

He studied her narrowly with a glint of curiosity in his dark eyes. 'I can't work out if you're a superior, head-in-the-clouds although accident-prone academic type or a rather exotic bundle of nerves.'

Harriet took a breath and actually managed to smile. 'If it's any help, neither can I. Goodbye, Tottie,' she added and patted the dog's head.

Damien Wyatt looked heavenwards as Tottie came as close as such a regal-looking dog could to actually simpering.

At the same time, Harriet said, 'Oh! I wonder where I put my glasses?'

'Here,' he remarked flatly, picking them up from the dining table and handing them to her. 'I'll see you out.'

Harriet hesitated. 'I'm sure I could see myself out.'

'Not at all. After you.'

So it was that Harriet preceded him out of the dining room and out of the house to the driveway. There was only one vehicle parked there: hers.

Damien Wyatt took one look at it and swore. 'You're not still driving that damn tank, are you?' he asked with furious incredulity.

Harriet coloured slightly. 'It just refuses to lie down. Anyway, it's not mine, it's Brett's, my brother's. It's very good over rough and sandy terrain.'

'I believe you.' Damien favoured the vehicle with a lingering look of malice then transferred his gaze to Harriet.

'Well, enjoy your stay at Heathcote, Miss Livingstone.' A tinge of irony entered his dark eyes. 'Don't go about kissing too many men at the same time as you're happy to remain fancy-free. Oh, and watch out for Charlie. He is, not to put too fine a point on it, a womaniser.'

Harriet drew a deep breath. 'Perhaps he takes after you?' she said quietly, and climbed into her battered old vehicle.

He waited until she'd driven off before saying to Tottie, 'What the devil do you make of all that? OK, I know you're on *her* side, but I don't ever recall kissing a girl I've—virtually—just met like that.'

Predictably, Tottie didn't answer; she only yawned.

Damien Wyatt shrugged. In fact I haven't kissed anyone quite like that for a while, he added to himself. Been too busy, been somewhat cynical about the whole tribe of women, to be honest. What I need, if that's the case, is someone nice and uncomplicated who knows the rules of the game—doesn't expect wedding bells in other words—rather than importuning an accident-prone, scholarly type who drives a horrible vehicle and has the nerve to suborn my dog!

'That's you, Tottie,' he said severely but Tottie remained serenely unaffected.

'Of course you could always kind of…keep an eye on her while I'm away,' Damien added. 'Heaven knows what "a left-handed syndrome" could lead her into.'

'Permission to speak,' a voice said and Charlie strolled onto the drive.

'Don't start, Charlie,' Damien advised.

'She's gone, I see.' Charlie came to a stop beside Tottie and his brother. He shoved his hands into his pockets. 'Unusual vehicle. For a girl, I mean. Not to mention some kind of an antique dealer, according to Isabel.'

'It's her brother's, apparently. Listen, Charlie—' he explained Harriet's background and the agreement they'd reached '—so leave her alone, will you?'

Charlie looked offended. 'Acquit me! Would I try to steal your girl?'

'Yes,' Damien said flatly. 'Not that *she's* my girl—not that she's *my* girl—' He broke off and swore. 'But she's got a job to do here and the sooner it's done, the better.'

Charlie frowned. 'Why do I sense a mystery attached to Miss Harriet Livingstone? Smashing pair of legs, by the way.'

'I don't know,' Damien said shortly. 'How long are you here for?'

'Relax, Bro,' Charlie said cheerfully. 'I'm due back at

the base in a week. By the way, you are now talking to
Flight Lieutenant Charles Walker Wyatt. Which is what
I dashed into the dining room to tell you, incidentally.'

'Charlie!' Damien turned to his brother. 'Congratulations!' And he shook his brother's hand then envel-
oped him in a bear hug.

'I suspect I got it by the skin of my teeth but, yeah!'

'Come in and I'll shout you a drink.'

It was just before they were called into dinner that Charlie said thoughtfully, 'There's something about that girl,
Damien. Easy to run onto the rocks there—take care.'

Damien Wyatt opened his mouth to deny that there
was any possibility of his running onto any rocks with
Harriet Livingstone but he closed it.

And he said musingly, 'I'm glad to hear you say
so because for the last few hours I've been wondering
what on earth got into me. So what do you think it is?'

Charlie shook his head. 'I don't know,' he said. 'But
some women just have an aura of...reserve, maybe, with
a dash of vulnerability, a tinge of heartbreak perhaps,
and that—' he waved his tankard '—certain something
you just can't put into words.'

'That *je ne sais quoi*,' Damien murmured. He
frowned. 'And you sensed all this about Harriet Livingstone in—roughly two minutes?'

Charlie looked wise. 'I once decided to date a girl
I saw riding past me on a bicycle. All I saw was the
curve of her cheek and all this shiny brown hair floating out behind her but it was enough. I chased her in

my car, persuaded her to pop the bike in the boot and have lunch with me. We dated for quite a few months.'

'What broke it up?' Damien enquired curiously.

'The Air Force. I didn't get to spend enough time with her. Anyway, getting back to you. After Veronica, well...' Charlie shrugged as if he didn't quite know how to go on.

'Veronica,' Damien repeated expressionlessly.

'Your ex-wife,' Charlie explained generously. 'Gorgeous girl, of course, but—tricky'

Damien raised his eyebrows. 'Good at hiding it, though.'

'Met her match when she ran into you, *however*,' Charlie declaimed. 'I—'

'Charlie,' Damien said gently, 'the only reason I've let the discussion get this far is because I'm feeling rather mellow on account of your promotion but that's enough.'

'Right-ho! Just don't say I didn't warn you!'

'Isn't that the guy you ran into?'

Brett Livingstone sat in a wheelchair in his pleasant room in the rehabilitation centre but his expression was troubled.

Harriet sat in an armchair opposite. She'd come straight from Heathcote with the news of the job she'd got—she hadn't told her brother anything about it before in case it hadn't come off.

'Yes. But that's all in the past and it's not only what I love doing, it comes with accommodation.'

'Are you safe with him?'

'Safe?' Harriet stared at him. 'Of course.'

Brett looked angry. 'He sounded like a thug and a bully.'

Harriet bit her lip. 'It was a very beautiful car. But look; his aunt lives there. So does his brother from time to time, and there's staff. And he has this marvellous dog. Her name's Tottie and she's very highly bred.'

Brett smiled reluctantly as he studied his sister's bright expression. 'Any kind of a dog could get you in, Harry.'

She grimaced. 'I suppose so. But really, Brett, it's the kind of job most people who do what I do would dream about. And—' she hesitated, wishing fervently she'd never told her brother about running into Damien Wyatt '—I'm not a very good waitress,' she added humorously. 'Can I stay and have dinner with you?'

'Sure. Hey—' Brett sat forward '—how can I ever thank you?'

Harriet had never lived in a caravan before but several weeks of it now had convinced her she wasn't cut out to be a gypsy.

Despite the fact that the van was clean and modern, she felt claustrophobic and found it hard to sleep. Of course her state of mind for the last few months hadn't helped.

Lennox Head was situated in the Northern Rivers District of New South Wales. Not on a river itself, it lay between the Tweed and Richmond Rivers, and as well as a distinctive headland that attracted surfers from around the world and hang-gliders too, it had a marvellous seven-mile beach.

Inland, the country was green, fertile and undulating until it came up against the Border Ranges. Sugar was grown on the coastal flats; coffee and custard apples amongst others further inland but the biggest crop of the district was macadamia nuts. It was pleasant country, home to huge camphor laurel trees and many colourful shrubs.

When she got back to the van, Harriet changed and went for a brisk walk then came back and sat on a bench.

It was a quiet evening.

She could hear the surf, she could see stars, but she had no sense of freedom.

And she still had Brett on her mind...

At twenty, he was six years younger than she was and their mother had passed away when he was a baby. Looking after and worrying about her little brother had been a way of life for Harriet for as long as she could remember.

For that matter, looking after their father was something she'd done as she'd got older. Until his death a couple of years ago, he'd been a delightful person, humorous, always devising little surprises for his children, telling them marvellous stories but otherwise quite hopeless when it came to the mundane things of life like saving and planning for the future.

Therefore they'd lived from day to day to a certain extent—when work was plentiful it was a lobster month he'd used to say, when it wasn't plentiful, mince on toast. And they'd moved a lot between capital cities and major and minor art galleries.

However, it was thanks to her father that Harriet had acquired much of her knowledge of antiques and art. She'd shared his fascination for them and some of her earliest memories were of visits with him to art galleries and art auctions, memories of reading art history books with him.

Brett couldn't have been more different. Athletic and with a love of the sea, he'd decided on a career as a professional surfer. And he'd been slowly making a name for himself when he'd been struck down by a freak accident and for a while no one had expected him to walk again.

But he was—just, if you could even call the sweat-soaked, painful inch by inch progress that.

But at least, Harriet mused, he was getting the best treatment now, and she had enough resources to ensure this treatment was maintained.

Which led her thoughts onto the subject of Damien Wyatt and the incredible turn of events of the afternoon.

A tremor ran through her as she remembered being in his arms and the powerfully sensual effect he'd had on her.

How could she have been so affected? she wondered. Was it simply the human contact and warmth she'd responded to?

It had to be something like that because hadn't she sworn never to fall in love again?

She grimaced at how melodramatic it sounded and wondered suddenly if she did project a neurotic image.

And how about scholarly or academic as well as accident-prone? Superior?

Or how about just plain lonely?

She bit her lip and blinked away a sudden tear.

CHAPTER THREE

TWO WEEKS LATER, memories of her time in the caravan
had started to fade and she'd fitted into the Heathcote
lifestyle easily.

The flat above the converted stable block was comfortable and self-contained. It had a galley-style kitchen
with all mod cons that appealed to Harriet. She was a
keen and innovative cook and it wasn't long before she
had a variety of herbs growing in pots on the window-
sills. There was a rather lovely old wooden refectory
table with benches.

The lounge area had comfortable armchairs and a
view of the sea. The one bedroom was home to a king-
sized bed, the lightest, warmest quilts and was rather
sumptuously decorated in shades of violet and thyme-
green.

Isabel had confessed to being the decorator and also
to having gone a bit overboard in the bedroom.

Isabel was becoming friendlier and friendlier. She
was Damien and Charlie's father's sister; she'd never
married and it was plain to see that she ran not only
the house but the estate with a lot of care and affection.

She'd confided to Harriet once that she knew every inch of the estate and every nook of the house because she'd not only grown up at Heathcote but spent most of her life there.

She certainly handled the small army of staff required—gardeners, cleaners, stable hands and one highly temperamental cook—with ease. Well, she'd confessed to Harriet that she suspected the cook, a Queenslander, was not only temperamental but that he drank and she really should sack him but he claimed to have six children under ten. He also cooked like an angel...

It hadn't required much insight on Harriet's part to see that Isabel doted on her nephews.

And she very early on discovered that Isabel always carried out Damien's instructions.

This discovery came, in fact, on the day Harriet arrived to take up residence at Heathcote. Isabel came up to the flat that afternoon to see how Harriet had settled in and at the same time she handed over a set of car keys.

Harriet looked at the keys with a frown. 'What are these for?'

'There's a blue Holden in the garage. It's not new but it's in great condition. It's for you to use while you're here. In fact, if you give me your car keys, I'll get your vehicle parked elsewhere.'

'Do I...do I detect the hand of Damien Wyatt here?' Harriet said ominously.

Isabel grimaced. 'You do.'

'Well, if he thinks he can—'

'I've been told to let you go if you don't agree to the Holden,' Isabel interrupted, and patted Harriet's arm. 'Much easier to drive, I'm sure. Besides, there's something about your vehicle that—upsets Damien.'

'I can understand that, but Damien is not here,' Harriet pointed out to his aunt.

'Damien is always here,' Isabel remarked with some irony. 'He seems to have a sixth sense about the place even if he's a million miles away. Please?' she added.

Harriet breathed deeply. 'If you must know, I can't help thinking he's a bit of a control freak!'

'Oh, definitely!' Isabel agreed. 'More than a bit, in fact. But it was—' she put her head on one side '—rather a thoughtful thing to do, don't you think?'

Harriet pursed her lips. 'I suppose so,' she said at length, and flinched inwardly a little to hear herself repeating the bit about it being *rather a thoughtful thing to do* to Brett that evening when she drove over in the blue Holden to see him.

'Thoughtful?' Brett repeated as she wheeled him out to the car park to look at it. 'You sure the guy's not sweet on you, Harry?'

'Quite s...' Harriet paused then said hastily, 'I think *your* car keeps reminding him of what I did to his beloved Aston Martin with it.'

'But he's not here to see it,' Brett objected.

'He has eyes in the back of his head—or something like that,' Harriet said gloomily, then forced herself to brighten up. 'How's it going?'

'I've got a new physio,' Brett replied. 'She's really cool. I'm walking a wee bit further every day.'

Harriet narrowed her eyes as she picked up a jaunty note she hadn't heard in her brother's voice for a long time. And she found herself crossing her fingers metaphorically and sending up a little prayer at the same time that this 'she', this new physio, might just be the one to provide her brother with the spark he needed.

The other aspect of life at Heathcote, of course, was Charlie. He didn't spend a lot of time on the estate during his furlough but when he did he always popped in to see Harriet.

It was probably during the third such visit that Harriet confirmed what she'd first suspected—that Charles Walker Wyatt treated her in rather a strange manner.

And she couldn't help mentioning it at the same time as she couldn't keep a straight face. 'Charlie,' she said with a chuckle, 'do I look as if I've popped down from Mars?'

'Mars,' he repeated, looking startled. He was lounging at the refectory table eating an apple plucked from her bowl when he wasn't watching her in that curiously assessing way he had. 'What makes you say that?'

'You have a way of looking at me and sort of…testing everything I say as if it has a hidden meaning or *I* have something about me you just don't understand.'

'Ah.' Charlie took a large bite of his apple. 'Well…' He munched and thought. 'I've never met anyone quite like you, I guess.'

He paused and studied her thoughtfully. She wore tight black shorts and a sapphire-blue tank top. Her hair was bunched up on top of her head and she wore her red-rimmed glasses as she studied a recipe she was planning to make for her dinner. It was an unexceptional outfit by any standards and yet it emphasised how trim and slim her figure was, how long her legs were.

No wonder Damien had got a bit carried away, Charlie found himself thinking as Harriet reached up and took down a pottery casserole dish.

Even used as he is to the crème de la crème, there's certainly something, well, subtly, but all the same eye-catching about Ms Harriet Livingstone, Charlie thought. Why on earth did I promise to leave her alone…?

'Charlie?'

He came out of his thoughts to find Harriet staring at him. 'Uh—I've certainly never met anyone who works as hard as you do. You were still working at midnight when I got home last night!'

'That's because I'd like to finish this project before your brother gets—' She stopped abruptly.

'Before Damien gets home? Why?' he asked simply.

Harriet shrugged.

'His bark is a lot worse than his bite, as I should know.'

'It may be but I…' She paused.

'And you certainly must have made quite an impression on him because, believe me,' Charlie said earnestly, 'he's usually intensely private about his affairs. I got put firmly in my place only a couple of weeks ago when all I did was mention Veronica's name. She's his ex-wife,' he added obligingly, and waited.

I will not rise to the bait, Harriet vowed.

'So am I—very private,' she said shortly then relented as Charlie's expression became wounded. 'Look, it was just one of those…things. He got furious with me over the accident. I got furious with him because I thought he was arrogant and high-handed and it all seemed to blow up again into—' She stopped and took a breath then said laconically, 'If I hadn't slapped his face I wouldn't have got myself so thoroughly kissed.'

'Slapped his face!' Charlie was wide-eyed and incredulously admiring.

'Yes,' Harriet replied shortly. 'Not that I'm proud of it, but he did call me Stretch, which is something I can't abide. And that is the last word I intend to say on the matter. So, off you go, Charlie, please. I need to concentrate on this recipe.'

The studio that had been converted from stables was a pleasure to work in. There was plenty of light, plenty of bench space, a lot of shelving, a sink, even a microscope as well as a computer.

But, of course, the other thing that made Harriet feel at home was Tottie's presence. The big dog became her constant companion. They went for walks together. They went down to the beach and they visited the stables together, where Harriet made special friends with one of the horses, a bubbly grey mare that went by the name of Sprite.

Stan, the stable foreman, offered to let her ride Sprite, if she rode, which she had as a child, but she declined and contented herself with taking the mare carrots every evening.

And there were other times when Harriet caught herself talking to Tottie as if she were human.

She'd wondered how Isabel would take this but it only amused her. 'She's always been Damien's dog,' she told Harriet, 'but of course he's away a lot so she doesn't get to see that much of him.'

So far as the business side of her stay at Heathcote went, one thing Harriet had insisted on was a system whereby all of Damien's mother's treasures were dual-catalogued. In other words, Isabel handled them first, kept her own record, then handed them over to Harriet.

'Did you think we'd not trust you?' Isabel had asked curiously when Harriet had suggested the scheme. 'You come so highly recommended.'

'It's always better to be safe rather than sorry,' Harriet had replied. 'This way we're both protected.'

And Arthur, who drove up from Ballina occasionally, agreed.

Three weeks after she'd arrived at Heathcote, it was a glorious summer's day and she and Tottie went down to the beach. No one else was home. Charlie had gone back to his base and Isabel, who sat on several committees, was in Lismore helping to co-ordinate a charity drive and was spending the night with a friend.

They were the only ones on the beach, she and Tottie, and they frolicked in the surf and played with a ball until finally Harriet called out that she had to get back to work.

But something else had engaged the dog's attention after she'd dropped the ball at Harriet's feet. She stiffened, growled low in her throat and then took off like a shaggy arrow in full flight.

Harriet turned and discovered there was a man standing beside her towel where she'd dropped it on the grass verge above the beach—a man Tottie obviously knew because she skidded to a halt in front of him, barked with obvious joy this time, and leapt up to lay her paws on his shoulders—Damien Wyatt.

Harriet froze. Then she swallowed nervously as their last encounter and the last thing she'd said to him, the insult she'd offered him, stood out clearly in her mind.

Plus, even from further down the beach she could see he was wearing a suit, just as he had the day of the accident when he'd been so angry.

She hesitated and looked down at herself. Her lemon and lime flowered bikini was reasonably modest but it was still a bikini and she would have much rather been wearing a boilersuit or a combat uniform with all its paraphernalia for this encounter.

There was nothing for it, however, than to stroll up the beach, to say hi as casually as she could and to pick up her towel and wrap it around her. Perhaps then she could say something along the lines of *You're home early!* or *Welcome home! I have enjoyed Heathcote*— Stop it! she commanded herself. Just do it...!

It was a nerve-racking trudge up the beach but, when she was halfway there, Tottie came prancing back to her with delight written into her movements and a smile on her doggy face.

In fact Harriet had to grin in spite of herself, so infectious was the dog's enthusiasm.

'Hello, Damien,' she said as she reached him, almost confident that Tottie had eased the situation for her. She certainly didn't trip or fall as she picked up her towel and wrapped it around her sarong-wise but then she glanced up at him and things changed.

He wore a grey suit with a white shirt and a dark blue tie but he'd loosened his tie and unbuttoned the top button of his shirt. His hands were shoved into his trouser pockets.

And it struck Harriet like a blow to her heart that she'd fooled herself over the past weeks. Fooled herself into believing she'd completely rationalised the effect Damien had had on her.

More than that; she'd buried herself in his mother's treasures and convinced herself she wasn't even thinking of him. Only to know now that he'd been there on the back roads of her mind all the time; he must have been because every intimate detail of the passionate encounter they'd shared came back to her.

Not only did they come back to her but they trapped her into immobility, with her breathing growing ragged and her senses stirring as she stared at him and thought of the feel of his tall body against hers, the delight his hands had wrought on her.

Trapped her staring at him as a sea breeze lifted his dark hair off his forehead and brought her out in goose bumps—was it the breeze or was it part of the effect he was having on her, so she couldn't speak, she couldn't tear her eyes away?

Then she noticed he was watching her just as intently

and there was a muscle flickering in his jaw that told a tale of its own as his gaze slid down to her legs, barely hidden under the towel.

Tottie came to the rescue. She bunted them both playfully, as if to say—*Come on, you two, don't just stand there!*

Harriet had to relax a little and smile. So did Damien.

He also said, 'I hope my dog has been taking good care of you?'

'She's been a very faithful friend these last couple of weeks.' Harriet squeezed out her hair. 'I didn't know you were coming home.'

'No.' His dark eyes lingered on her figure and her legs again below the towel. 'Something came up unexpectedly. You look...well.'

Harriet smoothed the towel. 'Thanks.' Her voice was husky and she cleared her throat. 'So do you.'

A smile appeared fleetingly in his eyes. 'We sound like a mutual admiration society, a stilted one at that. But anyway, how's your brother?'

He turned and indicated they walk up to the house.

'He's making good progress and I've enrolled him as an external student at the Southern Cross University in Lismore.'

'What subject?'

She grimaced. 'Sports Psychology. I was hoping to wean him away from that kind of thing but—no go.'

'Better than nothing—a lot better,' Damien commented.

'Yes—ouch.' Harriet stopped walking as she stepped on a stone in her bare feet.

He stopped immediately. 'All right?'

'Yes!' She stood on one leg and awkwardly tried to examine the sole of her other foot. 'Oh, it's nothing, I'll be fine.'

'Here.' And, before she knew what he was about, he'd picked her up and was carrying her towards the studio.

'You don't have to do this,' she protested after a silent, shocked couple of seconds.

'Too good an opportunity to allow to pass, on the other hand.'

'Mr Wyatt—'

'Ms Livingstone?' he parried. 'Surely we can go one step further—upstairs?' he asked as they arrived at the studio.

'Well, yes, but—'

'What I mean about one step further is surely we can use each other's given names now,' he said as he mounted the stairs and sat her down on the refectory table and examined the sole of her foot.

'Well, yes,' Harriet conceded and immediately felt like a broken record.

'Good. There's nothing wrong with your foot. You might have a bruise, that's all.'

'Thank you.' Harriet rested her palms on the table and could think of not another thing to say.

Damien Wyatt grimaced. 'OK,' he said. 'I seem to have rather bowled you over. Why don't we go our separate ways for the next couple of hours—I've got things to do anyway—then have dinner?'

Harriet licked her lips. 'I was planning to work.'

'Say that again.' Something rather chilly entered his eyes.

She blushed. 'I…' But she could only gesture helplessly.

'Still running away, Harriet?' he said softly.

'I…' She trailed off then gathered herself. 'There's nothing to run away from but—' she hesitated '—if you don't mind pasta you could come here for dinner.'

He looked surprised.

'What?' she queried.

'I guess I wasn't expecting that.'

'You may have some preconceived ideas about me that influence your judgement; you obviously do,' she retorted.

There was a challenging glint in her eyes as she continued. 'Uh, let's see.' And she started to tick off her fingers. 'Head-in-the-clouds, accident-prone, academic—oh, let's not forget superior and neurotic. No wonder you were surprised to be asked to dinner!'

His lips twisted and he looked about to reply, then as if he'd changed his mind. He did say, 'I'll look forward to it. Around six? I'll bring some wine. You can stay,' he added to Tottie, who was looking visibly torn as he walked to the door.

Harriet stared at the doorway for a long moment after he'd disappeared then she clicked her fingers and Tottie came to the refectory table and put her chin on Harriet's knee with a soulful sigh.

'You could have gone with him,' she said as she stroked the dog's nose. 'I'd quite understand. He may not appreciate divided loyalties. In fact I get the feeling he's a hard man with a lot of hang-ups.'

Tottie sat down and thumped her tail on the floor.

Harriet smiled then slid off the table and glanced at the kitchen clock and discovered she only had an hour to shower and change as well as produce dinner.

But when she reached the bathroom, she dropped the towel still wound round her and stared at herself in the mirror. Then she closed her eyes and breathed deeply as every sensation she'd experienced from the moment he'd picked her up in his arms and carried her upstairs to the moment he'd sat her down on the table—and beyond—came to her again.

The easy strength that had made her feel quite light despite her height. The movement of his muscles against her body, the feel of his heart beating against her as her own heartbeat had tripled. The hard wall of his chest that made her feel soft and so sensuous. The pure aroma of man she'd inhaled with delight...

She opened her eyes and stared at herself in something like shock as she thought—*this can't go on!*

It was a hurried shower she took. And she pulled on a pair of grey leggings patterned with white daisies and a white cotton shirt with puffed sleeves. She tied her hair back severely with a pink ribbon and didn't bother with any make-up, not that she needed any; walking in the sun and swimming in the sea the past few weeks had given her a golden glow.

'This is delicious but—correct me if I'm wrong—it's not pasta,' Damien said.

He'd changed into a denim shirt and jeans and they sat opposite each other at the refectory table that Harriet had set with blue woven mats, matching linen napkins and one of her herbs in a colourful pottery pot.

'Changed my mind,' she confessed. 'It's paella.'

'What's it got in it?'

Harriet rested her elbows on the table and dangled her fork in her fingers. 'Let's see, chicken and prawns, rice, saffron, of course, tomatoes, onions, garlic, baby peas—that's mainly it. I guess people have their own variations but that's mine.'

'If you'd told me I could have brought some Sangria.'

Harriet put her fork down and picked up her wine glass. 'It's a very nice Beaujolais.'

'Thanks. So,' he said thoughtfully, 'cooking is another of your accomplishments. You're a talented girl.'

'That's about the sum of it, though,' she said wryly. 'And I don't think I was born to cook. It came about through necessity.'

'How come?'

She explained about how she'd grown up.

'So that's why you're so protective of your brother,' he commented. 'I suppose in a way I'm the same with Charlie. Our father died when he was seventeen. I've been standing in loco parentis ever since.' He grimaced.

Harriet pushed her plate away and picked up her glass. 'Charlie's a honey,' she said warmly.

Damien narrowed his eyes. 'He hasn't been chatting you up, has he?'

'Not at all. He's been trying to pin me down, if anything. As in trying to work me out. He believes, he says, anyway, I'm not like anyone else he's met. Mainly, from what I can gather—' she shrugged ruefully '—because of my work ethic.'

'How's it going, work-wise?'

Harriet studied her wine. 'Another week should do it.'

'You would have finished before I came home, if things had run to schedule, in other words.'

Harriet took a sip of her wine, put the glass down and plucked a basil leaf from the herb pot and crushed it between her fingers. 'Yes.'

He shrugged. 'Still hell-bent on being fancy-free, in other words?'

'Ah.' Harriet got up and collected their plates. She took them to the sink then opened the fridge and withdrew a lemon meringue dessert. She put it on the table, together with a tub of ice cream.

'If that's meant to placate me,' he said with a sudden wicked gleam of amusement in his dark eyes, 'you've hit the right button, ma'am. I cannot resist lemon meringue. Just don't tell the cook. He believes he and only he can make a perfect meringue. Incidentally, I'm in his black books.'

Harriet looked a question at him.

'He wanted to cook dinner for me.'

She smiled absently and set a coffee pot on to percolate. 'You're popular.'

He didn't respond and she sat down and served his dessert in silence.

'What about you? Of course,' he said, 'you don't have a sweet tooth.'

She nodded and he ate in silence until he said, 'You know, you haven't tripped or spilled anything tonight, which means you must be feeling more at ease so—can I put a proposition to you?'

Harriet blinked several times. 'What?'

'That we at least agree we have a rather devastating effect on each other.' He paused as Harriet looked away at the same time as she coloured.

'Yes,' she said after a long moment, and started as the coffee began to perk.

'I'll get it.' He got up and, without much fuss, found mugs and milk and sugar. 'However,' he continued, 'for reasons best known only to us, we're not keen to—start anything.' He looked briefly amused. 'Sounds a bit juvenile, doesn't it, but you probably get my drift.'

Harriet nodded.

'Incidentally, why did you,' he said as he began to pour the coffee, 'ask me to dinner tonight?'

Harriet hesitated. 'I…I felt I owed you some explanation.'

He sat down. 'You don't "owe" me anything,' he said abruptly.

'Mr…Damien,' Harriet said sternly, 'you told me once you didn't appreciate being told what you should or should not feel, didn't you?'

He grimaced. 'Did I?'

'Yes! Well, I'm telling you I feel as if I owe you an explanation and that's that—damn!' she said with great feeling. 'Now you've got me all...' She trailed off frustratedly.

'Het up about nothing?' he suggested mildly.

She cast him a speaking look. 'Do you want to hear this or not?' she asked acerbically.

'Go ahead.'

'I fell in love. I...' She paused. 'I guess you could say I gave it my all. And we had...we did have some wonderful times. But then he noticed another woman and I could literally feel him slipping away from me. That's why...' She stopped.

'That's a fairly common thing to happen,' he said slowly. 'How long ago was this?'

'A year or so ago.' She shrugged.

'That's all?' he queried with a frown.

No, it's not all, Damien Wyatt, Harriet thought, but that's all you're getting, well...

'Well, I've wondered ever since whether I brought it on myself. I guess...' she twined her fingers together '...I may have been looking for someone to take over my life. No...' she frowned '...not that exactly, but someone I could depend on to make the right decisions for us. Rather than me having to, as I seemed to have grown up doing.

'But when it started to fall apart I couldn't help thinking I may have come across as too "needy" and it was probably a relief for him to get away,' she said with a wave of her hand. 'I still don't know the answer to that but, whatever, I'm not prepared to go through all that again. I thought…I should explain, though.' She hesitated because, of course, there was more but telling anyone was something she'd never been able to do yet…

Their gazes caught and held.

'But you don't seem to have that problem,' she said at last. 'I mean I get the feeling you'd be quite happy to "start something".' Her glance was very blue and tinged with irony.

He crossed his arms and studied her thoughtfully. 'Yes, but, to be perfectly honest, if there is such a thing as…' he paused as if searching for the right phrase '…*love ever after*, I don't think it's going to exist for me.'

Harriet's eyes widened. 'Your marriage…' She trailed off awkwardly.

He raised an eyebrow at her. 'Isabel?'

'No. Charlie.'

He looked heavenward. 'I might have known.' Then, 'Well, you probably don't need me to elaborate.'

'All he told me was her name—and that he'd got firmly put in his place for merely mentioning it a little while back.'

Damien grimaced. 'Sounds like Charlie.'

'Sounds like you, actually.' A faint smile twisted her lips. 'So, it left you disillusioned?'

'It did a lot more damage.' He looked across the room and his dark eyes were cold. 'But, yep, it certainly left me unwilling to repeat the experience—I know!' He raised his hand as Harriet opened her mouth. 'You're going to say with another woman it could be different. Perhaps. But not for me. I don't part easily from my grudges, be they personal or embracing an institution like marriage.'

Something like a shiver ran down Harriet's spine because she had a feeling his estimation of his character was correct...

'In a way, we're a bit alike,' he said then, drumming his fingers on the table. 'Too much responsibility at an early age, only it took us differently.' He paused, looking briefly humorous. 'You wanted someone to take over; I got too used to being in command to be able to bend at all.'

'How come?'

He shrugged. 'I was twenty-two when my father died. And we were about to be taken over so I had to stave that off and get us up and running again. That's when I made the dicey decision to expand into mining machinery when we'd always concentrated on agriculture and its machinery.

'Plus,' he said rather wryly, 'I think I was born with an "ornery" streak. Arthur agrees with me.'

'Talking of Arthur,' Harriet said with a smile, 'Penny is pregnant.'

Damien grimaced.

'You don't approve of her, do you?'

'I think she manipulates him shamelessly,' he said dryly, then grinned. 'He'll need plenty of support to get through this! He'll be a nervous wreck.'

Harriet laughed.

Damien put his coffee mug down and simply watched her. Her hair was tied back but becoming wayward as it escaped. Her skin was unbelievably smooth, her hands and wrists slender and elegant, and her eyes were like deep blue velvet and still sparkling with amusement.

He said slowly, with his dark gaze still resting on her, 'I don't know how the hell I didn't see it the first time we met but you're breathtaking when you laugh.'

'I had nothing to laugh about at the time,' she said, still smiling. But gradually it faded as she moved awkwardly and nearly knocked her coffee over.

'So nothing's changed?' he said barely audibly as his gaze tracked her awkward movements.

'N-no,' she stammered.

'It doesn't make it easier that we've both stated our cases and I think we've both indicated we're not talking love ever after?'

Harriet tilted her head as she studied him with a frown in her eyes. 'No,' she said slowly.

'Any special reason?' he enquired dryly.

'I'm—I don't think I'm like that. I seem to be an all or nothing kind of person. In that regard,' she said thoughtfully.

Damien Wyatt smiled in a way that brought to mind an unamused tiger. 'You shouldn't go around saying things like that, Harriet Livingstone.'

'Why not? I think it's true.'

'It's also an incendiary kind of statement,' he murmured dryly.

Harriet looked at him wide-eyed. 'I...I'm not sure what you mean...' She faltered into silence. Then a flood of colour poured into her cheeks as his meaning became plain and she jumped up so precipitously she took Tottie by surprise and she tripped over her.

This time Damien Wyatt was too far away to rescue her and she'd fallen to her knees when he got to her.

'It's all right, I can manage,' she panted and held a hand out as if to ward him off as she scrambled to her feet. 'I didn't mean to...to imply,' she went on, 'what you obviously thought I meant to imply.'

'What was that?' he enquired and looked as if he was having trouble keeping his face straight as he steadied her with his hands on her waist.

'That—oh! You know what I mean!' Her expression was seriously frustrated.

'That you're only great in bed when you believe you're in love?'

She nodded then shook her head, more frustrated than ever. 'I didn't say anything about being great in bed and—'

'I'd like to bet you are, though,' he broke in.

'There's no way you could possibly know that!' she said heatedly.

He gestured. 'You're talking to a guy who's kissed you, remember?'

Harriet subsided a little. 'Well,' she said uncertainly.

'And you did suggest you were an *all or nothing* kind of person in *that* regard, which suggests—which conjures up certain images,' he said gravely, but she just knew his dark eyes were laughing at her.

She took a distressed breath and formed her hands into fists. 'Don't laugh at me,' she warned.

'Or?' he queried, his hands still on her waist. 'You don't expect to slug it out with me, do you?' He eyed her clenched fists.

'I would like nothing better,' she confirmed with great feeling again.

'How about testing out the other side of the coin?' he suggested, and pulled her closer.

She stiffened and urged herself into battle mode. Resist this, she told herself fiercely. Don't fall under his spell as you did last time, don't get mesmerised again. Don't allow the somehow simply wonderful feeling of being in his arms to overcome you and make you dizzy with delight. Dizzy and delighted because he feels so strong, because he knows just how and where to touch you and arouse you... She started as he spoke again.

'How about—this?' And he slid his fingers beneath her top and cupped her breasts.

CHAPTER FOUR

HARRIET TREMBLED AND he felt it through his fingers.

'If it's nice for you, you only need to nod,' he said huskily. 'Believe me—' he moved his fingers across her nipples '—it's sensational for me.'

Harriet's lips parted and she unclenched her fists and grasped his wrists instead. She didn't nod but she did say, 'You have a way of doing that—that's breathtaking but—'

'You'd rather I didn't?' he suggested, narrowing his eyes suddenly.

Harriet closed her eyes briefly. 'I'd much rather fly to the moon with you, Damien Wyatt,' she said barely audibly, 'but I can't help knowing I'd regret it sooner or later.'

'Another incendiary statement.'

She bit her lip. 'I'm sorry, I'm really sorry.' And there were tears in her eyes.

He hesitated for a long moment then he withdrew his hands and smoothed her top down. 'You win,' he drawled.

Harriet flicked away the tears on her cheeks and

steeled herself for more mockery. It didn't come, not in the spoken form, anyway.

He turned away and sprawled out in one of the chairs at the table. 'Actually—' he ran a hand through his hair '—you're right, Ms Livingstone.'

But being right, Harriet discovered, didn't prevent him from subjecting her to a dark gaze full of dry amusement as he looked her up and down and mentally dispensed of all her clothes.

She bore that sardonic scrutiny and mental undressing for as long as she could, determined not to turn away and thereby give him the satisfaction of knowing he'd upset her, but was just about to protest when he spoke.

'Do you ride?'

Harriet blinked. 'Horses?'

'Well, I don't mean camels.'

'I have, as a kid,' she said cautiously.

He drummed his fingers on the table. 'Did you enjoy it?'

'Yes,' she replied but equally as cautiously as she wondered what was coming.

'Just tell me this, Harriet. Would it be purgatory for you if I suggested we get up at the crack of dawn tomorrow to take advantage of the low tide and go for a gallop down the beach? Tottie, I know, would love it.'

'If I could ride Sprite...' She paused and looked uncomfortable.

She saw him process this. 'So,' he murmured, 'you have a way with horses as well as dogs?'

Harriet spread her hands. 'Oh, I don't know.'

He raised an eyebrow. 'Sounds as if you've been chatting Sprite up already.'

'I suppose I have,' Harriet conceded ruefully.

'Then—are we on for tomorrow morning, about five?'

'I...' Harriet swallowed but nothing could stop the flow of images running through her mind of a dawn gallop followed by a swim then a huge breakfast. 'Yes,' she said.

'Good.' He stood up. 'Not—' he eyed her with a glint of pure devilry in his dark eyes '—that there'll be anything good about how to get to sleep tonight.'

It was no consolation to Harriet to reflect, as she tossed and turned in bed after Damien had gone, on one victory, one small victory perhaps, but all the same...

She'd successfully withstood the sensual onslaught Damien could inflict on her, although *inflict* wasn't the right word for it at all. But she had withstood the power of his masculine appeal, she'd tacitly told him to do his worst when he'd mentally undressed her—and then she'd gone and wrecked it all by agreeing to go riding with him.

'Damn!' She sat up in bed. 'I must be mad. Apart from anything else, I know he's only going to lead me to fresh heartache—I should be running for my life!'

At five o'clock the next morning she felt heavy-eyed and in an uneven frame of mind as she pulled on jeans, a jumper and sand shoes.

Twenty minutes later, trotting down the track from

the stables to the beach on the slightly fizzy Sprite, she was feeling marginally better, although only marginally, she assured herself.

By the time they reached the beach, the sun was turning the sky into a symphony of apricot as it hovered below the horizon and the placid waters reflected the colours back.

'Hang on,' Damien said as he took hold of Sprite's bridle and clipped on a leading rein so that she and Sprite were forced to adapt to his slower gait.

'What do you think you're doing?' Harriet asked.

'Taking precautions, that's all,' he replied.

'I can assure you, you don't need to!'

'You said you rode as a child. That could mean you haven't been on a horse for years.'

'I'm perfectly capable of riding this horse,' Harriet replied through her teeth.

'But you have to admit you're—well, if not exactly accident-prone, you do suffer from some weird syndrome that could cause all sorts of problems.'

'Mr Wyatt—' Harriet raised her riding crop '—don't say another word and let me go before I do something *you* might regret but *I* won't regret in the slightest!'

'Harriet,' he returned mildly, 'it's not very ladylike to keep attacking me.'

Harriet groaned. '*Let me go.*'

He hesitated briefly then unclipped the leading rein. Sprite, who'd been dancing around impatiently on the end of it, jostled his big brown horse, had the temerity to bestow a love bite on its neck, then, following Harriet's dictates, lengthened her stride and galloped away. Tottie raced after them joyously.

By the time they'd reached the end of the beach and galloped back, Harriet's mood had evened out—she was feeling far less grumpy and even of the opinion that this had been a good idea.

And, following Damien, she rode Sprite into the gentle low-tide surf. Both horses loved it and splashed energetically until finally they brought them out, led them to the edge of the beach and tied them loosely to trees.

'I'm soaked!' Harriet sank down onto the sand but she was glowing with enthusiasm as she sat cross-legged.

Damien cast himself down beside her and doodled in the sand with a twig. He hadn't shaved and he had a curious glint in his dark eyes as he looked across to study her.

'Tell me something,' he said. 'Are you not a morning person?'

Harriet opened her mouth, closed it, then she grinned. 'I am not. Well, not a very early morning person.' She was about to add—*and particularly not after a disturbed night*—but managed to hold that bit of information back. 'I take it you're the opposite?'

'Depends.'

'On what?'

'What's on offer in bed.'

Harriet looked heavenwards. 'Do men ever think of anything else?'

'Frequently.' He shot her an amused glance. 'Not,

generally, at five in the morning with a warm, compliant partner, however.'

Harriet frowned as the wheels of her mind worked through this. Then she turned to him incredulously. 'Did you get me up at that ungodly hour as a shot at me for not…for…not…for being…for not being in bed with you?' she said exasperatedly.

'If I did,' he said wryly, 'I had no idea the danger I was placing myself in. I'll probably think twice before I do it again.'

'Oh!' Harriet ground her teeth as she stared at him, so big, so relaxed, so attractive, even if he hadn't shaved and his hair was hanging in his eyes, not to mention the fact that he was teasing her mercilessly.

'But of course,' he went on before Harriet could speak, 'the real reason I got you up at the crack of dawn was because of the tide. You need a low tide and therefore firm wet sand to gallop on. By the way, where did you learn to ride like that?'

Harriet closed her mouth and subsided somewhat. Then she shrugged and smiled. 'My father decided it needed to be part of my education. He restored a couple of valuable paintings for a wealthy horse breeder who was once a jockey in exchange for riding lessons. He had a few other notions along those lines—I had tennis lessons under similar circumstances, not so successful; my—' she cast him a quirky glance '—weird syndrome interfered with me becoming a Wimbledon champion.'

He laughed and looked at her curiously again. 'You're full of surprises—docile and ladylike on one hand then quite a termagant.'

'Docile!' Harriet pulled a face. 'That sounds awful. So does termagant. I'm sure I'm not either of those.'

'You're also younger sometimes. The ladylike you could be ten years older.'

'That's ridiculous,' Harriet objected but found she had to laugh a little. 'You know, the art world takes itself very seriously sometimes, so one may get into the habit of *being* very serious-minded without quite realising it.'

He laughed then glanced at his watch. 'OK. I've got things to do.'

He got up and untied his horse but Harriet stayed where she was, quite unaware that she looked disappointed.

'Harriet?'

She looked up to see him frowning down at her.

'This is how you want it, isn't it?' he queried.

She froze then a heartbeat later she scrambled up. 'Sure! Let's go!'

But upstairs in the flat after she'd showered and was eating breakfast alone, it wasn't how she wanted it at all, she had to confess to herself.

She worked furiously for the next couple of days then Charlie came home for a long weekend and it was his birthday and he'd decided to have a party.

If she hadn't been so engrossed in her work, she'd have noticed the preparations going on in the big house, but she hadn't. Therefore it took her by surprise when Isabel asked her what she'd be wearing.

'Wearing?'

'To Charlie's birthday party.'

'When?'

Isabel clicked her tongue. 'Tomorrow. You're invited.'

'No I'm not.' Harriet put down the ivory figurine of a dolphin she was holding.

'But I put an invitation—' Isabel broke off, looked around and stepped over to the table beside the door where she picked up several items of mail, one of which she then brandished at Harriet, looking exasperated. 'Even if you didn't see this, surely you noticed that something was going on?'

Harriet coloured. 'No. I'm sorry. And thank you very much for inviting me—'

'Charlie did,' Isabel corrected.

'Charlie then, but I couldn't possibly come.'

'Why on earth not?' Isabel stared at her with the light of battle clearly lit in her dark Wyatt eyes.

Harriet heaved a sigh. 'I'm—I'm an employee, Isabel,' she said but tartly despite the sigh, 'and don't forget it! Look, I'm sorry if I sound snippy or rude but sometimes it's the only way to deal with you Wyatts.' To her horror, tears stood out in her eyes but she carried on relentlessly. 'I'm not coming and that's that.'

'Not coming where?'

Both Harriet and Isabel swung around to see Damien standing in the doorway.

'Charlie's party,' Isabel said bitterly.

Harriet turned away. There had been no more dawn rides on the beach; in fact she'd hardly seen Damien since that magical morning.

'That's OK,' Damien said easily. 'It's her choice.'

Isabel took a sharp angry breath. 'Men! You're all the

same; never there for you when you're needed. If anyone could have persuaded her, you could have. But, on top of being unreliable, most men are as thick as planks!' And she stormed past Damien and out into the night.

Harriet closed her mouth and blinked several times.

'Ditto,' Damien murmured. 'You wouldn't change your mind and come, would you, Harriet? If for no other reason than for me to regain some credibility in my aunt's eyes.'

Harriet hesitated then sighed. 'I might just put in an appearance. But that's all,' she warned.

'Far be it from me to urge you otherwise,' he said gravely. 'No, I wouldn't dream of persuading you to take part in what you might see as mindless revelry in some way beneath you—or whatever. So, good-night, Miss Livingstone,' he added reverently and he too stepped out into the night. He also closed the door.

Harriet discovered herself to be possessed of a burst of anger and she picked up an object to hurl it at the door, only to realise it was the ivory dolphin.

She lowered it to the table, breathing heavily, and she said to Tottie, 'That was a close call.'

Tottie wagged her tail and went back to sleep.

By eight o'clock the next evening, Charlie's party was starting to hum. The lounge had been cleared for dancing, a disco had been set up and the dining room hosted a magnificent buffet and a bar.

Guests from all over the Northern Rivers had descended on Heathcote, some from further afield like the Gold Coast.

Harriet got to know this because Charlie personally came to escort her to the party.

She looked down at herself just before Charlie climbed the stairs to the flat—not that she'd known he was coming. In fact she was grappling with nerves and the desire to find a hole to fall into. She was also hoping she wasn't over- or underdressed.

She wore a black dress with a loose skirt to just above her knees with white elbow-length sleeves and white panels in the bodice. It was a dress that emphasised the slenderness of her waist. With it she had on a ruby-red chunky necklace, her legs were golden and long and bare and she wore black suede high heels with ankle ties.

Her hair was pulled back into a knot but she'd coaxed some tendrils to frame her face. Her lips were painted a delicious shimmering pink and her eyes were made up with smoky shadow, her lashes just touched with mascara to emphasise their length.

'Holy Mackerel!'

Charlie stopped dead as he stepped into the flat and took in every detail about Harriet.

'Oh, boy!' he said then.

Harriet twisted her hands together. 'What's wrong?'

'It's not that, it's the opposite. Poor old Damien; is he in for…well. I hope you know what you're doing, Harriet.'

'Doing?'

Charlie blinked and frowned. 'You didn't set out to drive him wild?' He gestured to take her in from the tip of her head to her toes.

Harriet opened her mouth to deny this accusation but she closed it and coloured slightly. 'I haven't actually worn it before. Is it too…?' She didn't complete the sentence. 'I can change.'

'Don't you dare!' Charlie looked horrified. 'So you did set out to drive him wild?'

'I did not,' she denied.

'I wouldn't mind,' Charlie offered. 'I'm on your side.'

'I…' Harriet hesitated. 'He made a remark that cast me in the light of a docile priggish bore. So I thought I'd show him otherwise. But now, if you must know, Charlie, I'm sorry, but I really don't want to go to your party.'

'Made a remark, did he?' Charlie ignored the rest of her statement. 'He's done that to me. He has a way of doing it that makes you want to throw things—but what sweet revenge would this be. Come, my lady Harriet.' He held out his arm.

'Charlie…Charlie, this is not really me and I've changed my mind about…showing him anything.'

'No, you haven't,' Charlie disagreed as he led her to the top of the stairs. 'You've got a slight case of stage fright, that's all. But I'll be there!'

'So.'

Harriet stood on the terrace, sipping champagne and fanning herself.

There was a moon. There were also flaming braziers in the garden and the music flowing out was of a solid rock beat and loud enough to drown the sound of the surf beyond the garden wall.

'So,' she repeated without turning.

'You don't mind a dance, Miss Livingstone,' Damien observed, moving forward to stand beside her.

'I don't. At the right time and place,' she replied. She took another sip of champagne as she registered the fact that he was wearing a tweed jacket over a round-necked shirt, and jeans.

'I thought you were just going to put in an appearance.'

'I was. Your brother had other ideas.' She shrugged.

'You look—great. Quite unlike your alter ego.'

'Thank you. I suppose you mean my academic, neurotic—' she waved a hand '—and all the rest of it, side.'

'Well, certainly the you that looks as if you've stepped straight out of Christies or Sotheby's or a museum.' He paused then glanced across at her. 'What would happen if I asked you to dance?'

'Thank you so much, Damien, but—' she drained her champagne and put the glass down on the table beside her '—I think I've done enough partying,' she finished politely.

Their gazes locked. 'That's a pity.' He raised a dark eyebrow. 'Still scared and running, Harriet?'

Harriet put a hand to her throat. 'We've been through all this, Damien.'

He shrugged and studied his beer tankard. 'I don't think we made allowances for the effects of you looking so gorgeous and seriously sexy, you dancing, your legs on show; no sign of the eternal jeans or leggings you wear. It's almost as if you're issuing an invitation, Miss Livingstone.'

A tide of colour poured into Harriet's cheeks.

He studied it with interest. 'You are?'

'No. Oh! Look,' she said intensely, 'you persuaded me to come to this party. You then made—talk about an incendiary remark but in quite a different sense—you made my blood boil *in anger*,' she emphasised, 'with your comments about mindless revelry that I would find beneath me.'

'So you decided to show me a thing or two?' he hazarded.

'Yes,' she said through her teeth. 'Mind you—' she hesitated then decided she might as well go for broke '—I did intend only to put in an appearance, enjoy myself for a little while then retreat. The music got to me,' she added.

His lips twitched. 'I quite understand. The music is getting to me right now, as a matter of fact.'

Harriet narrowed her eyes and concentrated for a moment as she listened to the music, and grimaced.

'No good for you?' he queried as she barely restrained herself from moving to the beat.

'I couldn't exactly say that…'

'We could have a "no hands" agreement,' he suggested. 'We could just do our own thing,' he explained.

Harriet eyed him. 'What a good idea.' She smiled sweetly then laughed at his expression. 'It's OK. I'll take my chances.'

It was a phrase that was to haunt her during the rest of that night and the day that followed.

Because the fact of the matter was, she'd danced the rest of the night away with Damien.

She'd rocked and rolled, she'd been quiet and peaceful in his arms. She'd revelled in the feel of his hands on her, in the feel of his body against hers. She'd followed his lead and adapted her steps to his, once with a flourish that had flared her skirt out around her thighs so that she'd grimaced and pushed it down with a tinge of colour in her cheeks.

As she'd danced she'd recalled the last time she'd been in his arms and the intimacy of the way they'd kissed. And she'd wished they were alone as they'd been that day so she could run her fingers through the thick darkness of his hair and slide her hands beneath his jacket and shirt and feel those sleek muscles of his back...

And at the end she'd been wrapped in his arms, barely moving and loving it.

That was when the lights had come on. That was when people had started to leave. That was when she'd come to her senses, when she'd looked up into his eyes, when she'd seen the desire in them.

And when she'd freed herself urgently and fled from him, melting into the crowd of departing guests then running up the stairs to the flat, locking herself in and turning off all the lights.

She'd undressed shakily and thrown her dress onto the floor.

But as she'd climbed under the doona she'd known it was futile and ridiculous to blame a dress. She was the one to blame. She was the one who'd been unable to resist the feel of his arms around her, the one who'd got an incredible rush from matching her body to his as they'd danced. The one who had lost all her inhibitions at the hands of Damien Wyatt when she'd promised herself it was the last thing she would do...

There was no sign of Damien the next day.

In fact it was a curiously quiet day. Once the after-party clean-up had taken place, it was as if all the Wyatts and everyone else had melted away.

Isabel, at least, had explained that she was going to spend the night with a friend.

Charlie, Harriet assumed, had gone back to his base.

Not that she particularly wanted to face anyone after last night but it somehow added to her mood of doom and gloom to find herself feeling as if she were alone on the planet.

She'd just eaten her dinner when she heard footsteps on the outside stairway, and Damien arrived.

She half got up, sat down again and trembled inwardly at his expression.

Tottie was, of course, delighted to see him.

Harriet stood up again and collected her plate and knife and fork. 'I'm sorry,' she said. 'I don't know what got into me last night.'

'I didn't come to conduct a post-mortem into last night.' He looked at her sardonically. 'Any idea where Isabel is? She usually leaves a note.'

Harriet explained about the friend.

He looked even more irritated. 'Did she say which fr—?'

He stopped abruptly as Tottie growled suddenly and then, in a manner of speaking, all hell broke loose.

There was a whoosh of sound and the sky beyond the windows of the flat illuminated briefly in the direction of the house.

'What the devil...?' Damien shut his teeth hard then went on, 'It's the kitchen. Looks like the cook has finally decided to burn the place down.'

The cook hadn't—at least not consciously had he decided to burn the place down—but he had got drunk and he had allowed oil in a deep fryer to catch alight as he'd dozed with a bottle of bourbon in his fist.

He still had it—the bourbon bottle in his fist— when Harriet and Damien arrived on the scene as he stared, stupefied, from the relative safety of the vegetable garden, at the flames leaping out of the kitchen windows.

But within moments, or so it seemed, Damien had taken control. He'd rung for the fire brigade, he'd sent Harriet to waken Stan, the stable foreman, who was the only other person on the property, and he'd located several fire extinguishers, hoses and fire blankets. He also took a moment to attempt to send Harriet back upstairs to the flat.

'No,' she shouted over the crackling of the flames, 'I can hold a hose!'

'Yeah, but I don't want you tripping and falling over!'

'Listen to me, Damien Wyatt,' she yelled at him, 'it's only you who makes me do that—look out,' she screamed as a burning piece of wood fell from a window ledge right next to him.

He leapt away and she grabbed a hose and sprayed the sparks that had fallen on his boots and jeans.

'All right, listen,' he said. 'Be careful; be very careful.'

'I will, I will,' she promised fervently.

He stared down at her in the demonic firelight, then hugged her to him, and immediately turned away.

It was a frenetic scene as they tried to tame the leaping, crackling flames glowing orange against the background of a midnight-blue sky, a scene also of choking smoke pouring from the kitchen and a stifling charred smell.

And by the time the fire brigade arrived Harriet was blackened and soaked to the skin.

'Don't.' Damien loomed up in front of her and removed her hose from her hand. 'Don't do any more; you've done enough. It's under control now.'

'But…'

'Just do as I tell you, Harriet Livingstone,' he said and, without further ado, kissed her full on the lips. 'Be a good girl and go and get cleaned up.'

CHAPTER FIVE

HARRIET WENT, WITH the tips of her fingers pressed to her lips.

And she grimaced at the sight of herself as she went to take her third shower of the day. She dressed in jeans and a track top and concentrated on clearing away her dinner and putting a fresh pot of coffee on to perk.

Sounds of all the activity were starting to scale down as she worked, and finally she heard the fire engine drive away and an almost unnatural silence overtake Heathcote.

Not much later Damien and Tottie turned up, Damien also showered and in clean clothes, a grey track top and khaki cargo pants, and bearing a bottle of brandy.

Harriet reached for glasses. 'You must be a mind-reader.'

He grimaced. 'Nothing like a good fire to provoke the need for some Dutch courage.' He splashed two generous tots into the glasses.

'How bad is it?'

'The kitchen—cheers,' he said and touched his glass

to hers, 'the kitchen will have to be rebuilt. Thankfully, it didn't go any further.'

'How's the cook?'

Damien shook his head. 'A sodden wreck. Stan's looking after him. He's full of remorse and petrified he's going to lose his job.'

Harriet paused with her glass halfway to her mouth. 'He expects to keep it after nearly burning the place down?'

Damien shrugged and his lips twisted. 'According to Isabel, he's got six kids stashed away in Queensland so I'll get her to find him a position closer to home.'

Harriet looked surprised.

He looked wry. 'You didn't expect that?'

'Well, no,' she said. 'Sorry.'

'That's OK. I'm used to being in your bad books or, if not that, then suspected of some kind of dodginess or another.' He drained some of his brandy. 'Incidentally, we're going to have to use this kitchen until we get the house kitchen fixed.' He looked around.

'Oh. Of course.' She got up and poured the coffee and brought it back to the table. 'I don't suspect you of *dodginess*, whatever that means precisely.' She pushed his mug over to him and sat down with hers.

He drank some more brandy. 'You obviously suspect me of something, Miss Livingstone.'

Harriet grimaced. 'I did tell Isabel I thought you were a bit of a control freak.'

'What brought that on?'

Harriet looked at him askance. 'The car you insisted I drive.'

'Oh, that.' He lounged back and shoved his hands into his pockets.

Harriet studied him. His dark hair was still damp and there were blue shadows on his jaw. He looked perfectly relaxed and not as if he'd just fought a fire. For some reason, to have him so big and powerful and quite at ease in what she'd come to regard as her home annoyed her. 'Yes, that,' she said tartly.

He lifted his shoulders. 'I wouldn't be so far off the mark in believing you and your brother's vehicle were something of a menace on the roads but—' he sat up '—before you take umbrage, just the sight of it annoyed me enormously.'

Harriet stared at him.

'Does it make me a control freak to provide you with an alternative, though?' he mused gently. 'I don't believe so.'

Harriet continued to stare at him as several things ran through her mind. She'd experienced a maelstrom of emotions due solely to this man. She'd never stopped thinking about Damien Wyatt while he'd been away, even if she had been able to bury it in her subconscious. She'd been physically stirred by him. She'd told him some of her painful history. She'd cooked him dinner—she'd even made him a lemon meringue dessert.

She'd danced with him, ridden with him, been hugged and kissed by him—she could still feel the imprint of his mouth on hers, come to think of it—and her fingers went to her lips involuntarily at the mere thought of it.

Only to see that he was watching her intently.

She snatched her hand away as a tide of pink rose in her cheeks, then threw up her hands in serious frustration. 'Look,' she said levelly, 'because I'm not prepared to jump into bed with you doesn't mean to say I think you're dodgy, although it's just as bad but quite the opposite really.'

He frowned. 'What does that mean?'

Harriet bit her lip and could have shot herself—if ever she'd voiced an unwise utterance this was it...

'It doesn't matter,' she said stiffly.

'Oh, come on, Harriet,' he said impatiently, 'I can take it.' He looked briefly amused. 'Spit it out, Miss Livingstone.'

Harriet glared at him. 'If you must know, I suspect you of being far too good in bed, Mr Wyatt, for any girl's peace of mind.'

He sobered completely and stared at her narrowly. 'How, one has to ask,' he said slowly, 'did you work that out?'

Her eyes were full of irony. 'You're talking to a girl who's kissed you, remember?'

His lips twisted. 'So you did. Well—' he drained his glass and stood up '—on that note I think I'll leave you to your memories, Miss Livingstone, and I will take mine...somewhere else. Goodnight.' And he patted her on the head, told Tottie to stay put, and strolled out.

Harriet stared after him in a state of suspended animation. In other words, with her mouth open and her eyes huge and dark with disbelief.

Was this his retaliation for what she'd done last night?

Why did she feel disbelief, though? she found herself wondering. Because she'd been convinced he would
react differently to what had been—talk about incendiary!—another incendiary statement she'd made.

All the same, a true statement, she reasoned with
herself. She *was* deadly afraid that once she gave in to
Damien Wyatt she'd be hooked. She'd be on a round-
about, in love with a man who didn't believe in love,
who didn't believe in marriage...

As if she hadn't had enough trauma in that direction.

Damien Wyatt, after checking his property over thoroughly, and making sure the cook was in no position
to do any more damage, climbed the stairs and walked
into his bedroom but he didn't immediately go to bed.
He didn't even turn the light on.

He stood instead at the open window and listened to
the sea crashing onto the beach. From the sound of it, he
judged it to be high tide or close to it. And he could see
a tracing of phosphorous lying luminous on the beach
as each wave receded.

But he was only registering the phosphorous absently. He was thinking of Harriet Livingstone. He
could see her in his mind's eye, serving up her paella
and her lemon meringue with that slim tall figure in
daisy-patterned leggings and a white blouse.

Thinking of her last night as she'd looked lovely
enough to stir any man's blood. And had danced in her
own way, a way that was enough to tempt any man.

And tonight, soaked to the skin and her hands and

face blackened, then clean and neat again in jeans and a track top.

Hearing her saying the kind of things women who were not naïve couldn't say with a straight face—she was an all or nothing person in that direction. Sex and relationships, in other words. Accusing him of being too good in bed for her peace of mind...

He fingered the curtain then turned away and threw himself down in an armchair. The room was still in darkness but there was a lamp on the table beside the armchair. He pressed the button and soft light radiated from under the silk shade. And the bedroom came alive in its blue and gold trappings.

He'd inherited the master bedroom when his parents had passed away, although he hadn't moved into it until he'd married, and it still reflected his mother's taste. A four-poster bed, flocked wallpaper, tapestries—if it wasn't a superbly comfortable bed he'd have left the grandeur of this bedroom, which made him think it should belong in a French chateau, to darkness and silence after he and Veronica had separated.

Or, he mused, maybe it wasn't only the bed. Perhaps he continued to use the room as a warning to himself never to forget the trauma and betrayal Veronica had brought to him.

Maybe...

But where to place Harriet Livingstone in his scheme of things?

He moved restlessly. It was unfortunate but true, he had to admit, that he was extremely attracted to her, even if he couldn't quite analyse why.

What was more unfortunate about it was that he believed her when she said she wasn't built for affairs. Why he believed her, he couldn't say. Why he didn't see it as a ploy on her behalf to tell him she was an all or nothing girl, a ploy to set him on fire physically in a manner of speaking, he couldn't say either.

But what he'd considered the natural progression from a spontaneous attraction that had gripped them *both* was now fraught with all sorts of dangers...

It always had been from her point of view, he found himself conceding. She'd always known it was a road she couldn't, or shouldn't, travel.

He'd always thought, he conceded too with an inward grimace, that he could break her down or win her over to something that was fulfilling, pleasant but not too deep—no, not too deep.

'You're a fool, Damien Wyatt,' he told himself. 'Too blind to see that she is that kind of girl—a genuinely all or nothing girl. A girl who could be devastated if you had a relationship but didn't marry her—and now you've got to withdraw somehow.

'Why would it be so impossible to marry her?'

A pool of silence swallowed up his question.

Because he didn't believe he could trust any woman again? And therefore he didn't want to inflict the worst of his cynicism on Harriet Livingstone?

He stood up abruptly. The sooner he distanced himself from her the better.

Harriet, to her surprise, fell asleep as soon as her head touched the pillow and she slept deeply and dreamlessly the night of the fire.

As she studied herself in the bathroom mirror the next morning she couldn't help but notice that, despite that night of quality sleep, she looked tense. There seemed to be an undertone of worry to her expression.

'Damien,' she said softly to herself. 'Things between us are—a worry, aren't they? What am I going to do?'

She left the bathroom and suddenly remembered her kitchen would be on call and the least she could do was have some coffee ready.

It was Isabel who arrived first, looking shocked.

'Damien rang me earlier,' she told Harriet, puffing a bit after climbing the stairs. 'Thank heavens it didn't spread. I should have done something about Cook before now,' she added with a sigh. 'Thanks for helping to put it out.'

'I didn't do much, other than pointing a hose. Would you like some coffee?'

'Love some. I'm afraid you're stuck with me for meals and I'm not much of a cook,' Isabel confessed.

'That's OK. I enjoy it. In fact I was just going to cook some bacon and eggs for breakfast.'

'Yum! I'll stay put then.'

'What about Damien?' Harriet asked as she reached into the fridge for her breakfast ingredients.

'Oh, he's gone off again. Perth this time. Not sure when he'll be back. He's got some South African mining magnate he's dealing with.' Isabel waved a hand.

'Oh,' Harriet said.

'Didn't he mention it? I suppose he didn't have time,' Isabel continued without waiting for a response. 'He's

left me screeds of instructions to do with the kitchen—
you know, it did need renovating and modernising.'
Isabel chuckled.

Harriet smiled as well, but it wasn't really an amused
smile.

'So.'

It was late in the afternoon and she was sitting on a
bench with Tottie beside her on a small headland just
south of Heathcote homestead. It was an overcast day
with a cool breeze that was lifting Tottie's shaggy coat
and causing the seagulls to plane on the thermals.

They'd been for a long brisk walk and were on their
way home now.

'So,' Harriet said again. 'It's all off, Tottie. Your master has walked away without a word and I should be cel-
ebrating because I've always—almost—known I was
playing with fire just by being anywhere near him.'

'I'm not—' she put her arm around Tottie '—cele-
brating, though. I'm miserable. I feel abandoned. I feel
hard done by because he can come and go while I'm
stuck here because of his mother's collection, because
of Brett, not that I hold Brett responsible for anything…'

She stared out over the silvery sea. It was a choppy
seascape today with whitecaps that, if you knew anything about matters maritime, told you the breeze was
running at about twenty knots.

How did I know that? she wondered. Must have been
amongst quite a lot of the useless information I learnt
from Dad. Is any information useless, though?

She continued to stare out to sea and grimaced as

she saw a yacht sailing south and riding the waves a bit like a rocking horse. Then she felt Tottie stiffen and saw her nose quiver as she tested the wind. The final giveaway as the big dog bounded to her feet was the joyful bark she reserved for one person and one person only—Damien.

Harriet scrambled to her feet and there he was, climbing the headland towards them. Then she stood like a statue until he was right up to them and her eyes were wide and astonished because he wore a suit and a tie.

'I thought...I thought you were in Perth,' she stammered.

'I had planned to be,' he replied as he made a fuss of Tottie, 'but something wouldn't let me go.'

'What?' she asked huskily, her expression mystified.

'You.'

She blinked several times. 'I don't understand.'

'You once believed you owed me an explanation. I've come under the same compulsion.'

He paused and loosened his tie and once again the way the breeze lifted his dark hair gave her goose bumps.

'I thought it was best for us to—just cut this thing between us,' he said then, his dark eyes resting on the riot of curls in her hair the wind had whipped up. 'I thought that last night and right until I got to Sydney airport from Ballina this morning,' he said dryly. 'Then I changed my mind and flew back. Or, rather, it got changed for me by some arcane process I don't quite understand, but anyway—'

He stopped and looked around. 'Do you want to hear this here or back down—?'

'Here,' she broke in.

So they sat down on the bench and Tottie lay down at their feet with a look of pure contentment.

'It's about Veronica,' he said. 'She was, as Charlie insisted on putting it—' he looked heavenwards '—just gorgeous. Not only that; she was bright. She ran her own IT consultancy business. We had an affair, then we got married.

'I have to say,' he went on thoughtfully, 'that we fought as spectacularly as we did the opposite. But she wasn't cut out to stay at home and run things like Isabel does. That was something I often found irritating and often—' he shrugged '—held against her. Mind you, she had her own list of sins she held against me and, to be honest, the relationship was foundering. Then she discovered she was pregnant and, although she'd been rather secretive about it, I thought—it seemed to be a calming influence. I didn't realise she was simply subdued and—worried.'

Harriet looked down at her hands.

'And the baby came, a boy, no problems, until he was about six months old. Then he was diagnosed with a blood disorder and both Veronica and I were tested to establish our blood groups et cetera. That's when it emerged—' Damien stared out to sea for a long moment '—that I wasn't the baby's father.'

Harriet gasped.

'As you say,' he commented with some irony. 'At least that was my first reaction. Of course, after that, things got…much more animated. Accusations running thick and fast, along the lines of *Had she always been unfaithful?* Coming from me, that one,' he said. 'To be answered along the lines of *Who wouldn't be unfaithful to someone as cold and bloody-minded as me?* Hang on.'

He retrieved his mobile from his pocket, glanced at it and switched it off.

'So, as you can imagine, it was a shambles.'

'Yes,' Harriet breathed.

'It became even more so,' he said after a time.

'How?'

'It turned out she couldn't be sure *who* the father was but she'd reasoned I was the best bet, financially, anyway.'

Harriet put her hands to her face. 'She was…was she…?'

'She was promiscuous,' he said. 'That's probably a polite way of putting it. Of course I'd known I wasn't the first but it might be hard for you to imagine what it feels like to know you've been in a line of men even after the wedding, not to mention having some other man's child palmed off on you.'

'I'm surprised she kept the baby.'

'So was I,' he agreed, 'but I think she saw it as some kind of a hold over me if things got really tough between us. In the normal course of events, we may never have discovered he wasn't mine.'

'What happened to him?'

Damien stared out to sea. 'I made Veronica find out who the father was and these days, with DNA testing—' he shrugged '—you can do it and there's no way it can be denied. So I divorced her.' He stopped rather abruptly.

'Did you…did you have any kind of affection for the baby, when you thought he was yours?'

He frowned. 'I don't know if I had some premonition but no, not a lot. But I don't know if it was simply that I'm just not good with babies. Actually, I felt more for the poor kid when I found out he wasn't mine. And I've set up a trust for him and made sure that at least he'll know who his father is. I also paid for the procedures and treatment he needed and of course Veronica got a generous settlement. End of story.'

He got up and walked to the edge of the headland, staring out to sea with his hands pushed into his pockets and the breeze blowing his tie around.

'Of course not the end of the story,' he said over his shoulder and came back to sit down beside her.

'I didn't think it was,' Harriet said quietly, 'but—'

'Look,' he interrupted, 'if you're going to tell me it's highly unlikely it could ever happen for me like that again, you're right. The odds against it are enormous. I *know* that—intellectually. That doesn't mean to say I can make myself believe it in my heart. That doesn't mean to say I can bury all my cynicism, all my—' he broke off and shrugged '—disbelief that I could have been taken for such a flat.'

'Did you never suspect?' Harriet asked curiously.

'Sometimes. But she was good at diverting any doubts I may have had. And I'm not trying to say I was blameless myself. If anything was going to work for Veronica in a marriage, it was an anchorman. I could work that out, I could see,' he said intensely, 'that she was one of those high-powered people who often didn't know how to come down from the heights. But I couldn't... I—' he closed his eyes briefly '—just got more and more irritated and difficult to live with.'

Harriet looked across at him. His profile was rock-hard and she could see the tension in the set of his mouth and his shoulders. 'How can you be *sure* you're going to feel like this with another woman?'

'I've had a couple of—' he shrugged '—liaisons since then. They didn't last. I didn't want them to last because I felt stifled,' he said. 'I wanted to be free. I never, ever want to go through that kind of trauma again.'

He paused then he said sardonically, 'I would never have thought I was naïve going into marriage with Veronica; I certainly wasn't afterwards. I kept looking for signs, pointers, indicators that I was being taken for a fool again so that those liaisons became a nightmare of mistrust.'

He broke off and sighed. 'And I keep thinking of the consequences and how one innocent child got caught up in it all. That's why I'm better on my own. But I had to tell you this. Despite the fact that this attraction lies between us, it could never be more than that.'

He put his hand over hers. 'I'm sorry.'

Harriet blinked away a tear. 'That's OK.'

He paused then looked at her curiously. 'You really don't mind?'

Harriet smiled, just a gentle curve of her mouth.

'Yes, I do mind a bit but I always knew it couldn't work for me, so—'

'You're still in love with—whoever he was?'

Harriet considered and realised that until quite recently she might have believed that. Not any more, however. But it made no difference now. There was no future for her with Damien Wyatt...

She blinked several times as it hit her like a train all of a sudden that it mattered greatly to her to think there was no future for her with this man. He couldn't have spelled it out more clearly.

So, she thought, the tables have turned. I was the one who was eager to cut 'things' off between us; now I'm the one who...

'Harriet?'

'Uh—I don't know. But, for my own reasons, I really don't want to get involved like that again. You probably think I'm silly.' She stopped and shrugged.

There was a long silence. Then he said, 'Tottie will be devastated.'

Harriet smiled and blew her nose. 'Well, I ought to get back to work. Do you—' she hesitated '—do you want me to finish your mother's things?'

'Yes,' he replied promptly. 'I won't be here—no, I'm not going to try to go to Perth again today, but tomorrow I will.'

'Oh.' Harriet jumped up with a hand to her mouth. 'I'm cook tonight. I promised Isabel roast beef. Will you...?' She looked a question at him.

'Roast beef,' he repeated, his dark eyes full of amusement. 'Something else I can't resist.'

* * *

Harriet's roast beef was rare on the inside and dark brown on the outside. With it she served roast potatoes and pumpkin, green beans and a rich gravy.

'Mmm, that was delicious,' Isabel enthused as she put her knife and fork together. 'A girl of many talents!'

'She is,' Damien agreed and raised his glass to Harriet. 'If ever you need a job away from the job you do, you know where to come.'

'Apart from anything else, we know you won't burn down the kitchen,' Isabel said mischievously.

'On that subject, how is the gentleman—where is he?' Damien asked.

'I packed him off home to his wife and family today with three months' pay and a couple of contacts, both restaurants where he'd be too busy to get drunk and lonely. That wouldn't be sticky date pudding, by any chance?' Isabel asked of Harriet with equal proportions of trepidation and longing in her voice.

It was and it not only found favour with Isabel but also her nephew.

'Amazing.' he said, 'For someone who hasn't got a sweet tooth to produce such amazing desserts is quite—amazing.'

They all laughed.

'So you'll be in South Africa? For how long?' Isabel queried of Damien. 'Incidentally—' she frowned '—why did you come back today?'

'Something came up,' Damien replied. 'And I don't know how long I'll be in South Africa—a few weeks at least. As to why I'm going, there's a lot of mining in Africa.'

Isabel stood up and insisted on clearing the table and loading the dishwasher but she declined coffee and, with a yawn and her thanks for a perfect meal, she left them alone.

'You know—' Damien swirled the last of his Merlot in his glass '—I've been thinking. Why don't you stay on when all my mother's stuff is sorted? That's going to happen much sooner than your brother walking again by the sound of it. How is he doing?'

Harriet told him. 'He's got a new physio, a woman. I think he's fallen in love with her. Not too seriously, I hope.'

Damien grimaced. 'She's probably used to it and knows how to handle it. But if it's contributing towards his progress, it might be worth a few heartaches for him. Or...' he stretched his legs out '...who knows, it might become mutual. Anyway, to get back to this place, why don't you stay on? Isabel really enjoys your company. And I'm sure Charlie does too, when he's home.'

'I won't have anything to do, though,' Harriet objected.

Damien sat up. 'I've been thinking about that. Periodically, Arthur sends our paintings away to be cleaned. It's about that time now, so why don't *you* do it? Here.'

Harriet's eyes widened and her mouth fell open.

'Isn't that what your father did?'

Her jaw clicked as she closed her mouth. 'Yes. Well, he restored paintings too.' She stopped abruptly and bit her lip.

'Then?'

'I couldn't.' She clasped her hands on the table. 'I'd feel like a charitable institution.'

'Nonsense.' His tone was biting. 'It's a good business proposition. Arthur agrees.'

Harriet frowned. 'When have you had time to consult Arthur?'

'In this day and age of mobile phones it only took a few minutes. Did you think I had to rely on carrier pigeons or the bush telegraph?'

Harriet compressed her lips and looked at him mutinously.

'For crying out loud, just say yes, Harriet Livingstone.' He shoved his hand through his hair wearily. 'Thanks to you, I've been up since the crack of dawn, I've had to fly to Sydney and back again, not to mention loitering around Sydney Airport waiting for bloody flights.'

'I didn't ask you to do any of that!' she protested.

'Nevertheless, it was all due to you. Look, I won't be here, if that's what's worrying you. No coming home early this time.' He gazed at her ironically.

'But it could take me…a month!' She tried to visualise every painting in the house. 'It's very painstaking, careful work done properly.'

He pushed his wine glass away. 'I'll go on a safari,' he said flippantly. 'There's a lot of wildlife in Africa as well as mining.'

Harriet got up and put her hands on her hips. 'You're impossible.'

'That's what my wife used to tell me,' he drawled.

Harriet flinched then shrugged. 'She may have been right.'

'No doubt.' He watched her as she paced around the table. She'd changed into white pedal pushers and a loose apricot blouse with a distinctive pattern and a round neck. Her hair was tied back simply. 'Are you going to do it?'

'I don't know. I can't think straight!'

'Why don't you sit down and let me make you a cup of coffee? You could be more rational about things then.'

'I'm not being *irrational*,' Harriet said with extreme frustration. But she sat down and she didn't raise any obstacles when he got up to make the coffee.

And the wheels of her mind started to turn slowly rather than racing around uselessly.

It would be a solution.

It would provide not only the financial support she needed but, come to think of it, the moral support. She and Isabel had grown close. She also loved Heathcote. She was comfortable and secure here—and there were some marvellous paintings to work on when she finished her present job. Could she ask for more?

Despite her financial affairs being in much better repair thanks to Damien Wyatt's mother's treasures, once she wasn't earning, once she wasn't living rent free, living off her capital so to speak, she had a fair idea of how fast it would shrink.

But...

She looked across at his tall figure as he rounded up the coffee accoutrements, and had to marvel suddenly at how things had changed. How she'd hated him for his arrogance; how she'd hated the way he could kiss her without so much as a by-your-leave and leave her deeply moved. How she'd been so determined not to allow his effect on her to take root—only to discover that it had anyway.

But to discover at the same time why Damien Wyatt was so opposed to the concept of love ever after and the institution of marriage... A story that was painful even to think about.

She shivered suddenly and forced her mind away. And she asked herself if the wisest course of action for her peace of mind, if nothing else, was to go away from Heathcote as soon as she'd finished the first job.

But Brett! Brett—his name hammered in her mind. The more she could do for him, the more she could do to get him mobile again, the better and the sooner this nightmare would be over, for him as well as for her.

She held her peace for another couple of minutes until she had a steaming cup of Hawaiian coffee in front of her.

'I could do them,' she said slowly. 'The paintings. It would be one way to make sure Brett can stay on until his treatment is finished.'

'Good.' He said it briskly and in a way that gave her to understand it was a business deal between them and nothing more. And, before he could say any more, his phone rang.

'Excuse me, I'll take this downstairs; it's South Africa. Thank you for dinner, by the way.'

Harriet nodded and, moments later, she and Tottie were left alone.

'All sorted, Tottie.' Harriet dried sudden, ridiculous tears with her fingers. 'Dealt with, packed, labelled and filed away, that's me.'

She hugged Tottie then sat with her head in her hands for a while before she got up and resolutely put her kitchen to bed.

She was not to know that whilst Damien Wyatt might have sorted her out and locked her out of his life for the most part, his business life was about to become another matter. His PA, a man who'd worked closely with him for ten years, resigned out of the blue in order to train for his lifelong ambition—to climb Mount Everest.

If this wasn't trying enough, his South African trip was cancelled and the ramifications to his business empire as the lucrative business deal involved hung in the breeze were enough to make him extremely tense.

CHAPTER SIX

'TENSE, BLOODY-MINDED and all-round impossible,' Charlie said to Harriet one evening. 'That's Damien at the moment. It's like living under a thundercloud. I tell you what, I really feel for the poor sods he's interviewing for his PA position. I wonder if they have any idea what he might drive them to? I mean to say, it's got to be a pretty bizarre ambition, climbing Mount Everest.'

They were sharing what would have otherwise been a lonesome meal—Isabel was out and so was Damien.

Harriet had made hamburgers and chips, much to Charlie's approval.

Harriet had to laugh. 'I feel really guilty, though,' she said as she passed the ketchup to Charlie.

'You!' He looked surprised.

'I…' She hesitated. 'It was because of me that he didn't go to Perth and on to South Africa. I can't help wondering if that…if that—' she gestured widely and shrugged '—caused all this.'

Charlie frowned. 'Why "because of you" didn't he go?'

'Well, he missed his flight to Perth because he came

back to explain something.' Harriet bit her lip and berated herself for ever mentioning the matter but Charlie took issue with this.

'You can't open up a can of worms like that then play dumb,' he objected, 'but let me guess. You two had some sort of issue between you after my birthday party?'

Harriet sighed suddenly. 'Charlie, we've had issues between us since the day I smashed his car and his collarbone. Not to mention the day I slapped his face and he kissed me back. But his issues are...very complicated. And he wasn't supposed to be here while I finished the job,' she added, somewhat annoyed.

'Ah, well, so that explains—well, some of it! I didn't think some business deal hanging in the balance—I mean he's weathered a few of those before—was sufficient to cause this level of turmoil in my beloved brother.'

Harriet put her hands on her waist. 'That doesn't help me a lot, Charlie.'

'Or any of us! I think we'll just have to batten down the hatches and prepare for the worst. At least you can stay out of his way.'

This proved to be incorrect.

She was riding Sprite along Seven-mile Beach the next morning with Tottie at her stirrup. It was cool and crisp and the clarity of the air was amazing, dead flat calm water with hardly any surf, some pink clouds in a pale blue sky—and another horse riding towards her: Damien.

Her first thought was to gallop away in the opposite direction, and she started to do so but Sprite was no match for his horse and he caught her up.

By this time, some common sense had returned to Harriet and she slowed Sprite to a walk.

'Morning, Harriet.'

She glanced across at him as Sprite jostled his big brown horse and Tottie looked relieved. 'Hi, Damien.' Their breath steamed in the early morning cool.

'Running away again?'

'I guess that was my first intention,' she confessed and found herself curiously unsettled. He looked so big in a khaki rain jacket and jeans with his dark head bare. Not at all cuddly, she reflected, not at all affected by the post dawn chill, whereas she was bundled up in a scarlet anorak, navy track pants and a scarlet beanie.

'Why?'

'I think,' she said carefully and straightened the reins through her fingers, 'we're all a little nervous around you at the moment.'

He grimaced. 'That bad?'

She nodded.

'Of course things haven't exactly gone my way lately, business-wise,' he observed as they turned their horses onto the path from the beach.

'I'm sorry if I was—unwittingly—in any way the cause of that.'

He looked across at her. 'You weren't. Although, of course, you are part of the overall problem. After you.' He indicated that she should precede him through the archway that led to Heathcote and the stables.

But she simply stared at him with her lips parted, her eyes incredulous, so Tottie took the initiative and Sprite followed.

And it wasn't until they got to the stables that they took up the thread of the conversation.

They tied their steaming horses beside each other in the wash bay.

'What overall problem?' she asked at last as she hosed Sprite down.

'The one I have with going into the lounge, for example.'

Harriet turned her hose off and took a metal scraper off its hook. 'Why should that be a problem?' She scraped energetically down Sprite's flank then ducked under her neck to do her other side.

'Well, if I'd flown halfway around the world and was in another country I might have found it easier to think of other things than you at Charlie's party. At the moment, every time I walk into the damn lounge it strikes me again.'

Harriet dropped the scraper and it clattered onto the concrete at the same as Sprite moved uneasily and her metal shoes also clattered on the concrete.

Damien stopped hosing his horse and came round to see if Harriet was all right.

'Fine. Fine!' She retrieved the scraper and handed it to him. 'I think I've finished.'

'Thanks.' He hung up his hose and started to use the scraper on his horse.

They worked in silence for a few minutes. Harriet rubbed Sprite down with a coarse towel then she inspected her feet and finally threw a rug over her. But all the time her mind was buzzing. How to deal with this? How to deal with the fact that she still felt incredibly guilty about how she'd fled at the end of Charlie's party after...after...

Even days later, her cheeks reddened at the thought of how abandoned—that was about the only way she could describe it—she'd felt and how she'd run like a scared rabbit.

She clicked her tongue and backed Sprite out of the wash bay to lead her to her box, where there was a feed already made up for her thanks to Stan.

Perhaps it was that feed waiting for her that made Sprite a bundle of impatience to get to her stall, but she suddenly put on a rare exhibition that would have done a buck jumper proud, an exhibition that scattered Tottie and even caused Damien's horse, still tied in the wash bay, to try to rear and plunge.

'Sprite!' Harriet clung onto the lead with all her strength. 'Settle down, girl! What's got into you?'

'Tucker,' Damien said in her ear. 'I'll take her.'

And in a masterful display of horsemanship as well as strength, he calmed the mare down and got her into her box.

'Thank you! I was afraid I was going to lose her— another accident waiting to happen, to go down on my already tarnished record!' Harriet said breathlessly but whimsically.

Damien laughed as he came towards her out of the stable block and for an instant the world stood still for

Harriet. He looked so alive and wickedly amused, so tall and dark, so sexy...

And what he did didn't help.

He came right up to her, slid his hands around her waist under her anorak and hugged her. 'I wouldn't have held that against you,' he said, holding her a little away.

Without thinking much about it, she put her hands on his shoulders. 'No?' She looked at him with mock scepticism.

'No. I would have laid the blame squarely at the horse's feet. She's always been a bit of a handful. Hence her name. Typical female,' he added.

'Damn!' Harriet assumed a self-righteous expression.

He raised an eyebrow.

'I was full of approval for you but you went and spoilt it with your anti-feminist remark!'

'My apologies, Miss Livingstone. Uh—how can I make amends? Let's see, you did pretty damn good for a girl before I took over and—can I cook you breakfast?'

Harriet blinked. 'You cook?'

He shrugged. 'Some things. Bacon and eggs.'

'Only bacon and eggs?'

'More or less. Steak, I do steak as well.'

'I have both,' Harriet said slowly.

He laughed again, kissed her fleetingly on the lips, and removed his hands from her waist just as Stan came round the corner of the stables.

Fortunately Charlie turned up at the same time, wanting to know what all the hullabaloo was about and they repaired to the flat after Stan had offered to finish Damien's horse and put it in its box. And they had a jolly breakfast of steak, bacon and eggs.

Charlie even said, 'Notice how the sun's come out!'

Damien frowned. 'It's been up and out for a couple of hours.'

'I was speaking relatively,' Charlie said with dignity.

Damien narrowed his eyes as he studied his brother. 'I…think I get your drift,' he said slowly. 'My apologies.'

'That's all right. We'll forgive you, won't we, Harriet?'

She was clearing the table and about to pour the coffee but she couldn't help herself. She looked up and straight at Damien.

'Yes…' she said, but it sounded uncertain even to her own ears, nor could she mistake the ironic glint that came to his dark eyes as their gazes clashed.

So, she thought uneasily, he might laugh with me as he did this morning but I'm a long way from forgiven.

And although this lifting of the thundercloud, so to speak, over Heathcote, was much appreciated by Charlie and no doubt everyone else on the property, it brought Harriet mental anguish and confusion.

No longer was she able to keep Damien Wyatt on the back roads of her mind. Not that she'd been able to do that for a while but it seemed to have grown ten times worse day by day.

She was incredibly aware of him whenever he came within her orbit. He literally made her tremble inwardly and all her fine hairs rise. He made her tongue-tied now, never capable of thinking of anything to say.

He made the completion of the work on his mother's treasures and the paintings drag because she spent a lot of time day-dreaming.

Would she ever finish this job? she asked herself desperately once.

Then the kitchen was finished and Isabel organised a party to celebrate the fact.

'I don't think I've ever seen a renovation, especially not after a fire, be so swiftly and painlessly achieved,' Harriet murmured to Isabel as she was being given a tour of all the spectacular slimline stainless steel equipment and granite counters that now graced Heathcote's new bottle-green, white and black kitchen.

'Ever *seen* a renovation after a fire?' Isabel asked perkily.

'Well, no, but you know what I mean. By the way, you sounded just like your nephew—your older nephew,' she added.

Isabel laughed. 'Heaven forbid! Although he has been pretty good lately. But if you really want to know the reason for the speed and efficiency of this renovation, it's quite simple.'

'Your expert management of things?'

'Well, that too,' Isabel conceded. 'But it's money. It buys the best product, best workmen and in the long run it saves money.'

'Spoken like a true capitalist,' Harriet said but with affection.

'All right.' Isabel uncovered several platters on a long counter containing snacks. There were also plates and napkins plus bottles of champagne in ice buckets and gleaming glassware in amongst glorious vases of flowers.

'How many people have you asked?' Damien enquired as he pinched a smoked salmon savoury and had his hand slapped.

'Just the neighbours—don't,' Isabel replied.

'Just the neighbours!' Damien echoed. 'If you mean everyone we know around here that could be twenty to thirty.'

'Twenty-five. When has that ever been a problem?' Isabel enquired with her arms akimbo.

'Beloved, I was merely thinking that you must have done an awful lot of work. And I happen to know you don't like it.'

'Ah. I gave someone a trial run. She's applied for the cook's position. No, she's not here now,' she said as Damien looked around, 'but the proof will be in the pudding. There's plenty more to eat.'

One good thing about this party—people had been especially asked not to dress up since it was a kitchen party. So Harriet had been happy to attend in jeans and a lilac jumper. She'd been just as happy to leave after an hour although everyone else seemed to be content to stay on.

But it was a hollow feeling she encountered when she was upstairs in the flat. Hollow and lonely—hollow, ruffled and restless. And all due to watching Damien at his best.

Damien fascinating his neighbours with a blend of wit, seriousness, humour and setting not a few feminine pulses fluttering.

One of them was Penny Tindall, although she'd fought to hide it, Harriet thought with some scorn.

She almost immediately took herself to task for this uncharitable thought, not only uncharitable towards Penny but investing herself with a superiority she did not possess. If she did she wouldn't be feeling miserable, lonely, stirred up and generally like crying herself to sleep all on Damien Wyatt's account, would she?

But she knew herself well enough to know that sleep would not come, so she took herself downstairs, closed herself into the studio, drew the curtains and sat down on a high stool. She'd just finished notating a beautiful ivory chess set and she pushed it aside to study an object she wasn't all too sure about.

It resembled some giant curved tooth set on a brass base and embellished with scrimshaw of African wildlife—an elephant, a rhino, a lion, a cheetah and a buffalo.

She was handling it, turning it this way and that, when the door clicked open and Damien stood there.

They simply stared at each other for a long moment then he said, 'Can I come in?'

'Of course.' Harriet slipped off her stool and pushed her hair behind her ears. 'I…I…'

'Kitchen parties are not your cup of tea?' he suggested as he closed the door behind him.

'No. I mean…I haven't got anything against them really.' She grimaced. 'That sounds a bit weird.'

He didn't agree or disagree. He simply looked at her with patent amusement. Then he looked at the objects on the table and noticed the chess set.

'I was wondering where that had got to,' he commented. 'Charlie and Mum used to play a lot of chess. Charlie is a bit of a genius at it. Do you play?' He lifted a king, rotated it then set it down.

She nodded.

'Well?'

'Well enough.'

He studied her narrowly. 'Why do I get the feeling that's the guarded sort of response someone who is sensational at something gives you just before they set out to fleece you shamelessly?'

Harriet maintained a grave, innocent expression—for about half a minute, then she had to grin.

'You look like the proverbial Cheshire Cat,' he drawled. 'Did I hit the nail on the head?'

'I'm not bad at chess,' she confessed. 'I used to play with my father.'

'Don't think Charlie has had time to play for years.' He moved on and picked up the tooth-like object she'd been handling.

'Hello!' he said, as he picked it up. 'Haven't seen you for years!'

Harriet's eyes widened. 'You know it?'

'Sure,' he said easily. 'My mother showed it to me when she got it.'

Harriet's eyes widened further. 'So you know what it is?'

'Uh-huh. Don't you?'

'No. Well, a tooth of some kind from a whale maybe, but I can't find any paperwork that goes with it so I'm a little frustrated.'

He picked it up again. 'It's a tusk—a warthog tusk.'

Harriet's mouth fell open. 'Seriously?'

'Seriously. My mother was quite taken with African artefacts.'

Harriet frowned. 'Where are they?'

'Haven't you come across any more of them?'

'No. Apart from this, nothing.'

He sat down on the corner of the table. 'We'll have to consult Isabel.'

Harriet stared at the warthog tusk with its delicate scrimshaw. 'We'll have to get in an African expert,' she said.

'Couldn't you look it up?'

Harriet shrugged. 'Perhaps. How many do you think she had?'

'Hundreds,' he replied.

Harriet paled. 'But…that might mean I could be here for the next ten years!'

'Now that,' he agreed with a grin, 'could be a problem. Talk about growing old on the job.' But he sobered as she moved restlessly. 'Not to mention the other complications it would cause.' And the way his gaze roamed up and down her figure gave her no doubt that he meant complications in an extremely personal way.

'Uh—look, I'll think about it tomorrow,' she said hastily. 'Right now I should probably go to bed. I'll need—' she smiled shakily '—all my resources tomorrow if I'm to track down hundreds of things like wart-hog tusks.'

She laid the tusk back in its box, briefly tidied the table top, and came purposefully round the table towards the door.

Damien uncoiled his lean length from the stool and barred her way. 'Am I getting my marching orders, Miss Livingstone?' he said softly.

Her eyes flew to his. 'This was *your* idea—' She stopped abruptly and could have kicked herself.

'Mmm…' He scanned the way her breasts were heaving beneath the lilac wool. 'My idea for us to desist? So it was, but are you claiming you had another direction in mind for us?'

'No. I mean—' she bit her lip '—I don't know of any other way there could be and that's sad but probably a blessing in the long run.'

He put his arms around her. 'I didn't mean to make you sad. I could so easily…turn things around. Like this.'

His kiss, and although she'd known it was coming she did nothing about it, was like a balm to her soul.

She no longer felt hollow and lonely and restless. She felt quite different. Smooth and silken as his hands roamed beneath her jumper and his lips moved from hers to the hollows at the base of her throat to the soft spot where her shoulder curved into her neck.

Then he took her by surprise. He lifted her up and sat her on the table and she wound her legs around him—to have him grin wickedly down at her.

'If you only knew what your legs do to me,' he murmured, and his hands moved up to cup her breasts.

Harriet paused what she was doing, running her hands over the hard wall of his chest, and rested her hands on his shoulders. And she tensed.

'What?' he asked, his eyes suddenly narrowing.

'Someone coming,' she breathed and pushed him away so she could slide off the table and rearrange her clothes.

'Someone's always bloody coming,' he grated.

But whoever had been coming changed their mind and the footsteps receded.

Harriet let out a quivering breath.

'Would it matter if anyone saw us?' he asked abruptly.

She stirred. 'Surely it would complicate things even more?' She laced her fingers together. 'Damien...' She closed her eyes briefly. 'I'm sorry this happened. I'm sorry it keeps happening but if there's no future for us, if you're sure, I need—I need to go away from Heathcote.' Silent tears were suddenly coursing down her cheeks. She scrubbed at them impatiently. 'I have nearly finished your mother's things but if there are hundreds more...' She gestured helplessly. 'And the paintings. I don't see how I can stay. Surely you m-must—' her voice cracked '—agree?'

He took in her tear-streaked face and the anguish in her eyes. And for a moment a terrible temptation to say *Stay somehow we'll work it out, Harriet* rose in him. But another side of him refused to do it, a side that recalled all too clearly and bitterly how he'd been cheated and made a fool of...

'I'm sorry,' he said. 'This is my fault, what happened here tonight, not yours. It won't happen again, so please stay. Goodnight.'

He touched her wet cheek with his fingertips then he was gone.

Harriet took herself up to her flat and cried herself to sleep.

A week later their truce had held. Not that Damien had spent much time at Heathcote. But they were able to interact normally, or so she thought. As in the instance when she was explaining to him about his mother's artefacts.

'Isabel forgot to tell me,' she told him.

He lifted an eyebrow. 'What?'

'Oh, sorry, I should have started at the beginning. Your mother sold all her artefacts just before she…er… passed away. Somehow or other, the warthog tusk must have been overlooked.'

Damien grimaced and folded his arms across his chest. 'No doubt to your great relief.'

'Mostly,' Harriet said. 'I have to admit the thought of becoming an expert on apes and ivory et cetera was a little daunting.'

'Apes and ivory?'

'It comes from the Bible—Kings, First Book, chapter ten, verse twenty-two. *"…the navy of Tharshish bringing gold, and silver, ivory, and apes, and peacocks."* From Africa to King Solomon.'

'How did you come by that?' he queried.

'I did *some* research. It's fascinating.'

He studied her. She was now writing with her head bent and her expression absorbed. As usual, Tottie was lying at her feet. Her hair was loose and curly and she wore tartan trews and a cream cable stitch sweater. She looked at home on this cool autumn evening.

And if she wasn't close to becoming a part of Heathcote she wasn't far from it—or was she already? he wondered.

And was he mad not to make sure she stayed?

At the same moment his phone rang. He pulled it out of his pocket and studied it with a frown then he answered it tersely. 'Wyatt.'

Harriet looked up and she tensed as he said, '*What?*' and 'When and where?' in hard, clipped, disbelieving tones.

And she realised he'd gone pale and his knuckles around the phone were white, and a feeling of dread started to grip her although she had no idea what news he was getting.

Then he ended the call and threw his phone down.

'What?' she asked huskily. 'Something's happened.'

She saw his throat working and he closed his eyes briefly. 'Charlie,' he said hoarsely at last. 'His plane's gone down. Somewhere in the north of Western Australia. They either can't be more specific or it's classified information.'

He sat down and dropped his face into his hands then looked up. 'It's rugged terrain if it's the Kimberley. Rivers, gorges.' He drew a deep breath then crashed his fist on the table so that her coffee mug jumped and spilt. 'And there's nothing I can do.'

'I'm so sorry,' Harriet murmured and slid her hand across the table to cover his. 'I'm sure they'll be doing all they can.'

'There must be *something* I can do!' There was frustration written into the lines and angles of his face. He got up and looked around as if he had no idea where he was. He said, 'Excuse me, Harriet, but I can do more from my study and my computer.'

She rose hastily. 'Of course. I'll bring you a nightcap in a while if you like.' But she didn't think he'd even heard her as he loped down the stairs two at a time with Tottie hard on his heels.

Harriet marvelled at the dog's sensitivity; she obviously had no doubt where she was needed most tonight.

And to keep herself occupied and keep at bay images of a fiery crash and Charlie's broken body, she went downstairs to the studio to do some work of her own.

She was cleaning a delicate china figurine with a cotton bud dipped in a weak solution when Isabel, looking as if she'd aged ten years in the space of a few hours, came over from the big house.

'Any news?' Harriet asked.

Isabel shook her head and pulled out a stool. And she hugged her mohair stole around her.

'How's Damien?'

Isabel shook her head. 'He's…it'll kill him to lose Charlie. Me too, but more so Damien. They're really close, despite the way they josh each other. They got even closer after what happened with Veronica and Patrick.' Isabel stopped self-consciously.

'He's told me about her. So Patrick was the baby?'

'Uh-huh.' Isabel touched a finger to the figurine Harriet had finished cleaning and had dried. 'Hello, I remember you,' she said to it and again looked self-conscious. 'You must think I'm crazy,' she said to Harriet this time, 'but I do remember this figurine. It always sat on its own little circular table in the upstairs hall. That's where Damien's mother always kept it, but Veronica...' She trailed off.

Harriet said nothing.

Isabel shrugged. 'I don't know why I shouldn't tell you, seeing as you know some of it. It also helps to think of something else. If you've wondered why a lot of this stuff was more or less hidden, that was Veronica's doing. She didn't like antiques or objets d'art. A very modern girl was our Veronica, in more ways than one.' Isabel's tone was loaded with disapproval. 'Mind you,' she added, 'Damien said no to a lot of her plans for the modernisation of Heathcote.'

But then she sighed. 'One should never pass judgement on relationships because it's almost impossible to know the full story. And it's hard not to be biased, anyway.'

'How old is Patrick now?' Harriet asked.

'Let's see—nearly three.'

'I don't suppose Damien has any reason to have any contact with him?' She rinsed out a couple of cloths and suspended them from pegs from a dryer over the sink.

'No. Well, not directly.'

Harriet washed her hands and stood drying them

on a red and white checked towel as a frown grew in her eyes.

'He and Charlie worked out a plan. Because things are and always will be pretty tense between Veronica and Damien, I imagine—and because I can't quite hide my feelings—' Isabel grimaced '—Charlie sees Patrick fairly frequently. To make sure he's OK and to give him a constant man in his life, I guess you could say. Charlie somehow or other had a better understanding of Veronica than me or Damien. That sounds odd.' Isabel gestured a little helplessly.

'I don't think so. I think that's…Charlie,' Harriet said slowly. 'I wouldn't be surprised if Charlie keeps a sort of weather eye out for Damien.'

'Oh, I think he does.' Isabel rested her chin in her hands and studied Harriet. 'You're pretty perceptive yourself, my dear.'

Harriet grimaced. 'I don't know about that. So she—Veronica—didn't marry Patrick's father?'

Isabel shook her head. 'She hasn't remarried.'

'Is there any chance of them getting back together?'

'No.' Isabel said it quite definitely. 'It was one of those white-hot affairs that was too explosive to last, even apart from the drama over Patrick. Of course the double, triple even quadruple irony to it all is that Patrick was named after my father, Damien's grandfather.'

Harriet let the towel drop onto the counter. 'Oh, no!'

'Oh, yes.' Isabel shrugged. 'Not that there would be any point in changing his name and he'd been christened by the time they found out, anyway. But it does… it was such a mess.'

Harriet sat down. 'Do you think he'll ever marry again?'

Isabel stretched then she rocked Harriet to the core. 'Yes. If *you* would have him.'

Harriet shrugged. 'He's right, Isabel. He'll be thirty-three—'

Isabel smiled. 'So when the bould Harriet sets the cap
'Yes. 'cause' this' is her love back...'

CHAPTER SEVEN

'I…I BEG YOUR pardon?' Harriet stammered.

But Isabel simply looked at her wisely.

Harriet got up and did a turn around the studio with her arms crossed almost protectively. 'It couldn't work. The reason he came back from Perth—not that he ever got there—was to tell me why it couldn't work.'

'Why couldn't it?'

'He doesn't want to be married again. He's suspicious and cynical now and, even without any of that, he's a difficult, unbending kind of person and he admits that his habit of command was probably one of the reasons they fell out so badly.'

'Probably,' Isabel conceded. 'He's very much like my father, his grandfather, the first Patrick. The one who started it all. Dynamic, forceful—' Isabel nodded wryly '—difficult. Whereas my brother, Damien's father, was more interested in culture and the arts, passionate about sailing, that kind of thing. He was so nice—' Isabel looked fond '—but it's true to say we went backwards during his stewardship and it took all of Damien's grandfather's genes plus plenty of his own kind of steely determination to pull the business out of that slump.'

'The first thing that struck me about him,' Harriet said dryly, 'was how arrogant he was. I never felt more...more vindicated—that's not the right word, but it definitely was a release of some kind—when I slapped his face, although I got myself kissed for my pains.' She stopped and bit her lip.

'That first day you came to Heathcote?' Isabel queried and when Harriet nodded she laughed.

'Sorry,' she said, 'but I knew something had happened between you two. So did Charlie.'

'Charlie walked in on it,' Harriet said gloomily, 'that's how he knew.' Then she had to smile. 'If you could have seen his expression.'

But her smile faded and she put a hand to her mouth. 'Oh, God, please let him be OK!'

Isabel got up and came to put her arms around Harriet. 'I think we should go to bed. There's nothing we can do tonight. Goodnight, my dear.'

'Goodnight,' Harriet whispered back.

But, back up in the flat, Harriet had no desire to go to bed, she discovered, and not only on Charlie's account, although that feeling of dread was still running through her.

It was Isabel's bombshell that she also had on her mind. It was the fact that she'd been able to see it was no use denying to Isabel that she was helplessly, hopelessly in love with her nephew.

But how had she given herself away? She'd only admitted it to herself recently. Of course it had been bubbling away for longer than that; she just hadn't been aware of it.

'I must be incredibly transparent,' she murmured aloud. 'Maybe I do go around with my head in the clouds. Perhaps I was unaware of how I reacted when his name came up? Or perhaps Isabel and Charlie had been comparing notes? Did they see something in Damien, both of us, they hadn't expected to see?'

She shook her head and, with a heavy sigh, decided to take him a cup of cocoa.

What if he doesn't like cocoa? she immediately asked herself. He doesn't drink tea. They couldn't be less alike, tea and cocoa, however, but, if he needs some fortitude, what better than, say, an Irish coffee?

She found him in his study, staring out of the window.

The breeze had dropped and the sky had cleared so there was starlight on the water and a pale slice of moon.

He didn't move when she knocked softly; she didn't think he'd heard her.

She put the tray with two Irish coffees on his desk and walked over to him, making sure she approached from a wide angle so as not to startle him.

'Any news?' she asked.

He turned his head. 'No.'

'I brought us some—liquid fortitude.' She gestured to the tall glasses on the tray.

He glanced at them and sketched a smile—and held out his hand to her.

She hesitated for one brief moment then she took it,

knowing full well what was going to happen and knowing at the same time it was the least she could do for him because it all but broke her heart to see the suffering etched into his expression.

And she went into his arms with no hesitation at all. But he surprised her. He held her loosely and some of the lines left his face as he said, with a quirk of humour, 'There is something you could always put down on the plus side for me.'

'What?' she breathed, as his nearness started to overwhelm her.

'I'm taller.'

Her lips curved. 'Yes. You are.'

He raised a hand and traced the line of her jaw. 'Does it help? Or do you prefer your men shorter?'

'I do not,' she observed seriously. 'They make me feel like an Amazon. No, it's definitely a plus.'

'Good. I mean that makes me feel good. I was beginning to develop an inferiority complex. Not that I'll ever be able to even up the ledger.' He took a very deep breath. 'I'm talking nonsense but—what will I do without Charlie if it goes that way?'

Harriet slipped her arms around him and laid her head on his chest. 'Don't think like that. It hasn't happened yet, it may not happen.'

'It's so vast up there and if it's not dry and desolate, the shores and the creeks have crocodiles—I know, I've been fishing up there.' His arms tightened around her.

'But they must have very sophisticated tracking and search and rescue equipment. Don't give up hope.'

'You sound so sensible and sane. And you feel so good,' he added barely audibly.

'So...so do you,' she murmured back and raised her mouth for his kiss.

'This is getting out of hand,' he said some time later as they drew apart to take deep breaths and steady themselves. 'I hope you don't mind me doing this.'

Harriet regarded him gravely. 'It did annoy me, the last time.'

His eyebrows shot up? 'How come?'

She chuckled. 'You never asked me for my preferences in the matter. You just went ahead and did it.'

'Miss Livingstone,' he said formally, 'please tell me what your preferences are in the matter—*this* matter. So as not to be misunderstood.' He pulled her closer and cradled her hips to him.

Harriet took an unsteady breath. 'They appear to be very similar to yours in this instance.' And she linked her arms around his neck and stared into his eyes.

It was a long, compelling look they shared and Harriet strove to convey the sense that she understood his need and the starkness of his emotions and that she wanted to offer him some comfort.

He breathed urgently and said one word. 'Sure?'

'Sure,' she answered.

He looked around and gestured at the large comfortable settee. 'Here?'

'If you don't have a haystack or a loft?' she queried with laughter glinting in her eyes.

'I…' He hesitated then he saw that glint of laughter and for a moment his arms around her nearly crushed her.

'All right,' he said into her hair, and that was the last word spoken for a while.

But what followed didn't stop Harriet from thinking along the lines of, *I was right. I sensed that he'd know how to make love to a woman in a way that would thrill her and drive her to excesses she didn't know she could reach…*

Because that was exactly what happened to her. From a fairly timid lover—she suddenly realised this with a pang of embarrassment—she became a different creature.

She craved his hands on her body. She helped him to take her clothes off and she gloried in the way he touched and stroked her. She became impatient to help him shed his clothes.

She made no effort to hide her excitement as they lay together on the settee and he cupped her breasts and plucked her nipples, as he drew his fingers ever lower down her body.

And she clung to him as desire took her by storm and there was only one thing she craved—to be taken. So she moved provocatively against him and did her own fingertip exploration of him until he growled and turned her onto her back and made sure she was ready for him, then they were united in an urgent rhythm and finally an explosion of sensation.

'Oh!' she breathed, as she arched her body against him.

And he buried his head between her breasts as he shuddered to a final closure.

* * *

'Harriet?'

'Mmm…?'

'All right?'

'Oh yes.' Her eyes remained closed but she smiled a secret little smile.

He grinned and dropped the lightest kiss on her hair. 'Wait here.'

She moved in an urgent little protest. 'Don't go away.'

'I'll be right back.' But he checked his phone and glanced at his computer screen before he went out.

She looked a question at him but he shook his head.

And he was as good as his word; he was back in a couple of minutes with a sheet, a blanket and a couple of pillows. He'd also put on a pair of shorts.

He covered her and made sure she was comfortable.

Then he stopped. 'There are six bedrooms we could go to. I'm not sure why we didn't in the first place.'

'We weren't in the most practical frame of mind,' she suggested.

He sat down beside her and smoothed her hair. 'If I recall correctly, you were even talking about haystacks.'

'Silly talk.' She slipped her hand under her cheek. 'Love talk. Well—' she bit her lip '—you know what I mean—pillow talk, that's it!'

'Yes.'

Did he say it too soon? she immediately found herself wondering.

'Your Dutch courage drinks have gone cold,' he added.

Harriet grimaced.

'I'll get us something else.' He pushed his phone into his pocket.

'Don't.' Harriet sat up and pulled the sheet up. 'I mean, don't wake Isabel. She could be shocked even if she does think…' She broke off and hoped he didn't see the colour she felt rising in her cheeks.

But he appeared to notice nothing as he said, 'Isabel has her own apartment downstairs. It closes off and she doesn't hear a thing. I won't be long. Don't—' his lips twisted '—go anywhere.'

She didn't go anywhere but she did pull her knickers and her shirt on.

It wasn't brandy, as she'd been expecting, that he brought back—it was a bottle of champagne.

Harriet studied the dark green bottle with its gold foil and the two tall glasses on the tray that he deposited on his desk. 'Should we?' she asked tentatively. 'In the circumstances?'

His hair was hanging in his eyes. All he wore were shorts but he could hardly have been more magnificent as he picked up the champagne bottle, Harriet thought as she caught her breath. His shoulders were broad, his chest was sprinkled with dark hair, his diaphragm was flat, his legs long and strong. He was beautiful, she thought with a pang. How was she ever going to forget him…?

'In the circumstances,' he said as he unwound the wire around the cork, 'there is not only you and me to celebrate, there's Charles Walker Wyatt. Wherever you are, Charlie, may you be safe and sound!'

He popped the cork and poured the two glasses. He handed one to Harriet and clinked his against hers. 'Charlie,' he said.

'Charlie,' Harriet echoed. 'May you be safe and sound!'

His phone buzzed. He grabbed it and studied the screen, and breathed a huge sigh of relief as he read the message.

'They've found him. They've found the site where it came down and the crew are all alive. Charlie has a broken arm and leg and a few gashes but otherwise he's mostly OK.'

Harriet flew off the settee into his arms. 'Oh, thank heavens! Do you think they heard us, whoever is in charge of these things up there? I mean in heaven as well as North Western Australia? I think they must have!'

He laughed down at her. 'You could be right.'

'Where is he?'

'They're taking him to Darwin Hospital. They'll keep him there for a few weeks. Where's your glass?'

'Here.' She went to retrieve it from the end table beside the settee and he held it steady in her hand while he refilled it.

Then he looked down at her and raised an eyebrow. 'So—I'm over and done with, am I?'

Harriet looked down at herself. 'Not at all,' she denied. 'I just felt a little—undressed.' She grimaced. 'Not that I'm particularly—overdressed at the moment.'

'Stay like that,' he advised. 'Because I'll be right back. I'll just pass on the news to Isabel.'

* * *

She was sitting on the settee with the sheet covering her legs when he came back. He brought his glass over and sat down beside her. He dropped his arm over her shoulders.

'Cheers!'

'Cheers!' She sipped her champagne then laid her head on his shoulder. 'Any particular person in mind this time?'

'Yes.' He drew his hand through her hair. 'Us.'

'Well, we've both got brothers on the mend, so yes—to us!'

'True,' he agreed, 'but I meant a toast to what just happened here on this settee between us and the hope that it may continue to happen for us, not necessarily in a study or a haystack—a bed would do,' he said with a glint of humour. 'In other words, when will you marry me, Harriet Livingstone?'

Harriet, in the echoing silence that followed his words, asked herself why she should not have expected this. Because he'd *told* her he could never overcome the cynicism he'd been left with after the debacle of his first marriage?

'Harriet?' He removed his arm and put his fingers beneath her chin to turn her face to his. 'What?'

Her eyes were wide but dark and very blue. 'You said...' she began quietly.

'Forget what I said earlier,' he ordered. 'Have you never said or done something and almost immediately started to wonder why you did it?' He didn't wait for an answer. 'Well, I have and that was one of them. Anyway, things have changed.'

'Nothing's changed,' she denied.

'There you go again,' he drawled. 'You kissed me once and were all set to walk away from me. Don't tell me that modus operandi extends to making love to me as if—' he paused, and looked deep into her eyes '—your soul depended on it, then walking away?'

Harriet breathed heavily with great frustration. 'I don't have a "modus operandi" I employ like that,' she said through her teeth.

'So why did you make love to me like that?'

She opened her mouth then gestured, annoyed. 'I felt sorry for you—I felt sorry for *me*. It was so lonely and scary not knowing what had happened to Charlie; it was awful. That's—' she lifted her chin '—why I did it.'

'There had to be more than that.'

Harriet moved restlessly then she sighed. 'Yes. Of course. We obviously—' she shrugged '—are attracted.'

'Thank you,' he said with considerable irony. 'So why's it such a bad idea? We both appeared,' he said dryly, 'to have forgotten our inhibitions and our hang-ups as well.'

Harriet acknowledged this with a tinge of colour mounting in her cheeks but she said, 'Temporarily, yes, but you can't spend your life in bed. And I get the feeling marriage can create a pressure cooker environment for those hang-ups if they're still lingering.'

'Don't,' he advised, 'come the philosopher with me, Harriet Livingstone.'

She bristled. 'Don't be ridiculous! It's only common sense.'

He grinned fleetingly. 'OK. How about this, then? If you won't marry me, would you consider a relationship? That should give our hang-ups the freedom to rattle in the breeze rather than build up all sorts of pressure.'

Harriet sat up. 'No, I will not! And I'll tell you why. You've got me on your conscience again, haven't you? You couldn't change so suddenly otherwise. Well, you don't need to. I'll be fine.'

He sat up, all trace of amusement gone. 'Listen,' he said harshly, 'if I have got you on my conscience, I've got good reason. You came here to Heathcote obviously traumatised—I wouldn't be surprised if you were traumatised the day you ran into me. You were as skinny as a rake—and all because some guy had passed you over for another girl—'

'Not just another girl,' Harriet threw in. 'My best friend.'

Damien paused.

'Someone I loved and trusted,' she went on. 'We met in our last year at school. I hadn't made any close friends up until then because we moved around so much. That's why I think she meant so much to me. Then Carol and I went to the same college and we did everything together. We backpacked around Europe. We did a working holiday on a cattle station; we did so much together.

'And all the while we dated guys, but not terribly seriously until I met Simon and she met Peter. And for a few months we double-dated. But then we drifted apart. Simon and I were talking marriage. Carol and Pete weren't so serious.' She stopped and shrugged.

'And then Simon wasn't so serious,' Damien contributed.

Harriet nodded. 'I think Carol tried to avoid it but it didn't work. And *they* got married. So you see, it was a double betrayal. That's what made it so painful. And in the midst of it all my father died and my brother had this accident…and…I was alone. Everything that meant the most to me was gone or, if not gone, terribly injured. I don't know how I got myself together but, once I did, I decided I was the only one I could rely on.'

'I see—I do see,' he said gently.

'And it's not something I want to go through again, any kind of a betrayal. And that's why—' she turned to Damien '—I'm not prepared to marry you or be your mistress because you've got me on your conscience.'

'I—'

'No.' She put her hand over his. 'I'm certainly not prepared to fall in love with you, only to find you don't trust me, to find you don't and never will believe in love ever after.'

'What you need,' he said after a long, painful pause, 'is someone like Charlie.'

Harriet jumped in astonishment.

'I don't mean Charlie per se,' he continued, looking annoyed with himself. 'I mean someone uncomplicated, with no hang-ups and no habit of command. No back story.'

He pushed the sheet aside and stood up.

Harriet stared up at him, her lips parted, her eyes

questioning. 'What…what's going to happen now?' she queried unevenly.

Damien Wyatt looked down at her and his lips twisted. 'Nothing.'

'Nothing,' she echoed.

'What did you expect?'

'I…I don't know,' she stammered.

'That I'd kick you out?'

'Well, no. I mean—not precisely.' Harriet reached for her pedal pushers and stepped into them.

'I'll be off to Darwin first thing tomorrow and I'll stay with Charlie for as long as he needs me. Then—' he grimaced '—I'll rearrange my Africa trip. Whilst you can finish my mother's things and start on the paintings.'

'I'm not sure if I can do that.'

'You should. I'm sure it'll do your brother good to have you around.'

Harriet bit her lip.

He watched her intently.

She became conscious of his scrutiny. And it seemed to bring back the whole incredible sequence of events as they'd unfolded in this very room, not the least her passionate response to his lovemaking. It did more than that. It awoke tremors of sensation down her body and a sense of longing in her heart—a longing to be in his arms, a longing to be safe with him, a longing to be beloved…

She closed her eyes briefly because, of course, that wasn't going to happen. All the same, how to leave him?

'I don't know what to say,' she murmured.

'Not easy.' A smile appeared fleetingly in his eyes. 'Thanks but no thanks?' he suggested.

Harriet flinched.

'Or maybe just, from me, anyway—take care?' he mused. 'Yes, in your case, Harriet Livingstone, I think that's particularly appropriate. Don't drive into any more Aston Martins, or anything, for that matter; you take care now. By the way, if there are any consequences you wouldn't be so head-in-the-clouds as not to let me know?'

Harriet took a sobbing little breath, grabbed her shoes and ran past him out of the door.

CHAPTER EIGHT

'HARRIET, YOU'RE WORKING your fingers to the bone!' Isabel Wyatt accused as she stood in the studio doorway, shaking raindrops off her umbrella a couple of weeks later. 'It's Sunday,' she continued. 'Even if you're not religious, you need a rest. What is the matter?'

'Nothing! Come in. I'll make you a cuppa. I'm just working on the Venetian masks. It's a pity they got so dusty. Look at this lovely Columbina!'

Harriet held up a white porcelain half-mask studded with glittering stones and dyed feathers.

'Where does the name come from?'

'A Columbina is a stock character in Italian comedy, usually a maid who's—' Harriet shrugged '—a gossip, flirty, a bit of a wag and in English known as a soubrette.'

'Obviously not above disguising herself with a mask for the purpose of delicious secret liaisons,' Isabel said.

Harriet paused her dusting operation as the word *liaison* struck a chord with her, and for a moment she wanted to run away to the end of the earth as she thought of Damien Wyatt.

But she forced herself to take hold.

'Something like that,' she murmured. 'There are examples in this collection of all the different materials used to make masks, did you know? Leather, for example.' She held up a mask. 'Porcelain, as in the Columbina, and of course glass. Did you know the Venice Carnival goes back to 1162, when the Serenissima, as she was known then, defeated the Patriarch of Aquileila?'

'I did know that bit, as a matter of fact.' Isabel took the leather mask from Harriet. 'I've been to the Venice Carnival. It was also outlawed by the King of Austria in 1797 but no one knows exactly what prompted the population of Venice to be so exceedingly taken up with disguising themselves. Come along.'

'Where?'

'Upstairs to your kitchen, where *I* will make you a cuppa. Now don't argue with me, Harriet Livingstone!'

'What happened?' Isabel asked about twenty minutes later when they both had steaming mugs of tea in front of them on the refectory table as well as a plate of rich, bursting with cherries fruitcake.

'You mean…?' Harriet looked a question at Isabel.

'I mean with you and Damien—I'm not a fool, Harriet,' Isabel warned. 'Look, I wasn't going to say anything but you're so obviously…upset.'

Harriet frowned. 'We wouldn't suit, that's all.'

'And that's why you've been working all hours of the day and night and looking all haunted and pale?' Isabel looked at her sardonically.

'I need to get this job finished,' Harriet said sharply. 'It's really started to drag—I just couldn't seem to get on top of it! Even the kitchen's been rebuilt whilst I didn't seem to be getting much further forward! But I need to put Heathcote behind me and I wish I'd never laid eyes on Damien Wyatt.'

'I'm glad you didn't say all the Wyatts.' Isabel stared at her.

Harriet looked away. 'I'm sorry. No, of course not you, Isabel. Or Charlie. But, ideally, I'd like to be gone before Damien and Charlie get home from Darwin. Look—' she turned back to Damien's aunt '—it's impossible for us to be in the same place now. Believe me.'

Isabel opened her mouth, hesitated, then said, 'So you're not going to do the paintings?'

'I…I…no.'

'How about your brother?'

Harriet licked her lips. 'He's making…progress.' But of course Brett was at the back of her mind, and how much easier it would be to make ends meet if she did stay on and do the paintings. But all the guilt in the world associated with Brett couldn't make her stay, not now, not after…

She sighed inwardly and pushed the plate of fruitcake towards Isabel. 'I made it to welcome Charlie home,' she said desolately and stood up abruptly to cross over to the window and stare out at the dismal, rainswept landscape. 'He loves fruitcake.'

'They'll be home shortly.'

'Autumn has come with a vengeance,' Brett said.

Harriet huddled inside her coat and agreed with him.

They were outside, despite the chill—Brett loved being outdoors whenever he could so she'd pushed him in his wheelchair to a sheltered arbour in the grounds. The breeze, however, had found its way around the arbour and it wasn't as sheltered as she'd thought it would be.

'I want to show you something,' he said.

Harriet looked enquiring and hoped he didn't notice that she was preoccupied but she couldn't seem to help herself. She was not only preoccupied but she was trying to dredge up the courage to tell him she was going back to Sydney...

'Here.' He took the rug she'd insisted on draping over his legs and handed it to her.

'Oh, I'm all right,' she protested.

'Actually, you look half-frozen,' he responded with a grin, 'but all I want you to do is hold it for a couple of minutes.'

And, so saying, he levered himself out of the wheelchair and, with a stiff, slightly jerky gait but, all the same, walked around the arbour completely unaided and came to stand in front of her.

Harriet's mouth had fallen open and her eyes were huge.

'What do you think of that?' he asked with obvious pride.

Harriet jumped up and flung her arms around him. 'Oh, Brett,' she cried joyfully. 'That's such an improvement! When? How? Why? I mean...' She stopped. 'You've been holding out on me!' she told him.

'Yes. I wanted it to be a big surprise.' He hugged

her back then rocked slightly. 'There's still a way to go, though.'

'Sit down, sit down,' she insisted immediately, 'and tell me all about it. I think I can guess a bit of it, though. Your new physiotherapist?'

Brett sat down in his chair and nodded. 'Yes. Ellen has made a huge difference, but not only as a physio. She—' he paused '—she got me talking. See, I seemed to reach a plateau that I couldn't get beyond and she asked me one day if there was anything I was worried about, other than the obvious. And I found that there was and it was something that made me feel helpless and hopeless.'

'What?' Harriet asked fearfully.

He smiled at her and put his hand over hers. 'You,' he said simply.

Harriet gasped.

'Because of all the things you gave up for me,' he said. 'Because I didn't know how I could ever repay you. Because I didn't much like the sound of this guy you went to work for but there was not a damn thing I could do about it.'

'Oh, Brett!'

'And somehow I found myself telling Ellen all this— she said the best thing I could do for you was to walk again. It just seemed—' he shook his head '—to put the fire back into me,' he marvelled. 'But there's still a way to go.'

'And will Ellen be with you down that road?' Harriet asked.

'I think so. I hope so. She...we—' he managed to

look embarrassed and uplifted at the same time '—really get along.'

Harriet hugged him again. 'I'm so glad. So glad,' she repeated, 'because I'm going back to Sydney tomorrow. I know, I know,' she said to his look of surprise, 'it's a bit out of the blue but I've finished the job at last! And I'd like to look around for another one. Also, I told you about his brother?' Brett nodded. 'Well, they're due home from Darwin in a couple of days and it'll be a family time, I'm sure.'

Brett stared at her. 'What's he done to you?'

'Done?' She blinked.

'Yep,' Brett said grimly. 'Damien Wyatt.'

'Nothing! He's been quite—he's been quite kind, all things considered—'

'Don't give me that, Harry,' Brett said concernedly. 'I can see with my own eyes that you look all haunted.'

Harriet put a hand to her mouth. 'Do I really—? I mean, am I really that easy to read—? I mean—'

'Yes, you are. For someone who goes into her own little world quite frequently, you're amazingly easy to read,' he said somewhat dryly.

Harriet bit her lip then took a deep breath. 'If there's any trauma, he didn't cause it,' she said. 'I did. And I want you to believe that and—' she stood up '—I want you to put it out of your mind and continue this…this marvellous recovery. Ellen is right, you see; it's the *very* best thing you could do for me.'

'I can't let you go like this,' Isabel said the next morning as she watched Harriet pack her stuff into Brett's battered old four-wheel drive. 'Damien will never forgive me!'

It was another blustery autumn day.

'Stop worrying about it,' Harriet advised her. 'Between the two of you, you'll have enough on your minds helping Charlie to get better without worrying about me. Besides which, I'm not that bad a driver,' she added with some asperity.

'There could be differing views on the matter.' Isabel looked mutinous. 'Look, take the Holden!'

'I couldn't possibly take the Holden,' Harriet argued. 'It doesn't belong to me!'

'Ah!' Isabel pounced on an idea. 'It could be said to belong to *me*, however!'

Harriet didn't stop packing up her vehicle.

'What I mean is,' Isabel continued, 'I have a share in Heathcote, which includes all the equipment and machinery, so I am able, equally, to dispose of—things. Therefore I can gift you the blue Holden!' she finished triumphantly. 'Isn't that how they phrase it these days?'

Harriet put the last of her bags into the four-wheel drive and closed the back door.

She walked over to Isabel and put her arms around her. 'I'll never forget you,' she said softly. 'Thank you for being a friend and—I have to go. I can't explain but don't blame Damien.'

Isabel hugged her then took out her hanky.

But a parting just as hard was still to come.

Tottie was sitting disconsolately beside the open driver's door.

'Oh,' Harriet said softly as a knot of emotion she'd

been hoping to keep under a tight rein unravelled and her tears started to fall. 'I don't know what to say, Tottie, but I will miss you so much.' She knelt down and put her arms around the big dog. 'I'm sorry but I have to go.'

A few minutes later she was driving down the long, winding drive.

In her rear-view mirror she watched Isabel hold on to Tottie's collar so she couldn't chase after Harriet, then the house was out of sight and the double gate-posts were approaching and the tears she'd held on to so tightly started to fall.

There was a sign on the road to be aware of a concealed driveway entrance to Heathcote.

There was no sign inside Heathcote to the effect that the portion of the road that went past the gates was hidden from view due to some big trees and a slight bend in it.

Still, Harriet had negotiated this many times so perhaps it was because that she was crying and had misted up her glasses that accounted for the fact that an ambulance driving into the property took her completely by surprise and caused her to swing the wheel and drive into one of the gateposts.

Damien put Harriet carefully into a chair and said in a weary, totally exasperated way, 'What the hell am I going to do with you?'

'Nothing,' Harriet responded tautly and eyed him with considerable annoyance.

They were in the flat above the studio, where all

Harriet's belongings had been unloaded from Brett's vehicle and where she now sat in an armchair with one foot swathed in bandages and resting on a footstool.

The ambulance had picked Charlie and Damien up from Ballina airport because, due to his casts and stitches, fitting into a normal vehicle would have been difficult for Charlie.

The ambulance had escaped unscathed from the incident at the gate. So, yet again, had Brett's four-wheel drive. The gatepost was another matter. It had collapsed into a pile of rubble. And Harriet had somehow sprained her ankle.

The male nurse accompanying Charlie had attended to it.

'Nothing,' Harriet repeated, 'and I would appreciate it if you didn't tower over me like that or treat me like an idiot!'

'My apologies,' Damien said dryly and sat down opposite her. 'It's not the first time this has happened, however.'

'And it might not have happened if…if people hadn't made…hadn't cast aspersions on my driving or if I hadn't been…' She shook her head and closed her eyes. 'It doesn't matter.'

'Been crying?' he suggested.

Her lashes lifted. 'How did you know that?'

He grimaced. 'You looked as if you'd been crying—red eyes, you still had tears in your eyes, as a matter of fact, and tearstains on your cheeks.'

There was a longish pause, then she said, 'It was

only Tottie I was crying over.' She paused. 'And perhaps Isabel.'

'Despite her aspersions on your driving?'

'How did you know *that*?'

'She told me. She feels very guilty and has asked me to apologise.'

Harriet shrugged. 'She meant well,' she said gruffly.

'So there's no possibility there was a skerrick of regret in you about leaving me?'

An uneasy silence developed until Harriet said carefully, 'You know it could never have worked, Damien.'

'I know I made a tactical error in asking you to marry me there and then. My intentions were the best, though.'

'Yes.' Harriet looked across at him. 'You thought I'd go into a decline if you didn't. You thought it could all be worked out on a pragmatic basis. Above all, you had me on your conscience again.'

'Maybe,' he said. 'But look, we're both stuck here for a while so we need to come to an arrangement.'

Harriet raised an eyebrow. 'You're staying?'

He nodded. 'I've postponed Africa while Charlie recovers.'

'I should be fine within a week at the most. It's only a sprain.'

'It's quite a severe sprain. The nurse told you to take it easy for at least a fortnight.'

'I could go crazy in a fortnight,' Harriet said gloomily.

'Not if you start on the paintings.'

She turned her head to look out of the window at the

scudding clouds. 'Back to the paintings again. They're starting to haunt me.'

'Of course we could spend a few days in Hawaii or Tahiti.' His glance was ironic. 'Together,' he added and favoured her with a loaded glance.

Harriet took a sharp breath but what she was about to say went unuttered as Tottie was at last allowed into the flat, with Isabel close behind.

And Damien Wyatt observed the reunion between his aunt, his dog and—the thorn in his side?—not a bad description, he decided, and found himself feeling so annoyed on all fronts, he took himself off to, as he told them, go and see how Charlie was.

But Charlie still had the nurse with him, checking him out.

So Damien continued on to his study, but that wasn't a good idea either. That brought back memories of a girl who'd loved him in a way that could only be described as 'all or nothing'.

It also reminded him that he still fancied Harriet Livingstone, although he was undoubtedly angry with her. Angry with her for turning him down again? Angry with her for driving into the gatepost?

'Just plain angry with her,' he mused and, coming to a sudden decision, reached for the phone as he swung his feet up onto the desk.

Fortunately Arthur answered. Exchanging inanities with Penny would have been too much for him, Damien decided.

'Arthur,' he said, 'Damien. Can you spare a bit of time up here at Heathcote?'

Arthur rubbed the bridge of his nose. 'Well, Penny is pregnant so I don't like to leave her, not for too long anyway.'

'How pregnant *is* Penny?'

'About five months.'

For crying out loud, Arthur, Damien thought but did not say, she's going to keep you dancing attendance for the next four months!

He cleared his throat. 'Uh...of course. It's just that Harriet could do with some help.'

'Harriet?' Arthur repeated. 'I thought she was fine and almost finished.'

'She was. She is finished but I've suggested she cleans the paintings for us rather than sending them away.'

'Wonderful idea,' Arthur responded heartily. 'I'm sure she'd do a great job!'

'Yes, well, she doesn't quite see it that way and that's probably because she's a bit incapacitated at the moment. But I thought if you could come up and go through them with her—you know, if she had someone to discuss them with, someone who really knows what they're talking about, it could help.'

There was a short silence then Arthur said on a curious note, 'Incapacitated?'

'She's sprained her ankle.'

'How?'

Damien grimaced. 'She...ran into the gatepost. In that...tank.'

A sudden silence came down the line, then, 'I don't believe it! The girl's a menace behind the wheel.'

'Uh, there may have been extenuating circumstances.'

'What?' Arthur enquired. 'A dog or two that escaped completely unscathed?'

Damien's lips twisted. 'No. But anyway, she's a bit down in the dumps and I didn't—' he paused and was struck by a brainwave '—I didn't believe Penny would like to think of Harriet like that.'

'Of course not,' Arthur agreed. 'I'll come up tomorrow morning. How's Charlie?'

Damien put the phone down a few minutes later. Then he lifted the receiver again and proceeded to order not one but two wheelchairs, and two pairs of crutches.

CHAPTER NINE

'How's Penny?'

Harriet and Arthur were in the dining room and Arthur was pushing her around in a wheelchair from painting to painting. Harriet was taking notes.

'Well, we were expecting morning sickness, of course, and *some* form of—I don't know—maybe emotional highs and lows, some weird cravings like pickles on jam, but she doesn't seem to have *ever* been better.'

Harriet hid a smile. Arthur sounded quite worried.

'That's *good* news,' she said. 'Sounds as if she's having an uncomplicated pregnancy. Oh!' Harriet stared at a picture on the wall. 'I can't believe I never noticed that before.'

'Tom Roberts. Heidelberg School. One of my favourites. I was lucky to get that,' Arthur said complacently

'I love his beach scenes,' Harriet said dreamily. 'Where did you find it?'

Arthur pushed her a bit further on and into the hall as he told her the story of how he'd acquired the Tom Roberts for Damien's father. Harriet listened, genuinely fascinated, and they spent a pleasurable couple of hours going through the Wyatt collection.

In fact, when they'd finished and he'd wheeled her back to the studio, Harriet said energetically, 'Arthur, I'll need—'

'I'll get all the stuff you need, Harriet. It's quite some time since they were last done—I've been urging Damien to do it for a while so I'm really pleased he's asked you. You seem to—' he eyed Tottie, who was lying next to the wheelchair '—fit in here really well, too.'

Harriet opened her mouth to dispute this but that could only sound churlish, so she simply nodded.

He went shortly thereafter but sought Damien out before driving off.

He was up in his study, which gave Arthur a sense of déjà vu.

'Come in,' Damien responded to his triple knock.

'Mission accomplished,' Arthur said. 'She's going to do them. She even sounds quite enthusiastic about it now.'

'Thanks, mate.'

Arthur fingered his blue waistcoat with purple airships on it as he pulled up a chair. 'Unusual girl that, you know.'

Damien couldn't help a swift glance at the settee across the room, and made the sudden unspoken decision to have it moved elsewhere. 'Yes, I do, as a matter of fact,' he replied dryly.

'Penny reckons it's a case of still waters running

deep with Harriet Livingstone and she doubts she'll ever get over Simon Dexter.'

Damien frowned. 'I thought they hadn't seen each other since college when they bumped into each other, Penny and Harriet?'

'They hadn't, but word gets around and Penny has quite a network of old friends, so when Harriet bobbed up—she did some research, you might say. And—'

'Simon *Dexter*,' Damien interrupted. 'Elite golfer who's earned himself a million dollars recently, playboy, heart-throb—that Simon Dexter?'

Arthur nodded. 'Can't imagine what brought them together in the first place. I mean, she's not a groupie type, she's not a sporting type. The way she keeps running into things suggests she may even be a bit uncoordinated, not to mention short-sighted.'

'Suffers from a left-handed syndrome, in fact,' Damien supplied.

'Never heard of it.'

'That makes two of us. Uh...hasn't Simon Dexter been on the news lately—for other reasons?'

'Could well have been; I haven't been much tuned into the news lately. And I should be getting home.' Arthur stood up. 'You'll have your hands full, what with Charlie and Harriet, but at least her—er—incarceration, if you could call it that, is only for a couple of weeks.

'Yes.'

And, to Arthur's surprise, after that single yes, Damien seemed to fall into some kind of reverie and didn't appear to notice his departure.

By the time Arthur had gone, Harriet was also deep in thought for a time.

Along the lines of wondering whether she'd been conned into staying on and doing the paintings.

Surely not. She could hardly be in Damien Wyatt's good books at the moment, after knocking back both his proposals as well as knocking down his gatepost.

But he had rung Arthur and Arthur had tapped into her love of art and managed to imbue her with a feeling of enthusiasm, even eagerness for the project.

Why, though? Why would he want her to stay on?

She shook her head and her thoughts returned to Arthur and how, despite his waistcoats, she enjoyed talking to him about art.

Arthur, she thought with a fond little smile. How on earth was he going to get through the rest of Penny's pregnancy, let alone the birth?

The next morning her ankle was more swollen than it had been, and more painful, so Charlie's nurse conceded that there might be something broken and she should have an X-ray. Isabel drove her in to Lismore, where an X-ray revealed a hairline fracture and a cast was applied to her ankle. She was warned to keep her weight off it while it healed.

Easier said than done, as she discovered. She was exhausted after hopping up the stairs to the flat on one foot, even with Isabel's help.

'We'll have to do something about this,' Isabel said worriedly. 'You can't go through this every time you want to get out or home. Damien should have thought of that. I'll speak to him.'

'Don't worry about it,' Harriet told her. 'Just please say hello to Charlie. And tell him in a few days I'll actually get to see him.'

Isabel went away, still looking worried.

And, an hour or so later, Isabel, Stan and Damien mounted the steps to the flat and moved Harriet and her belongings down to the ground floor of the house.

She didn't protest. She didn't have the energy.

Her new quarters were a guest suite, with a sitting room and separate bedroom, pretty and floral and comfortable, with a view over the garden.

Isabel unpacked for her and brought her a cup of tea but she was alone when Damien came in with a knock and closed the door behind him. He didn't beat about the bush.

'What's wrong?'

Harriet stared up at him, and licked her lips. 'What do you mean?' she asked huskily. 'I...I've broken a bone in my ankle.'

He sat down opposite her wheelchair. 'I know that but I was wondering—' he paused '—whether you'd heard that Simon Dexter and his wife Carol have split up.'

Harriet gasped and her eyes widened.

'It's been on the news. He's a newsworthy figure nowadays. More so perhaps than when you knew him?'

'Yes.' She stared at him. 'I...I...no, I hadn't heard.'

'Do you play golf?' he asked.

'Oh, no!'

'I thought you might have had golf lessons in similar circumstances to your riding lessons.'

'No.' She shook her head.

'So how did you and Simon Dexter get together?'

Harriet looked away and clasped her hands in her lap.

'Don't tell me,' Damien said softly as a tide of pink entered her cheeks, 'that you ran into him?'

She said stiffly, 'Not with a car. Well, not exactly a car.'

'I hesitate to wonder what "not exactly a car" could be,' he marvelled.

Harriet tossed him an irate look. 'A golf buggy, of course.'

'Of course! How dumb can I get? How did it happen?'

'My father did play golf. I was going around with him one morning when he asked me to drive the buggy up to the green while he made a shot from the rough and then took a shortcut not suitable for buggies, to the green. I'd never driven one before but it seemed pretty simple.' She raised her eyebrows. 'Famous last thoughts.'

'You obviously didn't kill Simon or maim him.'

'No.' Harriet paused and a frown grew in her eyes. 'How did you know it was Simon Dexter? I didn't think I mentioned his surname.'

Damien studied his hands for a moment then grimaced. 'Arthur.'

'Arthur doesn't know him.'

'Penny, then.'

'Penny doesn't know him either,' Harriet objected.

'Ah, but Penny runs this spy ring, MI55. She's actually M in disguise, or—' he raised an eyebrow '—is she Miss Moneypenny?'

Harriet went from bristling to calming down to smiling involuntarily. 'I still don't understand how it came up,' she said, though.

'We were worried that you seemed to be down in the dumps.'

She took a breath and sat back. 'I don't know how I feel. I—it's terribly sad actually, isn't it?'

He didn't agree or disagree. He posed a question instead. 'So what is it?'

'What is what?'

'If it's not Simon Dexter, what's making you look as if your heart's breaking?'

Harriet swallowed. 'I didn't know I was. Look, it's probably just my ankle, bound up with feeling like a fool and...' She tailed off.

He raised his eyebrows. 'In what way?'

Harriet sighed. 'Surely I don't have to spell it out for you?'

He rubbed his jaw. 'You're regretting knocking back my offers of marriage?' Sheer irony glinted in his dark eyes.

'I'd be a fool to want to be married to you after...after what happened with your first wife—and how it affected you,' she said slowly. 'No. I feel stupid, that's all.'

Damien studied her thoughtfully. Her hair was clipped back to within an inch of its life—no wavy tendrils today, as there'd been on the night of Charlie's birthday party, no discreet make-up to emphasise her stunning eyes, no shimmering lipstick rendering those severe lips doubly inviting.

No gorgeous dress that showed off those amazing legs—not only tracksuit trousers today but a cast on her ankle... So what was it about her that made how she looked a matter of indifference to him?

It struck him suddenly that she was the most unaware girl he'd ever known. She certainly didn't flash her legs. She didn't bat those long eyelashes except when she was thinking seriously and tended to blink.

Was that why it didn't matter whether she was dressed up or down—he still fancied her? Then he was struck by a thought.

'You're not,' he said at last, with his eyes suddenly widening, 'pregnant, are you?'

Harriet opened and closed her mouth. 'No.'

'I'm sorry,' he said dryly. 'That wasn't a very good way of phrasing things, but if you are—'

'I'm not,' she broke in.

'Sure?'

Harriet eyed him. 'Yes.'

They stared at each other for a long moment, she with a spark of anger in her eyes, he suddenly completely inscrutable.

'Harriet,' he said, 'there's no point in hiding it from me.'

'I'm not hiding anything from you!' she protested. 'It was—unlikely, anyway.'

'That has been a trap for the unwary since time immemorial,' he said dryly. 'We both stand convicted of thoughtlessness there, however.' He shrugged and a glint of humour lit his eyes. 'Could we blame Charlie?'

'Blame Charlie for what? Thanks, mate,' Charlie said to his male nurse as he was pushed into the guest suite. 'Harriet! I can't believe we're both in wheelchairs!'

'Charlie!' Harriet had to laugh because, from the neck up, it was the same old Charlie and his infectious smile and mischievous expression hadn't changed. Otherwise, he had his right arm in a cast and a sling and his left leg stretched out in a cast.

'Oh, Charlie!' She hoisted herself out of her wheelchair and hopped across to him on one foot to kiss him warmly. 'I'm so glad to see you, even if you did render us thoughtless! Oh, nothing,' she said to Charlie's puzzled look. 'Nothing!'

They had dinner together that night.

The new cook produced barbecued swordfish on skewers with a salad, followed by a brandy pudding.

'Mmm,' Charlie said, 'if he doesn't burn down the kitchen, he may be as good as old cookie.'

'She,' Isabel contributed. 'I decided there'd be less chance of that with a woman.'

I can't believe I'm doing this, Harriet thought. I can't believe I'm sitting here like one of the family after actually driving away from Heathcote and planning to stay away for ever. I can't believe Damien is doing the same!

She glanced across at him but found his expression difficult to read, except to think that he looked withdrawn.

* * *

After dinner, however, everyone seemed to go their separate ways.

Charlie's nurse insisted he go to bed. Isabel went out to a meeting after wheeling Harriet into the guest suite and Damien went up to his study.

Harriet sat for several minutes in the wheelchair then decided she was exhausted. She used the crutches Damien had hired to get herself changed and finally into bed.

She was sitting up in bed arranging a pillow under her foot when she remembered she hadn't locked the door and she was just about to remedy this when the outer door clicked opened and Damien walked in.

Harriet went to say something but her voice refused to work and she had to clear her throat.

He must have heard because, with a light tap on the open door, he came through to the bedroom.

'OK?' He stood at the end of the bed and studied her in her ruffled grey nightgown.

Harriet nodded. 'Fine, thanks. Have you come to...?' Her eyes were wide and questioning.

'I haven't come to take up residence,' he said rather dryly. 'I've come to talk.'

'Oh.'

His lips twisted. 'What would you have said if I'd indicated otherwise?'

Harriet swallowed. 'I'm not sure.'

He studied her comprehensively then turned away and pulled a chair up. 'If you're worried about staying on to do the paintings, can I make a couple of points?'

He didn't wait for her approval. 'You really seem to enjoy this place, you love art and I guess—' he grimaced '—it's not a bad place to convalesce.' He paused and listened for a moment, then grinned and got up to let Tottie in.

She came up to the bed and rested her muzzle next to Harriet.

Harriet's eyes softened as she stroked the dog's nose. 'I've left you once, with disastrous consequences,' she murmured. 'Could I do it again?'

'You don't have to,' Damien said. 'There's something else you could do. I told you Charlie plays chess?'

She nodded after a moment.

'He's going to need some help to get through this period. Obviously he can't spend the whole time playing chess, but you two might be able to come up with ways to keep each other occupied—you're going to have the same problem for a while. You can't spend your life cleaning paintings.'

Harriet looked up at him. 'What about you?'

'What about me?'

She sat up and plaited her fingers. 'Will you be here?'

'Yes. But I'll be busy. Africa is coming to me, you see.'

Harriet blinked several times. 'Come again?'

He grimaced. 'I've reversed things. Instead of taking my machinery there, I've invited this company I'm dealing with to come here. I may not—' he paused then continued gravely '—be able to offer them wildlife safaris with lions, leopards, buffalo, elephants and hippos, to name a few, but there's the Great Barrier Reef, the

Kimberley, Cape York, Arnheim Land and some wonderful fishing. If they feel like a bit of danger there are plenty of crocodiles to dodge.'

Harriet blinked again then had to laugh. 'Is that what big business is all about?'

'That's better... It has a part.'

'What's better?' Harriet asked curiously.

He shrugged after a moment. 'It's the first time I've seen you laugh since you demolished the gatepost.

'But look, I'll obviously be here at times. If you're worried I'm liable to harass you on the subject of...on any subject, don't be.'

Harriet turned her attention to Tottie, still sitting patiently beside the bed, and wondered at the reaction his statement brought to her. It had a familiar feeling to it...

But Damien didn't elaborate. He felt in his pocket for his phone, and glanced at the screen. 'Sorry,' he murmured. 'I need to take this. Sleep well.' And he walked out, switching off the overhead lights so that she only had her bedside lamp to deal with. Tottie pattered after him at a click of his fingers. He closed the door.

She lay back after a moment and turned the bedside lamp off. And she pulled the spare pillow into her arms and hugged it as she examined that familiar feeling she'd experienced only minutes ago on hearing he didn't intend to harass her.

Why should that make her feel hollow and lonely at the same time as she felt ruffled and restless? It didn't make sense. She should be relieved if anything. The last thing she should feel like was crying herself to sleep.

It could never work—any other arrangement with

Damien could never work; she knew that in her heart and soul, didn't she? It would hurt her dreadfully if she came to be mistrusted because he couldn't help it now; if she could never get right though to him, if she lost him…

But how to cope with *this* hurt. Living in the same house with him, even if he wasn't home a lot, wanting him, wanting to be special to him, loving him…

CHAPTER TEN

THREE MONTHS LATER there were no more wheelchairs or crutches at Heathcote.

Both Charlie and Harriet were recovered, Harriet completely, Charlie almost there; and Damien Wyatt had been as good as his word. Then again, he'd hardly spent any time at Heathcote at all.

But he came home one evening, three months on, with the news that he'd swung his South African deal at last, which was exceedingly good news, he told them, but he needed a break.

'So I'll be home for a while,' he said, laying his napkin down on the table. He still wore a grey suit with a blue shirt but he'd discarded his tie. 'By the way, that dessert was almost up to your standards, Harriet,' he added.

'It was up to her standard—it was hers,' Isabel said.

Damien looked down the table at Harriet. 'How come?'

'Uh…' Harriet hesitated.

'The new cook proved to have light fingers in more ways than one,' Charlie said. 'She was a good cook, made marvellous pastry, actually, but when we began to discover we were missing minor amounts of money—you know what it's like, at first you think maybe you were mistaken and you didn't have it or you'd spent it or whatever, but then not only did it happen more often but she got bolder and took larger amounts.'

'So you fired her,' Damien said to Isabel.

'I didn't exactly fire her; she has an elderly mother to support. I...I let her go. I haven't found anyone to replace her yet, so Harriet very kindly stepped into her shoes.'

'What would we do without Harriet?' Damien murmured. 'But what is it about Heathcote that attracts either arsonists or petty thieves?'

'Cookie wasn't really an arsonist,' Isabel argued. 'Just...careless.'

Damien grimaced then pushed back his chair. 'OK, well, thanks, Harriet. And could you spare me a few moments of your time? I'll be upstairs in my study.'

Isabel said she would deal with the dishes and Harriet closed herself into the flat above the studio. She'd insisted on moving out of the house once she was mobile again.

Her emotions now, three months on and having received what had almost amounted to an order to beard Damien in his den, were hard to define.

He'd almost made it sound, she marvelled with clenched fists, as if she'd gone out of her way to make herself indispensable to the Wyatt family; as if she had a secret agenda to her own advantage.

When, if she was honest, the last three months *had* had a secret agenda, they'd been mostly sheer torture for her.

When he'd been home she'd had to use all her will-power to be normal and unaffected in his presence. When he'd been gone, it had taken all her willpower not to pack her bags and run for cover. But that would have meant deserting not only Brett but Charlie.

The other sticking point had been the Heathcote paintings. Her estimation of a month to clean them had proved to be optimistic. Even if she'd worked as tire-lessly as she had for the most part over his mother's treasures, she'd have taken longer than a month.

But trying to keep Charlie occupied at the same time—until she'd had a brainwave—had slowed her down a lot. The brainwave had been to introduce Char-lie to Brett. They'd hit it off immediately.

Her other sticking point with the paintings had been the generous amount she'd already been paid—Damien had simply paid the money into her account without consulting her.

The result was she felt honour-bound to either finish the job or pay the money back. But Brett still had some treatment to go through…

All this, though, she reasoned as she pulled on a blue cardigan over her shirt and jeans, was minor compared to the other inner havoc she'd experienced. The lonely nights when he was only a few steps away from her—that knowledge had kept her tossing and turning.

The lonely nights when she had no idea where he was—or who he was with.

The frisson that ran though her every time she walked through the dining room and recalled their first meeting and that passionate embrace. Recalled the feel of him, the taste of him, his wandering touch that had lit a fuse of sensation within her—if he had a problem with the lounge, her nemesis was the dining room, the memory had never gone away...

And now this, she thought.

A hard, bright, difficult Damien who'd ordered her up to his study as if she were a schoolgirl. A room she hadn't been in since the night Charlie...don't even think about it, she warned herself.

Despite the stern warning to herself, she stood outside the study for a couple of moments, trying to compose herself. Then she knocked and went in. Tottie followed her.

He was lounging behind his desk. There was a silver tray with a coffee pot and two cups on the desk. The windows were open on an unusually warm spring night and there was the sound and the salty air of the sea wafting in.

'Ah,' Damien said. 'I see you've brought your reinforcement.'

Harriet pushed her hair behind her ears. 'If you don't want her here—'

'Of course I don't mind her being here,' he said irritably. 'She *is* my dog. Sit down.'

Harriet looked around and froze. There was no longer the settee where they had... She stopped that thought in its tracks. Instead there were two elegant chairs covered in navy leather.

'You... I...' She turned back to Damien. 'I mean... nothing.' She swallowed and pulled one of the chairs up but was unable to stop herself from blushing a bright pink as she sat down. Tottie arranged herself at her feet.

Damien steepled his fingers beneath his chin and studied her meditatively. 'You think I should have kept it, the settee? As a memorial of some kind?'

Harriet's blush deepened but she said, 'No. I mean—' she gestured '—it was entirely up to you. What did you want to see me about?'

He stared at her then said abruptly, 'What are we going to do?'

'Do?' Harriet blinked.

'I hesitate to remind you, Harriet Livingstone, but that's exactly what you said to me once before in highly similar circumstances. The day we first met here.'

Her eyes widened.

'I asked you what we were going to do and you repeated "do" as if—as if nothing had ever happened between us or, if it had, it meant nothing,' he said savagely.

'Y-you—' her voice quivered and, to her amazement, she heard herself go on '—got rid of the settee. As if it meant nothing.'

'I didn't get rid of it,' he denied. 'I had it moved to my bedroom, just in case I should be plagued by any erotic images of you during a business meeting.'

Harriet blinked and this time her cheeks grew so hot she had to put her hands up to cover them. 'I can't believe I...said that.'

He looked darkly amused for a moment. 'Maybe your

innermost sentiments got the upper hand. Harriet, we can't go on like this. I can't anyway.'

He sat back and Harriet was suddenly shocked to see how tired he looked.

She opened her mouth but he waved a hand to forestall her. 'Don't say it. I know what you'll say anyway. You'll offer to go, just like you did the last time. Well, it's been a couple of times now but I can't guarantee a gatepost for you to drive into this time.'

'Wh…what do you suggest?' she asked. 'You say we can't go on like this but you don't want me to go.'

'Marry me,' he said after a long tense pause. 'I've given you three months to recover from Simon Dexter and your best friend Carol.'

Harriet gasped. 'You didn't have to—' She stopped abruptly. 'I mean…I mean there's still Veronica, there's still the way you feel—'

His dark eyes were mocking. 'You have no idea how I feel. I had no idea what it was all about so there was no way you could have known,' he said.

'I don't understand.' Harriet blinked almost frenziedly.

'Then I'll tell you.' He sat forward. 'I can't cope any more.'

'I still don't understand.'

'Harriet—' he fiddled with a pen for a long moment then looked into her eyes '—can I tell you a story?'

She nodded.

'I couldn't…right from the beginning I couldn't get you out of my mind. I told you that was why I agreed to see you again?'

'Two months later, though. I mean—I don't mean to nit-pick but it was that.'

He grimaced. 'You're entitled to nit-pick. But from then on I couldn't get you out of my mind. I couldn't believe you were still driving that ghastly old tank and I had to do something about it. I couldn't believe how much I worried about you. I couldn't believe how I kept coming up with jobs for you. I couldn't believe,' he said dryly, 'how the thought of your legs kept interfering with my sex life.'

Her lips parted. 'You mean...?' She looked incredulous.

'It's true. After I kissed you the first time,' he said wryly, 'I decided I'd either gone a bit mad or I needed some nice girl who understood the rules—no wedding bells, in other words—and I found a couple. But the trouble was, they had ordinary legs.'

Harriet put a hand to her mouth. 'I don't believe this,' she said indistinctly.

'You should,' he replied. 'Of course, it wasn't only their legs. I simply didn't seem to be attracted to anyone any more—anyone who wasn't you, that is.'

'Are you serious?'

He studied her wide eyes and the look of shock in them. 'I've never been more serious, I've never been as confused, as I was for a while, in my whole life. I've never felt as rejected as I did the night of Charlie's accident when you...'

'Don't.' Harriet closed her eyes briefly. 'I felt terrible then, and the night of his birthday party.'

'Good,' he said gravely but his eyes were wicked.

She bit her lip. 'I did seriously not want to be on your conscience, though, I still do,' she said then with more spirit. 'I mean I still don't want to be—there,' she elucidated.

'I know what you mean and you're not. It's something else altogether and it only started to come home to me when you ran into the gatepost.'

'Don't,' she pleaded. 'Don't bring up those things. They meant nothing.'

'Maybe not to you but they did to me. They were all part of the picture, you see.'

'What picture?' She frowned at him.

'The picture I loved. I *loved* you, Harriet Livingstone. That's why I cared so much about you. The thing I'd thought could *never* happen for me, had snuck up and hit me on the head, and I realised I was going to spend the rest of my *life* worrying about you.'

They gazed at each other and she thought he suddenly looked pale.

'And loving you because I just can't help myself. All the rest of it, all my grudges and heaven knows what else, they suddenly counted for nothing.'

'Damien,' she whispered.

'Nothing had the power to change that or flaw it or make the slightest difference to how I felt about you. Remember the night you told me you weren't pregnant?'

She nodded.

'I couldn't believe how disappointed I was.'

Harriet stared at him with her lips parted. 'But…but you went away. You told me you wouldn't be harassing me on—on any subject.'

He grimaced. 'And I even managed to stick to that. But don't forget you told me that same day that you'd be a fool to want to be married to me after Veronica and how it had left me. You also hadn't had time to absorb the news about Simon Dexter and your best friend. And I thought—' He stopped abruptly.

'What?' she asked.

'That I could never get you to believe me.' He looked suddenly irritated to death. 'Especially after I'd told you *why* it was no good us contemplating any future together.' He gestured. 'I was also afraid that you could never love me.'

'Never love you?'

He froze as she repeated the phrase as if it had never occurred to her.

'Harriet,' he said ominously, 'you told me at the beginning that you were quite happy to remain fancy-free and you never, even after you slept with me, changed your position other than to a slight tinge of regret when I told you about Veronica!'

'Damien,' she said, 'can I tell you my story? It's not as long as yours but that slight tinge of regret you sensed when you told me about Veronica was in fact a torrent of sudden understanding. I *was* determined to stay "fancy free", I'd fooled myself into thinking I had but it suddenly hit me—that I'd fallen head over heels in love with you and it was the saddest moment of my life.'

He got up and came cautiously round the desk, almost as if he was feeling his way in the dark. 'You said you were sad about Simon.'

'No.' She shook her head. 'I was sad for Carol.' She shrugged.

'So.' He sat down on the corner of the desk. 'Have I been living in hell for these long months because I was a blind fool?' He pulled her upright and into his arms.

'I wouldn't say that. I guess we both had our demons.' She put her hands on his upper arms and all restraint suddenly vanished as they were consumed by an overwhelming hunger.

Harriet felt the blood surging through her veins as if she were on fire at his lightest touch. She felt incredibly aware of her body and of his. But it was more than that for Harriet, more than a sensual arousal that rocked them both; it was a feeling of safety, as if she'd come home, as if a part of her that had been wrenched away had been restored to her.

And when they drew apart she was crying as well as laughing, she was in a state of shock that told Damien more than words could how deep her feelings were.

'Harriet. Harriet,' he said into her hair as he cradled her in his arms, 'it's OK. We've made it. Don't cry.'

'I can't help it. I'm so happy.'

'Come.' He picked her up.

'Where?' she queried.

'You'll see.'

He took her to his bedroom, not the one his parents had used, not the one he'd shared with Veronica—a different room but with a familiar settee along one wall.

'See?' He put her down on it and sat down beside her.

Her tears changed to laughter. 'I couldn't believe how that upset me, the thought that you'd got rid of it!'

His lips twisted. 'You've no idea how good that is to hear.'

'Why?' she queried innocently

'Well, this old settee has brought back some memories.' He allowed his dark gaze to roam over her figure.

'I thought it might be something like that.' Her eyes glinted with humour but only for a moment, then desire replaced the humour and she put her hands on his shoulders, and hesitated.

He frowned. 'What is it?'

'Some other memories. The first time you kissed me it crossed my mind that you knew how to make love to a woman in a way that thrilled her and drove her to excesses she didn't know she could reach... I was right. That night and this settee proved it to me. It had never happened to me like that before. I didn't—' she smiled wryly '—quite recognise myself, even if I had believed I was an all or nothing person.'

Damien stared into her eyes for a long, long moment.

'Harriet,' he said finally, in a husky voice unlike his own, 'if you continue to make incendiary statements like that—we may never get off this settee.'

She laughed then they sobered and their need for each other was so great it wasn't only the settee that became involved but the floor then the bed.

'So you will marry me?' he said when they were lying in each other's arms, sated and in the dreamy aftermath of their passion.

'Yes.' She ran her fingers through his hair.

'Tomorrow?'

Harriet laughed softly. 'I don't think you can do it that fast but if you could I would.'

'On the other hand, coming back to reality, if we're going to do this,' he reflected, 'we might as well do it with style. Not big but with style.'

'Do you think I look all right?' Harriet said to Isabel two weeks later.

She was dressed and ready for her wedding.

She wore a white dress with lacy sleeves and a bouffant skirt that skimmed her knees. Her hair was fair, glossy and coaxed into ringlets. But she stared at herself in the bedroom mirror and sighed.

'You look beautiful,' Isabel replied. She'd been in a state of constant excitement ever since the wedding had been announced.

Harriet sighed again, however, as she continued to gaze at her reflection in the mirror.

'What?' Isabel queried as she produced a pair of new shoes out of a box for Harriet.

'It's just that when I first met Damien I looked a mess. Then, the next time we met, I looked like an attendant out of a museum. I'm just wondering if he doesn't prefer me looking—unusual.' She sat down on the bed to put her new shoes on.

'Honey,' Isabel said, 'believe me, he will love this you as much as all the others.'

'*You* look lovely,' Harriet said, taking in Isabel's camellia-pink linen suit. 'And I can't thank you enough for...for everything. You've been marvellous.'

Isabel sat down on the bed next to Harriet and picked up her hand. 'I knew someone once,' she said. 'I thought he was my north and my south but I wasn't prepared to play second fiddle to his career. And it would have meant a lot of time on my own. It would have meant bringing up our kids virtually on my own, it would have meant being the other woman to a career that was almost like a mistress to him. So I said no when he mentioned marriage.'

Isabel paused and looked into the distance. 'I sent him away and I've regretted it ever since.'

Harriet caught her breath. 'Can't—surely you could have—wasn't there some way you could have got together again?'

Isabel shook her head. 'By the time I'd realised what I'd done, and it took a few years to *really* realise it, he'd married someone else. So—' Isabel patted Harriet's hand again '—to see you and Damien so much in love and getting married when I was afraid it wasn't going to happen, when I thought it all was going to fail, means a lot to me.'

'Now you've made me cry!'

'Here, just fix your make-up and you'll be fine. But first, let me do this.' And she hugged Harriet warmly.

It was a beautiful day and the garden was looking its finest.

There was a table set up for the marriage celebrant with a cloth of gold and a marvellous bouquet of flowers fresh picked from the garden that morning. There were chairs set out for the guests on the lawn and there was a sumptuous buffet laid out on the veranda.

The guests, more than Harriet had expected, comprised close family friends and, of course, family. Charlie was there—apart from the slightest limp, he was quite recovered from his accident and he'd brought along a stunning brunette. He was also the best man.

Brett Livingstone was there, also almost fully mobile now and engaged to his physiotherapist. It was he who was to give Harriet away.

Arthur and Penny Tindall were there. Arthur wore a morning suit.

Harriet drew a very deep breath as she stepped out from her guest suite and paused for a moment.

Brett was waiting for her. And Damien who, thanks to Isabel's sense of tradition, she had not seen since yesterday, was waiting at the table in the garden with Charlie by his side.

'Ready?' Brett mouthed, his eyes full of affection as he held out his arm.

She nodded and something brushed against her legs—Tottie. Tottie, with a ribbon in her collar and a wide smile, as if to say, *It's OK. I'm here.*

Then she was beside Damien, who was looking quite breathtakingly handsome in a dark suit. And Brett stepped back, leaving her to her fate...

They exchanged a long glance that sent tremors through Harriet because that was the effect Damien had on her and always would, she suspected. Then his lips twisted and a wicked little glint lit his eyes. 'I like your dress. I was afraid you'd wear something long.'

'I was afraid you mightn't marry me if I did,' she whispered back.

'For crying out loud, who mightn't marry whom? Don't tell me you two are having second thoughts!' Charlie intervened, although sotto voce. 'I'm a nervous wreck already.'

'Why?' Damien and Harriet asked simultaneously.

'In case I lost the ring or dropped it or did something otherwise stupid.' He ran his finger round his neck inside his collar. 'Damn nerve-racking business this getting married bit. I might have second thoughts about it myself!'

Both Harriet and Damien laughed and the marriage celebrant cleared her throat and asked if she could proceed.

All three participants in front of her replied in the affirmative in a rather heartfelt manner, so she did.

Not many minutes later, Damien Richard Wyatt and Harriet Margaret Livingstone were pronounced man and wife and the bridegroom was told he might kiss the bride.

Damien put his arms around her. 'I *love* you,' he said and bent his head to kiss her lips.

But, at that moment, Penny Tindall, who had a rather penetrating voice, said, 'Arthur...Arthur, the baby's coming!'

And before the bemused gaze of the whole congregation plus the bridal party, Arthur Tindall sprang to his feet, and fainted.

'Things are running true to form,' Damien said to

Harriet. 'There's something about us getting within a cooee of each other that just invites chaos!'

They laughed together and went to rescue Arthur.

'It was always my deepest fear,' Arthur said that evening as he clutched a glass of brandy, 'that I would have to deliver the baby. That's what did it. That's what made me faint.'

In fact Penny's baby had been delivered in a maternity ward, as planned, admittedly after a rather fast trip in an ambulance, but both mother and daughter were fine.

* * * * *

WAVES OF TEMPTATION

BY
MARION LENNOX

Marion Lennox is a country girl, born on an Australian dairy farm. She moved on—mostly because the cows just weren't interested in her stories! Married to a 'very special doctor', Marion writes Mills & Boon Medical Romances, as well as for Mills & Boon Cherish. (She used a different name for each category for a while—if you're looking for her past Romances search for author Trisha David as well.) WAVES OF TEMPTATION is Marion Lennox's one-hundredth romance novel.

In her non-writing life Marion cares for kids, cats, dogs, chooks and goldfish. She travels, she fights her rampant garden (she's losing) and her house dust (she's lost). Having spun in circles for the first part of her life, she's now stepped back from her 'other' career, which was teaching statistics at her local university. Finally she's reprioritised her life, figured out what's important and discovered the joys of deep baths, romance and chocolate. Preferably all at the same time!

For Marion

PROLOGUE

SHE WAS HUDDLED as far from the receptionist in the funeral parlour as she could get. Curled into one of the reception area's plush chairs, she looked tiny, almost in a foetal position.

Her dirty, surf-blonded hair was matted and in desperate need of a cut. Her cut-off-at-the-thigh jeans were frayed, her too-big windcheater looked like something out of a charity bin and her bare feet were filthy. Her huge grey eyes were ringed with great dark shadows.

In ordinary circumstances, Matt Eveldene would have cast her a glance of sympathy. He might even have tossed her a few coins to get a decent meal.

Not now. Not this girl.

He knew as much about her as he'd ever want to know. Her name was Kelly Myers. No. Kelly Eveldene. She was seventeen years old and she was his brother's widow.

She rose as she saw him. She must know what he'd been doing—identifying for himself that the body lying in the funeral home's back room was indeed his brother's.

'I...I'm sorry,' she faltered, but she didn't approach him. Maybe his face stopped her. It was impossible to conceal his anger. The white-hot rage.

The waste...

He'd just seen Jessie. His beloved big brother. Jess, who'd laughed with him, teased him, protected him from the worst of their father's bullying.

Jessie, who was now dead, aged all of twenty-four. Jessie, who for some crazy, unfathomable reason had married this girl two weeks before he'd died.

'How can you be married to him?' he snapped. It was a dumb thing to ask, maybe even cruel, but it was all he could think of. He knew so little of what Jessie had been doing for the last few years. No one did. 'You're only seventeen.'

'He wanted to marry me,' she said, almost as a ghost might talk. As if her voice was coming from a long way away. 'He insisted. He even found my father and made him give permission. I guess...my father's still my guardian, even if—' She broke off and sat down again, hard, as if all the strength had gone out of her.

But Matt had no room left in his head for pity. Not now. He'd loved his big brother. Jess had been wild, free, bordering on manic, but he'd lit their lives. Or he'd lit Matt's. In the big old mansion overlooking Sydney's famous Bondi Beach, with its air of repressed elegance and propriety, and its walls echoing with his father's displeasure, it had always been Jess who'd brought in life.

But that life had been more and more out of control. The last time Matt had seen him he'd been in a rehabilitation ward in West Sydney. Jess had been twenty-two. Matt had been eighteen, confused and desperately frightened at the state of his big brother.

'I can't go back home, Matt,' Jess had told him. 'I know what Dad thinks of me and it always makes it worse. The black dog...depression...well, when you're older maybe you'll understand what it is. When I get out of here I'm heading overseas. Following the surf. The surf gets me out of my head like nothing else can. If I'm to stay off the drugs, that's what I need.'

What had followed then had been two years of intermittent postcards, the occasional press clipping of minor success in surf competitions, and demands that his parents didn't try and contact him until he'd 'found' himself.

Had he found himself now, on a slab in a Hawaiian mortuary? Jess... He thought back to the last time he'd seen his brother, as a recovering addict. Recovery had been for nothing, and now he was facing this girl who was calling herself Jessie's wife.

His anger was almost uncontrollable. He wanted to haul up her sleeves to expose the tracks of the inevitable drug use, and then hurl her as far as he could throw her.

Somehow he held himself still. He daren't unleash his fury.

'He wanted to be cremated,' the girl whispered. 'He wants his ashes scattered off Diamond Head, when the surf's at its best. At sunset. He has friends...'

Matt bet he did. More like this girl. This...

No. He wasn't going to say it. He wasn't going to think it.

Married! His father was right—he needed to pay the money and get rid of her, fast. If his mother knew of her existence, she might even want to bring her home, and then the whole sad round would start again. *'Please go to rehab... Please get help. Please...'*

He was too young to face this. He was twenty years old but he felt barely more than a child. His father should be here, to vent his anger, to do what he'd ordered Matt to do. Matt felt sick and weary and helpless.

'Can you afford cremation?' he demanded. The

girl—Kelly—shook her head. Her grey eyes were direct and honest, surprising him with their candour.

'No,' she replied, her voice as bleak as the death that surrounded them. 'I hoped... I hope you might help me.'

In what universe could he help a woman who'd watched his brother self-destruct? Even if she looked...

No, he told himself. Don't think about how she looks. Just get this over and get out of here.

'I'm taking my brother home,' he told her. 'My parents will bury him in Sydney.'

'Please—'

'No.' The sight of his brother's body was so recent and so raw he could barely speak. Dear God, Jess... He needed to be alone. He felt like the world was closing in on him, suffocating. How could his father demand this of him? This was killing him.

Maybe his father was punishing him, too. Punishing him for loving his big brother?

Enough. He had to leave. He hauled a chequebook from his jacket and started writing.

The girl sank back down into her chair, tucking her feet back under her, assuming once again that position of defence. Her eyes became blank.

The cheque written, he handed it to her. Or tried to. She didn't put out her hand and he was forced to drop it onto her grubby knee.

'My father had an insurance policy in my brother's name,' he said, struggling to hold back his distress. 'Even though we doubt the validity of your marriage, my father acknowledges that you may have a claim on it. This pre-empts that claim. This is the total value of the insurance policy, given to you on the condition that you make no contact with my parents, that you never attempt to tell my mother that Jess was married, that you keep yourself out of our lives, now and for ever. Is that clear?'

She didn't pick up the cheque. 'I would like to write to your mother,' she whispered.

'I can think of a hundred reasons why you shouldn't contact my mother,' he said grimly. 'The top one being she has had heartbreak enough and doesn't need to be lumbered with the mess you've made of your life as well. My father has decided not to tell her about the marriage and I understand why.'

She closed her eyes as if he'd struck her, and he found his fury fading.

This was unfair, he conceded. This girl was a mess, but, then, Jessie's life had been a mess, too. He didn't need to vent his grief solely on her—but he had to get out of there.

'Use the cheque,' he said. 'Get a life.'

'I don't want your cheque.'

'It's your cheque,' he said, anger surging again. 'It's nothing to do with me. All I want is for you—his *widow*—' and he gave the word his father's inflection, the inflection it deserved '—to sign the release for his body. Let me take him home.'

'He wouldn't have wanted—'

'He's dead,' he said flatly. 'We need to bury him. Surely my mother has rights, too.'

Her fingers had been clenched on her knees. Slowly they unclenched, but then, suddenly, she bent forward, holding her stomach, and her face lost any trace of remaining colour.

Shocked, he stooped, ready to catch her if she slumped, concerned despite himself, but in seconds she had herself under control again. And when she unbent and stared straight at him, she was controlled. Her eyes, barely twelve inches from his, were suddenly icy.

'Take him home, then. Give him to his mother.'

'Thank you.'

'I don't want your thanks. I want you to go away.'

Which fitted exactly with how he was feeling.

'Then we never need to see each other again. I wish you luck, Miss Myers,' he said stiffly. Dear God, he sounded like his father. He no longer felt like a child. He felt a hundred.

'I'm Kelly Eveldene.' It was a flash of unexpected fire and venom. 'I'm Mrs Eveldene to you. I'm Mrs Eveldene to the world."

'But not to my parents.'

'No,' she said, and she subsided again into misery. 'Jess wouldn't have wanted his mother hurt more than she has been. If you don't want to tell her, then don't.' Her face crumpled and he fought a crazy, irrational impulse to take her into his arms, to hold her, to comfort her as one might comfort a wounded child.

But this was no child. This girl was part of the group that had destroyed his brother. Drugs, surf, drugs, surf... It had been that way since Matt could remember.

Get out of here fast, he told himself. This girl has nothing to do with you. The cheque absolves you from all responsibility.

Wasn't that what his father had said?

'Sign the papers,' he told her roughly, rising to his feet with deliberation. 'And don't shoot the entire value of that cheque up your arm.'

She met his eyes again at that, and once again he saw fire.

'Go back to Australia,' she said flatly. 'I can see why Jessie ran.'

'It's nothing to do—'

'I'm not listening,' she snapped. 'I'll sign your papers. Go.'

Kelly sat where she was for a long time after Matt had left. The receptionist would like her gone. She could understand that, but she was the widow of the deceased. The funeral home would be repatriating the body to Australia. It'd be a nice little earner. It behoved the receptionist to be courteous, even if Kelly was messing with the décor.

She needed a wash. She conceded that, too. More, she needed a change of clothes, a feed and a sleep. About a month's sleep.

She was so tired she could scarcely move.

So tired...

The last few days had been appalling. She'd known Jess's depression had deepened but not this much, never this much. Still, when he'd disappeared she'd feared the worst, and the confirmation had been a nightmare. And now... She'd sat in this place waiting for so long...

Not for him, though. For his father. She hadn't expected a man who was scarcely older than she was.

Matt Eveldene. What sort of a name was Eveldene anyway?

A new one. She stared at the bright new ring on her finger, put there by Jess only weeks ago. 'You'll be safe now,' he'd told her. 'It's all I can do, but it should protect you.'

She'd known he was ill. She shouldn't have married him, but she'd been terrified, and he'd held her and she'd clung. But she hadn't been able to cling hard enough, and here she was, in this nightmare of a place.

She'd been here for almost twenty-four hours, waiting for whoever came as the representative of Jess's family. She knew they'd have to come here.

She had to ask.

'If ever something happens, will you scatter my ashes out to sea, babe?' Jess had asked her. Had that only been a week ago? It seemed like a year.

She'd failed at that, too. Matt had simply overridden her.

Like father, like son? Jess had told her of his bully of a father. She'd been gearing herself up to face Henry Eveldene, but Matt's arrival in his father's stead had thrown her.

She'd failed.

'I'm sorry,' she said to the closed door behind which Jessie's body lay. 'I'm so sorry, Jess.'

There was nothing more she could do.

She rose and took a deep breath, trying to figure how to find the strength to walk outside, catch a bus, get away from this place of death. Nausea swept over her again but she shoved it away. She didn't have the energy to be sick.

'Mrs Eveldene?' The receptionist's voice made her pause.

'Yes?' It was so hard to make her voice work.

'You've dropped your cheque,' the girl said. She walked out from behind her desk, stooped to retrieve it and handed it to her. As she did, she checked it, and her eyes widened.

'Wow,' she said. 'You wouldn't want to lose this, would you?'

Matt stood outside the funeral parlour, dug his hands deep into his pockets and stood absolutely still, waiting for the waves of shock and grief to subside. The image of Jess was burned on his retinas. His beautiful, adored big brother. His Jess, wasted, cold and dead on a mortuary slab.

He felt sick to the core. The anger inside him was building and building, but he knew deep down that it was only a way to deflect grief.

If he let his anger take hold he'd walk right back in there, pick up that piece of flotsam and shake her till her teeth rattled, but it would do no good at all. For that was all she was, a piece of detritus picked up somewhere along Jessie's useless mess of a life.

What a sickening waste.

But suddenly he found himself thinking of the girl inside, of those huge, desperate eyes. Another life heading for nothing.

But those eyes...that flash of anger...

That was more than waste, he thought. There was something that Jess had loved, even a kind of beauty, and, underneath the anger, part of him could see it.

He could turn around and try and help.

Yeah, like he'd tried to help with Jess. Useless, useless, useless.

He'd given her money to survive. 'Don't waste it all,' he found himself saying out loud, to no one, to the girl inside, to the bright Hawaiian sun. But it was a forlorn hope, as his hopes for Jessie had always been forlorn.

Enough. It was time to move forward. It was time to forget the waif-like beauty of the girl inside this nightmare of a place. It was time to accompany his brother's body home for burial.

It was time to get on with the rest of his life.

CHAPTER ONE

SHE HAD THE best job in the world—except right now.

Dr Kelly Eveldene was the physician in charge of the International Surf Pro-Tour. For the last four years she'd been head of the medical team that travelled with the world's top surfers. She was competent, she was popular, she understood the lingo, and she knew so many of the oldtimer surfers that the job suited her exactly.

There were a couple of downsides. This year the pro tournament had moved to Australia for the world championships. She wasn't happy about coming to Australia, but Australia was big. The other Eveldenes lived in Sydney and the surf championship was to be held on the Gold Coast in Queensland. Her chances of running into...anybody were minuscule.

She'd done the research now. Henry Eveldene—her ex-father-in-law—was a business tycoon, rich beyond belief, and Eveldene was an uncommon name. Still, surely the presence in the country of a couple of inconspicuous people with similar names wouldn't come to his attention.

Her other quibble was that Jess was competing this year, his first time out of juniors. He was seventeen years old, surf mad and as skilled as his father before him. She couldn't hold him back and she didn't want to try. Her son was awesome. But now, at this level, with the surf so big and Jess trying so hard, she had qualms.

She had qualms right now.

She was in the judging tent on the headland, as she always was during competition. There were paramedics on jet skis close to the beach, ready for anything that happened in the surf. In the event of an accident she'd be on the beach in seconds, ready to take charge as soon as casualties wcrc brought in. If it looked like a head or spinal injury—and after long experience with the surf she could pretty much tell from seeing the impact what to expect—she'd be out there with the paramedics, organising spinal boards from the jet ski, binding open wounds so they didn't bleed out in the water, even doing resuscitation if it was needed.

The job had its grim moments, but at this professional level she was seldom needed for high drama. What she dealt with mostly were cuts, bruises, rashes and sunburn, plus the chance to combine her medicine with the surfing she loved. It was a great job.

But now Jess was competing and her heart was in her mouth.

He had thirty minutes to show the judges what he could do. The first wave he'd caught had shown promise but had failed to deliver. It hadn't given him a chance to show his skills. He'd be marked down and he knew it. He hit the shallows, flagged down an official jet ski and was towed straight out again.

Then there was an interminable ten minutes when the swell refused to co-operate, when nothing happened, when he lay on his board in the sun while the clock ticked down, down. Then, finally, magically, a long, low swell built from the north-east, building fast, and Kelly saw her son's body tense in anticipation.

Please…

She should be impartial. She was an official, for heaven's sake.

But she wasn't impartial. She wasn't a judge. For this moment she wasn't even Dr Eveldene. She was Jessie's mother and nothing else mattered.

He'd caught it. The wave was building behind him, swelling with a force that promised a long, cresting ride. The perfect wave? He rode to the lip and crested down, swooped, spun, climbed high again.

But…but…

There was another wave cresting in from the south-east. The surfers called this type of wave a rogue, a swell that cut across the magic wave that had seemed perfect for the best of the rides.

Jess wouldn't be able to see it, Kelly thought in dismay, but maybe it wouldn't matter. Maybe his wave would peak and subside before it was interfered with. And even the waves crashed together, surely he'd done enough now to progress through to the next stage.

But then…

Someone else was on the rogue wave.

The surf had been cleared for the competition. No one had the right to cut across a competitor's wave. Only the competitors themselves were in the catching zone—everyone else was excluded. But a pod of enthusiastic juniors had set themselves up south of the exclusion zone, lying far out, hoping to get a better view of the surfer pros. This must be one of those kids, finding a huge swell behind him, unable to resist catching it, too much of a rookie—a grommet—to see that it would take him straight into a competition wave.

Uh-oh. Uh-oh, uh-oh, uh-oh.

The judges were on their feet. 'Swing off. Get off,'

the judge beside Kelly roared. His voice went straight into the loudspeaker and out over the beach but the surfers were too far out, too intent on their waves...

Jess was in the green room, the perfect turquoise curve of water. He'd be flying, Kelly knew, awed that he'd caught such a perfect wave at such a time, intent on showing every ounce of skill he possessed. He'd be totally unaware that right behind...

No. Not right behind. The waves thumped into each other with a mighty crest of white foam. The grommet's surfboard flew as high as his leg rope allowed, straight up and then crashing down.

She couldn't see Jess. *She couldn't see Jess.*

That impact, at that speed...

'Kelly, go,' the judge beside her yelled, and she went, but not with professional speed. Faster.

This was no doctor heading out into the waves to see what two surfers had done to themselves.

This was Jessie's mother and she was terrified.

'Matt, you're needed in Emergency, stat. Leg fracture, limited, intermittent blood supply. If we're to save the leg we need to move fast.'

It was the end of a lazy Tuesday afternoon. Matt Eveldene, Gold Coast Central Hospital's orthopaedic surgeon, had had an extraordinarily slack day. The weather was fabulous, the sea was glistening and some of the best surfers in the world were surfing their hearts out three blocks from the hospital.

Matt had strolled across to the esplanade at lunchtime. He'd watched for a little while, admiring their skill but wondering how many of these youngsters were putting their futures at risk while they pushed themselves to their limits. No one else seemed to be thinking that. They were all just entranced with the surfers.

Even his patients seemed to have put their ills on hold today. He'd done a full theatre list this morning, but almost half his afternoon's outpatient list had cancelled. He'd been considering going home early.

Not now. Beth, the admitting officer in Accident and Emergency, didn't call him unless there was genuine need. She met him as the lift opened.

'Two boys,' Beth told him, falling in beside him, walking fast, using this time to get him up to speed. 'They're surfers who hit each other mid-ride. The youngest is a local, fourteen years old, concussion and query broken arm. It's the other I'm worrying about. Seventeen, American, part of the competition. Compound fracture of the femoral shaft, and I suspect a compromised blood supply. I've called Caroline—she's on her way.'

Caroline Isram was their vascular surgeon but Matt knew she was still in Theatre.

'He'll need both your skills if we're going to save the leg,' Beth said. 'Oh, and, Matt?'

'Yeah?'

'Coincidence or not? His surname's Eveldene.'

'Coincidence. I don't know any seventeen-year-old surfer.'

Kelly was seated by the bed in Cubicle Five, holding Jess's hand. It said a lot for how badly he was hurt that he let her.

He had enough painkillers on board to be making him drowsy but he was still hurting. She was holding his hand tightly, willing him to stay still. The colour of his leg was waxing and waning. She'd done everything she could to align his leg but the blood supply was compromised.

Dear God, let there be skilled surgeons in this hospital. Dear God, hurry.

'They say the orthopaedic surgeon's on his way,' she whispered. 'The emergency doctor, Beth, says he's the best in Australia. He'll set your leg and you'll be good as new.' *Please.*

'But I'll miss the championships,' Jess moaned, refusing to be comforted.

The championships were the least of their problems, Kelly thought grimly. There was a real risk he'd lose a lot more. Please, let this guy be good.

And then the curtains opened and her appalling day got even worse.

The last time Matt had seen his brother alive Jess had been in drug rehab. He'd looked thin, frightened and totally washed out.

The kid on the trolley when Matt hauled back the curtain was...Jess.

For a moment he couldn't move. He stared down at the bed and Jessie's eyes gazed back at him. The kid's damp hair, sun-bleached, blond and tangled, was spreadeagled on the pillow around him. His green eyes were wide with pain. His nose and his lips showed traces of white zinc, but the freckles underneath were all Jessie's.

It was all Matt could do not to buckle.

Ghosts didn't exist.

They must. This was Jessie.

'This is Mr Eveldene, our chief orthopaedic surgeon,' Beth was telling the kid brightly. The situation was urgent, they all knew it, but Beth was taking a moment to

reassure and to settle the teenager. 'Matt, this is Jessie
Eveldene. He has the same surname as yours, isn't that
a coincidence? Jess is from Hawaii, part of the pro-surf
circuit, and he's seventeen. And this is his mum, Kelly.
Kelly's not your normal spectator mum. She was Jessie's treating doctor on the beach. She's established circulation, she's put the leg in a long leg splint and she's
given initial pain relief.'

He was having trouble hearing. His head was reeling. What were the odds of a kid called Jessie Eveldene
turning up in his hospital? What were the odds such a
kid would look like Jess?

Sure, this kid was a surfer and all surfers had similar characteristics. Bleached hair. Zinc on their faces.
But…but…

The kid's green eyes were Jessie's eyes, and they
were looking at him as Jess's had looked that last time.

Make the pain go away.

Focus on medicine, he told himself harshly. This
wasn't his older brother. This was a kid with a compromised blood supply. He flipped the sheet over the
leg cradle and it was all he could do not to wince. The
undamaged foot was colourless. He touched the ankle,
searching for a pulse. Intermittent. Dangerously weak.

'We took X-rays on the way in,' Beth told him.
'Comminuted fracture. That means there's more than
one break across the leg,' she said, for Jessie's benefit.
'Matt, he needs your skill.'

He did. The leg was a mess. The compound fracture
had been roughly splinted into position but he could see
how it had shattered. Splinters of bone were protruding
from the broken skin.

'Blood flow was compromised on impact,' Beth said
softly. 'Luckily Jess has one awesome mum. It seems

Kelly was on duty as surf doctor. She went out on a jet ski and got Jess's leg aligned almost before they reached the shore. The time completely without blood couldn't have been more than a few minutes.'

So it was possible he'd keep his leg. Thanks to this woman.

He glanced at her again.

Kelly?

It was impossible to reconcile this woman with the Kelly he'd met so briefly all those years ago. This couldn't possibly be her.

But then her eyes met his. Behind her eyes he saw pain and distress, but also…a hint of steel.

Kelly. A woman he'd blamed…

'Well done,' he said briefly, because that was all he could think of to say. Then he turned back to the boy. If they had a chance of keeping this leg, he had to move fast. 'Beth, we need an ultrasound, right away. Tell Caroline this is priority. This blood flow seems fragile. Jess…' He had to force himself to say the name. 'Jess, you've made a dog's breakfast of this leg.'

'Dog's breakfast?' Jess queried cautiously.

'Dog's breakfast,' Matt repeated, and summoned a grin. 'Sorry, I forgot you were a foreigner.' Gruesome humour often helped when treating teens, and he needed it now. The anaesthetist needed Jess settled—and he needed to settle himself. 'It's slang. A working dog's breakfast is usually a mess of leftovers. That's what this looks like.'

'Ugh,' Jess said, and Matt firmed his grin.

'Exactly. We need to pin it back together and make sure enough blood gets through to your toes. That means surgery, straight away.'

The kid's sense of humour had been caught despite

the pain. 'Cool...cool description,' he said bravely. 'Do you reckon someone could take a picture so I can put it on Facebook? My mates will think "dog's breakfast" is sick.'

'Sure,' Beth said easily. She'd stepped back to snap orders into her phone but she resurfaced to smile. Beth had teenage boys of her own. Priority one, Facebook. Priority two, fixing a leg. She waved her phone. 'I'll snap it now if that's okay with your mum. But then it's Theatre to make you beautiful again.'

'If your mother agrees,' Matt said.

Jess's mother. Kelly. Doctor in charge at the world surf championships.

Kelly Eveldene. The undernourished waif curled up in a funeral director's parlour eighteen years ago?

The images didn't mesh and Matt didn't have time to get his head around it. The boy's leg was dreadfully fractured, the blood supply had already been compromised and any minute a sliver of bone could compromise it again. Or shift and slice into an artery.

'You have my permission,' Kelly said, her voice not quite steady. 'If it's okay with you, Jessie?'

What kind of mother referred to her kid for such a decision? But Kelly really was deferring. She had hold of her son's hand, waiting for his decision.

Jessie. This was doing his head in.

Maybe he should pull away; haul in a colleague. Could he be impersonal?

Of course he could. He had to be. To refer to another surgeon would mean a two-hour transfer to Brisbane.

No. Once he was in Theatre this would be an intricate jigsaw of shattered bone and nothing else would matter. He could ignore personal confusion. He could be professional.

'Matt, Jessie's mother is Dr Kelly Eveldene,' Beth was saying. 'She's an emergency physician trained in Hawaii.'

'Mr Eveldene and I have met before,' the woman said, and Matt's world grew even more confused.

'So it's not a coincidence?' Beth said. 'Matt...'

Enough. Talking had to stop. History had to take a back seat. These toes were too cool.

'Jess, we need to get you to surgery now,' he told the boy. There was no way to sugar-coat this. 'Your leg's kinking at an angle that's threatening to cut off blood supply. Caroline Isram is our vascular surgeon and she's on her way. Together we have every chance of fixing this. Do we have your permission to operate? And your mother's?'

Finally, he turned to face her.

Kelly Eveldene had been a half-starved drug addict who'd been with his brother when he'd died. This was not Kelly Eveldene. This was a competent-looking woman, five feet six or seven tall, clear, grey eyes, clear skin, shiny chestnut curls caught back in a casual wispy knot, quality jeans, crisp white T-shirt and an official surf tour lanyard on a cord round her neck saying, 'Dr Kelly Eveldene. Pro Surf Medical Director.'

Mr Eveldene and I have met before.

'Are you a long-lost relative?' Jess asked, almost shyly. 'I mean, Eveldene's not that common a name.'

'I think I must be,' Matt said, purposely not meeting Kelly's eyes. 'But we can figure that out after the operation. If you agree to the procedure.'

'Dr Beth says you're good.'

'I'm good.' No place here for false modesty.

'And you'll fix my leg so I can keep surfing?'

Something wrenched in him at that. Suddenly he

heard Jess, long ago, yelling at his father over the breakfast table. 'All I want to do is surf. Don't you understand?' And then saw Jessie arriving home from school that night, and finding his board in the backyard, hacked into a thousand pieces.

But now wasn't the time for remembering. Now wasn't the time to be even a fraction as judgmental as his father had been.

'I'll do my best,' he said, holding Jessie's gaze even though it felt like it was tearing him apart to do so. 'Jess, I won't lie to you—this is a really bad break, but if you let us operate now I think you'll have every chance of hanging ten or whatever you do for as long as you want.'

'Thank you,' Jess said simply, and squeezed his mother's hand. 'Go for it. But take a picture for Facebook first.'

She'd been a doctor now for nine years, but she'd never sat on this side of the theatre doors. She'd never known how hard the waiting would be. Her Jess was on the operating table, his future in the hands of one Matt Eveldene.

Kelly had trained in emergency medicine but surfing had been her childhood, so when she'd qualified, she'd returned. Her surfing friends were those who'd supported her when she'd needed them most, so it was natural that she be drawn back to their world. She'd seen enough wipe-outs to know how much a doctor at the scene could help. Even before she'd qualified she'd been pushing to have a permanent doctor at the professional championships, and aiming for that position after qualification had seemed a natural fit.

But she'd spent time in hospitals in training, and she'd assisted time and time again when bad things had happened to surfers. She knew first-hand that doctors weren't miracle workers.

So now she was staring at the doors, willing them to open. It had been more than three hours. Surely soon…

How would Jess cope if he was left with residual weakness? Or with losing his leg entirely? It didn't bear thinking about. Surfing wasn't his whole life but it was enough. It'd break his heart.

And Matt Eveldene was operating. What bad fairy was responsible for him being orthopaedic surgeon at the very place Jess had had his accident? Wasn't he supposed to still be in Sydney with his appalling family? If she'd known he was here she would never have come.

Had she broken her promise by being here?

You keep yourself out of our lives, now and for ever.

She'd cashed the cheque and that had meant acceptance of his terms. The cheque had been Jessie's insurance, though. Her husband's insurance. Surely a promise couldn't negate that.

The cheque had saved her life. No, she thought savagely. Her Jess had saved her life. Her husband. Her lovely, sun-bleached surfer who'd picked her up when she'd been at rock bottom, who'd held her, who'd made her feel safe for the first time. Who'd had demons of his own but who'd faced them with courage and with honour.

'We'll get through this together, babe,' he'd told her. 'The crap hand you've been dealt…my black dog… We'll face them both down.'

But the black dog had been too big, too savage, and in the end she hadn't been able to love him enough to keep it at bay. The night he'd died…

Enough. Don't go there. In a few minutes she'd have to face his brother, and maybe she would have to go there again, but only briefly, only as long as it took to explain that she hadn't broken her promise deliberately. She and Jess would move out of his life as soon as possible, and they'd never return.

It took the combined skill of Matt Eveldene, a vascular surgeon, an anaesthetist and a team of four skilled nurses to save Jessie's leg.

'Whoever treated it on the beach knew what they were doing,' Caroline muttered. Gold Coast Central's vascular surgeon was in her late fifties, grim and dour at the best of times. Praise was not lightly given. 'This artery's been so badly damaged I have no idea how blood was getting through.'

She went back to doing what she was doing, arterial grafting, slow, meticulous work that meant all the difference between the leg functioning again or not. Matt was working as her assistant right now, removing shattered slivers of bone, waiting until the blood supply was fully established before he moved in to restore the leg's strength and function.

If Caroline got it right, if he could managed to fuse the leg to give it the right length, if there'd not been too much tissue damage, then the kid might…

Not the kid. Jessie.

The thought did his head in.

'I think we're fine here,' Caroline growled. 'Decent colour. Decent pulse. He's all yours, Matt.'

But as Matt moved in to take control he knew it was no such thing.

This kid wasn't his at all.

The doors swung open and Matt Eveldene was in front of her. He looked professional, a surgeon in theatre scrubs, hauling down his mask, pushing his cap wearily from his thatch of thick, black hair. How did he have black hair when Jessie's had been almost blond? Kelly wondered absent-mindedly. He was bigger than Jess, too. Stronger boned, somehow...harsher, but she could still see the resemblance. As she could see the resemblance to her son.

This man was Jessie's uncle. Family?

No. Her family was her son. No one else in the world qualified.

'It went well,' he said curtly from the door, and she felt her blood rush away from her face. She'd half risen but now she sat again, hard. He looked at her for a moment and then came across to sit beside her. Doctor deciding to treat her as a mother? Okay, she thought. She could deal with this, and surely it was better than last time. Better than brother treating her as a drug-addicted whore.

The operation had gone well. She should ask more. She couldn't.

There was only silence.

There was no one else in the small theatre waiting room. Only this man and her.

There were so many emotions running rampant in her mind that she didn't have a clue what to do with them.

'Define...define "well",' she managed, and was inordinately proud of herself that she'd managed that.

'Caroline had to graft to repair the artery,' he told her. 'But she's happy with the result. We have steady pulse, normal flow. Then I've used a titanium rod. You know about intramedullary nailing? There wasn't enough bone structure left to repair any other way. But the breaks were above the knee and below the hip—

well clear—so we've been able to use just the one rod
and no plates. He has a couple of nasty gashes—well,
you saw them. Because the bone fragments broke the
skin we need to be extra-cautious about infection. Also
Caroline's wary of clotting. He'll spend maybe a week
in hospital until we're sure the blood flow stays steady.
After that, rest and rehabilitation in a controlled environment where we know he can't do further damage.
You know this'll be a long haul.'

'It'll break his heart,' Kelly whispered. 'It's going to
be six months before he's back on a surfboard.'

'Six months is hardly a lifetime,' Matt said, maybe
more harshly than he should have. 'He'll have some
interesting scars but long term nothing a surfer won't
brag about. Depending on his growth—at seventeen
there may or may not be growth to come—we may
need to organise an extension down the track but the
rod itself can be extended. Unless he grows a foot he
should be fine.'

So he'd still be able to surf. She hadn't realised quite
how frightened she'd been. She felt her body sag. Matt
made a move as if to put a hand on her shoulder—and
then he pulled away.

He would have touched her if she'd been a normal
parent, she thought. He would have offered comfort.

Not to her.

It didn't matter. He'd done what she'd most needed
him to do and that was enough.

She made to rise, but his hand did come out then, did
touch her shoulder, but it wasn't comfort he was giving.
He was pressing her down. Insisting she stay.

'We need to talk,' he said. 'I believe I deserve an
explanation.'

She stilled. Deserve. *Deserve*!

'In what universe could you possibly deserve anything from me?' she managed.

'Jessie has a son!'

'So?'

'So my brother has fathered a child. My parents are grandparents. Don't you think we deserved to know?'

'I'm remembering a conversation,' she snapped, and the lethargy and shock of the last few hours were suddenly on the back burner. Words thrown at her over eighteen years ago were still vividly remembered. 'How could I not remember? Make no contact with your parents. Do not write. Never tell your mother Jess and I were married. Keep myself out of your lives, now and for ever. You said there were a hundred reasons why I should never contact you. You didn't give me one exception.'

'If you'd told me you were pregnant—'

'As I recall,' she managed, and it hurt to get the words out, 'you didn't want to know one single thing about me. Everything about me repelled you—I could see it on your face.'

'You were a drug addict.'

She took a deep breath, fighting for control. 'Really?' she asked, managing to keep her voice steady. 'Is that right? A drug addict? You figured that out all by yourself. On what evidence?'

He paused, raking his long, surgeon's fingers through his thatch of wavy, black hair. The gesture bought him some time and it made Kelly pause. Her anger faded, just a little.

The present flooded back. This man had saved her son's leg. Maybe she needed to cut him some slack.

But it seemed slack wasn't necessary. He'd gone past some personal boundary and was drawing back.

'No,' he said. 'I made…I made assumptions when Jess died. I know now that at least some of them were wrong.'

Her anger had faded to bitterness. 'You got the autopsy report, huh?'

'You need to realise the last time I saw Jessie alive he was in drug rehab.'

'That was years before he died.'

'He told you about it?'

'Jess was my husband,' she snapped. 'Of course he told me.'

'You were seventeen!'

'And needy. Jess was twenty-four and needy. We clung to each other.' She shook her head. 'Sorry, but I don't have to listen to this. You never wanted to know about me before, and you don't now. Thank you very much for saving my son's leg. I guess I'll see you over the next few days while he's in hospital but I'll steer clear as much as I can. I need to go back to our hotel and get Jess's things, but I want to see him first. Is he awake?'

'Give him a while. We put him pretty deeply under.' He raked his hair again, looking as if he was searching for something to say. Anything. And finally it came.

'You weren't on drugs?'

'You know,' she said, quite mildly, 'years ago I wanted to hit you. I was too exhausted to hit you then, too emotionally overwrought, too wrecked. Now I'm finding I want to hit you all over again. If it wasn't for what you've just done for Jess, I would.'

'You looked—'

'I looked like my husband had just died.' Her voice grew softer, dangerously so. 'I was seventeen. I was twelve weeks pregnant and I'd sat by Jess's bedside for twenty-four hours while he lost his fight to live. Then I'd sat in the waiting room at the funeral home, waiting for you, hour upon endless hour, because I thought that it'd be his father who'd come to get him and I didn't think a message to contact me would work. I couldn't risk missing him. And then you walked in instead, and I thought, yes, Matt's come in his father's stead and it'll be okay, because Jess had told me how much he loved you. All I asked was for what Jess wanted, but you walked all over me, as if I was a piece of pond scum. And now... now you're still telling me I looked like a drug addict?'

There was a long silence. She didn't know where to go with this. She'd bottled up these emotions for years and she'd never thought she'd get a chance to say them.

Somewhere in Sydney, in a family vault, lay Jess's ashes. She'd failed the only thing Jess had ever asked of her. She hadn't stood up to his family.

She should hate this man. Maybe she did, but he was looking shocked and sick, and she felt...she felt...

Like she couldn't afford to feel.

'I'll grab Jess's things and bring them back,' she said, deciding brisk and efficient was the way to go. 'It's only ten minutes' walk to the hotel. I should be back before he's properly awake. The rest of the surfers will be worried, too. There are a lot of people who love my Jess—practically family. Thank you for your help this afternoon, Matt Eveldene, but goodbye. I don't think there's single thing left that we need to talk about.'

There was. She knew there was. She walked down the hill from the hospital to the string of beachside hotels where most of the surfers were staying and she knew this wouldn't end here.

Why did Jess look so much like his father? Why had she called him Jess?

Why had she kept her husband's name?

'Because it was all I had of him,' she said out loud, and in truth she loved it that her son was called Jessie, she loved that he loved surfing, she loved that when she looked at him she could see his father.

But not if it meant…loss?

Her husband had told her about his family, his father in particular. 'He controls everything, Kelly. It's his way or no way. He loathed my surfing. He loathed everything that gave me pleasure, and when I got sick he labelled me a weakling. Depression? Snap out of it, he told me, over and over. Pull yourself together. I couldn't cope. That's why I hit the drugs that first time.'

She knew as much as she ever wanted to know about Jessie's father—but he'd also told her about his brother, Matt.

'He's the only good thing about my family, Kell. If anything ever happens to me, go to him. He'll help you.'

Well, he had helped her, Kelly thought grimly. She thought of the insurance cheque. It had been tossed at her in anger but she owed everything to it.

'So Jess might have been wrong about him being a nice guy, but he's had his uses,' she told herself. 'Now forget about him. You have enough to worry about without past history. For instance, the surf tour's moving on. You'll need to take leave. You'll need a place to stay, and you'll need to figure a way to stop Jess's heart from breaking when he learns that he's no longer part of the surf circuit.'

He felt like he'd been hit with a sledgehammer.

Matt walked up to the hospital rooftop, to the cafeteria area that looked out over the ocean. He leant on the rail overlooking the amazing view, trying to let the enormity of what had just happened sink in.

Jessie had a son. Somehow, his brother wasn't dead.

Okay, that was a crazy thing to think but right now that was how it seemed. He knew if he phoned his mother—'You have a grandson. He's named Jess and he looks just like our Jessie'—his mother would be on the next plane. She'd broken her heart when Jess had died, and she'd never got over it. Always a doormat to her bully of a husband, she'd faded into silent misery. Matt worried about her, but not enough to stay in Sydney, not enough to stay near his father.

Should he tell his mother? He must. But if he told his mother, his father would know, too. There was the rub. Could you fight for custody of a seventeen-year-old boy? No, Matt thought, but knowing his father, he'd try. Or, worse, he'd let loose the anger he still carried toward his older son and unleash it on Kelly and his grandson.

The thought of his father bullying Kelly...

As he'd bullied her...

He thought back to the appalling funeral parlour scene and he felt ill.

He'd been a kid himself, a student. The call had come late at night; Jess had had a fall and died. Yes, it seemed to be suicide. His body was at a Hawaiian funeral home and a woman calling herself his wife was making the arrangements.

His father had exploded with grief and rage. 'Stupid, idiotic, surfer hop-head. You needn't think I'm heading off to that place to see him. You do it, boy. Go and get him, bring him home so his mother can bury him and there's an end to it.'

'They say he's married?'

'He's been off his head for years. If there's a marriage get it annulled. We have more than enough evidence to say he was mentally incapable. And don't tell
your mother. Just fix it.'

But Jess had never been mentally incapable. The
depression that had dogged him since adolescence had
been an illness, the same way cancer was an illness. Underneath the depression and, yes, the drugs when he'd
been using, he'd still been Jess, the gentle, soft-spoken
big brother Matt had loved.

He might have known he'd have married a woman
of spirit.

But a seventeen-year-old?

He'd judged her back then because of her appearance and obvious desperation, but things were making
horrible sense now.

All apart from the age. Surely seventeen was under-
age for marriage in Hawaii? They'd have needed special permission.

Had they done it because Kelly had been pregnant?

These were questions Matt should have asked years
ago, not now.

The questions had been there, though. He'd flown
home with Jessie's body and the questions had rested
unanswered in the back of his mind. The image of a girl
curled in utter misery, of a cheque floating to the floor,
of a desperation he'd done nothing to assuage, these images had stayed with him. The questions had nagged
while he'd qualified as a doctor, while he'd got himself
away from his domineering father, while he'd attempted
his own marriage... While he'd come to terms with life,
as Jessie never had. Just as Kelly had obviously come
to terms with her life.

He remembered his relief when he'd found the cheque

had been cashed. Now I don't need to feel guilty, he'd told himself. But the questions had stayed.

They had been answered now—almost. She'd used the cheque, but to what purpose?

To train herself in medicine?

To raise another surfer like Jess?

If his father found out... To have a grandson addicted to surfing...

Better not to tell him. Better to leave things as they were, just get this kid well and on his way.

But he looked so much like Jess...

So? He'd be in hospital for a week or so and then an outpatient for longer with rehab. He'd see him a lot. He had to get used to it.

And his mother?

Her image haunted him. In truth, her image had haunted him for years and now there was this new image juxtapositioned on the old.

Should the new image make the haunting go away?

A surf doctor. What sort of doctor was that?

What sort of woman was that?

A woman with spirit.

How could he know that?

He just...knew. There was that about her, an indefinable strength. A beauty that was far more than skin deep.

Beauty? He raked his hair again, thinking he wasn't making sense. He was too tired, too shocked to take it in. He needed to go home.

At the thought of his home he felt his tension ease. Home, the place he'd built with effort and with love. Home with his dogs and his books.

His house was the only place where he was at peace.

His home mattered. He'd learned early and learned hard; people only complicated that peace.

He needed to go home now and put this woman and her son out of his head.

He needed to be alone.

CHAPTER TWO

THE SURF CHAMPIONSHIPS lasted for two more days and Kelly worked for both of them. There were gaps in the day when she could visit Jess, but she had to work for as long as she could. She needed the money.

The surfing community looked after its own, but there wasn't a lot they could do to help. They'd need to employ another doctor for the next round of the championships in New Zealand. As soon as Jess was well enough for Kelly to rejoin the tour, the position was hers again, but pro-surfing ran on the smell of a surf-waxed rag, and they couldn't afford to pay her for time off.

And she would not use the trust fund.

She needed to move from the hotel. One of the locals offered her a basic surfer's squat and she accepted with relief. She'd find a decent apartment when Jess was released from hospital but until then she'd live in her surf squat and focus on Jess's recovery.

From Jessie's charts and from information she drew from junior doctors, she could track Jessie's progress. There was therefore no need to talk to Matt Eveldene. The advantage of Matt being head of the orthopaedic ward was that where Matt went, students followed. She could always hear him coming so she could give Jess a quick hug and disappear.

'Here come the medical cavalry. It's time to make myself scarce.'

'He looks at me funny,' Jess said sleepily on the second day, and she hugged him again, feeling defensive about leaving him.

'Surgeons are a law unto themselves,' she said. 'If he only looks at you funny, you're getting off lightly. These guys spend their days looking inside people, not practising social skills.'

The surf tour moved on. She spent a couple of hours of her first free day moving into her dreary little apartment. Back at the hospital she found Jess awake and bored, so she spent an hour going over the results of the championship he'd missed out on, talking future tactics, as if those tactics might be useful next week instead of in six months.

Finally he went to sleep. What to do now? She knew how long rehabilitation would take. She had weeks and weeks of wondering what to do.

Okay, do what came next. Lunch. She slipped out to find some—and Matt was at the nurses' station.

Was he waiting for her? It looked like it. His hands were deep in the pockets of his gorgeous suit, he was talking to a nurse but he was watching Jess's door. As soon as he saw her, he broke off the conversation.

'Sorry, Jan,' he said to the nurse, 'but I need to speak to Mrs Eveldene.'

'That's Dr Eveldene,' she said as he approached, because her professional title suddenly seemed important. She needed a barrier between them, any barrier at all, and putting things on a professional level seemed the sensible way to achieve it. 'Do you need to discuss Jessie's treatment?'

'I want lunch,' he growled. 'There's a quiet place

on the roof. We can buy sandwiches at the cafeteria. Come with me.'

'Say "please",' she said, weirdly belligerent, and he stared at her as if she was something from outer space.

But: 'Please,' he said at last, and she gave him a courteous nod. This man was in charge of her son's treatment. She did need to be…spoken to.

They bought their lunches, paid for separately at her insistence. He offered but she was brusque in her refusal. She followed him to a secluded corner of the rooftop, with chairs, tables and umbrellas for shade. She spent time unwrapping her sandwich—why was she so nervous?—but finally there was nothing left to do but face the conversation.

He spoke first, and it was nothing to do with her son's treatment. It was as if the words had to be dragged out of him.

'First, I need to apologise,' he said. As she frowned and made to speak, he held up his hands as if to ward off her words. 'Hear me out. Heaven knows, this needs to be said. Kelly, eighteen years ago I treated you as no human should ever treat another, especially, unforgivably, as you were my brother's wife. I accused you of all sorts of things that day. My only defence was that I was a kid myself. I was devastated by my brother's death but my assumptions about him—and about you—were not only cruel, they were wrong.'

'As in you assumed Jess was back using drugs,' she whispered. 'As you assumed I was the same. An addict.'

'I figured it out almost as soon as I got back to Australia,' he said, even more heavily. 'The autopsy results revealed not so much as an aspirin. I should have contacted you again, but by then I was back at university and it felt…' He shook his head. 'No. I don't know how it felt. I was stuck in a vortex of grief I didn't know how to deal with. Somehow it was easier to shove the autopsy results away as wrong. Somehow it seemed easier to blame drugs rather than—'

'Unhappiness?'

'Yes.'

'Jess was clinically depressed,' she said. 'You're a doctor. You know it's different. He wasn't just unhappy; he was ill.'

'No antidepressants showed up either.'

'He wouldn't touch antidepressants,' she said, not sure where this was going, not sure that she wanted to go with him. 'He'd fallen into addiction once and it terrified him. In all the time I knew him, he took nothing.'

'How long did you know him?'

She shouldn't say. She didn't owe this man an explanation, and her story hurt. But it was also Jessie's story. It hadn't been told and maybe…maybe Jess would want his brother to know.

'Get in touch with Matt if anything happens to me,' he'd said to her, more than once. *'He'll look after you.'*

If anything happens to me… He'd obviously been thinking suicide. It still played in her mind, and it was still unbearable. So many questions… The questions surrounded her, nightmares still.

But maybe she had to expose a little of that pain. Matt was waiting for her to speak, and after all these years his gaze was non-judgmental. He wanted to know.

Eighteen years ago he hadn't asked, and she'd hated him. But then he'd been young and shocked and grieving, she conceded, and shock could be forgiven.

Almost. There was still a part of her that was that cringing seventeen-year-old, remembering this man's fury.

'I met Jess when I was sixteen,' she said, forcing herself to sound like the grown-up that she was. 'And I was a mess. But not because of drugs. I was just…neglected. My father was interested in surf and booze and nothing else. My mother disappeared when I was four—at least, I think it was my mother; my father never seemed sure. It didn't matter. It was just the way things were. I was dragged up in the surfing community. There were good people who looked out for me, but they were itinerant and there were lots who weren't so good. But all of them came and went. I stayed.'

'It must have been a tough upbringing,' he said quietly, and she nodded.

'You could say that. And then, of course, I reached my teenage years. I matured late, thanks be, but finally at sixteen I became…female, instead of just a kid. Then things got harder. Unprotected and often homeless, camping as we often did, I became a target and my father was little use. I was a little wildcat, doing my best to defend myself, but it couldn't last. Then Jess arrived. He set up on the outskirts of the camp, seemingly intent on surfing and nothing else. I didn't think he'd even noticed us but there was an ugly scene one night when someone offered my father money. I remember someone grabbing me as if he owned me.'

'You were so alone.'

'I… Yes.'

'With no one?'

'No one who cared.'

'Kelly—'

'It was a long time ago,' she said, and she even smiled a little. 'You know, when you spoke then, you sounded just like Jess. Just as angry on my behalf. That night he appeared out of the dark, out of nowhere, and he was furious. I hit out—and Jess moved in before the guy could retaliate. He just…took over.'

'Jess was always bringing home strays,' Matt said. His instinctive anger seemed to have settled and his tone gentled. *Strays.* The word drifted in her mind. She knew no offence had been meant and none had been taken, because that's exactly what she'd been. A stray. Living in temporary surf camps. Going to school when the surf camp had been close enough or when her father had been capable of taking her. Living hand to mouth, the only constant being the surf.

But then there'd been Jess.

'He was the best surfer,' she said, pain fading as she remembered the way he'd transformed her life. 'He'd only just arrived but everyone there respected him. He was also…large.' She eyed Matt's strongly built frame, his height—six three or so—his instinctive anger on her behalf—and she remembered Jess. For some reason it made her want to reach out and touch this man, comfort him, take away the pain behind his eyes.

She could do no such thing.

'He told me he hadn't seen his family for years,' she went on, trying to ignore the urge to comfort Matt. 'By the time you saw his body the depression had left its mark. He hadn't been eating for weeks. But imagine him as I first saw him. He lived and breathed surfing. He was beautiful. He was built like a tank. No one stood up to him—and yet he stood up for me.'

'You became his lover?'

There was a moment's pause. She really didn't want to go there, but she needed to tell it like it was. For Jessie's sake. He'd been her hero, not some low-life who'd picked up teenage girls.

'No,' she said at last. 'Believe it or not, I was sixteen and that was how Jess treated me. Dad and I were living in a rough beach shanty, but Dad left soon after Jess arrived, looking for better surf on the other side of the island. He came back every so often, but Jess built a lean-to on the side of our hut and we stayed put. Jess said it was to protect me and that's what he did. He surfed with me, but it wasn't all fun. He pushed me to go to school. I'd been going intermittently but Jess insisted I go every day. He gave me money for clothes. He stopped Dad…well, he kept me safe. He was my gorgeous big brother. But then the black dog got too much for him.'

'The depression.'

'He called it his black dog. He said that's what Winston Churchill called it and that's what it felt like. A great black dog, always shadowing him. He said it'd been shadowing him since he was a kid, something he was born with. He told me how his dad hated it, thought he was weak because of it. He told me about how'd he'd tried to escape with drugs when he was in his late teens, and what a mess that had been. I think that was a way of warning me, because drugs were everywhere in our scene. But Jess wouldn't touch them. Never again, he said, even near the end when the depression was so bad and I pleaded with him to get help. "They'll only give me pills," he said, "and I'm not going down that road again."'

'If I'd known…'

'Jess said you didn't want to know,' Kelly said gently. 'Jess said you and he were close, but after rehab… He knew that shocked you. After he got his life together and the surfing was helping, he said he sent you the airfare to come and have a holiday together during your university holidays, but you wouldn't come.'

Matt closed his eyes and she saw the pain wash over him. No. It was more than pain. Self-loathing.

'He'd come out of rehab and gone straight back to surfing,' Matt managed. 'I thought—'

'You know, surfing and drugs don't really mix,' she said gently. 'There are always the fringe dwellers, people like my dad who surf a bit but who love the sun-bleached lifestyle more than the skill itself. But to be a real surfer you're up at dawn, day after day. The sea demands absolute attention, absolute fitness. You need to work as Jess did—he did casual bricklaying to pay bills—but he surfed at dawn and then he was back at dusk to surf every night, falling into bed with every single part of him exhausted. Jess used the surf to drive away his demons and it mostly worked. He had no time for drugs. I swear he wasn't taking them. I swear.'

'I believe you,' Matt said heavily. 'Now. But back then…I'd just found out my brother had killed himself and, what's more, that he'd married a seventeen-year-old just before he'd died. What was I to think? And then…pregnant?'

'That was my fault,' she said evenly, but he shook his head.

'Seventeen was hardly old enough to consent.'

'In those last months Jess wasn't fit enough to think of age differences,' she said evenly. 'The depression was so bad he just…went away. Physically he left for a couple of weeks and when he returned to camp he looked gutted. I was terrified. He was limp, unable to make any decisions. He didn't want to surf. He didn't want to do anything. If I told you all he'd done for me… Well, I was so grateful, I loved him so much, and the state he was in, I was terrified. Anyway, I did everything, anything I could think of to pull him out of it, and in the end I just lay down and held him. I held him all I could, every way I could, and when he finally took me I was happy because I thought he was coming out of it. I thought…he must be.'

'Oh, Kelly…'

'And I'd bought condoms—of course I had—and we used them, but that first time, well, I had the experience of a newt and I guess I was doing the seducing and I didn't do it right and then I was pregnant.'

'You told him?'

'He guessed. And for a while that woke him up. We had this first morning when we knew… I'd woken up sick and he waited until I was better and we took the boards out beyond the surf break to watch the dawn. And we lay there talking about our baby like it might really exist, about this new life that was so exciting. Life for both of us had been crap but this new life… we planned for it. And Jess told me I'd be an awesome mother and he'd try, he'd really try. But that was the last time…'

Her voice trailed off. 'The last time. We came back to shore and Jess found my dad and forced him to sign consent. We married but the dog was back, and with such force that Jess couldn't fight it. He…he went away. I searched and searched but then the police came to find me. And the rest you know.'

The rest he knew?

The rest he guessed.

He'd left a pregnant kid, his brother's widow, to fend for herself.

He'd left her with money. At least he'd done that.

But that had been the least he could do, and it had been her money anyway.

He should have brought her home.

To what? He'd still been a medical student; he'd had no income himself. He'd been sent by his parents to bring his brother's body home, not his brother's widow. If he'd arrived back with Kelly…his father could have destroyed her.

She was twisting a curl round and round her finger. It was a nervous gesture, showing she was tense. He suddenly wanted to reach out and take her hand in his. Hold her still. Take away the pain he'd helped inflict.

He didn't. He couldn't.

'Don't beat up on yourself,' Kelly said gently. 'Matt, it was eighteen years ago. We've moved on.'

'How did you manage?'

'You left me a cheque, remember? I stood outside that day, staring at this obscene amount on a slip of paper, and I wanted to rip it up. And then I thought, this wasn't my money, it was Jess's, and I was carrying his baby. And I kept thinking of what Jess said to me over and over—"Babe, you're awesome, you can do anything." I thought of the biggest, best way I could keep his baby safe. "Go back to school." Jess had said it and said it. So I got a room with some surfing friends close to the high school and I went back.'

'And had a baby.'

'I had to stop for six months when Jessie was born,' she told him. 'But friends helped me out. I got choosy and I got stronger. My home was where my friends were, and I've made some good friends. It wasn't the easiest existence but finally I qualified and we were safe. Then, just after I got my first job in ER, a kid was hurt in an appalling surf accident. The surf pro-tour was in town and the kid had been hit in the neck by a stray board. He was moving after the accident, but he'd fractured C3. The bones shifted as he was being moved and he died almost as he reached us. The pro-tour organisers were so appalled they decided to fund a full-time medic. Career-wise it was my best fit, so here we are.'

'And what about Jess? Doesn't he go to school?'

'When we're in Hawaii. Otherwise he studies online. He's okay.'

'Online? That cheque was enough for a home,' Matt said roughly. 'It was enough to set you up for life.'

'I told you,' she said, and her voice wasn't rough but it was as determined as Matt's. 'My home's where my friends are. Jess and I have never needed bricks and mortar. Besides, that money is for Jess. Yes, I used some of it to become a doctor but I'm paying it back. By the time Jess turns twenty-one, his father's fund will be intact. He'll have an inheritance.'

'But what sort of career? Once my parents know—'

'Why would I want your parents to know?' She met his gaze, strong, sure, defiant, and he wondered how to answer that.

If his parents knew...

For his mother it'd be the most amazing gift. But his father...

Matt considered his bully of a father, and faltered.

He looked across the table at this amazing woman, and he thought...he thought...

'Tell me about Jess's leg,' Kelly said.

And he thought, yes. Medicine, that was easiest. Retreat to what he knew.

'It's looking okay,' he said. 'The open wounds are healing. We want him on IV antibiotics for another few days. The risks of bone infection after a compound fracture are too great to do otherwise. Caroline's positive about the arterial graft. The physiotherapists are already

working with him—you'll have seen that. We're thinking minimal weight bearing in a couple more days, and
then a slow rehab. Another few days in hospital until
Caroline's happy and then six weeks as an outpatient.'

'I'd like to take him back to Hawaii.'

'You know the dangers of blood clots and swelling. Caroline will concur. Six weeks minimum before
he flies.'

She'd known it. It was just hard hearing it. She'd have
to get a decent apartment and it'd cost a bomb. She bit
her lip, trying to hide her emotions.

There were always glitches. From the time she'd
been born she'd been faced with glitches. Everybody
faced them, she told herself. It was just that some of her
glitches were a bit more major than others.

'Kelly—'

'My name is Dr Eveldene,' she snapped, and then
flinched. She had to be polite. 'Sorry. This is not your
business. You fix Jess, I'll do the rest.'

'I'd like to help.'

'You already did,' she said brusquely. 'You helped
save Jess's leg and more. Eighteen years ago you threw
me a cheque. It took me through medical school and
it gave Jess and me a life. That's enough. I don't need
more from your family.'

'It was,' he said slowly, 'your money.'

'You gave it to me.'

'I threw it at you, yes, but whatever I said at the time
it was legally yours. My father made out insurance poli-
cies the day we were born—he values his assets, does
our father, and he insures them all. But the policy was in
Jess's name, which meant once Jess was married it was
legally yours. If Dad had imagined that Jess intended
marriage he'd have changed the policy in an instant, but

you can't change the policy after death. Jess's marriage meant you inherited.' He hesitated. 'Jess knew about the policy. He must have known…'

'That I'd be safe,' Kelly whispered. 'Maybe that was even why… Oh, Jess…' She closed her eyes but then she opened them, moving on with a Herculean effort. 'All that's in the past,' she said. 'I need to look forward. I need to figure what to do for Jess.'

'You're broke?' he asked, and she flinched.

'I have money if I'm desperate, but I don't want to use it.' And then she took a deep breath, recovered, and fixed her gaze on his. 'I told you. I used Jess's insurance to put me through medical school, to get us a future, but I used as little as possible and I treated it as a loan. That money's sitting there waiting for Jess to need it as I needed it.'

'When he finally realises he can't spend his life surfing?'

Whoa. Where had that come from? Shades of his father?

'What are you saying?'

'He can't surf all his life.'

'That's his business.'

She was on her feet, backing away. 'Matt, if I hear you slight my son's lifestyle to him then, medical need or not, he's out of here. Your brother told me your father cares about possessions and power, and that's all. When he was ill, I suggested he might go home and you know what he said? "My father's home is where his things are. Home is where he can gloat over what he's achieved." But home for Jess and me is where my friends are. Our friends and the sea. And that's what we need now. We don't need your money or your judgement, Matt Eveldene. Leave us alone.'

CHAPTER THREE

HE SPENT A day letting her words sink in.

He spent a day feeling like a king-sized rat.

He also spent a day being proud of her. That she'd pulled herself up from where she'd been... That she was repaying her legacy... That she had the strength to stand up to him...

He was deeply ashamed of himself, but he was awed by Kelly.

'Jess married some woman!'

He was talking to himself while he walked on the beach near his house. His home was on a headland north of the town, surrounded by bushland and ocean. It hadn't rained for weeks. The country was parched but the scent of the eucalypts and the salt of the sea were balm to any man's soul.

And right now he needed balm.

His two dogs were by his side. Bess was a black Labrador, teenage-silly, joyfully chasing gulls, racing in and out of the waves as she tore along the beach. Spike was a fox terrier, a battered little dog from the lost dogs' home, and he went where Matt did. Spike put up with Bess's company when Matt was at work but when he was at home Spike belonged solely to Matt.

Spike was a dog a man could talk to.

'But why's she letting the kid go down the same road as his father?' Matt asked, stooping to scratch an ear Spike was having trouble reaching. He'd hurt Kelly. He knew he had and he hated it, but still he worried. 'All he seems to know is surfing. The first couple of days he was in hospital there were kids clamouring to visit. Now the tour's moved on, he's watching hour upon hour of surf videos. That's all he does. He's as fixated as Jess was.'

But the kid *was* Jess. The duplication of his brother's name was doing his head in. The likeness was doing his head in.

Kelly was doing his head in.

He'd noted her change of address on Jessie's medical records and he was appalled. Yesterday she'd moved into some kind of apartment at the back of an ancient Queenslander, a big old house up an enormously steep hill from the hospital. On his 'accidental' drive-by he'd decided it looked like it could blow down at any minute. It looked a dump.

She was spending most of her days with her son, but Jess was either sleeping or watching videos or playing video games. What sort of life was that for her? She had a couple of months of the same in front of her.

Dreary months.

It wasn't his business. She'd said that clearly. Back away.

How could he back away?

But to get involved…

See, there was the problem. Kelly had been right when she'd said his family cared for things rather than people. He did, too, but not for his father's reasons. His father accumulated possessions and gloated over them. Matt simply valued his home.

When he'd been a kid, Matt's older brother had been
the centre of his world, and he'd been forced to watch as
he'd slowly disappeared into his tortured illness. In defence Matt, too, had disappeared, surrounding himself
now with his medicine and his home—a real home as
opposed to the mausoleum his parents occupied.

His home, though, was solitary. For many, home
meant family but it didn't for Matt. One failed marriage had shown him that.

Jenny had been a year younger than him, a colleague,
ambitious and clever, warm and fun. His father had been
critical but his father was always critical. His mother
had approved.

'She's lovely and she's loving, Matt. You make sure
you love her right back.'

He'd thought he had. They'd married. They'd bought
a beautiful apartment overlooking Sydney Harbour and
brought in an interior designer with the brief: 'We want
it to be warm. We want it to be a home.'

They'd filled the house with gorgeous furniture and
hundreds of books. They'd had separate studies, separate careers, but every night they'd slept together and
Matt had felt like he had it all.

When Jenny had pulled the plug he'd been stunned.

'Matt, you love me but it's like I'm your imitation
fireplace,' she'd told him. 'For decoration only. I want
to keep you warm, but you have your own form of central heating. You're self-contained. You don't need me.
I've tried to fit in with your beautiful life but I can't.
Now I've met a farmer from west of nowhere. I'm off
to be a country doctor, and raise sheep and kids, and
have a very messy life and be happy. Good luck, Matt.
I'll always love you a little bit. I'm just sorry that you
couldn't love me a lot.'

That had been six years ago. He still didn't fully understand but after this time he conceded that maybe Jenny had been right. He wasn't husband material.

He'd moved to Queensland. He'd built a house he was immensely proud of and his career had taken over the gap that Jenny had left until he couldn't quite see where she'd fitted.

His parents' marriage was a disaster. He'd lost his brother and then he'd lost Jenny. There was no need to go down that emotional roller-coaster again. He was obviously a loner—except right now he wasn't. He kept thinking of a kid called Jess.

And he kept thinking of a woman called Kelly. A woman who twisted her curls around her fingers when she was tense. A woman he wanted to touch...

No. That was a road he wasn't going down. He needed to focus on practicalities.

And the foremost practicality? She was living in a dump because of some noble idea of saving her son's inheritance.

So what to do? Offer to pay for somewhere better? He thought of Kelly, of the fire in her eyes, of the hundred reasons she had to hate him, and he knew she'd refuse.

What, then?

He turned to stare up the cliff at his house.

Invite them to stay?

His house had a self-contained apartment, built so his mother could visit now and in the future. Wheelchair access. A veranda overlooking the surf. Its own television and internet access. Everything a disabled kid needed.

What was he thinking? Did he want them here?

Even if he offered, Kelly would refuse.

But if she didn't...

If she didn't then a kid called Jessie would be living in his house. Six weeks of Jess/Jess. Jess, his big brother. Jess, his nephew.

His nephew. His family.

He had to offer.

But when Jenny had accused him of self-containment, she'd been right. He didn't want to feel...the way he was feeling about Jess. Then there was Kelly. She was a woman he couldn't look at without feeling racked with guilt.

And then there was the way he felt when she twisted her curls...

The situation was doing his head in. He walked and walked, and when his cell phone rang and Beth was on the line, saying there'd been a car crash and he was needed, he was almost grateful.

Work, dogs, home, he told himself. They were all that mattered.

Except something else mattered. Someone else. Two someones.

He just needed space to get his head around it.

The car accident had been avoidable, appalling and tragic. One kid had a fractured pelvis but was so drunk it'd be morning before Matt could operate safely. He immobilised his damaged joint but that was all he could do for now. One kid had broken ribs and lacerations to his face. The broken ribs weren't life-threatening. The plastic surgeons would need to take over with this one.

The final casualty—the boy Beth had called him for because his spine was shattered—died just as he arrived.

So in the end there was little for him to do. Matt

headed for the door, skirting the cluster of shattered parents, thanking heaven counselling wasn't his role.

Then he paused.

It was nine o'clock. Visiting hours ended at eight. He might be able to drop in and check on Jess without Kelly being present. Without being surrounded by students.

He might be able to talk to Jess by himself.

Why would he want to?

Because... Because...

There was no because. He had no reason, but almost before he thought it, he was in the orthopaedic ward, greeting the nurse in charge, shaking his head as she rose to accompany him, heading down the corridor alone to Jessie's room.

The nurse looked interested and he knew this visit wouldn't go unreported. The hospital grapevine was notorious. Having a kid in here who looked like him *and* shared his name had sent the rumour mill flying.

So what? Rumours didn't affect him and it was normal to visit patients after hours. Even a kid who looked like his...son?

But he was his nephew. Kelly had told Jess who he was. She'd obviously not told him the bleakest parts of their history, though, because the kid always greeted him with friendly interest. It was as he found it intriguing to have an uncle.

Uncle. The idea unnerved him.

Jessie's door was slightly open. He knocked lightly, not enough to wake him if he was sleeping, and pushed it further.

Jess was asleep, but he wasn't alone. Kelly was sitting by the bed, and even by the dim nightlight she looked ill.

'Kelly?' He said her name before he could stop himself. She wanted to be called Dr Eveldene. He'd tried to remember it. But now... What was wrong?

'Kelly,' he repeated, heading for the bedside, looking down at Jess, expecting something dire.

But Jess was deeply asleep. He had a good colour and his breathing was deep and even. Matt flicked back the bedclothes at the end of the cradle and checked the lower leg, using the small torch he often used for evening rounds. Good circulation. No problem.

He glanced again at Kelly. Problem.

She was wearing jeans and a light windcheater. Her curls were hauled back in a ponytail. Her eyes were deeply shadowed, as if she hadn't slept.

A row of welts ran from her chin down her neck and underneath the cover of her windcheater.

The doctor in him went straight into diagnosis mode. Shingles?

He tried to look more closely but she put her hands up to cover her neck. Defensively.

'Yes?' she said, and it was a dismissal in itself. *Yes, what do you want, how soon can you get out of here?*

'What's wrong?'

'Why are you here?'

'Nightly ward round,' he said as if he always did an evening round. He often did, he conceded. Just not to patients who were recovering nicely.

'You don't come in at night.'

'I do when I'm needed.' He relented. 'Car accident. Alcohol. Stupid. There was a death. An eighteen-year-old. Fractured spine, and he died before I could get here. I thought...'

And she softened, just like that.

'Oh, Matt,' she said, her tone suddenly understanding. 'I do that, too. See a kid's death, hug another kid.

After I had Jess, that's where I'd be after trauma. Hugging. Jess always knows when I've had a bad day when the hugs are too tight. But...'

'But I have no right to hug Jess?'

'You don't,' she said flatly, but then she relented again. 'Kids killing themselves is the hardest thing.'

'Yet you let him surf.'

There was a moment's silence and when she finally spoke he could hear in her voice that he'd gone over that line again. 'You want me to pack him in cotton wool?'

'I... No. But he should have something other than surfing.'

'Butt out, Matt,' she said ominously, and he should. But right now he was facing a woman with an obvious problem. Even if her name hadn't been Kelly Eveldene, he couldn't walk away. There was something...

'You want to tell me what's wrong?'

'No,' she said, but he moved before she could react, caught her hands and dragged them down from her neck.

Down the left side of her throat were red weals, clumping in groups of three, some so large they were running into each other. The mass was expanding as it disappeared under her windcheater. Heaven knew what sort of a mess was under her clothes.

'What's this?' He ignored her jerk of protest and concentrating on the welts. It looked like shingles, and yet not. These were angry clumps rather than the mass of irregular swelling that shingles caused.

She looked so unwell...

'Kelly, what did this?' he said gently. 'Can I help?'

'No.'

'Now, that's dumb,' he told her. 'If it's shingles we

need to get antivirals on board right away. The sooner
it's treated, the shorter the period of discomfort.'

'I know that,' she snapped. 'But it's not shingles.'

'Then what?'

'Bed bugs,' she said, goaded. 'I was dumb. You'd
think I'd suspect. Haven't I lived in enough rough places
in my time?' She wrenched away from him in sudden
anger but the anger seemed to be self-directed. 'Leave
it. I'm treating my room. These'll fade.'

'These'll give you hell,' he said, looking at the dark
pools around her eyes. 'Did you get any sleep last
night?'

'No, I—'

'They must be driving you crazy. Come down to
Pharmacy and I'll get you antihistamines. I'll also get
you an anaesthetic cream to give you immediate relief.'

'I don't need—'

'You do need,' he told her, and without waiting for
agreement he took her hand and tugged her to her feet.
'Suffering's for those who have no choice and you have
a choice. Jessie's asleep. He doesn't need you to look
after him now, Kelly. You, however, do need to look
after yourself.'

How long had it been since things were taken out of
her hands?

They hadn't been. Ever. She looked out for herself.
Apart from that one blessed time around her briefest
of marriages, she'd been alone.

Even when she'd been tiny, when she'd been sick
she'd coped herself, and she was coping now. She'd
woken in the small hours covered with bed-bug sores.
She'd spent hours trying to rid her dump of an apartment of the creatures, knowing how hard it was to

eradicate them from ancient crevices. She should find another place to stay but the thought of paying any more for accommodation when Jess was still in hospital horrified her. The insurance was Jessie's money, college money, and it had to stay intact.

But the thought of going back there tonight made her feel nauseous. Or maybe she felt nauseous because she'd had so many bites. All she knew was that Matt Eveldene suddenly had her by the hand and was tugging her through the hospital toward his goal, the pharmacy. So, on top of nauseous, she felt helpless as well.

She wasn't stupid. She'd taken an antihistamine that morning. She managed to tell him.

'What strength? Do you have them in your purse? Show me.'

'Matt, I'm a doctor.'

'Show me,' he growled again, and it was too much trouble to argue. She just did.

'You took one of these this morning?' He looked at the packet with contempt. 'One?'

'I had stuff to do. I couldn't afford to be sleepy.'

'Yeah, you might go to sleep. What a disaster. This stuff won't even touch the sides. You can take much stronger medicine now, and stronger still when you're home in bed. But not in that bed.'

'I've sprayed.'

'It's a dump.'

'What business is that of yours?'

'You're my sister-in-law,' he growled. 'Family.'

'You are not my family!'

'Try telling that to every member of staff in this hospital.' She had to shut up then, while he threw orders to the woman in charge of Pharmacy. But even as he did, Kelly had to concede that he was right. She'd been aware of sideways glances and there'd even been straight-out questions. Now the pharmacist was filling Matt's scripts but she was looking from Matt to Kelly and back again, as if she could see family ties in the flesh.

Family? No way. She wasn't about to play happy families with an arrogant surgeon.

'Thank you,' she said stiffly, as the pharmacist handed over pills and cream. 'I'll pay—'

'I'm paying,' Matt snapped. 'And we need to get some of that cream on fast. I'll take you down to Emergency and we'll find a cubicle…'

'To do what?'

'Those welts are on your back. You can't reach them.'

'You're not putting cream on my back!'

'Don't be ridiculous. I'm a doctor.'

The pharmacist was watching them with interest, clearly enjoying herself. Clearly enjoying the sparks flying.

'I'll manage,' Kelly said stiffly.

'That's pig-headed.'

'You're not touching me.' She took the pills and cream from Matt's hands and backed out the pharmacy door. Matt followed, and she forced herself to stay still, to wait until the pharmacy door closed. She wanted to head straight for the exit but she had to be polite. This guy was Jessie's surgeon and he'd helped her. There was no need for her hackles to rise.

'Sorry,' she managed as the door closed behind them. 'I'm…I'm a bit of a private person.'

'How are you going to get that cream on your back?'

'I've been putting sunburn cream on my back for years. I'm a surfer, remember?'

He remembered. She could see it in the way his face closed down. And from the past…

'My family hates my surfing.' She could still hear Jess, her Jess, whispering to her all those years ago when he'd been in the throes of blackness. *'Don't they understand? When I'm surfing, I'm free.'*

She'd studied depression now; of course she had. When she'd first met Jess she'd had no clue, but she had enough knowledge now to know that he'd been treated the wrong way. Depression was an illness. If his surfing had been time out it should have been encouraged, not rejected. If he'd been encouraged to surf when he'd been a teenager, he might be alive now.

And now…

'Don't you dare judge,' she snapped, and Matt blinked and took a step back.

'I'm not judging.'

'Yes, you are. I can see it in your eyes. Surfing's a waste of space for you and your family.'

'It's a great sport,' he shot back. 'I surf myself. But you can't spend your life surfing.'

'You can if it's the only option,' she snapped. 'If your parents hadn't been so blind they'd have seen… they could have a kid who surfed or no kid at all. They gambled with their son's life and they lost.'

'Is that why you're letting Jessie surf?'

'You think that's why anyone wants to surf? Because they're ill? Butt out.'

'Kelly…'

'You know nothing.'

'I know plenty.' He raked his hair.

And she thought suddenly, he looks tired. Stressed. Of course he did. He'd coped with road trauma tonight—a dead kid, grieving parents. And now she was laying ancient history at his door.

It wasn't his fault Jess had died. He'd been younger than Jess. The damage had been done by others, not by him.

'Kelly, I want you to come and stay with me,' he said, and her thoughts cut off dead right there.

Stay. With him?

'No.' It was an instinctive rejection; a gut reaction.

'Why not?'

'Because you're Jessie's doctor, nothing more. Because my problems are nothing to do with you.'

'We both know that's not true,' he said wearily. 'Kelly, my big brother loved you. I loved him. I wasn't there for you eighteen years ago and I should have been. There's not much I can do for you now, but I do have a large house with an invalid-friendly self-contained guest apartment. My mother comes to stay sometimes but it's free now. My housekeeper keeps the kitchen stocked and I have two dogs who need walks and company. There's a spare Jeep you can use, as long as you're comfortable driving on the left side of the road. It's a straight ten-minute drive to the hospital. I'm out most of the day. We'd hardly see each other. And best of all, last time I looked I didn't have a single bed bug.'

'No,' she said again, but she didn't sound as sure. She didn't feel as sure.

It was a great offer. Why say no?

Instinct, she thought. Pure animal instinct. There was something about this man that seemed…dangerous.

'Besides,' he said gently, 'I'd really like the opportunity to get to know your Jessie. I'm his uncle. I know he's had no one in the past…'

'He's had me. He's had the surfing community.'

'Don't you think he should be given the chance to have more?'

'Not if it messes with his head,' she said bluntly. 'Not if it means one trace of judgement.'

'There won't be judgement.'

'There already is. You're judging me for letting him surf.'

'I won't judge him.'

'No,' she said again, but she was faltering.

Her son was an Eveldene. Her son was this man's nephew.

Somewhere there was a bully of a grandfather, a man she never wanted to meet, but Jess had loved Matt— and his mother.

Her son had a grandmother, too.

Family was such an alien concept. She'd never had so much as a cousin.

Actually, probably she had. It was just that by the time she'd been old enough to know them her father had driven them away.

As Matt's father had driven his son away?

My mother comes to stay sometimes. That's what he'd said. Nothing about a father there.

But maybe there were similarities between Matt and his father. There were definitely similarities between Matt and his brother. Maybe that was why she was look- ing at him now and feeling...feeling...

She didn't know how she was feeling.

Matt looked like her husband, like her son. Maybe that was it—but she knew it wasn't. It was the way he looked at her, as if he was as confused as she was. As vulnerable?

That was a nonsense. He was a chief orthopaedic sur-

geon, successful, gorgeous and at the top of his game.
Vulnerable? Ha!

And he really was gorgeous. Long, lean and ripped.
He looked…

Um, no. This wasn't what she should be thinking
right now. Or thinking ever. Move on, she told herself. The hormonal rush she was feeling must be her
emotions flaring up at his similarities to her long-dead
husband, surely. Surely it had nothing to do with Matt.

Concentrate. She'd just been thrown an offer. If she
accepted she wouldn't have to go back to her dump of
an apartment tonight.

She shouldn't be so pig stubborn about the trust
money, she told herself, not for the first time, but there
was still the remembrance of that cheque, thrown at her
in anger. Her initial urge to rip it in half was still with
her. Only the thought of the baby inside her had stopped
her. And now… She didn't want to use Eveldene money.
She didn't want Eveldene hospitality.

She was also just a little bit scared of how this man
made her feel.

'Come home,' Matt said, quite gently, and she realised he'd been waiting patiently for her to come to
a decision.

'Home is where Jess is,' she said, too fast, and he
grinned.

'There's not a lot of room in his hospital bed,' he said.
'You sound like you've had a lot of temporary homes.
What's wrong with making one of them with me?'

'Matt…'

'I know, every part of me repels you,' he said ruefully. 'And I understand that. But for now, what I'm offering is sensible. Let's go find an all-night supermarket
and buy you what you need.'

'I can collect my stuff.'

'It'll have to be fumigated before we transfer it.'

'How do you know?'

'I'm a dog owner,' he said. 'I'm used to fumigating.'

'You want to fumigate me?'

'A shower and a washing machine might do the job.'

A shower and a washing machine…

Of all the seductive things Matt could have said to her, that was the one most likely to succeed. A shower and a washing machine…

She knew her gear would be infected by bed bugs. She'd thought of doing a massive laundromat clean today but the thought of taking bedding by taxi had seemed too hard. She'd wanted to be with Jess, and she'd felt ill.

'You have a washing machine?' she said weakly.

'A really big one,' he said, like it was a siren lure, and it was. He smiled and his smile was suddenly tender, as if he'd realised she'd reached the end of her protests. 'Enticement by washing machine,' he said, echoing her thoughts. 'Come home with me, Kelly Eveldene, and see your washing go round and round and round.' He reached out and touched her then, tracing a long, strong finger down her cheekbone. It was a feather-light touch, a touch that meant nothing, but for some reason it made her want to sink against him. Dissolve…

'Give in, Kelly,' he said softly. 'I'm not threatening your independence. I'm not threatening anything. But I am offering you respite, a clean bed and a machine with six wash cycles. Let me take you home.'

And what was a girl to say to that? She looked up at him and tried to speak but for some reason she was close to tears and she couldn't.

It didn't matter. Matt took her shoulders and turned her round and steered her out the back to the hospital car park.

And took her home.

CHAPTER FOUR

THE LAST TIME Kelly Eveldene had felt completely out of control had been the night she'd had Jess. She felt out of control again now.

She was sitting in Matt Eveldene's gorgeous Aston Martin, heading out of town towards who knew where? On the back seat was a parcel of stuff bought at the late-night supermarket, an oversized T-shirt and knickers, toothbrush, toothpaste, a hairbrush. In the trunk was her duffel bag, carefully sealed in two layers of plastic.

The antihistamine was kicking in. She didn't feel quite as itchy but she felt...dirty.

She still wanted to scratch but she wasn't going to scratch in this man's car. Imagine if she dropped a bed-bug egg into the leather?

'If you scratch, you risk infection,' he said, and she glanced across and realised he'd been watching her hands clench and unclench on her lap.

'I won't scratch,' she muttered.

'Good girl.'

'I don't think an Aston Martin with bed bugs would suit your image.'

'I'm thinking you'll have showered this morning and given those clothes a good shake before you put them on. My risk is minimal.'

'Yet still you took it,' she muttered. 'Jess always said you were hero material.'

'Did he?' he said, and she saw his hands grip hard on the steering-wheel.

'He said you stood up to your father.' She might as well say it. It took her mind off the itching—or some of it.

'Jess couldn't,' Matt said grimly. 'Or rather when he tried it didn't work. It wasn't that I was a hero. It was just that when Dad hit me I refused to fall over. I figured from the time I was tiny that showing hurt made me more vulnerable. I just…dissociated myself. Jess, on the other hand, didn't have it in him to dissociate himself. Every punch, it was like it was killing him inside.'

'Your father punched?'

'Yes,' he said curtly.

'Do you still see him?'

'Seldom.'

'But you still see your mother?'

'When Dad's overseas. But she's never had the courage to leave him. I sometimes think she would have, but after Jess died any shred of self-worth she had died with him. She's just…shrivelled. Dad doesn't hit her. He hasn't needed to. Sometimes I think there are worse ways of controlling than physical violence.'

'And that's why Jess…'

'Got sick? Who knows with mental illness? But if I had to take a punt I'd say it certainly didn't help matters. And I hardly supported him either.' There was anger behind his words, impotent fury, and his knuckles on the steering-wheel showed white. But then he seemed to make an effort to recover, forcibly relaxing his hold, forcibly relaxing the muscles around his mouth. 'Sorry. Ancient history.'

'You blame yourself? You were four years younger. But your father—'

'I said it was ancient history,' he snapped again.

'If your mother's still with him then it's current affairs.'

'Current affairs I can't do anything about. Except protect you from him.'

'Why would I need protecting?'

'You might,' he said grimly, 'if he knew he had a grandson…'

'You won't tell him?'

'No.'

'Thank you,' she said in a small voice. She was feeling more and more out of control.

They were heading into what looked like dense bushland. Where was he taking her?

The car swung off the main road onto what looked like a private driveway, but this was no manicured garden. It was still bushland but solar lights nestled among the trees on either side of the track, some glowing brightly, some just faint traces of light, depending, she guessed, on how much sun they'd received during the day. The effect was strangely beautiful.

Isolated and beautiful.

She was heading into nowhere with a man called Matt Eveldene. If she had been back in her surfing days all her senses would be telling her to get out of the car now. But she wasn't a kid and she was no longer defenceless—she hoped.

But still…

'You're quite safe,' he said, guessing her thoughts, and she flushed.

'I never thought…'

'You'd have been foolish not to have thought. This

looks like the end of the earth, but in the morning you'll wake up and look over the ocean and you'll almost see Hawaii. Almost home.'

Almost home.

Home... There was a word to give her pause.

A home was what Jess needed now, for a while. But apart from their shoebox studio apartment back in Hawaii, where was home?

Home was work. Home was childcare when Jess had been little, school, university, libraries where she'd studied, with Jess reading or drawing pictures beside her, public playgrounds, beaches, friends' houses. Home was the surf, dawn and dusk. Home was where Jess was.

'Hawaii's hardly home any more,' she said, thinking aloud.

'Where is it, then?'

'Wherever Jess is. Wherever the surf is.'

'No roots?'

'I don't believe in them,' she said, and then for some reason she continued, revealing stuff she didn't normally reveal. 'As a kid I had a stuffed rabbit. Wherever Bugs was, that was home. Then when I was about eight one of my Dad's mates used Bugs to stoke a campfire. Home's never been anywhere since.'

'Hell, Kelly...' And there it was, that retrospective anger on her behalf. Jessie had reacted to stories of her past with fury. But who'd been angry on her behalf since?

No one. But it didn't matter, she told herself. And this man's concern shouldn't make her feel... She wasn't sure how she was feeling.

Push past it, she told herself. She didn't need this man feeling sorry for her. She didn't need this man looking at her with concern.

'It's no use worrying about what's in the past,' she managed. 'And what good did your fancy home do you or Jess? You need people. You don't need homes.' She meant it, too—but then they rounded the last bend in the driveway.

'This is home,' Matt said in a voice she hadn't heard before. 'I'm thinking this home almost equates to Bugs.'

Maybe it did. Sort of.

The house was long and low, nestled into the surrounding bushland almost as if it was part of it. It was built of sand-coloured stone, with wide verandas and a low-pitched roof, with tiny solar lights all around the veranda. Two dogs stood on the top step like two sentinels. A couple of battered surfboards leaned on the rail and a kayak lay near the steps. It looked like the perfect seaside homestead. It was picture-postcard perfect, though in postcards the dogs might have matched. These two were polar opposite, one a boof-headed Labrador, one a pint-sized fox terrier.

The dogs stood perfectly still until the car came to a halt, and then they whirled down the steps like a firecracker had exploded behind them. They raced round and round the car like crazy things until Matt opened his car door. The Labrador kept on whirling but the little dog timed it perfectly. Her circuit ended in a flying leap, straight onto Matt's knee. She gave an adoring yip, and then ceased all movement and gazed enquiringly at Kelly.

She had to laugh. What the little dog meant couldn't have been plainer if she'd been able to speak.

Matt, I'm really, really pleased to see you, but who is this? I need an introduction before we proceed.

'Spike, this is Dr Eveldene,' Matt said gravely, and

to Kelly's delight Spike raised a paw and waited, just as gravely, for it to be shaken.

'Call me Kelly,' Kelly said, and Matt grinned.

'Does that go for me, too?'

'I...' She sighed. 'Of course. Sorry.' And then she couldn't say anything else because the Labrador was now in the car, welcoming them both home with far less refinement and far more exuberance than Spike had shown.

Matt grabbed her gear. He dumped her plastic-shrouded duffel bag on the veranda—'That'll wait until morning'—then escorted her, with Spike leading the way, to his guest quarters.

He opened the door, flicked on the lights and she gasped in delight.

It was a self-contained apartment, furnished simply but beautifully. Polished wooden floors were softened with Persian rugs. The furniture looked comfortable and even a little faded, as if the curtains were left wide every day and the sun was left to do its worst. There were two bedrooms leading off the small sitting room. Matt led the way into the first, and flung open wide French windows while Kelly looked longingly at the truly sumptuous bed.

'All this for your mother?'

'Friends come here from Sydney, too,' he said briefly. 'I like them to be self-contained and I like my independence. You'll need to have breakfast with me tomorrow because I didn't think to get supplies, but from then on you can do your own thing. Leave the windows wide for a while—it's a bit musty in here. Would you like a drink? Anything?'

But she was still looking longingly at the bed, and

through the door to the bathroom. A long, cool shower to get the heat out of the bites…

'Make sure the water's no hotter than body temperature or you'll make it worse,' Matt said, following her gaze. He dumped her stuff on a luggage stand and put the pharmacy items on the dresser. 'Are you sure you can put this cream on after your shower?'

'I… Yes.'

'I'll leave you to it, then,' he said. 'Goodnight, Kelly. Come on, guys, let's leave the lady to sleep.'

And he clicked his fingers and he was gone. The dogs went with him and he closed the door behind him.

Good. Excellent. She had all the privacy a girl could ask for.

Shower. Bed.

Home?

She didn't do home; she never had. To invest in a permanent base would have meant spending all the money she'd had, and it had seemed wrong. The money had never seemed hers. It was her son's, and it would stay intact for him.

So she'd rented places that would do. On the surf circuit, as part of her job, they'd stayed in decent hotels, but nowhere as good as this.

This was pure comfort. She could sink into bed right now, if she didn't feel so dirty.

She flicked off the lights, stripped naked and tossed her clothes out onto the veranda. She'd cope with them in the morning. Then she headed for the shower. No tiny bed-bug egg was going to get into this place—it'd be a travesty.

Still, there was a niggle. Matt had given her this.

She'd be beholden to him, and she didn't want to be any more beholden than she already was.

But... 'I don't owe Matt,' she told herself. 'The insurance was Jessie's. He's done nothing for me but hand me what was rightfully mine.'

He'd saved her son's leg. She'd studied the X-rays. She'd even—heaven forgive her for her lack of trust—scanned them and sent them to a guy she'd trained with who'd gone on to specialise in orthopaedics in the US. The response had come back, loud and clear.

'These before-and-after X-rays are truly impressive, Kelly. That's one hell of a break. Whoever did the repair has saved Jess a lifetime of limping.'

So, yes, she was grateful and here she was, in his home. She was in his bathroom, to be precise, because she'd wasted less than ten seconds getting from naked to under the water.

Matt was right through the wall. Jess's brother.

Was that what was doing her head in? The similarity between Matt and her husband?

It must be, she thought. There was no other explanation, because she was feeling...strange.

Out of control?

It was the bed bugs, she told herself, and the weariness, and the shock of the last few days. Even so, sitting by Matt in the car, following him as he'd strode through the supermarket, figuring out what she needed, knowing that he was...caring...

He didn't care. He was simply doing the right thing for once.

But the concept of caring was insidious. If he did...

He did. He'd been angry on her behalf. And he'd looked at her in such a way...

'Oh, stop it,' she told herself, lathering her hair for

the second time with the gorgeous shampoo provided. She must have soap in her eyes. She was getting teary, and she didn't get teary. For some reason the thought of someone caring was almost overwhelming in its sweetness.

She coped alone. She'd always coped and she'd cope again. But for now...for now it was enough to stand under Matt's wonderful shower and then fall into Matt's wonderful bed...

Um...

Another image. Not a wise one. A totally stupid one, in fact. One started by his concern and moving to something else.

Matt was Jessie's brother. You did *not* have fantasies about your husband's brother.

Jess had been dead for eighteen years.

There'd been the occasional fling since—of course there had. Kelly was no black-clad widow, mourning her husband for ever. In fact, sometimes it seemed to her that Jess had been less her husband and more a wonderful, loving friend, someone who'd taken her out of a bad place but who'd been in a dreadful place himself. They'd been two kids fighting demons and Jess had lost.

She'd mourned him but she'd got on with her life, and occasionally a guy had turned up in her orbit. Never seriously, though. She was too busy, too preoccupied, not interested enough.

But Matt...

'Stop it,' she said out loud, and lathered her hair for a third time for good measure. 'Of all the times to indulge in fantasies... Inappropriate, inappropriate, inappropriate. Get yourself dry and into bed.

'Yes, Doctor,' she told herself, and managed a grin. Ooh, that bed...

As if on cue, one of the bites on her back stabbed with pain. Ouch. She turned the water colder and winced.

She had Matt's cream. Dry yourself off and get it on, she told herself. Bed's waiting.

Matt took the dogs for a fast walk out to the headland and then headed back to the house. For some reason he needed to be near. He'd told Kelly she could be independent but…but…

It didn't quite work. He'd like to be making her supper, making sure her bites were coated, making sure she was safely in bed.

Bed. His mind went all by itself to the memory of Kelly looking longingly at the bed.

A bed built for more than one.

Was he out of his mind? He was not interested in her like that. Not!

She was Jessie's wife. If he thought of her as his sister-in-law…

Logically it should help.

It didn't.

He headed back up the veranda and saw her open windows. Her clothes were heaped outside. He grinned. Very wise. He gathered them gingerly and took them to the laundry where he'd dumped her duffel bag.

Did bedbugs escape from laundries?

On impulse he tossed the clothes into the washing machine then unzipped her bag. Clothes only, he told himself; he wasn't looking at anything else.

He could do this. Confirmed bachelors—or confirmed divorcés—were good at laundry.

Most of her stuff was coloured. It all went into the machine. Her delicates—cute delicates, he noticed, before admonishing himself once again—went into the tub to soak. Then he found a can of insecticide, sprayed the room to within an inch of its life and carefully closed all the doors. No sucker would get out of there alive.

Job done. He should go to bed himself. He had an early start in the morning.

Instead, he found himself out on the veranda again, glancing along, seeing Kelly's windows were still open.

Her light was still on.

Why? She was dead on her feet. She should be in bed by now.

When she went to bed was her business—or maybe she slept with the light on.

Maybe there were shadows in her past that demanded nightlights.

Yeah, that didn't bear thinking of. Her past didn't bear thinking of. Thank God Jess had been able to help her.

And suddenly something lightened just a little inside him. His grief for his older brother had stayed raw, even after all this time. What a waste. The mantra had played over and over in his head—the thought that because his father had rejected his illness, Jess had died alone. Jess had had no one.

But he hadn't died alone. He'd had Kelly. She'd held him and loved him and she'd told him she was bearing his child. And Jess had known of the insurance. No matter how ill he'd been, Jess would have known Kelly would be provided for. He'd have known she and her child would be safe.

And in that moment the gaping bleakness of Jessie's loss lessened, faded. It shifted to a corner of his mind where he knew it could stay in peace for the rest of his life. What a gift! And Kelly, this slip of a girl who'd turned into a woman of such strength, had given it to him.

Kelly, whose light was still on. Because of demons? Because…?

He heard himself call out before he knew he intended to. 'Kelly? Are you all right? Is there anything you need?'

There was a moment's silence. The dogs by his side seemed to prick up their ears, as if they, too, were listening for a response. And finally…

'I'm not as clever as I thought,' she said, sounding exasperated. She was just through the window.

'You want to expand on that?' he asked cautiously.

'Fine,' she said, goaded. 'I've always been able to put sunburn cream on myself. All over. But some time over the last few years, being with Jess rather than alone, I must have lost the knack. "Do my back," I'll say, and Jess does. There are bites on my back that are driving me nuts and I can't reach them.'

'You want help?'

There was a moment's silence. Then: 'I've only got a T-shirt and knickers on.'

'And if I'm to help you'll need to get rid of the T-shirt. Kelly, I'm a doctor.'

'Yes, but—'

'I'll do it with my eyes closed,' he told her, and she snorted.

'Right.'

'You want help or not?'

Another silence. Another moment's hesitation. Then, finally, the French windows were thrust wider and Kelly appeared in the light.

This was a Kelly he hadn't seen before. Her curls were damp and tangled. She was wearing her oversized man's T-shirt. Underneath she'd be wearing the cheap knickers the supermarket stocked, but that was all.

The T-shirt material was cheap and thin. A bit too thin. The shower had been cold...

'You said you wouldn't look,' she said coldly, and he shut his eyes.

More silence.

'Matt?'

'Yes?' he said cautiously. She was sounding...even more goaded.

'I'm a patient,' she said. 'I'm going to lie face down on the bed and pull up the T-shirt and you're required to apply medication.'

'It'd be better if you took the T-shirt off altogether.'

'Better for who?'

'I'm a doctor,' he reassured her. 'And you know I'm right. The night's warm. You're better sleeping with nothing on at all.'

'I might,' she conceded. 'After you leave.'

'After the doctor has done what he needs to do,' he agreed. 'Kelly...'

'Yes?'

'Go lie on the bed and we'll get this over with.'

She stripped off her T-shirt with her back to him—asking him to leave the room again would have seemed... prissy. Then she lay face down on the crisp, clean sheets and waited for him to do his worst.

His best? Surely his best. She needed help. All he had to do was take the cream from the bedside table and rub it in.

She heard him lift the tube, imagined him squeezing the cream onto those gorgeous surgeon's hands...

What was she doing, thinking of those hands?

She was actually thinking of more than his hands.

You're a sad case, Kelly, she told herself. One good-looking guy wanders into your orbit and your body reacts like...

Her body certainly did react. The moment his fingers touched her skin, she felt every sense respond. It was like her body lit up from within, as if the place on her back where he touched was suddenly the centre of her entire being, and all of her wanted to be there.

What the...? Could she have an orgasm because someone was touching her?

This was crazy. She was feeling super-sensitive because of the bites. She'd been without sex for far too long.

Surely this had nothing to do with the fact that it was Matt Eveldene who was doing the touching. Surely if an elderly woman with body odour was applying the cream she'd be feeling the same.

Liar, liar, pants on fire. She was face down in her pillow, muffling thoughts, muffling everything, but all she could see was Matt, with his gorgeous dark hair and his long, sensitive fingers doing indescribable things to her, making sure every last part of her back was covered with the anaesthetic cream. Suddenly, dumbly, she found herself wishing she hadn't worn knickers to bed last night and the bites had gone lower.

Uh-oh. She needed to get a grip fast. She was a mature woman, the mother of a seventeen-year-old son, a competent doctor. She did not grip her pillow and stifle groans because some strange man was applying cream to her.

His fingers stopped and to her horror she heard a whimper of protest. Surely that wasn't her?

It was. Was she out of her mind?

But luckily, thankfully, he misinterpreted it. 'These are bad,' he said. 'Kelly, stay still, I'm going to find some ice. I've made them warm again, putting the cream on. We need to get all the heat out of them so you can get some sleep.'

We. Plural. The word was seductive all by itself.

There wasn't a we. There had been never a we.

Matt left and for some stupid reason she found herself thinking of the night Jess had been born. She'd been staying with friends on the far side of the island. They'd promised to be with her for the birth but Jess had come two weeks early. They'd gone out and she'd had no car.

She'd taken the local bus, an hour's bumpy ride in the dark. She'd walked four blocks to the hospital and she'd delivered her baby with no one but too-busy hospital staff in attendance.

Why think of that now?

We. It was the word; it penetrated her deepest thoughts.

The only *we* she knew was herself and her son.

And then Matt was back. She hadn't moved. Her world seemed to be doing weird, hazy things. Maybe it was the antihistamines—how much had Matt given her? Or maybe it was the toxic effect of so many bites. No matter, she couldn't have moved if she'd tried. She didn't speak, just lay absolutely still while Matt applied ice packs wrapped in soft cloth to her inflamed skin.

The feeling was incredible. She no longer felt like whimpering. She felt incredibly, amazingly peaceful, like this was right, like this was where she ought to be.

Like this was home.

There was a dumb thought. Home. For her, the concept didn't exist.

'You know, if you rolled over I could ice your front,'

Matt said conversationally, and she finally managed to rouse herself.

'In your dreams, Matt Eveldene,' she managed. 'I can ice my front all by myself. Thank you very much. I'll go to sleep now.'

'Are you sure? I can give you—'

'If you give me anything else I'll never wake up. I'm medicated to my eyeballs. Thank you, Matt, and goodnight.'

'Goodnight, Kelly,' he said softly, but he didn't go. For a long moment he simply stood by her bed.

She wanted to roll over. She wanted, quite desperately, to look up at him.

She was naked from the waist up. A girl had to have some sense.

And it seemed Matt had sense, too.

'Goodnight,' he said again, and then, before she knew what he intended—how could she ever have guessed?— he stooped and kissed her lightly on the head.

'You're the bravest woman I've ever met,' he told her. 'Thank you for loving Jessie. It's the greatest gift you could ever have given me.'

'Is that why you kissed me?' she managed, and what sort of question was that? Dumb, she thought, but equally…important.

'No,' he said at last. 'It's not. But it needs to be.'

She was his sister-in-law. Jessie's wife. He had no business thinking of her…as he was thinking.

Why had he kissed her?

It had been a feather kiss, the kiss one might give a child to say goodnight.

It had meant nothing.

Wrong. It had meant…more.

She hadn't felt like Jessie's wife and she hadn't felt like a child. She'd felt—and looked—every inch a woman.

He left the house and walked down to the beach again, to watch the moon sending its slivers of silver ribbon over the waves. The dogs were silent by his side, as if they knew how important it was that he be given time to think.

There was nothing to think about.

There was everything to think about. A woman called Kelly, a woman lying half-naked in his guest room, a woman responding to his touch...

She had responded. That hadn't been a doctor/patient treatment. The whole room had crackled with sexuality. With need.

His need?

'It's because I'm guilty and grateful,' he said out loud, but he knew it was much, much more.

It couldn't be more. This situation was complicated enough. It didn't need testosterone as well.

'Back off,' he told himself harshly. 'There's so much to be sorted before you can...

'Before you can what?'

Before you can nothing. He raked his hand through his hair and felt weariness envelop him. The family ramifications were enormous. How to let his parents know?

It'd be easier if he didn't. He'd promised Kelly...

But...but...

'Stop it,' he told himself. 'One step at a time. They're both safe now and that's all that matters. She's asleep and you need to take a cold shower.' He was still talking aloud and the dogs were paying attention. Like what he was saying was important.

He looked down at them and gave a rueful chuckle.

'Okay. With the amount of drugs Kelly has on board, she'll sleep until morning, and I need to, too. So go to bed,' he told himself. 'You have a full list in the morning. You have more to think about than Kelly.'

Kelly. Not Jessie's wife. Kelly. It suddenly seemed important to differentiate the two.

The dogs were getting restless. His unease was communicating itself to them. Bess put a tentative paw on his knee and whined.

'Right,' he said, hauling himself together. He picked up a piece of driftwood and hurled it up the track toward the house. Bess bounded after it. Spike looked towards Bess and back toward Matt and whined.

Both dogs were worrying about him.

'Okay, I'm discombobulated,' he told Spike. 'Do you know what that means? No? Well, maybe I don't know either. Maybe all I know is that I need to get on with my life. Home, bed, hospital, medicine. Get your priorities back in line, Eveldene, starting now.'

CHAPTER FIVE

WHEN SHE WOKE, sunshine was pouring in through the open windows. She could hear the waves crashing on the beach below the house.

Two dogs' noses were on her bed.

Bess was so big the dog's nose was practically beside hers. Spike was standing on his haunches, his nose just reaching the top of the mattress.

Both their tails were going like helicopter blades. *Look what we've found—a person! A person in our house!*

She grinned and stretched and it was enough. Spike was up on the bed with her, as if her stretching had been a command. Bess, obviously trained for restraint, stayed where she was. She was sitting and waiting but her tail was still going a mile a minute.

She felt…

She felt…

She glanced at the bedside clock and felt stunned.

Ten o'clock? She'd slept for almost twelve hours!

Visiting hours started at the hospital at ten. She should be there. Jess would be expecting her.

Actually, Jess wouldn't be expecting her. He'd started gentle physio yesterday. She'd supplied him with a week's worth of surfing videos. Talking to his mother would come far down his list of the morning's priorities.

She therefore had nothing to do but lie in this gorgeous bedroom and be sociable to these very nice dogs.

Where was Matt? There was the question and it was a biggie.

It was Monday morning, she told herself. He'd be back in the hospital, where he belonged.

She had his house to herself.

Cautiously she tossed back the covers, apologising to Spike as she did so. 'Sorry, little one. I should have woken earlier and given you more cuddle time.'

But Spike just wiggled and hopped off and headed out the French windows, as if his job had been done. They'd said good morning and now both dogs were off to enjoy the day.

She followed, but only to where the curtains fluttered in the warm breeze. She wasn't exactly respectable. Actually, she wasn't respectable at all. She did a quick rethink and a bit of sheet-wrapping and then dared to explore further.

The dogs were on the veranda.

The view took her breath away.

Wow. Wow, wow and wow. The Pacific Ocean stretched away as far as she could see. The house was nestled in a valley, and the valley broadened out, sweeping down and spreading to a wide, golden beach. Promontories at either end of the beach reached far out to the sea, forming what Kelly thought looked like perfect surf breaks.

The beach looked deserted but civilisation must lie close by, for there were surfers at each headland, drifting on the sun-washed sea, waiting for the right wave.

An ancient cane settee lay along the end of the veranda, covered with saggy cushions and dog hair. Kelly looked at it and thought that of all the perfect places for Jess to convalesce, this was the best.

She'd have to hide the surfboards, though.

Um…what was she thinking? She shouldn't stay here for his whole convalescence.

Why not? Matt was Jessie's uncle. Family. He owed her.

No. He didn't owe her, she reminded herself. He'd been a kid when his brother had died and he'd been shocked and sick. The words he'd flung at her should have been forgiven long ago.

Maybe they had been.

But still she couldn't suppress a grin. If a bit of guilt made it possible for Jess to stay in this place…

Don't try and manipulate. Not Matt.

Involuntarily she tightened her grip on her sheet. What she'd felt last night…

It was only because she'd been exhausted, she told herself, and the mass of bites had been making her feel nauseous. And the antihistamines had been messing with her head.

It was a wonder she hadn't jumped him.

Good grief. She peered cautiously under her sheet, just checking, and saw the welts had subsided. The angry red had faded.

She was still a bit itchy, but it was manageable.

What she needed, though, was coffee. Her apartment might be gorgeous but it didn't have coffee.

Matt must have a kitchen. Matt must be at work.

Matt must have coffee.

The three together were a deal-breaker. Off she went, wearing her sheet. A couple of steps down the veranda she changed her mind, went back and donned the too-

thin T-shirt, wound the sheet around her a bit tighter
and tried again.

She needn't have bothered. She found Matt's kitchen
and it, too, was deserted.

A note lay on the kitchen bench.

Help yourself to anything you need. The keys to
the Jeep in the driveway are on top of the fridge.
Assuming you have an international driving licence, feel free to use it. Don't forget to drive on
the left. The pills in the yellow packet are daytime
antihistamines. They won't make you sleepy. Take
two. My housekeeper, Mrs Huckle, will be here at
ten. I've phoned her and she'll cream your back.
I've washed your clothes and they're out in the
sun. In this breeze they'll be dry by lunchtime.
Take it easy until then. M.

She'd stayed in lots of friends' houses. She'd been
left lots of notes. What was it about this one that made
her tear up?

He'd done her laundry?

'You must be Kelly.'

She whirled and found a wiry little woman beaming
across the room at her. The housekeeper?

'I'm Sally Huckle.' She was in her fifties or early six-
ties, skinny, sun-worn, wearing skin-tight jeans and a
shirt with too much cleavage showing. The woman took
her hand and shook it like it might come off.

'A woman on her own,' she said, still beaming. 'Excellent. Too many dratted couples stay here. Only his
mother comes by herself and what use is that? He needs
a single friend. You're American? And Matt says you
have bites. Where's the cream? Matt says you'll need

help to put it on and he's told me to apply ice packs as well. Talk about orders. And if you weren't awake I wasn't to wake you but when you did could I please make you pancakes for breakfast.'

She beamed, and her beam was widely enquiring. 'I'm not Matt's friend,' Kelly said stiffly, before the woman could keep going. 'I'm his sister-in-law.'

'His sister-in-law?'

If Jess was coming here to stay, why not say it? 'Yes. My son's had an accident on the Gold Coast. He's still in hospital but he's coming back here to convalesce.'

'Your son? You're Matt's sister-in-law?' The woman sounded incredulous. 'You're Jessie's wife?'

'I... Yes.'

'Your son is Jessie's son?'

'Yes.' Where was she landing herself?

'Does his father know about you?'

'No.'

'Then God help you when he finds out,' she said bluntly. 'Are you sure it's a good idea to stay here?'

'Matt doesn't seem to have given me much choice.' She hesitated. 'But what's wrong with his father knowing?'

'Do you know about your father-in-law?'

'Not much.'

'Then take a look,' the woman said, and crossed to an alcove holding a desktop computer. 'I'm just the hired help but everyone in Australia knows about the Eveldenes.' She hit the browser and in seconds Henry Eveldene's face filled the screen.

'This was written as a Sunday papers feature a couple of years back,' Sally said. 'As far as I can figure, it's accurate. Take a read while I make pancakes. The man makes my hair stand on end. I've never met him but

Matt's mother comes here while he's overseas and that's enough. Downtrodden's too big a word for it. Sit. Read.'

'I don't need pancakes.'

'Matt might not be as scary as his father,' Sally said, 'but he's my boss. He's still an Eveldene and what he says goes. Sit. Read. Pancakes.'

Two hours later Kelly was driving cautiously—why didn't the whole world drive on the right?—trying to take in everything she'd learned about Matt's family.

Jessie's family, she reminded herself. Henry Eveldene was Jessie's grandfather.

He was also a giant of industry, owning and operating a huge consortium of paper mills.

He was also a greedy, avaricious bully.

The page Sally had found for her to read had pulled no punches. It spoke of a man to whom money was second only to power. He operated on a knife edge between legal and illegal. He coerced, bullied, blackmailed, and his competitors had gone under one by one.

The article hadn't stopped at his dubious business practices, though. It had talked of the beautiful, wealthy girl he'd married, and how she'd faded from sight and was now practically a recluse.

The article was careful. Kelly could see litigation concerns all over it, but the implications were everywhere. It described two sons, the expectation that they'd move into the family dynasty and take orders from their father, the older son's breakdown and suicide, the younger son's decision to move into medicine, and the subsequent estrangement.

The picture emerged of a solitary megalomaniac who tried to destroy everyone who opposed him.

What would he do if he discovered he had a grandson?

She shivered and went back to concentrating on the road. Stupid left-hand drivers.

But this was a cool little Jeep, fitted with roll bars to make it into a dune buggy. She could have fun with this machine.

She scolded herself. It wasn't hers.

Hey, but it was, for the time she was staying with Matt. She had visions of putting Jess in the back seat and heading out to explore the local coast. There were places she'd read about around here where they could drive on the beach. They could look for surf spots where they could return once his leg was healed.

Jess's convalescence was looking a lot brighter because of Matt.

Matt... An enigma. Matt, who caused her stomach to clench and she couldn't figure out why.

Matt, who'd done her laundry. Matt, who'd put cream on her back last night, who'd kissed her hair and who'd made her feel...

Enough. She didn't feel like that. She was solid, sensible Dr Kelly Eveldene and if only she could avoid the odd oncoming car she was off to visit her recuperating son and live happily ever after.

Matt's theatre list took him all morning and into the afternoon. He finished at two, rid himself of his theatre scrubs, figured he needed to do a ward round but first he'd grab a sandwich. Maybe he'd take it up to Jessie's ward to eat.

Was it wise to get any closer to Jess? Maybe it wasn't but the decision had been taken out of his hands the moment he'd offered accommodation to Kelly. Besides, he had a nephew. The thought was unnerving but it wasn't something that'd go away.

The minute he'd seen him he'd known this was Jessie's son. Now, come hell or high water, he'd look out for him.

And if he was to look out for him then he needed to get to know him.

As an uncle.

As a friend to his mother?

He'd look out for Kelly, too, but it wasn't just because Jess had married her. It seemed more.

Except he couldn't define more.

He pushed open Jess's door, balancing sandwiches and coffee. Two faces turned to him. Jess and Kelly.

Jess was so like his father that it made Matt's heart twist.

Kelly was so like…Kelly that for some stupid reason his heart twisted even further.

'Hi,' Jess said shyly. 'Come in.'

'I'm not here on business,' he told them. 'No poking and prodding, unless there are any problems?'

'No problems,' Jess said. 'But thank you for looking after my mom.'

That took his breath away. So someone else was looking out for Kelly.

'I told her yesterday she had to get out of that crappy apartment,' Jess said. 'Thanks for picking her up and forcing her.'

'Do you need to pick her up and force her often?' Matt asked, and Jess grinned.

'If you only knew. She's stubborn as a brick, my mom. Immovable. And stupid about money. She has some dumb idea—'

'Jess!' Kelly intervened. 'Let's not be telling Dr Eveldene our family business.'

'Yeah, but Dr Eveldene *is* our family,' Jess said, shy again. 'Isn't that right, sir?'

'I... Yes. But not so much of the "sir".'

'Uncle Matt?'

'Matt.' The uncle bit did his head in.

'Take a seat,' Jess said, relaxing. 'We're watching the next leg of the surf circuit in New Zealand. This guy coming up next is pretty good. He's getting a bit old, though. I reckon his knees might start crumbling soon.'

'How old is a bit old?' Matt asked, perching on the spare visitor's chair.

'Twenty-eight,' Jess said, and Matt choked on his coffee and grinned and looked across at Kelly and found she was grinning as well.

'Yep, you and I are well and truly on the scrap heap,' she said. 'It's a wonder we can still see our knees.'

'Speak for yourself. I do push-ups,' Matt told her. 'Every morning. I reckon I'll be able to see my knees until I'm at least fifty.'

'Dream on,' Kelly said, grinning back. 'Knees don't exist when you're fifty.'

'Especially old knees in neoprene,' Jess said, and shuddered. 'Old guys in wetsuits...ugh.'

'Thank you,' Kelly said with asperity. 'Shall we talk about something else? Like when Dr Eveldene will let you out of hospital?'

'Call me Matt,' Matt said sharply.

'Matt,' Kelly said, as if making a concession, but then she smiled and he thought...he thought...

Concentrate on Jess, he told himself. Concentrate on what mattered. Jess was his family. Kelly wasn't.

'The vascular surgeon and I concur, a week in hospital,' Matt managed. 'And we talked yesterday about surfing. You know it'll be six months before you can

safely surf again. Have you had any thoughts about what
you might do while you convalesce?'

This was a conversation he often had with patients.
As an orthopaedic surgeon, he often treated people with
passions—paragliders, trail bike riders, skiers, people
who pushed their bodies to extremes.

Not fronting that question—What will you do while
your body recovers?—was an invitation to depression,
and with Jessie's family background there was no way
Matt was ignoring the risk.

'I'll sulk,' Jess said, with an attempt at lightness that
didn't quite come off. He saw Kelly glance at her son
sharply and then look away. So she was worried, too.

'When did you leave school?' Matt asked. 'If you're
interested, you might be able to go back for a bit. A
couple of subjects might hold you in good stead if you
decide you need a career when your knees go.'

There was silence in the room. His suggestion had
been presumptuous, Matt knew, but, then…his big
brother had had nothing but surfing. To see this kid go
the same way…

'I've done with schooling for a while,' Jess said, turning back to the surfing on television. 'Mom and I made
a deal. No more study.'

What sort of deal was that—letting your son do nothing but surf? But he'd pushed the boundaries as far as
he could. Mother and son both suddenly seemed tense
and there was no way he could take it further.

'I might learn to play snakes and ladders,' Jess said,
attempting lightness but his words weren't light at all.

'I'll buy you a set,' Matt told him. 'No,' he said, as
his offer was met by silence. He put up his hands as if
to ward off protests. 'I insist. As an uncle it's the only
appropriate thing to do.'

Jess chuckled and went back to watching what the surfer was doing on television. Kelly cast him a look of relief and Matt unwrapped his sandwich and wondered where to go next. What was the role of an uncle?

And then his phone went.

Of course. This was part of his job. How many times had meals been interrupted by his phone? At least this was just a sandwich.

He tossed Kelly an apologetic glance—no need to send one to Jess, who was engrossed again in his surfing world—and answered.

Trouble.

He tossed his sandwich in the bin and headed for the door.

'What?' Kelly demanded.

'Work.'

'Yeah, but it's a biggie,' she said. 'I'm a doctor, too, remember? I know the drill. If you get a minor call, you rewrap your sandwich. You ditched your sandwich so I'm figuring it's major. I shouldn't ask but—'

'Bus crash,' he said curtly. 'A self-drive bus of tourists mucking about off road in the sand dunes. They copped a head-on with a council grader on the far side of a crest. Deaths and multiple casualties. We'll be pushing to get staff to cover it. See you tomorrow, Jess.'

'Matt, can I help?' Kelly asked sharply.

'I don't see how.' He had the door open; he needed to leave.

'Matt, as surf-pro physician I have provisional registration to work in almost every country we visit,' she said, talking fast. 'In emergencies I can stay hands on. In hospitals I require overall supervision from local medics, but I'm a doctor, I'm another pair of hands and I'm available. Do you need me?'

Matt hesitated. An unknown doctor, overseas trained...

But this accident involved twenty or more tourists, Beth had said, and she'd sounded desperate. They were evacuating some to Brisbane but there was only one chopper and most were coming by road. This was the first and only place that casualties could be stabilised.

He steadied. He did know her. He trusted her. He needed to check, though, for the sake of the patients she'd be treating.

'Can you prove your registration?'

'My paperwork's in my travel wallet with my gear at your place,' she told him, as if she'd expected the question. She hauled a card from her purse. 'But you can ring this number. Quote my name and my registration number. They'll confirm fast.'

She'd done this before, he thought. She'd acted as a doctor in a foreign setting. Then, he thought, *of course she had.* Kelly—or the organisation she worked for— would have set up temporary registration from the moment she entered the country, so in an emergency, if there weren't enough medics on hand, she could act as a doctor without repercussions.

'Phone while we hit the lift,' she said.

'Thank you.' There was nothing else to say.

They left Jess to his surfing and headed for Emergency. They didn't speak on the way down. He'd phoned and was listening to someone in officialdom telling him Kelly was fine.

A small army seemed to be waiting for them, but they were mostly nurses. Matt glanced around and saw only three qualified doctors, Beth, Frieda and Emma. Beth and Frieda were good but Emma had only passed her final exams last month. She wasn't confident at the best of times, and now she was looking terrified.

'I'm trying to get more hands here,' Beth told him as she saw his visual sweep of the room and guessed his thoughts. 'But everyone seems to be in the middle of something urgent. Brisbane's on standby. We're pulling in another chopper, but for now it's down to us.'

'Kelly's offered to help. She's an emergency physician accredited for work here under supervision. I've done the checks.'

'Excellent,' Beth said with relief. 'Matt, can you do a fast tour, show her what's needed and find her some scrubs. Kelly, can I put you on triage with Rachel, our senior nurse? Direct the straightforward ones to Emma, the harder ones to the rest of us.'

Kelly nodded. Matt saw her assessing the teams of nurses, checking the doctors, then glancing at Emma, who looked like she was about to faint.

'Maybe Emma and I could work together,' Kelly suggested. 'With Rachel's help, we could do triage and urgent stabilisation as a team. I'm supposed to work under supervision if Australian doctors are present so it'd cover all the bases.' Then, as Emma visibly relaxed at the thought of not working alone, Kelly moved on. 'Do you have an anaesthetist?'

'That's Frieda,' Matt told her, signalling to a grey-haired woman currently tossing orders to nurses on the other side of the room. 'If we need 'em, intubation and tracheotomies are her specialty.'

'I can do trachies in my sleep.' Frieda threw her a friendly grin. 'We're always short-staffed, but this is looking crazy hard. Glad to have another Eveldene on board.' She gave a brief smile.

'I hope you don't need me,' Kelly told her, but then

the scream of an ambulance outside announced the first arrival and there was room for no more talk.

They needed Kelly. They needed everyone.

This was war-zone stuff.

Kelly had trained as an emergency physician. She'd done mock-ups of this type of scenario but she'd never been in one. Nevertheless, her drilled-in training kicked in, making her reactions instinctive. By her side the very junior Emma was visibly shaking. Emma supervising Kelly? Ha!

The first arrival, a girl of about sixteen, had a deep gash running from under her arm to the small of her back. Her blood pressure was dangerously low—the drip wasn't going fast enough. The other casualty coming through was a spinal injury with breathing difficulties. Matt and Frieda took that case, while Beth headed out to greet whoever was coming next.

That was almost the last time Kelly had time to see what everyone else was doing. She focused only on the kid under her hands.

She reached for the adrenaline, showed Rachel—thankfully capable—where to apply pressure, and snapped orders to Emma. 'Get another line in. We need as much fluid as we can.'

Emma's hands shook as she tried to do as ordered.

'Stop,' Kelly said, grabbed the young woman's hands and held for one harsh moment. 'Deep breath. Emma, you will not mess this up. You can't. The only wrong way is not at all. You know how to do this. Move to automatic pilot. Don't think of the consequences. You've had years of training. This is what you're here for, Emma. Do it.'

And Emma met her gaze, took a deep breath and visibly steadied. She picked up the syringe and inserted it into the back of the girl's hand. It went exactly where it was supposed to go and she didn't even pause for breath before turning to grab bags of plasma.

From fifteen feet away, where Matt and Frieda were working on a woman who probably wouldn't make it but had to be given every chance, Matt saw and felt a jab of relief. Yeah, he'd watched. He had too much on his plate, but he'd assured Beth that Kelly was qualified. Lives were in her hands and it would have been negligent not do a fast visual check.

Two minutes in he was completely reassured. Not only did she work like an efficient machine but she'd settled Emma, so instead of one terrified novice, they had a team of two steady, intent doctors.

'It has to be cervical spine fracture,' Frieda barked. 'Get her straight through to Imaging.'

And then the woman's shallow breathing ceased. Kelly was forgotten, everything was forgotten as they fought to get her back—and lost.

And when they surfaced from defeat there were more casualties waiting. A couple more doctors arrived. The department looked even more like a war zone.

He lost sight of Kelly. He lost sight of everything except trying to save lives.

CHAPTER SIX

By NINE THAT night there was nothing left for Kelly to do. Patients had been transferred, to Theatre, to wards, to other hospitals at need. A couple were in the morgue. That was a gut wrenching she could never get used to. In emergency situations Kelly worked on the front line, but eventually surgeons, anaesthetists, paediatricians, neurologists, even grief counsellors, moved in and took over.

But sometimes Kelly thought she needed counselling herself. She felt like that now, but she'd done what she'd needed to do. When the last patient was wheeled out, Beth thanked her and told her to go home.

'We wouldn't have had the outcome we did without you,' she told her. 'And the way you hauled Emma together...your help today meant we had five doctors instead of three.'

'Emma's a good doctor,' Kelly said, wishing, stupidly, that Matt was still here, but Matt was an orthopaedic surgeon, one of those who kept working after emergency imperatives had been met. He'd probably be operating until morning.

'She's good *now*,' Beth told her. 'Thanks to you, she worked well, and she'll never be as terrified again. And as for you, if you'd like part-time work while you and

Jessie are stuck here, just say the word. It'd be a huge pleasure to have two Eveldenes working in this hospital.'

Two Eveldenes… That was a weird concept.

She and Matt.

Something was twisting inside her. What?

Today she'd been part of Matt's team. Matt had vouched for her and she'd worked in his hospital. Beth was referring to them as the two Eveldenes.

Strangely it felt like she had family, and the feeling was weird.

She found herself wishing she could go home with Matt now. She'd seen him as they'd wheeled the last patient out of Emergency to Theatre. He was facing multiple fractures. He'd be working all night.

And he'd looked haggard already.

He was nothing to do with her.

Wrong. He was an Eveldene.

Family?

Needing to ground herself, she headed back to Jessie's room. Jess was deeply asleep. She sat by his bed, just watching him. Settling herself in her son's presence.

After a while the nurse in charge of the ward popped in. 'I've been sent to take care of you,' she said, efficiency overlaid with kindness. 'Would you like tea and a sandwich? Or something hot? The whole hospital knows what you've done today and we're grateful. We can heat you some soup if you like. Anything.'

'Thank you, no.' She rose, feeling bone weary. There was no point in staying here. 'I need to go home.'

'And you're staying with Matt. You're his sister-in-law, the wife of his brother who died. That's awfully sad.'

'It was a long time ago,' Kelly said repressively, but

knowing hospital grapevines were the same the world over. She had as much chance of hiding her history as flying.

'But still...' The woman glanced at Jess. 'They say he's just like his dad, and you've brought him up in America but finally you've brought him home.'

'This isn't home.'

'You just said it was,' the woman said gently. 'And we all think you're wonderful already. If Jess needs an uncle and you need roots, why not stay? Heaven knows, Matt needs a family.'

'Matt has a family.' She was sounding curt to the point of rudeness now but the woman wasn't noticing. What was it about the medical world that made its inhabitants think they could intrude into their colleagues' lives? It happened the world over and here was obviously no exception.

'One failed marriage, one wimp of a mother and one bully of a father,' the nurse said softly, thoughtfully. 'The whole hospital's been trying to get our Matt paired off for ever. We'd practically given up.'

'I'm his sister-in-law, not a potential girlfriend,' Kelly snapped, and the nurse grinned.

'Of course you are,' she agreed. 'But as you said yourself, all that was a long time ago. And our Dr Matt is gorgeous.'

Our Dr Matt is gorgeous.

The problem was that he was.

Kelly drove home in the dark. She normally needed all her attention to stay on the left, but the road was quiet and there was a fraction of her mind free to stray.

She'd been acutely aware of Matt today. Beth was in charge of Emergency but she'd almost unconsciously deferred to Matt. He'd worked like two men, one part working to salvage mangled limbs, the other watching what was going on in the rest of the room. He'd snapped curt orders, not just for the patient he was treating but for others as well. He didn't interfere with any other doctor's treatment, but he was covering the room, making sure equipment, plasma, saline, everything needed was on hand.

Supply should have been a full-time role but there hadn't been enough medical hands on deck to cover it. Matt had done it seamlessly, as well as ensuring at least two people didn't need amputation. As well as reassuring frightened patients. As well as fielding a call from the overseas parents of the girl who'd died under his hands. The hospital counsellors had moved in to take most of the calls but for that one the counsellor had approached him.

'They know their daughter didn't die instantly. They have visions of her dying in agony. Matt, if you could…'

Matt could. He'd stepped to a corner of the room near where Kelly had been working and she'd heard him speaking, quietly, gently, as if he'd had all the time in the world.

'With the blow to the head as well as the spinal injury she'd have been instantly unconscious and not frightened or in any pain. Apparently they were having a wonderful time in the bus. It started slipping on the dunes and everyone thought it was fun. The passengers thought it was supposed to happen, so there was no terror. Yes, she was alive when she was brought into hospital but the paramedics assure me she was deeply unconscious from the moment of impact.'

And then… 'No. I'm so sorry but even if we'd been able to save her, her brain damage would have been

massive and the spinal injury would have meant total
paralysis. Of course I'm available to answer any questions you might have in the future, and certainly if you
decide to come to Australia to take your girl home, I'll
talk to you then. Or before. That goes for any of our
staff. The paramedics who brought her in, the counsellors, any one of the men and women who've cared for
her, we're all here for you.'

Kelly hadn't been able to hear the other end of the
conversation but she'd listened to Matt's reassurances
and she'd thought somewhere on the other side of the
world devastated parents would put down the phone
knowing everything that could have been done for their
girl had been done.

She'd been in caring hands.

Caring...

She thought of the Matt she'd met eighteen years
ago. Caring was the last word she'd have thought to
apply to him.

That had been a long time ago. So...what?

Her thoughts were drifting and she wasn't sure
where. Or maybe she did know but it scared her. She
needed to think of someone...of something else.

She'd been offered a job. That was a good thought.
If she could work and earn, maybe she wouldn't have
to stay in Matt's house.

But Jess would love staying in Matt's house, and
Matt was Jessie's uncle. Did she have the right to refuse
to let them get to know each other? A week ago she'd
have said yes. After tonight, seeing Matt's skill, seeing Matt's inherent kindness, she thought: possibly not.

But where did that leave her? The way she was feeling...Matt's skill and kindness was doing her head in.

Was that down to his likeness to her husband?

Possibly not, she thought. She'd been widowed for eighteen years and her memories of her husband had been obscured by time. He was a loving ghost at her shoulder, but he wasn't one who reminded her to mourn. Neither was he one who claimed ownership.

He'd be troubled that she'd never had another serious relationship, she thought, and she struggled to conjure him up. What would his advice be?

Do what's right for today, Kell, he'd say. *Don't let tomorrow's monsters scare you. Tomorrow they'll look like minnows. You can kick them away with the pleasure you gain from today. Especially from today's surf.*

Maybe she needed a surf.

Now? In the dark?

Maybe not.

What she needed now was bed. What she needed now was to make the confusion in her head go away.

'You'll all be minnows tomorrow,' she told her doubts, but the image of Matt on the telephone superimposed itself.

There was no way Matt Eveldene would ever be a minnow.

Matt slept badly. He always did after tragedy. While he'd trained he'd thought eventually he'd get used to it but he never had. The anger at the waste of life, because one unskilled driver had thought it would be fun to gun a busload of kids over cresting sand dunes... The grief it caused... The grief that would go on and on...

Like the grief he felt for his brother.

He thought of the woman presumably sleeping just through the wall from him and the grief she'd endured. He could have helped her.

There was yet more grief.

He found himself thinking of his mother in that appalling mausoleum of a house, afraid to walk away from her husband, afraid of her own shadow. But maybe she wasn't afraid, he thought. Maybe she couldn't escape grief wherever she went, so why try? He brought her here when his father was away but she was totally passive. She sat on the veranda and stared out to sea, and as soon as her husband was due home, she packed and left.

He'd tried to persuade her to seek help. He'd made appointments for her with psychologists, but no one had been able to break through.

Could Kelly?

Could Jessie?

There was another worry keeping him awake. If he let his mother know of Jessie's existence, it'd bring joy, but it'd also set loose the full force of his father. Kelly was one strong woman but no one could face down his father.

He slept fitfully, and finally it was dawn. He dropped a hand to greet the dogs at the side of his bed—and found nothing.

Traitors, he thought, remembering they hadn't bounded out to greet him last night either. They'd be with Kelly.

They'd be just through the wall. By her bed.

This was driving him crazy. He'd head down to the beach before work, he decided. At least the waves might clear the fog.

He grabbed his swimmers, headed out to the veranda and paused.

Someone was surfing just below the house. His dogs were on the beach, standing guard as they did when he surfed.

He gazed along the veranda to where two surfboards

usually lay, one short and light for when he wanted to push himself, the other a long board, stable and easy to paddle, for times when he wanted to lie behind the breakers and catch the occasional wave with ease.

The small one was gone. It took skill...

She had skill.

He stood and watched in the soft dawn light. A rolling breaker was coming in. The sea was silk smooth, glimmering in the sun's early rays. The breaker was a dark shadow, moving swiftly, building height as it neared the shallows.

She caught its force at just the right time, at just the right angle. In one smooth movement she was on her feet, sleek and light, her feet at one with the board, working it like a lover.

She wasn't content to simply ride the wave to shore. She crested to the lip and swooped, she flipped a turn, then cruised under the breaking foam. Finally she dropped full length, dipping her head so the wave wouldn't push her backwards, and started paddling, easily and smoothly, out to catch the next wave.

She was wearing a simple black costume. Her hair was a tangle of dripping curls. She looked...she looked...

No. There were a hundred reasons why he shouldn't think how she was looking.

He thought of how she'd been when Jess had found her. Seventeen. She'd been a wild creature, he thought. Maybe she still was.

Why would he prefer to see her as a wild creature? Someone who could never fit into a life like this?

Still, she shouldn't be surfing alone.

He glanced across at the headlands and was almost disappointed to see other surfers in the water. It was an unwritten rule that surfers looked out for others when they could see them. She wasn't actually alone.

But now she'd seen him. He must be obvious, standing on the veranda, watching.

He didn't want to intrude but she waved as if she was including him in her morning—and then the next wave rolled in and she went back to concentrating on the surf.

How could he resist? He couldn't. He had two hours before he needed to leave for work and Kelly was surfing on his beach. Even his dogs were waiting.

Putting away the hundred reasons why he shouldn't, he grabbed his long board and went to join her.

For Kelly, surfing was as natural as breathing. It was her release, her escape. She surfed with friends, she surfed with Jess, but their presence didn't matter.

It was also okay to surf with Matt, for he understood silence.

She'd met chatty surfers and they drove her crazy. It was okay to lie out behind the waves and solve the problems of the world after a long morning's surf, but to choose to talk rather than surf...

Matt didn't. He simply paddled out to her, raised a hand in greeting and concentrated on the next wave.

He caught it with ease, rose, steadied, then manoeuvred the big board with skill and rode it until the wave shrank into the shallows.

A surfing surgeon.

He wasn't as skilled as a pro, but he was more than competent. He was riding a big old board, because she had his good one. He looked good on it. No, he looked great. She'd thought he was married to his medicine but his body was tanned and ripped and he couldn't be as good as this without practice.

A wave swelled and swept past—and she'd missed it. It was a beauty. Matt caught it and in seconds he was in the green room, that gorgeous sapphire tube of perfectly looped water.

If he'd had his good board he could have stayed in there for the length of the ride. As it was, he emerged and glanced back at her and said, 'If you're going to waste waves like that, I want my board back.'

She chuckled and glanced behind and caught the next one, and somehow things had changed between them again.

Something had settled.

This was her husband's brother, she told herself as the morning grew brighter, as they caught wave after wave, as the silence deepened and strengthened between them. He was Jess's uncle.

But she knew, at some deep level, he was becoming much, much more.

It should scare her, but it didn't. She rode her waves and Matt rode behind, before or beside her, and it didn't matter.

Something had changed. Somehow, for this moment, she felt peace.

The morning had to end. Matt had patients waiting. 'Stay if you want,' Matt told her, but she shook her head. In truth, she wasn't as fit as she used to be. Two hours' surfing was enough.

'Do you want to leave the boards in the dunes?' Matt said. 'The surfers at the headlands never come this far. No one comes along here but us. You...*we* could surf tomorrow.'

There was a promise. She managed a wavery smile in return.

'The short one's yours tomorrow.'

'No way. My skills don't match yours. Right now I can blame the board and that's the way I like it.'

She chuckled and they headed up to the house.

If I was a teenager I might reach out and take his hand, Kelly thought, and then hauled herself back under control.

Yeah, but you're not a teenager. You have a whole lot more hormones—and Matt needs to go to work.

Matt.

But...but...

'You're smiling because...?' Matt asked, and she found herself blushing from the toes up.

'Yeah,' Matt said. 'Me, too.'

Me, too? Really? *Really*?

'Not appropriate,' she managed.

'No.'

Okay. That was decided.

'Not when I have a theatre list in forty minutes.'

Hmm. There was enough promise in that statement to take a woman's breath away. 'You get first shower,' she told him, feeling suddenly breathless. 'Unless there's enough water pressure for two showers.'

'There's not," he said.

"Go. I'll make breakfast.'

'I'll grab a coffee at the hospital.'

'You can't surf for hours and then operate on an empty stomach. Surgeon fainting mid-list? Not a good look.'

'Toast, then,' he said, and she nodded.

'Toast. Go.'

'Kelly?'

But his nearness was doing things to her. He was too

big, too broad, too almost naked. His chest was still wet. Water was still dripping from his hair. He looked…

'Toast,' she said, and if she sounded desperate, who could blame her? 'But shower, now. Go!'

He ran his shower cold. Really cold. If he could have added ice it would have been a sensible option. He dressed with care, thinking it'd be better if he was consulting rather than operating this morning because then he could dress formally in suit. He could always take his jacket off later, but for some reason it seemed imperative that he be completely, carefully dressed when he saw Kelly again. If he didn't have a suit jacket and tie on it would be so easy to…

No. Any minute now it'd be another cold shower.

Breakfast. Toast. He headed for his kitchen, thinking he should have made it clear to Kelly that he'd eat on his side and she could do whatever she wanted on her side, but he hadn't made it clear and he copped the smell of eggs and bacon before he got there. *In his kitchen.*

Kelly was frying bacon. She had a beach towel wrapped round her like a sarong. Her feet were still sandy. Her curls were tangled damply around her shoulders.

Every part of him froze.

Every part of him wanted.

No. A man had to work!

Sensibly, though, a man also had to have breakfast. Treat this as ordinary, he pleaded with himself. He walked in and she turned and smiled at him and handed him a loaded plate of eggs, bacon, fried tomato and toast.

'A boy's fantasies are all coming together right here,' he managed. He had the plate in his hands. That helped.

He couldn't reach out and touch her. But she was still too close and that towel was tucked simply into itself right at her breast and he knew underneath was that simple slip of black Lycra...

'Seduction by bacon,' she said demurely. 'Things your mother never taught you.'

'No.' He hesitated, trying to figure how to get this electric charge out of the room. History, he thought. Remember bleakness. 'Your mother never taught you much by the sound of it,' he tried.

'No,' she said, and the smile slipped a little. 'But I've been around enough surf camps in my life to know a great feed after surfing is a sure way to a man's heart. You'll still have forgotten me by lunchtime, though. You'll see. The lady in the cafeteria will smile at you as she hands you your turkey sandwich and you'll change allegiances, just like that.'

He thought of Tilda in the hospital canteen, fair, fat and fifty. He looked again at Kelly's bare toes and the sand in her cleavage and the way one curl was just trailing downward...

'I think you just won,' he said, and he couldn't keep his voice steady.

'Love's more fickle than you think,' Kelly said serenely, turning back to cook her own breakfast.

'You mean no one ever fell for you after Jessie?' He tried to keep the question casual—and failed.

'Sure they did,' she said. 'I've cooked so many breakfasts I couldn't possibly count.'

'Kelly...'

She turned. The bacon sizzled in the pan behind her. She looked at him.

'I don't do light stuff,' she said in a voice that was anything but light. 'My dad was promiscuous, living with woman after woman after woman. I'm Jessie's mother. That comes first. It always has and it always will.'

'Jess is growing up.'

'And he still needs to respect his mom.'

'How can he not respect you?'

'Eat your breakfast,' she told him, and deliberately turned away. She finished cooking hers, served it out and then sat on the opposite side of the table. They ate in silence. Things were happening between them, and he didn't have a clue what.

I don't do light stuff. It was a warning to back off.

He didn't—necessarily—want to back off, but the complications of falling for this woman were immense.

Was he falling for her?

Had he already fallen?

He'd only known her a few days. She was his brother's wife.

'I need to go,' he managed, thinking he needed space, and, thank heaven, medicine could supply it. 'I'm doing Gloria Matterson's hip replacement this morning. She's been waiting for two years in the public queue and she doesn't need to wait longer.'

'Of course you do. And this… Maybe this morning wasn't a good idea,' Kelly told him.

And he thought, she needs space, too.

What was happening between them? Exactly nothing. They hadn't even kissed.

He rose and carted his plate to the sink. He'd have coffee on the way to work. There was a drive-through…

He turned and Kelly had risen with her plate and she was just…there. Right in front of him.

She looked adorable.

He took the plate from her grasp and put it in the sink behind him. He did it without turning. For some reason it seemed imperative that he didn't break their locked gazes.

I don't do light stuff.

This wasn't light. This was a force he'd never felt before, a sensual pull stronger than any he'd ever known. He wanted to take the beach towel and tug it to the floor. He wanted to run his hands over the curve of her beautiful hips. He wanted...

He'd just have to want. Gloria Matterson wanted, too, and she'd have been given pre-op drugs already.

'I need to go,' he said hoarsely.

'Of course you do.'

'Kelly...'

'Just go.'

'I will,' he said, and if it sounded like a vow, maybe it was. Then, because he couldn't help himself, because there was no way he could stop himself, he took her shoulders in his hands, drew her to him and kissed her.

She should not be kissing Matt Eveldene. Not!

For eighteen years she'd hated this man. She'd hated his family, she'd hated everything he represented. She'd sworn never to have anything to do with him or his ghastly family ever in her lifetime. And now she was in his arms, her mouth was on his, and she was being soundly, solidly kissed.

No. Not soundly. Not solidly. There was nothing about those two words that came near to describing what was happening to her right now.

She was being...subsumed.

Was that the word? Actually, who cared? His mouth was warm on hers, his hands were hugging her close, her breasts were moulding against him and the kiss... oh, the kiss...

It felt like fire. It felt like pure, hot fusion. She could taste him, feel him, melt into him.

He was large and strong and sure. The soft wool of his gorgeous suit was whispering against the bare skin of her shoulders. His hands were in the small of her back, pressing her closer. His strong, angular face was hard against hers.

Her hands rose seemingly of their own accord and ran through his thick, black hair to tug him closer, close enough so she felt their mouths were welded together, a fusion growing stronger by the moment.

As was the heat building through her body. She was on fire.

She wanted this man, right here, right now, but he was already putting her away because Gloria Matterson was waiting and there were medical imperatives and this was…this was…

Crazy.

Her towel slipped. It lay in a puddle on the floor and she thought of what might have happened if there had been no surgical list waiting. She could…

She couldn't. Somehow she managed a deep breath. Yes, that's what she had to do. Recover, think things through and get on with…what she had to get on with.

'Uh-oh,' she managed, but she didn't quite recognise the husky whisper that came out. 'I knew my cooking was good but not that good.'

'There's a lot about you that's good.'

'You…don't know me.'

'There is that. We should have started this as online dating. I'd know your star sign then.'

'So what's yours?' She wasn't making sense, even to herself.

'Libra.'

'Uh-oh. I'm Aries. I'll walk all over you. Favourite music?'

'Wagner.'

'Really?' She choked.

'Um, no.' He grinned, lightening the room with his devastating smile. 'Assuming this is online dating data, I threw that in to scare away the hip-hops. But classical, yes.'

'But mine *is* hip-hop,' she said mournfully, trying to smile back, carefully retrieving her towel and rewrapping it. 'So we're doomed from the start. Take this no further, Dr Eveldene. Go to work.'

'Until tonight?'

'I should move out,' she said worriedly. 'I don't think—'

'Don't move out.'

'Because?'

'Because I don't want you to.' His smile faded. He cupped her chin in his hand and kissed her again, hard and fast. 'You're right, we don't know each other. We have baggage that is certain to get in the way. Hip-hop, classic—problem, but there are always earphones. Kelly…my home is special and I wish to share it with you. Please stay.'

'I'll stay,' she said, and he had to go. She stood and watched as he headed out the door, into his car and out of sight. Her hand stayed on her lips as if she could keep the taste of him just by holding it there.

He disappeared and reality set in. But not regret.

She'd just kissed her husband's brother. For years she'd regarded him as the enemy. Kissing him should have seemed like a betrayal and yet…it hadn't. It had felt right.

More, it felt like the bitterness that had stayed with

her for all those years had melted in that kiss. Ultimate forgiveness? Ultimate moving on?

But what had he said? *My home is special.* It was an odd line for a guy to use. Seduction by interior design?

She glanced about her at his stunning home. She glanced into the living room at the great rock mantelpiece, the exquisite rugs, the floor-to-ceiling windows framing the ocean beyond.

My home is special.

'I'd have stayed anyway,' she whispered, still touching her lips. 'The way you kissed me seems to have wiped away the awfulness of the past. And in such a kiss, I might not have noticed your home.'

She hardly noticed places. No, that wasn't true. She could certainly appreciate that Matt's house was beautiful. It was just that she saw houses—homes—as transient.

My home is special...

It was such an odd statement that she found herself thinking again of the inherent, basic differences between them. Classic, hip-hop. Aries, Libra. Nomad, house-loving. Internet dating wouldn't have stood a chance.

My home is special...

She thought back eighteen years, to her beloved Jess, trying to explain about his family.

'All my dad ever thinks about is things. His home. His possessions.'

Jess had rejected those things and so had she.

'Dad controls people with his possessions,' Jess had told her. *'We don't need them.'*

She still didn't. She'd been fiercely independent all her life, and nothing was changing now. Just because one man had kissed her...

Oh, for heaven's sake. Stop worrying, she told herself crossly. She should take a shower and then head to the hospital. She had a son to visit. Beth had promised to talk to her about a job. She had enough to do today without thinking of possessions controlling her. She had enough to do without thinking of the incompatibility between the two Drs Eveldene.

And in any gaps in her day, qualms or not, she had a kiss to remember.

CHAPTER SEVEN

'HOW ABOUT TRIAGE in Emergency?' To say Beth was enthusiastic about employing her was an understatement. 'The local surf competitions come straight after the world tour so we're overrun with surfing casualties. Plus, it's school holidays, which always sees us busy. Could you work mornings from eight to one? That's when most surf casualties come in. Your provisional registration means you're supposed to be supervised, but with your skills I'm happy to supervise from half a hospital away. From what I gather, you can cope with most surf injuries in your sleep.'

So it was settled. Excellent. Wasn't it?

How had her life changed so dramatically? She was living in Matt's house. She was working in Matt's hospital.

She'd been kissing in Matt's kitchen.

Giving in to temptation...

Um, temptation wasn't exactly what she needed to be considering, when the woman in front of her was offering her a job.

'I coped with a kid impaled on a surfboard once,' Kelly told her, trying hard to feel and sound professional. 'A grommit—a learner surfer—thought it'd be a great idea to make his surfboard stand out. He drew the eyes and the razor teeth of a swordfish and whittled the snout to a sharp point. He came off, his leg rope jerked him onto the point and the whole thing went through his thigh. He came into ER with fibreglass still attached.'

'Yikes,' Beth said. 'Happy ending?'

'A textbook surfboard-ectomy.' Kelly grinned, relaxing into the medicine she loved. 'He lived to surf another day.'

Beth grinned back. 'A woman who performs surfboard-ectomies is my kind of doctor. So, do you want the job?'

'Surely you need to check up on me.'

'Matt already did. He phoned your previous bosses this morning. You have glowing credentials from everyone.'

'How did he know who to ask?' Kelly gasped.

'Your son, of course. Apparently Jess thinks it's cool that you'll be working here.'

'Matt asked Jess?'

'He's his uncle, isn't he?'

There was a statement to make her catch her breath. It suggested that Matt had a relationship with Jess that had nothing to do with her. Maybe he did, but...

My home is special and I wish to share it with you.

She couldn't get rid of that stupid statement. Why did the words keep coming back and why did they make her feel edgy? Like the walls were closing in?

She was being paranoid, she decided. She and Jess were accepting Matt's kindness while Jess recuperated. That was all. And it was fine that Jess had told Matt where she'd trained.

And the kiss?

The kiss had been an aberration, she told herself—

a momentary temptation and weakness. So why had it felt like a beginning?

'So, do you want the job?' Beth asked brightly again. 'There's a heap of forms to complete if you do. You can take them with you and fill them in while Jess watches his surf videos.'

'How do you know Jess watches surf videos?'

'Matt told me. He took him some sci-fi movies and Jess politely declined. Matt thinks he's a bit obsessed.'

'He told you he thinks Jessie's obsessed?'

'Hey,' Beth said, and held up her hands as if in surrender. 'I'm a mother of three teenagers. I understand obsession. Matt doesn't.'

'But he told you. It's none of his business.'

'Maybe he wants it to be his business,' Beth said mildly. 'But as for me, I'm butting out, right now.'

'So Matt's been lending you sci-fi movies?'

Kelly had made herself wait a whole half-hour before casually asking the question, and Jess didn't look up from the television when she did.

'Yeah. They were dumb. He didn't mind, though, when I refused. It's not like he bought them or anything—they're borrowed. I told him I had more surfing stuff than I could handle but he didn't seem interested. Do you know if he can surf?'

'He can. He's not bad.'

'I guess with Dad for a brother he must know how. A surfing surgeon. That's pretty cool. He was telling me about Dad when he was a kid. Mom, they're saying I can go home tomorrow as long as I come in every morning for physiotherapy. Matt says there's loads of room at his place and he dogs and I can see the surf. And Beth… she's the doctor in Emergency and she's cool…she has a son who's fourteen and a surf nut but he's teaching himself from videos. She asked if I might have time to talk him through them. She'll bring him out to Matt's.'

Right. All organised. This was good. So why did it feel like the ground was sliding away from under her? Why was she feeling like she was more out of control that she'd ever been?

'That's great,' she managed. 'And I have a job.'

'I know that, too,' Jess said. 'Or I knew they were going to offer. Everyone knows everything around here, even the janitor.' He looked up at her then, with that shy, warm smile that was so like his father's it still did her head in. 'If I had to wipe out, it was pretty lucky I wiped out here. It almost feels like home.'

Home. There was that word again.

She shook off her unease and checked the colour of Jess's toes, not because she needed to—she was sure even a minuscule change wouldn't have escaped Matt's attention. But she needed to be doing something.

She wished she could start work this morning instead of in two days' time when the forms had been cleared. She wished...

She wished she was doing something that wasn't controlled by Matt Eveldene and his hospital and his home.

She wished she wasn't tempted.

There was no way Kelly was raiding Matt's refrigerator again. She and Jess would be independent. So after leaving the hospital she headed to the supermarket Matt had taken her to that first night he'd taken her to his place.

After stocking up on provisions, she made for home. No, she corrected herself, she made for *Matt's place*. Why the differentiation was important she didn't know, but it was. She did Jess's washing then, looking for something else to do, she took the dogs for a walk on the beach.

She wished Jess wasn't so fiercely independent. If he was younger and less fierce about his boundaries she could go back to the hospital and talk to him or read, or even help while he did his physio.

If Matt offered, would Jess let him help?

'The kid needs a father.' Various people had said that to her over the years, or variations on the theme. 'How does he cope without a father figure?'

He'd coped fine. She was proud of him.

So why was she stalking along the beach like she was angry? Was she angry?

If the Eveldenes had been supportive all those years ago, if they'd offered a home and family to her and her son, would she have wanted it?

Did she want it now?

She wasn't making sense, even to herself.

Disconcerted, she headed back to the house. She felt aimless, totally disoriented.

She could surf, but for once there was no one surfing at the far headlands and one of her rules was not surfing without other surfers in sight. She'd made that rule up for Jess. As a kid she'd surfed whenever she'd wanted, but becoming a mother had changed the ground rules. Tempting as it was, if she surfed alone then Jess would, too.

She needed to ask Matt not to, she decided. There was already a hint of change of allegiance in Jess's attitude. She could hear him in her imagination.

'If Matt surfs alone, I don't see why you're worried.'

Oh, for heaven's sake, get over yourself, she told herself. She was worrying about shadows. She turned

her back on the ocean and headed for her little kitchen.
What to do? What to do?

Bake?

She never baked. She didn't even cook much. In their
shoebox of an apartment in Hawaii she had a two-ring
burner and a microwave.

'If this place is "home" then I might as well pretend
it really is,' she told herself. 'And what do normal people do at home? Bake.'

So she would. She'd make a welcome-home cake for
Jess. How hard could it be?

'I'll need a pinafore,' she told the dogs, egging herself into the role of cook-extraordinaire. 'And maybe
some fluffy slippers and hair curlers.'

The dogs wagged their tails, bemused, as well they
might be. Kelly cooking? Kelly was a bit bemused herself.

Matt climbed out of the car, taking a breath of the sea
air to ground himself—and smelled burning. Smoke
was wafting from the windows at the end of the house.
He ran, grabbing his phone so he could call emergency
services, imagining the worst.

It wasn't the worst. Kelly was at her kitchen bench,
surrounded by smoke, staring mournfully at something
that looked like a withered, black pyramid.

She looked totally, absolutely crestfallen.

The pyramid was oozing the smoke. It smelled of
burned citrus. It was surrounded by flour, eggshells,
milk cartons, cream cartons, splattered…mess. The
dogs were cruising, obviously hoovering up a week's
worth of treats in one hit. Bess was doing better than
Spike because she could reach higher. Whatever had
splattered had hit walls as well as floor.

'I think I know what the problem is,' Kelly said mournfully, not taking her eyes from the pyramid. 'I should have put the orange syrup on after it was cooked, not before. It sort of spilled over the sides and the bottom of the oven started to smoke. And then flame. And it cooked so fast...'

She had mixture on her face, through her hair, on her jeans and T-shirt. She looked...

Delicious.

'Argument with the mixer?' he ventured, trying desperately not to laugh, and she glared at the offending object as if it was totally to blame.

'I wanted to check if it was thick enough. I lifted the beaters for a second. And your oven's faulty. The recipe said three-fifty degrees for three-quarters of an hour and your oven only goes to two hundred and eighty. But look what it did after fifteen minutes?'

He couldn't help it. His mouth twitched.

'Don't you dare laugh.'

'No,' he said, and walked—or rather squelched—to the bench. She had her laptop sitting on the fruit bowl, where it had, luckily, been shielded from the mixer by fruit.

He read the screen. Yep, the instructions read three-fifty degrees for forty minutes. But this was an American site. An American recipe.

'You ever heard of Celsius versus Fahrenheit?' he asked.

She stared at him, her eyes widening in dawning horror. 'Celsius...'

'And we drive on the left side of the road, too,' he said apologetically. 'Whoops.'

'Celsius! That'd be...' She did a quick calculation

in her head. 'A hundred and seventy. Oh, my… Why didn't they say?'

'Because *they're* American.'

'That's crazy.'

'Americans *are* crazy. Almost the whole world— apart from Americans—uses Celsius.'

'Now you're insulting my country as well as my cooking.'

He grinned, took a dollop of goop from the bench and tasted. 'I'm not insulting your cooking. This is good. Ganache?'

She peered suspiciously at the recipe and checked. 'Yes,' she conceded.

'Did you try and layer it into the cake before you cooked it?'

She glowered. 'I'm not completely dumb. It's still in the bowl. Or at least,' she corrected, 'most of it's still in the bowl.'

'So…' He went back to the recipe, fascinated. 'We have Grand Marnier ganache, some of it still in the bowl, plus chocolate orange cake, slightly singed.'

'Stupid recipe,' she muttered. 'If I can track neural pathways and get high distinctions for forensic pathology, I should be able to follow basic instructions. But no. And now you're making things worse by being supercilious. Go away. Do something useful, like look up cake shop addresses online.'

'You want a welcome-home cake for Jess?'

'That's the idea.'

'I can cook.'

'Right.'

'Honest.' He folded his arms and surveyed cook and kitchen with glinting amusement. She was cute, he thought. She was really cute. And with ganache on her nose he had a strong desire to…

Um…his thoughts had better change direction fast.

'We still have heaps of ganache,' he said. 'We could try again.'

'Again? Are you out of your mind? Your oven needs a jackhammer. I might need to buy you another one.'

He opened the oven. Orange syrup, baked on hard…

He rolled up his sleeves. 'This is men's work,' he said, feeling the need to beat his chest a little. 'Nothing to it.'

'You're lying.'

'I'll prove it. You scrub the walls, I'll scrub the oven.'

'I'd rather fence off the whole area and let it moulder.'

'What would you do if you did this at home?' he demanded, startled.

'Move. We only ever rent.'

He looked at her with incredulity. 'I can't imagine how you get references.'

'I'm a good tenant,' she said with dignity. 'I just don't rent ovens. Apartments with ovens cost more and now I see why. They're lethal.'

'They're fun.'

'Says the man who's offering to scrub one? Matt, it's okay. I made this mess. I'll clean it up.'

'You won't,' he said, suddenly serious. 'I've left you to face enough messes on your own. The least I can do is help you with this one.'

He wouldn't take no for an answer. He changed into jeans and T-shirt and locked the dogs outside, then for half an hour they scrubbed and cleaned. She grew more and more mortified. Then, the last wall wiped, the last pot cleaned, he hauled ingredients and pots and bowls out again and she forgot about being embarrassed, regarding him with horror.

'Matt, this recipe is lethal.'

'This recipe looks great.'

'It could have killed me. I could be a smouldering pile of ash on top of what remains of your glorious home right now.'

'Let's not get carried away.'

'It has it in for me.'

'You just lack the necessary qualification. Did I tell you I'm a surgeon? Precision is my byword. You want to be second in command?'

'No,' she said. 'Think of me as the janitor. Washing up's my forte.'

'I need an assistant,' he said. 'As of now you're employed by Gold Coast Central. As senior surgeon I have the right to tell junior staff what to do. I want two fifty grams of plain flour measured out into a bowl. The scales are in metric. Don't you dare think about conversion. Get to it now, Dr Eveldene. Flour. Weigh. Stat!'

And there was nothing else for a woman to do. Flour. Weigh. Stat.

This man was a surgeon and that was how he approached his cooking. He treated it as a tricky piece of surgery, like reconstructing a child's knee, with meticulous attention given to detail at every stage.

He insisted on scrupulous cleanliness. Measurements had to be correct almost to the closest gram. Tins were to be lined with perfect circles of baking paper—when her circles were a bit wobbly he made her cut more. Instructions were read aloud by his 'assistant' then checked by Matt, then rechecked as soon as the procedure was complete. There was not a sliver of room for error. And pity any recipe writer who got it wrong, because Kelly could hardly imagine what Matt's reaction would be if he didn't get it right first time.

But, of course, he did. An hour and a half later they were sitting at the kitchen table, admiring a cake that looked better than the picture on the internet. All they had to do when Jess arrived was slice it and insert the ganache.

'And I'll do that,' Matt said sternly.

'You're the surgeon,' she admitted. They were eating toasted sandwiches, which Matt had kindly allowed her to make—under supervision. She grinned. 'There's no need to keep looking at it. I can only cope with so much smugness before I crack and put the ganache where it really oughtn't to be put.'

'It's hard not to be smug about perfection.' He looked even more smug and she lifted the ganache bowl. He grinned back at her and held his hands up in surrender. 'Hey, I'm not being smug about *my* work. I'm being smug about *our* work.'

'Very generous. When did you learn to cook?'

'When I was a kid. We had a cook-housekeeper. Mrs Marsh. Jess used to escape to the surf, but while I was too young to go with him, the kitchen was my refuge.'

'Your childhood was tough, huh?'

'Poor little rich kids,' he said dryly. 'It was better for me than for Jess. He was the elder so he was expected to take over the business. The pressure on him was enormous but I learned to stay out of the way.' He hesitated. 'When I was really young I'd try and intervene. I remember screaming at my father, "*Leave my Jess alone.*" I was belted for my pains and Jess told me he'd do the same to me if I ever tried to interfere again. Not that he would. But I learned…the only way was to disappear.'

'It's a wonder you're still in Australia.'

'Once I got my medical degree I had some form of protection.' He hesitated. 'Even that was down to Jess, though. When I was due to start university my father was so angry with Jess he hardly noticed what I was doing. Jess was the oldest, Jess had to pull himself together and take over what was expected of him. While I was at university he thought I was still under control. I put my head down and kept out of his way. That feels bad now. I should have deflected more of his anger.'

'I think there's been enough guilt,' Kelly told him. 'Jess would have hated you to carry more.'

'He would have wanted me to care for you.'

'I didn't need to be cared for,' she said with some asperity. 'Or maybe I did, but Jess did enough. He married me, he settled my future and he knew I had the strength to take his legacy forward.'

'He knew how strong you were,' Matt said, and lifted his hand and touched her face, a whisper of a touch, tracing her cheekbones and sending all sorts of weird currents through her body, and not one of them bad. 'His independent Kelly.'

If he kept touching her... If she just leaned forward...

'I feel like a surf,' she said, pushing her plate away, striving desperately to push away the longings this man was starting to engender. 'We have an hour before dark. Would you like...?'

'I would like,' he said gravely, and his eyes didn't leave hers. 'I would like very much.'

There was only so much temptation a woman could resist.

They surfed as they'd surfed that morning, but things had changed. They lay out on the sunset-tinged waves, waiting for the next wave to carry them in, but tonight, by unspoken mutual consent, they caught the same waves. And there was no fancy surfing from Kelly. Even though she had the zippy short board, even though her board would have let her run rings around Matt, she was content to ride the force into the shallows beside Matt.

Over and over they caught the waves, but there was no speaking. There seemed no need. It seemed all the talking had been done, everything they needed to know had been discovered, and what was before them now was predestined.

The sun sank low over the hills, sending fire out over the waves. The moon rose over the sea, hanging low, promising ribbons of silver when the sun's rays stopped competing for air play.

Night. The rays would come in to feed. Visibility was dropping by the second. It was time to leave.

They rode the last wave to the beach, tugged the boards up past the high-water mark and left them there. Matt took her hand and led her up to the house and still no words needed to be spoken.

This is right, Kelly thought, a great wash of peace settling over her as her body tingled with anticipation of what was to come.

That was a dumb thought. It was a thought that had to be shelved, and it was, because how could she think of anything but Matt as he led her into the shower off his bedroom? Matt, as he stepped into the shower with her...?

She couldn't think past his body. The rippling muscles of his chest, the traces of sand in the hollows at his shoulders, the way the water ran from his smile right down to his feet. She could see every long, gorgeous inch of him. The water from the shower ran over them, and for this night, for now, every single thing in the world could be forgotten except that this was Matt and he was here, now, and for tonight he was hers.

Nothing else could matter.

'You know this is not a one-night stand,' he muttered thickly into her hair as they stood under the warm water, as somehow their costumes disappeared, as somehow their bodies seemed to be merging into each other.

Not a one-night stand. What was he saying?

It didn't matter, though, because she wasn't thinking past right now, this minute, as Matt flicked off the shower, grabbed towels and started, deliciously, to dry her. This minute, as Matt hung the towels—okay, she did allow herself a moment to be distracted here and think that even now the man was house-proud—but she didn't allow herself to be distracted for more than a millisecond.

Because Matt was lifting her, holding her hard and tight against his body, skin against skin, and it was the most erotic sensation in the world.

And Matt was carrying her back to the bedroom, setting her down on crisp, cool sheets, gazing down at her, taking in every inch of her as she was doing right back to him.

And finally he came down to her. Finally he gathered her into his arms and he made her feel as she'd never felt in her life before.

He made her feel as if she'd found her home.

CHAPTER EIGHT

MATT TOOK A couple of hours off work the next day so he could help bring Jess home. Jess lay with his leg stretched out in the back seat of Matt's car and he signalled his approval as soon as they turned into the main gates.

'Neat place.'

His approval grew even stronger when he saw his room, the veranda—and Matt's indulgent, toys-for-boys media room.

'Can we stay here for ever?' he demanded, and Matt quirked a brow at Kelly and Kelly blushed from the toes up. Why? What was wrong with her?

She knew exactly what was wrong with her.

She'd been tempted and she'd caved right in.

Matt had organised decent crutches, which made Jess pretty much independent. The bathroom in their apartment had obviously been built with Matt's mother in mind. Its easy access and built-in seat catered for the needs of an elderly woman now and in the future, so it was perfect for Jess. Jess checked it out and was obliged to use his approval rating's highest score.

'Über-neat. Now I don't need anyone fussing.'

'Certainly not me,' Kelly agreed, and went and made them all sandwiches. She could at least make sandwiches, she thought ruefully. She wasn't completely useless.

But, then…last night's cake disaster had turned into a success.

Define success?

Success was a highly edible, orange ganache gateau, she told herself, carrying the amazing creation out to the veranda where they'd settled. Nothing else.

'Wow,' Jess said, eyes wide. 'Where did that come from?'

'Your mother made it,' Matt said with aplomb, and Jess looked at him as if he'd lost his mind.

'Not in a million years. Mom struggles with hamburgers.'

'I do not,' Kelly said hotly. 'Or at least, not very much.'

Both guys grinned. Identical smiles.

It did something to her heart. It made her feel…

'You cut,' Matt said, handing her the knife, and she shook her head.

'You're the surgeon.'

'And you're the mother,' Matt said softly. 'You're the mother welcoming her kid home.'

Matt went back to work. Jess went to sleep. Kelly took a book and she and the dogs headed for the beach.

She couldn't read. She walked the dogs but it didn't help. Even a swim couldn't clear her head.

What was happening was some strange, sweet siren song. Temptation plus. Come home… Come home…

What was wrong with it? Why was she so nervous?

Matt was gorgeous. She was pretty sure he wasn't making love to her out of pity or some weird misguided attachment to his long-dead brother. She was pretty sure he'd stopped seeing her as Jess's widow, as she'd

stopped looking at him as Jess's brother. He was just…
Matt. The past was forgotten, or maybe not forgotten
but so far in the past that it was simply a shadow that
could be tucked away and left to lie in peace.

Last night had been awesome, and today… The way
he'd kissed her before he'd left for the hospital this
morning… The way he'd looked at her as she and Jess
had laughed over their cake… There was the promise
of more. Much, much more.

Home.

See, that was the problem. That was what was making her nervous.

Home.

Matt had outpatients all afternoon. This was the day
of the week he liked best. It was his day when patients
came for their final check-up after major surgery.

He saw sixty-year-old Lily Devett who'd fallen over
her cat and broken her arm. Yes, it had been a nasty
fracture but the bones hadn't splintered or broken the
skin. Pinning the bones together had been relatively
easy.

She brought in chocolate cookies, a bottle of truly excellent whisky and gave him a hug that almost squeezed
the breath out of him. 'I can't believe how good it is.
When I broke it I thought that's it, it's a downhill road
to the nursing home, but it's as good as new. I can even
carry my cat again.'

'Just don't fall over it again.' He smiled, and moved
on to see Doug Lamworth.

Doug was fifty-two and had tripped while playing
a tricky golf shot. The ball had landed on the other
side of a creek, the ground was rough and unstable
but Doug had refused to play a drop shot. He'd fallen

and ended up with an appalling hip injury. It had taken Matt tense, difficult hours in surgery to ensure Doug wouldn't walk with a limp for the rest of his life, but his gratitude wasn't forthcoming.

'It still aches,' Doug snapped. 'After six weeks you'd think it'd be right. I don't know what you fellas did in there but you've mucked me round worse than the fall. The bruises…hell. And now your blasted registrar won't give me any more of that codeine stuff. I need it. I tell you, I've just about had enough.'

He left without a script for more of the highly addictive drug, complaining he didn't have time for the physiotherapy Matt told him would work much better than painkillers. He left promising he'd sue the pants off Matt if he wasn't better by the time he and his mates left for their Thailand holiday, and telling him that, by the way, he needed a certificate to try and get a compassionate upgrade to business class.

He left and Matt found himself grinning. He thought he'd enjoy telling Kelly about it tonight.

Telling Kelly… There was a thought. Going home tonight and finding Kelly waiting for him.

And suddenly he found himself thinking of his ex-wife. He'd loved coming home and finding her there. He'd loved the concept of wife and family. It was just that Jenny hadn't wanted to fit in. She'd wanted another sort of life and he'd never really understood what.

Was this his second chance?

Things were better. Things had changed since Jenny.

He knew now that things would never have worked out between him and Jenny. They'd been incompatible, and the thought gave him pause. How could things be different with Kelly? One night's passion wouldn't make a long-term commitment.

But the way she'd felt... The way her body had responded to his... It had felt more than right. It had felt as if he'd been waiting all his life to find her.

His next patient was Herman Briggs, who had a list of complaints a mile long. Apparently his knee replacement should have cured all his ills. At Matt's insistence he'd lost weight before the operation but he'd put it back on with interest. Now his hip was playing up, he had a sore back and his other knee was hurting. What was Matt going to do about it?

Matt organised X-rays, sent him back to the dietician and looked forward to going home to Kelly.

She wasn't sure of the rules.

'Why are you pacing?' Jess demanded. He'd abandoned his video game, distracted by his mother's distraction. 'Is there a problem?'

'I'm not pacing.'

'You look like you're pacing.'

'I'm waiting for Matt.'

'Why?'

The question brought her up short. She turned from the window and stared at her son.

Jess was stretched out on the settee. His gaming console was linked to the television. He'd been using a remote to control cartoon characters doing surf stunts. He looked content.

Jess. Her lovely, placid Jess who took what came, who'd been her life for so long.

Why was she pacing?

There'd been illnesses and injuries before, of course there had. This might be an upmarket place to find themselves in while he recovered but essentially things were the same. Jess got on with his life, she got on with hers, but they were there for each other.

She was his mom. Today was Jess's first day home from hospital. It was well after seven and she hadn't even thought about dinner.

Why? Because she was waiting for Matt?

She was thinking about Matt rather than thinking about her son.

And suddenly she felt like she'd been hit by ice-cold water.

Was she nuts? She'd just met a man again whom she'd thought a toe-rag for years. She'd changed her mind. More than that, she'd fallen in lust for him and now she was mooning about, waiting for him like a lovesick teenager.

Or the little wife. When he got home would she invite him in, cook for all of them, start being a family?

It's a wonder she wasn't standing by the door, slippers in one hand, pipe in the other.

The vision was so ridiculous that she chuckled and Jess looked at her curiously. 'What's the joke?'

'Me being dumb.'

'You're dumb all the time. What makes now something to laugh over?'

She grimaced, grabbed a cushion and tossed it at him. 'Dinner?'

'Yes,' Jess said cautiously. He knew her cooking skills and this seemed a place where take-out seemed unlikely.

'Hamburgers,' she said, and he relaxed.

'Yay.'

She headed for the apartment kitchenette and thought that from tonight she needed to step back. To slow down and think of Jess first.

She needed to close the dividing wall between the apartments until she'd settled her hormones into some sort of sensible, working order.

Matt got home at eight and the apartment side of his house was lit. His side of the house was in darkness.

The dogs came to greet him as he garaged the car but they weren't there instantly, as they normally were. He stooped to pat them and their coats were warm, as if they'd just emerged from somewhere cosy.

He looked at the apartment windows, and then looked at his.

Separate houses?

Kelly emerged onto the veranda and walked along to meet him.

'Hey,' he said, and reached for her. She let him hug her, she responded to his kiss, sinking into him, but only briefly and the kiss was less than quarter baked before she tugged away.

'Um…Matt, no.'

'No?'

'Jess's home.'

'Right.' He wasn't sure how to take that. 'So that means…'

'It means we need to step back,' she said, slightly unevenly, as if the kiss had unsettled her—as well it might. It had sure unsettled him. He had an urgent desire to lift her up and carry her into his den, caveman style. He wanted, quite desperately, to have his wicked way with her—and let her have her wicked way with him.

But there was no humour in her eyes, and the passion of the morning had been subdued.

'Jess has known you less than a week,' she told him. 'He hardly knows you.'

'Is that another way of saying you hardly know me?'

'I guess it is,' she whispered. 'Matt, you're my husband's brother. I don't know why I'm responding to you like I am and I need time to figure it out.'

'You don't want to figure it out together?'

'But where does that leave Jess?' she asked. 'He's smart. He has eyes in the back of his head where I'm concerned. He knows I'm conflicted about seeing you again, even though he knows very little about our history. So now he needs to get to know you—as his uncle. I'm not throwing his mother's lover into the equation.'

'Kelly...'

'It won't hurt,' she said, but he knew it did. Her voice wobbled a bit and he thought that for all her planning she was still unsure. Still tempted. 'It can't hurt to step back a bit.'

Wrong. It hurt a lot. The hunger inside him was primitive. He wanted this woman and he wanted her now, but she was making sense.

She was right. His brother's son was just through the wall. There were complications.

And in the middle of these complications...one man and one woman who wanted each other.

'Give us time, Matt,' Kelly pleaded. 'Let things settle. Let Jess get to know you—as his uncle.'

He didn't want it to make sense, but it did.

'Not...after he goes to bed?' he said without much hope, and she snorted.

'Um...we're talking seventeen-year-old with friends on the other side of the world,' she said. 'Teenage sleeping habits. You want me to try tucking him into bed at nine and sending him to sleep with a bedtime story?'

'A really boring bedtime story?' he suggested without much hope, but at least her smile was back. She chuckled.

'Yeah? Like that'll work. He'll be checking tweets over my sleeping body.'

'That's my plans shot,' he said morosely, and she chuckled.

'Not for ever,' she said lightly. 'We just need to take our time.'

'I'll slope off and take a cold shower, then.'

'Come over and have leftover hamburgers with Jess afterwards.'

'I have the makings of steak and peppercorn sauce.'

'See, there's the divide between us,' she told him. 'Unless you've bought your peppercorn sauce in a bottle, we have a chasm a mile wide.'

'We can bridge it.'

'We might,' she said, and stood on tiptoe and kissed him lightly on the cheek, then stepped back fast before he could respond. 'But it'll take time, and both of us need to be patient.'

He showered. He cooked and ate his steak—with his sauce that didn't come out of a bottle. Then he wandered along the veranda. The French doors of Kelly's apartment were wide open, and he could hear the sound of waves crashing inside.

Waves. Inside. Huh?

He didn't need to knock or call out because the dogs had been by Jessie's side by the settee. They bounded across to him as they sensed his presence.

Kelly was curled in an armchair, reading. Jess was sprawled on the settee, controlling surfers on the television. Waves. Lots of waves.

He put down the remote and grinned. 'Hey, Matt.'

Would it be easier or harder if he was less like his brother? Matt wondered. The way his heart twisted…

'Hey, yourself,' he said, as Kelly looked up and smiled and his heart did a little more twisting. 'You guys look comfortable,' he managed.

'We're good at making transitory places home,' Kelly told him, and he looked at the scattered jumble of teen-age detritus, the piles of obviously to-be-read books and comics on the table, the bunch of wildflowers popped randomly into a tall drinking glass, already starting to drop petals.

'You look like you want to tidy us up,' Kelly said, and he caught himself. That was dumb. He'd just been… looking.

'It's your apartment for the duration. You're welcome to do what you want with it.'

'Thank you,' Kelly said, and put her book aside. 'It will be neat when we leave. We were about to have hot chocolate. You want some?'

'I… Thank you.'

'My pleasure.' She headed for the kitchenette while Jess lay back on the settee and regarded him with eyes that were curiously assessing. How much could the kid guess about what had gone on with his mother?

'Neat freak, huh?' he asked, but his tone was friendly.

'I guess I have to be. Non-neat surgeons tend to do things like leave swabs inside people.'

'So no swabs in me?'

'Not a snowball's chance in a bushfire. Can I check your leg?'

They both relaxed at that. Doctor-patient was a rela-tionship they both understood. They knew where they were.

And the examination was even more reassuring. Jess

was healing with the resilience of the young. His leg looked better than Matt had hoped, and he set the blanket back over it, feeling good.

'So when's the soonest I can surf again?' Jess asked, and the question oddly threw him. Suddenly he no longer felt good.

Memories of his brother were surfacing. 'When can I surf?' The words had been a constant in his childhood, a desperate plea. Surfing had been an escape for Jess, but for the much younger Matt Jess's surfing had meant long days alone with a seething father and a mother who'd suffered because of his father's anger.

It wasn't surfing's fault. Matt had found his own ways of escape, but for Jess surfing had become an obsession. He looked down at his brother's son, and he saw evidence of the same.

Surfing was an obsession for this kid, too.

'In three months you can cope with gentle surf and no tricks,' he told him, struggling to rid himself of shadows. 'But you need to wait for six months for the big-boy stuff. If you get hit again before your leg's completely healed, you risk lifetime damage.'

'Six months *is* a lifetime,' Jess groaned.

'You could always do something useful in the meantime.'

There was a sudden stillness in the room. Kelly had been stirring the hot chocolate. The stirring stopped.

'Like what?' Jess said. His face had gone blank.

So had Kelly's.

Step back, Matt told himself. This was none of his business.

But, then, he was this kid's uncle. Who else did this boy have looking out for him except a mother who was clearly surf mad herself?

What better time to present an alternative than when Jess was looking at an enforced six-month break? Did he intend spending the whole six months playing computer games? Staring out the window at distant surfers, aching to join them?

'I did suggest you might go to school here,' he said diffidently. 'Make some friends. Maybe even pick up a few subjects that might be useful for later.'

'Later when?'

'When you're old enough not to want to spend every minute surfing.'

There was another silence, even more loaded this time. Jess suddenly looked mutinous. 'Mom and I have a deal.'

'What sort of deal?'

'I'll surf and she keeps off my back about anything else.'

What sort of a deal was that? 'It seems a bit one-sided to me,' he said mildly.

'Yeah, and Mom says my grandfather hated surfing, too,' Jess snapped.

'I don't hate surfing.'

'You want me to do calculus and history instead?'

'It's not my business.'

'It's not, is it?' Kelly said from the kitchenette, and she set down the mugs she'd been about to carry across to them. 'What Jess and I do is for us to decide. Matt, we're incredibly grateful for the use of this apartment but if you're about to try forcing Jess back to school then the deal's off. We'll manage without.'

'I'm not forcing anyone anywhere.'

'Good,' she snapped. 'Your family's done enough damage as it is.'

What followed was another one of those loaded silences, but it was worse this time. 'I'm not my father,' he said at last, because it was all he could think of to say.

'No,' she said. 'And as far as I know, uncles have no jurisdiction over their nephews.'

'They don't. I'm sorry.'

'Will you be judgmental about Jess's surfing the whole time we're here?'

'Of course not.' He raked his hair in exasperation. How to mess with a relationship in two short minutes.

'I don't need school,' Jess growled. 'I've done enough study.'

The kid was seventeen! 'For ever?'

'This is none of your business,' Kelly snapped. 'Do you want a hot chocolate or not?'

She lifted the chocolate and he wasn't sure where she was offering to send it. As an air-based missile?

'I seem to have put my foot in it.'

'You have,' she said cordially. 'Jess and I do things our way and we don't take kindly to interference from the Eveldenes.'

'My family has hardly interfered.'

'They haven't, have they?'

'You sound like you resent that.'

'I contacted your father when your brother was ill,' she said, and every trace of warmth was suddenly gone. 'You have no idea how hard that was, for a seventeen-year-old to find the courage to phone the great Henry Eveldene. I thought if we had a little money I could persuade Jess to see a psychiatrist. But you know what your father said? "I'm not sending money to that waste of space. Tell him to give up surfing and come home." That's it. And now here you are…'

'I'm not withdrawing help because Jess wants to surf.'

'No,' she said flatly. 'And for that we're grateful. But Jess doesn't need to go to school.'

He was going about this all the wrong way. He raked his hair again, exasperated. They were living in their own little world, these two. Sure, Kelly had been hurt by his family, but did that allow her to be a negligent parent? Encouraging her son not to go to school?

'You hurt your leg,' he told Jess, struggling to keep things on an even keel. 'It seems this time you've been lucky and you'll get back to surfing. But eventually you'll want security, a home.' He gestured around him to the house he'd built with such care, the house that had become his refuge. 'Somewhere like this. You won't earn this from surfing.'

'Does it matter?' Kelly demanded. 'That we don't have a home?'

'Of course it matters. Look at the mess you're in now.'

'We're not in a mess,' she snapped. 'We're independent. We don't need anyone and we can handle our issues ourselves. Our only problem now is that we seem to have a judgmental landlord. That doesn't matter. We've coped with landlords before. If they're bad we move on.'

'Hey, don't threaten that yet,' Jess said, startled. 'Mom, he's being a stuffed shirt, that doesn't mean we need to move. This place is ace. We can manage a bit of aggro.'

'I'm not being aggressive!'

'Nah,' Jess said thoughtfully. 'But pushy. I'd have thought Dad's brother might be more laid-back. Mom, cut him some slack. Matt, have a drink and move on. I want to stay here.'

'I'd like to stay here, too,' Kelly said. 'But not if Matt's controlling. Not if he intends to bully you.'

'I'm not bullying,' Matt snapped. 'And I'll back off. But I'll have a drink next door, thank you.'

'Are you taking your bat and ball and going home?' she demanded. 'Just because we won't let you be like your father?'

'I am not like my father!' His words were an explosion, and even the dogs responded. Spike even whimpered and headed under Jessie's rug. What a traitor!

'Of course you're not,' Jess said at last, as the echoes died. 'Have a hot chocolate and forget about it.'

'I need to sleep. I have work tomorrow.'

'Bat and ball,' Kelly snapped, and he glared, clicked his fingers at the dogs and headed for the door.

The dogs didn't follow. He reached the veranda and looked back. Every single one of them was looking at him with reproach—even the dogs.

Jess went back to his computer game. Kelly went into her own room, lay on the bed and stared at the ceiling. She'd have liked to walk on the beach but there was no way she was risking meeting Matt again.

They should leave. If Matt intended to even think about controlling Jess... He mustn't.

She'd been so careful, for all her son's life. Her Jess adored surfing. She knew what it meant to him, so she'd worked her life and his around it. She'd had to. She'd seen what denying that passion had done to his father. So far Jess had shown no signs of his father's depression and that was the way it was staying.

Even if it meant walking away from Matt Eveldene?

Even that. Of course that. If he put one more step wrong... If he tried to control...

Even if she wanted him?

'And that's something you need to forget about,' she

told the ceiling. 'Temptation is just plain stupid. From now on, you go back to being a mom. You go back to protecting Jess, no matter what the cost.'

CHAPTER NINE

HE WAS THEIR landlord. They were his tenants. From that night on, that was the way things needed to operate. He'd keep out of their lives. What he said or thought was none of their business, and vice versa.

Luckily, things were frantic at work. King tides meant the surf was huge. Every novice surfer in the country seemed to be daring themselves past their limit—and ending up in Gold Coast Central. Almost all the injuries were orthopaedic. Matt was needed full time.

He stopped surfing in the mornings. He walked his dogs at dawn and then left for the hospital before there was any movement next door. He did his paperwork in his office instead of taking it home. Normally he wouldn't—it wasn't fair on the dogs—but the dogs seemed to be having a fine time with Jess. When he did get home they bounded out to meet him, but they were always toasty warm and he knew where they'd been.

'Are you avoiding us?' He got home one night and Jess was on the veranda settee, watching the sunset surfers with fieldglasses.

'Just busy,' he said briefly. 'You have a follow-up appointment in two days. I'll see you then.'

'It seems dumb only to see you at the hospital.'

It did.

'I crossed a line,' he said. 'I thought I should back off.'

'Just don't cross the line again,' Jess said cheerfully. 'You make Mom mad. We have doughnuts. You want to come in and have supper?'

'Does your mother want me to?'

'Mom's got her knickers in a twist about you. She needs to get over it.'

'Well, when she gets over it, I'll join you.'

'She's being weird.'

'Then it's best we leave it,' Matt told him. 'We wouldn't want to upset your mother.'

Only he did want to upset Jess's mother. Or something. It nearly killed him to have things hanging in limbo. Each day that passed it seemed worse, like there was tension hanging over his home and his hospital.

Kelly, on the other hand, seemed remarkably unperturbed.

'She's a great doctor,' Beth told him. 'The best. Kids are brought into Emergency and she manages to get the priorities sorted and reassure everyone at the same time. Kids relax with her. We had a boy come in yesterday with concussion and a broken collar bone. He was in pain and his mother was hysterical. The kid had fallen through a roof he'd been forbidden to climb and his mum was so out of it she was saying, "I'll kill him, I'll kill him." Kelly had them sorted in minutes. "Don't you just hate it when they scare you like this?" she said to the mum. "But no killing, not yet. Let me patch him up and then he's all yours." The woman finally ended up giggling. She got the kid smiling, too. Can we keep her?'

'She's only here until her own kid gets better.'

'Then put on a heavier cast and prescribe twelve months of Australian physiotherapy. Keep her. She's good.'

He had an irrational urge to see for himself. The orthopaedic department was too far from Emergency and for the first time in years he found himself wishing he could change specialties. But he was occasionally needed there. Later that morning Beth called him to assess X-rays of a guy who'd come off a motorbike. He was about to leave when noise at the entrance caught his attention.

Paramedics had brought in a child, barely more than a toddler, and Matt saw at once what the problem was. She had her big toe stuck in a bath outlet. The pipe had been cut and she'd been brought in with the pipe still attached.

The noise was deafening. The little girl was hysterical with fear and pain. Her sobbing mother could hardly be prised away, and her father was shouting random commands at the top of his lungs. 'Elly, keep still. Get the thing off. How much longer? I thought you called yourself a hospital. I'll call the fire department, they'll be more use.'

Kelly had obviously once again been paired with Emma, and Emma was struggling to make herself heard. Kelly was struggling to get past the mother and assess the situation. She was attempting to calm the little one, while Emma was trying to hold the irate father back. 'Please, if you could leave her to us...'

The paramedics weren't helping. The situation was escalating.

Was it time for an orthopaedic surgeon to step in, even if it wasn't his patch?

'What's the child's name?' he asked the closest paramedic.

'Elly Woodman, aged two. They've all been screaming since we reached them but we need to go. We have a coronary call waiting.'

'Her parents' names?'

'Sarah and Ben Woodman. The dad's a lawyer and he's already threatening to sue. Good luck, mate.'

The paramedics left. Kelly glanced up, saw him and sent him a silent plea.

There was nothing for it. Matt took a deep breath and dived right in.

'Mr Woodman.' His deep growl cut across the commotion like a harsh blow. He aimed himself directly at the little girl's father, no one else.

'There are too many people in here,' Matt said, fixing his gaze on the young lawyer. 'We need to settle your daughter so we can give her an anaesthetic, but we need space. Therefore her mother stays and that's all. Dr Kellerman—Emma—will take you to Administration, where you can fill in admission details. Please leave.'

'But I'm supposed to be—' Emma ventured, but Matt cut her off with a placatory glance.

'I'm taking over assisting Dr Eveldene.' He laid a hand on the mother's shoulder. 'Stop crying,' he said, and it was a command, not a plea. 'You're scaring your daughter.'

'I can't...' the woman sobbed.

'Stop crying or leave with your husband. Your daughter needs you to be a sensible woman, not a watering can. Hold Elly's arm, Doctor,' he ordered Kelly, but Kelly was already moving.

Matt's commands had distracted the child enough for Kelly to take hold. She manoeuvred Elly before her mother could hug her close again. Before the little girl had time to react, Matt took her arm and held it.

They worked as a team, almost instinctively. Kelly swabbed fast while Matt held. She lifted the anaesthetic syringe from the tray and administered it. The syringe was out of sight before the child knew what had happened.

Kelly relaxed. A hysterical child was a nightmare. The thrashing had been making her foot swell even more and the metal groove of the plug was digging in deeper. The department had been stretched to the limit, there'd been no nurses available and coping with only the inexperienced Emma had been impossible.

But Matt's intervention had the situation under immediate control. The fast-acting injection of relaxant and painkiller took effect almost instantly. Already the little girl was slumping back in her mother's arms.

Emma had successfully steered the lawyer dad away. There was now only the four of them, and as Elly stopped struggling, her mother relaxed.

'I'm...I'm sorry,' she whispered.

'There's no need to be sorry,' Kelly told her, making her voice deliberately soothing. The time for snapping orders was over. 'But now Elly's nice and sleepy we need to move. How do you suggest we go about this, Dr Eveldene?'

'I'm thinking Elly needs a good sleep while we assess the situation. Sarah, keep cuddling Elly,' Matt told the mum. 'We'll elevate her foot to relieve the swelling but we won't do anything until she's totally relaxed. Meanwhile, we'll cover you with blankets so we can make this as cosy as possible. A bit of storytelling might be called for, all about a bear who gets his toe stuck. You can tell her all about the handsome doctor who slips it off while she's asleep.'

'Handsome?' Kelly queried.

'I like incorporating fact with fiction.' Matt grinned and the young mother gave a wobbly smile and things were suddenly okay.

More than okay.

'You're both Dr Eveldenes?' the young woman asked, looking from Kelly's lanyard to Matt's and back again. She'd relaxed now as Elly snuggled peacefully against her. 'Are you married?'

'Um…no,' said Kelly.

'They just live together.' Beth had come in behind them, obviously wanting to check that things were okay. 'They share a house and a name. They have a kid and two dogs so I don't know why they don't just get married and be done with it.'

Whew.

Despite his shock, Matt understood why Beth had said it. Beth had been in the next cubicle, coping with the guy who'd come off his motorbike. She'd have heard what was happening but not been able to help. Now she was adding her bit, distracting the mother still further. 'There's a spare bed in cubicle five,' she told the young mum. 'It's the quietest. You snuggle down with your little one while these two discuss marriage. There. All problems solved. I do like a happy ending, don't you?'

And she beamed and chuckled and headed off to cope with the next crisis.

Once Elly was deeply asleep things were straightforward.

Elevation and lubrication didn't work but Plan B succeeded. They wound a fine, strong thread down the length of the tiny toe, over and over, with each round of thread placed hard by the next so the toe was enclosed and compressed. Then Kelly managed to manoeuvre an end through the ring. Then they lubricated the thread and gradually started unwinding, using the thread to push the metal forward as they went.

To everyone's relief the toe gradually worked free. Matt gave a grunt of satisfaction—cutting the metal would have been much harder. The thing was done.

Matt patted the kid's head, said his goodbyes and headed back to his work.

It was after her knock-off time. Kelly was free to go.

But not quite. Jess's physio session was running late. The therapist glanced up as Kelly arrived, and waved her away.

'We need an extra half an hour, Dr Eveldene. Jess is doing great.'

Jess was struggling, Kelly could see that, and it was hurting. He was balancing between two standing bars, trying to bear weight.

Kelly knew her son well enough to understand that he wouldn't want her to watch. She waved and left them to it, then headed up to the rooftop cafeteria. She bought a sandwich and headed outdoors to eat it—and Matt was there.

The rooftop was deserted. There was Matt and one table. There were a dozen more tables to choose from.

Don't be pathetic, she told herself, and sat at his.

'If you're about to talk about what sort of flowers you want our bridesmaids to carry, I'm out of here,' Matt said, and she stared at him and then, to her surprise, found herself chuckling.

'Well, it did work,' she conceded. 'It made Sarah focus on gossip instead of what a bad mother she was for letting Elly get her toe stuck. The only problem is it was overheard by half the emergency staff and rumours have probably reached London by now.'

'You need to stop wearing a wedding ring.'

She looked down at the slim band of gold on her finger, very slim, the cheapest wedding ring they had been able to find all those years ago.

'No.'

'You've been faithful to him all these years?'

'You know I haven't,' she said evenly. 'But I still love him.'

'So do I.'

'I think,' she said quietly, hearing his pain, 'that your loss must have been as great or even greater than mine. I was able to mourn him. I was surrounded by people who loved him. More, I've always been able to talk of him with pride, whereas you...'

'I was proud of him.'

Deep breath. 'If you were proud of him you wouldn't be talking to your nephew about wasting his life surfing.'

'I only suggested—'

'It's not your place to suggest.'

'Kelly, he'll have nothing,' he exploded. 'Heaven knows whether he can get that leg strong enough to go back to competitive surfing but even if he can, there'll be more accidents, there'll be the natural aging of his body, there'll be life. How can he possibly earn enough to buy himself a decent home, a decent future.'

'He's able to sort that himself,' she snapped. 'He's a smart kid and he knows what he's doing. But even so... is a decent future predicated on a house like yours?'

'Yes,' he said, sounding goaded. 'It'd be his, something he can control, a sanctuary that can't be taken away from him.'

'Lying on the surfboard at dawn is something that can't be taken away from him as well. Friends, a community, that's something, too.'

'It's not enough. You need a home.'

'We never have.'

'I don't know how you've existed.'

'We've done more than exist. We've been happy.'

'So you're condemning him to a lifetime of being a nomad?'

'Me?' She met his gaze head on. 'You think I should be dictating my son's life? As your father dictated yours?'

'He didn't.'

'I think he did,' she said evenly. 'He drove Jess away and he made you so fearful that you put your home above everything. It's not your retreat, Matt, it's your prison.'

'How can you say that?'

'This hospital is a goldfish bowl.' If he was going to make assumptions about her son, she could throw a few home truths back. 'Everyone talks about everyone. They say you spend more time with your house and your dogs than with your friends—that you don't get close. They say your marriage didn't last because you held yourself aloof. You have a reputation for being a loner, for helping others but never asking for help yourself. You care for your patients but you care for solitude above all else.'

'Is that what everyone says?'

'Yes,' she said evenly. 'And I reject your life plan. My son is a lovely social kid who cares about the world. He's surrounded by his friends. Even though he's a long way away, he has people Skyping him on the computer at all hours. He's not depressed, like his father. He's not

obsessed with possessions, like his uncle. Do you think
he'd be desolated if he was living in that dreary little
apartment I found first? As long as we'd got rid of the
bugs he'd hardly notice.'

'He loves my home.'

'Yes, but if you asked him to choose home or his
friends, it'd be his friends in a heartbeat. That's how
I've raised him, and I'm proud of the man he's turning
into. He's healthy and he's happy and I won't have you
judging him.'

'We're worlds apart on this one.'

'Yes, we are,' she said, and somehow she managed to keep her voice even, she managed to keep her
twisted heart under some sort of control. She'd held
this man in her arms. For a short time she'd thought…
she'd thought…

Well, enough of thinking. She needed to act on evidence, not emotion.

'We are worlds apart,' she told him sadly. 'I guess it
doesn't matter, though. We've lived in separate worlds
all our lives. As soon as Jess is better we'll do so again.
But, please, until then keep your judgement under control. I'd love Jess to know he has an uncle; a link with
the father he never knew. If you can figure some way
to relate to him without your prejudices getting in the
way, it'd be great, but don't interfere. I won't risk him
ending up like you or his father. As for you and me…
what was between us must have been only that. Temptation. Sex. A stupid rush of blood to the head. So now
we put it aside. I need to keep Jess safe and if I'm to do
that, you and I don't take what's between us any further.'

Did she think he was a danger to Jess? Did she think
he could pressure the kid into illness? The thought left
him cold.

'What's between you and Mom?' Jess asked him. It was a Sunday. He was out on the veranda, watching Kelly walking down on the beach, when Jess thumped his way out to talk to him.

'What do you mean?'

'I mean every time you're near she puts on this weird smiley face and takes the first excuse to escape. I know things have been non-existent between Dad's family since I was born but now Mom's acting as if you're a threat.'

'I can't see that I'm a threat.'

'You did threaten to send me back to school. I'm over that, but Mom still seems scared.'

Scared... Over and over the word echoed.

Eighteen years ago he'd blamed himself when his brother had died. He hadn't done enough.

He should step back now.

'Maybe it's my family,' he offered. 'Your grandfather's a powerful man. He likes control. If he knew you existed he'd want some sort of control.'

'He doesn't control you.'

'It's taken a lot to get away from him.'

'He wouldn't control us, and I don't think Mom's scared of him. I think she's scared of you.'

'She has no reason to be.'

'That's what I told her,' Jess said. 'But, still, whenever you're near she sort of freezes. I don't understand.'

'Neither do I.'

'Then talk to her about it,' Jess said, irritated. 'It's messing with my serenity.'

'Your serenity?' Matt said, startled, and the boy grinned.

'She's cool, my mom,' he said. 'But she's supposed

to worry about me, not the other way round. I'd appreciate it if you could fix it.'

He headed back to his video games, leaving Matt to his thoughts.

Fix it. How was he supposed to do that? A chasm seemed to have opened up between them that he didn't have a clue how to cross. Okay, he understood her fears, but how could she not see how important a home, a base, was? Jess was at risk of ending up with nothing.

Matt's career and his home had given him power over his father. For Jess not to have that same power seemed appalling. Kelly was scared, but there was more than one path to disaster.

This was a deep divide and it meant he couldn't do what Jess wanted. It was messing with Jess's serenity, but it was also doing more. It was causing a man and woman to stand apart.

Maybe it was just as well. He'd had one failed marriage and he still didn't fully understand the cause. Maybe he was meant to be a loner. He had his dogs and his home and his career. What more could a man want?

A woman like Kelly?

No.

He went to work, he came home and he avoided Kelly. She was always on the edge of his consciousness but he'd made a decision.

He'd been a loner for ever and it couldn't stop now.

If it wasn't for Matt Eveldene she might even be enjoying this forced pause in her life, this time dictated by Jess's accident. Her days were full. Every morning she dropped Jess at the hospital rehab unit. He spent the next few hours working with the physios, exercising to keep his muscles from wasting and making friends in the process. Jess enjoyed his mornings and so did she. Her work in Emergency was varied. She was often run off her feet. She felt useful, the staff were friendly, and it was only Matt's occasional presence that caused her unease.

She didn't know how to handle the way he made her feel. When he walked into the ward it was like she had brain freeze. She had no idea why he made her feel like that, but he did and she didn't like it.

She liked the afternoons, when she took Jess home, when they had the house and the beach to themselves and she knew Matt was at work and wouldn't disturb their peace. Jess mostly snoozed and played computer games. She swam and read and felt…like she was home?

It was a great place, she conceded. It was indeed a lovely home. But for Matt to say it was all-important… For Matt to pressure Jess because he might not be able to afford a home like this… It clearly showed the gulf between them—the gulf that had killed Matt's brother?

Things weren't important. Her attitude to Matt was right. She tried to tell herself that. His house—his *home*—was amazing, but it couldn't be put above all else.

Forget it.

But she couldn't relax. Her body didn't know how to. As soon as Matt returned she retreated to her side of the house. He was her landlord; anything else was too threatening.

Until the day of the suicide.

Mid-morning. Friday. Outside the day was gorgeous. 'I hate not being able to surf,' Jess had grumbled as she'd driven them both to the hospital, and she'd agreed.

Today was a perfect day to be outside. A perfect day to live.

But for the boy who was wheeled into Emergency at six minutes past ten the day must have seemed anything but perfect. The ligature marks on his neck were raw and appalling. The paramedics were still working frantically as they wheeled him in, but Kelly took one look and knew they were too late.

Beth did the initial assessment and Kelly, standing behind her, ready to move into resuscitation mode the moment Beth said the word, was relieved that it was Beth who had to shake her head, Beth who had to remove the cardiac patches, close her eyes briefly and say, 'I'm so sorry, guys, but we've lost this one. Thank you for trying.'

The police arrived.

And Matt.

She briefly remembered that Beth had called Matt down to see to an elderly patient's hip fracture. He stood at the inner door to Emergency and took the scene in at a glance. They were wheeling the kid into a private cubicle but everyone still seemed paralysed with horror.

A middle-aged couple came through the outer entrance. They stopped and stood still, as if terrified to enter. The boy's parents? The man was in work overalls and heavy boots, clothes that said he was a builder or similar. The woman was all in white, dressed for lawn bowls. They were holding each other for support but not giving it to each other. They looked bewildered, shocked to the point of collapse.

Kelly took a deep, fast breath. She glanced through to Beth, knew she was caught up with the police, and knew the job of caring for the parents fell to her. She walked towards them, signalling to a nurse to help.

The nurse stepped forward but then stopped, put her hand to her mouth and shook her head wildly. She retreated fast.

Vomiting was what Kelly felt like doing. The angle of the boy's neck...the horror of that ligature...

He was, what? Twenty maybe? Young enough to be the nurse's brother.

Or husband?

Hold it together, she told herself harshly. You're no use if you can't keep emotion in check. If you can't suppress history flooding back.

The older of the paramedics was still there, grim faced and silent. She took his clipboard and searched for what she needed.

Toby Ryan. Aged nineteen. Found by the surf-club manager in the club storeroom half an hour ago.

'Positive ID?' she asked, and the paramedic nodded.

'The surf-club manager knows him. Seems he's been a club member since he was a nipper.'

There was no question, then. She knew what she had to do. She turned back to face the parents.

'Mr and Mrs Ryan?'

It was the woman who found the strength to nod.

'Y-yes.'

What had they been told?

Assume nothing.

'Toby's your son?'

'Yes.' The woman closed her eyes and put her hand up as if to ward off what was coming.

'Come through where we can be private,' she said gently.

They already knew. Someone must have phoned them; someone from the surf club? The woman's legs were giving way under her.

Kelly moved to catch her before she sagged, but Matt was there before her, catching her under the arm, holding her upright.

'I have her,' he said. 'You help Mr Ryan. This way, sir.'

Together they led them into the counselling room, set up for just this purpose. It held a settee and two big armchairs and a maxi box of tissues. The woman slumped onto the settee, stared at the tissues and moaned. Her husband sat beside her, clasped his hands and stared at the floor.

'I knew it'd come to this,' he whispered. 'We've been dreading this day. Was it…was it quick?'

'Yes,' Kelly said, thinking of the snapped vertebrae. 'Almost instant.'

'Did a good job, then,' the man said heavily.

'Sir…' Matt said, but the man glared at him as if he was the enemy.

'Call me Doug,' he snapped. 'And Lizzie. We're Toby's Mum and Dad. There's no "sir" about it. No bloody formality today. No bureaucrats. No one helped our Toby. No one could.'

'We knew it was coming.' Lizzie was talking to herself. She was a dumpy little woman in crisp bowling whites, and the life seemed to have been sucked out of her. It was as if a ghost was talking.

'He was born with it, we reckon,' she whispered. 'The black dog. It wouldn't let up. Wherever he went, whatever he did, it kept coming back. Black, black, black. We couldn't help him. His sisters, his brother, all our family. We love him so much. We love him and love him and we can't help. We don't know what to do.'

Her segue into the present tense, where her son was still alive, where problems were still here, still now, seemed to catch her, and for Kelly it was too much.

Professional detachment be damned. She was down on her knees, gathering the woman into her arms and hugging her close.

'There's nothing more you can do except keep on loving him,' she whispered, as she held and the woman sobbed and the man beside her groaned his anguish. 'You've done everything you could and Toby knows that. You love him and that's all that counts. The disease has killed him, but that's what it was, a disease. It's tearing your heart out, but what stays is your love for your son. You did everything you could. You couldn't defeat it but no matter what's happened, Toby's love will stay with you for ever.'

Matt had an afternoon of consultation booked but he cancelled. His secretary took one look at his face and didn't ask questions. Kelly finished at one, and he was in the car park, waiting for her. Jess was already in the car.

'Disaster of a morning,' he'd told Jess. 'A kid of your father's age when he died was brought in. Suicide. And your mother had to deal with it. We're taking her home. We'll come back later and pick up the Jeep.'

'Mom's tough,' Jess said. 'Stuff doesn't upset her much.'

Yeah? Matt saw his Kelly's face as she emerged from Emergency and he knew Jess was wrong. A cameraman and a reporter were waiting at the door. Toby had been a surf coach, popular and involved in the community. His death would hit the local news. The camera flashed, the reporter pressed forward but she extricated herself, fast.

She was some woman.

'Kelly?' He headed toward her, ignoring the media. She glanced up and saw him and her face relaxed a little.

'I need to fetch Jess.'

'We're both here,' Matt said gently. 'We're taking you home.'

'There's no need.'

'There's every need.'

'Hey, Mom,' Jess said, as she reached the car.

Her face crumpled then. She'd been keeping up a front, he saw. She'd probably been planning to keep on the same coping face she'd used for her son for years, but Jess's concern had slipped behind her defences.

She reached out and hugged him and Jess let himself be hugged.

Then she had herself together, hauling back, swiping her face and giving a shame-faced smile.

'It's okay. It's just…'

'Matt says a guy died just like Dad.'

'I… Yes.'

'I can't imagine how you must feel,' Jess said, and Matt looked at Jess and thought this kid was seventeen but suddenly he sounded like a man.

He wanted to hug them both. A lot.

He couldn't. He was on the outside, looking in.

'I'm playing chauffeur,' he asserted. 'The crutches get to ride up front with me. You guys travel in the back.'

'I can drive,' Kelly said. 'I don't need—'

'You do need,' he said harshly. 'You've needed for eighteen years and I've done nothing. Get in the car, Kelly, and let me help.'

She did. He drove them home, the back way, not past the surf club, where police cars would still be clustered, but through the hills behind town. Jess set up a stream of small talk in the back seat, though actually it wasn't small talk, it was all about his rehabilitation, about what

Patsy, the rehab physician, had told him, about how the strengthening exercises were going and what he could reasonably hope for as he healed. Getting such information from a teenager was normally like pulling teeth, so Kelly was forced to listen, forced to respond, and Matt saw a tinge of colour return to her face.

He gave Jess a thumbs-up via the rear-view mirror, and Jess gave him a return man-to-man nod and went right on distracting his mother.

He was a kid to be proud of, Matt thought. A son to be proud of?

And right there, right then, he realised how much he loved the pair of them. What was he on about, pushing the kid to do what he thought was important? He watched the pair of them and he thought they knew what was important. If they wanted to surf every day of their lives, who was he to judge? Whatever they did, it was okay by him.

And more. Whatever they did, he wanted to join them.

But now wasn't the time for declarations. Now was simply the time for being in the background, giving them space, but he glanced back and saw the way Jess held his mother's hand, saw the way she tried to smile at him, saw the deep concern in the kid's eyes for his mom and he thought...

He thought for the first time in his life, he desperately wanted to share.

CHAPTER TEN

SHE SPENT THE afternoon trying to work things out in her own mind. Matt was nowhere to be seen. She made Jess hamburgers for tea, and then, as he settled in with Matt's dogs and his computer games, she gave him a hug and made her decision.

'I need to go talk to Matt.'

'Of course you do,' Jess said, not taking his eyes from his game. 'He's shattered, too.'

'You think?'

'Yeah,' Jess said. 'When he came to get me in physio he looked like he'd been wiped out and held under for ten minutes. Well, maybe not ten,' he corrected himself, 'but three. Time enough to see his life rolling before his eyes.'

'What do you know about life rolling before your eyes?' Kelly demanded, startled, and Jess grinned.

'Hey, I've lived through a Very Bad Accident. When I felt that board crack against me I thought of all the levels of *Major Mayhem* I had yet to play. It was a sobering experience.'

She gave him a pretend slap to the side of the head and chuckled.

'So you don't mind if I go and see Matt now?'

'Stay the night,' Jess offered. 'I'm a big boy now.'

'Jess!'

'Seriously, Mom,' Jess said, and finally he turned away from his computer game. 'Matt's great and he cares. Don't let me—or Dad—get in the way of something beautiful.'

'Beautiful?' she choked.

He grinned. 'Heart and flowers and violins. Yuck.' But then he sobered. 'Or just real good friends. Go for it, Mom. Think of yourself for once.'

Right.

It was a discombobulating little speech, and she was still feeling discombobulated when she headed out onto the veranda.

Matt was sitting on the settee, holding a beer, staring out at the moonlight.

'Pa Kettle,' she said cautiously. 'You need to make that settee a rocker.'

'I need my dogs,' he said. 'Traitors.'

'Jess has popcorn. No contest.'

He grinned and went to rise.

'Don't get up.' She perched beside him. 'I need to talk.'

'So do I.'

'Me first,' she said, and then she paused because all of a sudden it seemed hard. Matt watched her in the moonlight, then left her and came back with a glass of wine. She took it and swirled it in his gorgeous crystal glass and thought of all the chipped and cracked kitchenware she and Jess had used over the years. And then she thought, it didn't matter. It didn't matter one bit.

People were what was important. This man was important.

Up until now her hurt had all been about herself and her son. Somehow today had made her see that long-ago devastating scene in the funeral parlour in a different light. It made sense of the tie Matt had with things rather than people and it had exposed the knot of hurt and pain this man had carried for years.

Today she'd looked at the shattered parents and she'd known that she couldn't protect Jess, any more than Matt could have protected his brother.

'You know it wasn't your fault,' she said into the stillness, and the words seemed to freeze and hang. 'What happened to Jess... Today I looked at Toby and I saw a kid who had everything. Loving parents. Sisters and brother who adored him. After you left Toby's sister came in and she talked and talked, and I had time to let her. Toby was loved. Whatever he did was fine by them. He had his beloved surf club. He had his whole community behind him, but the depression, the illness wouldn't let go. His family knew this was coming, she said. It was like watching a slow train coming toward them and not being able to get off the track. Doctors, treatments, everything that could be done was done. And yet the depression won.'

'Kelly—'

'No, let me say it,' she said. 'I've been angry. I lost my Jess and then you came and you were the embodiment of all the things I thought had caused Jess to die. Jess used to talk about your house, the Eveldene mansion. He used to talk about all the things he had, all the things your family valued, as if they were the cause. So when you came, I hated you and I hated what you represented. I swore my Jess would never learn your values. Then...what happened between us...somehow it felt like a betrayal, and what you said to Jess made it worse.

'But today, maybe for the first time, I figured out how unfair my anger was. Your suggestion that Jess study was just a suggestion. It was nothing to make a big deal over. And as for eighteen years ago… You were a kid yourself. You were doing what your father should have done, but even that's immaterial. What matters is that today I let go of my anger. Eighteen years and it's finally gone.'

'One kid's death…' he said slowly, but she shook her head.

'No. It's lots of things. How the hospital staff react to you. Your kindness toward your patients. The fact that you care. The way you've treated Jess, and then stepped back when you realised you'd hurt him. And this afternoon I finally figured it out. You've been hurting as much as I have. It's a no-brainer yet finally I've seen it. You loved Jess. You lost him and now you hold on to things instead. Like this house. This place. Your career. Tangible things are important but it's not because you're impersonal. It's anything but. It's because once upon a time you saw your brother on a slab in a mortuary and part of you died.'

And something within him twisted, so hard it was as if things were ripping apart. The pain of the last eighteen years. The way he'd reacted to this woman the first time he'd seen her, with such unforgivable anger. The aching helplessness of knowing his big brother had been self-destructing and there hadn't been a thing he could do about it.

Something changed.

He stood abruptly, knocking the beer at his feet so it spilled its contents. Who cared? He didn't. Where to go from here? So many emotions, coalescing in one morning's tragedy. In one woman's words.

'Kelly, maybe that was what I was going to tell you,'

he managed. He was trying to figure it for himself. How to put it into words.

'I did blame myself,' he said. 'I was four years younger than Jess and I ached for him, but every time I tried to do anything I had to retreat. My dad reacted with anger, but Jess himself retreated. I ached because he asked me to come to Hawaii when I finished school. He sent me the plane fare. But I was eighteen. I thought he was on drugs. My father was apoplectic when I even suggested it. It was too hard and I've hated myself for ever because I didn't have the courage to stand up to my father. But today I saw that it wouldn't have made one bit of difference. Nothing I said or did...'

'Nor me,' Kelly said, and she stood beside him and slipped her hand in his. 'We both loved him and somehow we ended up hating each other because of his death. It was dumb. We both ended up rejecting...something that's important.'

He turned to her then, taking her hands so they were locked together in the moonlight.

'You mean...important as making a go of...us?'

'We could give it a try,' she said softly. She ventured a faint smile. 'I might learn to love this house as well.'

'It's a great house.'

Her smile faded. 'Matt...'

'I didn't mean,' he said, 'that this house is as important as people. I didn't mean this house is as important as you.'

'Or happiness?'

'Or happiness.'

'We need to take things slowly.' She bit her lip, looking up at him in the moonlight as if she was trying to read his mind. 'And, Matt...despite what I just said I won't have you lecturing Jess. You need to respect that he's his own person.'

'I will respect that.'

'The truth's in the doing,' she said with a touch of asperity. 'But you're stuck with us for another few weeks. If you let us hang around, I'll see what you're made of.'

'And I'll see what I'm made of, too.'

'No judging?'

'Just loving.'

'It seems,' she said uncertainly, 'that loving's the given. It's fitting everything else in that's the problem.'

'You mean you might love me?'

'I think I might,' she said with all seriousness, and then she gasped as he tugged her close. 'Matt, we have all sorts of stuff we need to work out first.'

'We will work it out. Give us time.' But he spoke thickly because his face was in her hair. He was kissing her, tugging her tightly into him. 'We'll sort it.'

'Matt…' She still sounded worried.

'Let the past go,' he told her, sure of himself now, holding his woman in his arms and knowing nothing else was important. 'There's just us.'

'And Jess and our careers and your dogs and your house…'

'Kelly?'

'Mmm?'

'Is Jess likely to disapprove if I pick you up, cart you to my lair and have my wicked way with you?'

'Jess practically ordered me to submit,' she said. 'And he's just reached the next level in his game. Who's noticing?'

'I'm noticing,' he said, as he swung her into his arms and kissed her, a long, deep kiss that held all the promise of life to come. 'I'm noticing a lot,' he said, as he pushed the door open with his foot. 'I'm noticing and noticing and noticing. But, Dr Kelly Eveldene, all I'm noticing is you.'

'So are we happy-ever-aftering?'

It was the morning after the night before. Kelly was making pancakes on her side of the beige door. She was demurely dressed in her respectable bathrobe. She'd showered, she'd brushed her hair and she was trying hard to look like nothing had changed. She was a mom looking after her kid.

She was different.

'What?' She plated two pancakes for her son. 'What do you mean?'

'I mean you look like the cat that got the canary. Smug R Us. Does Matt look the same?'

'I… He might.' She tried to fight it but she could feel herself blushing from the toes up.

'Excellent,' Jess said. 'He's cool.'

'Didn't he tell you to go back to school?'

'Yeah, but it was only past history that made me react,' he said. 'The way you told me Grandpa treated Dad. I've thought about it. Judging someone because of what happened years ago might be dumb. If we tell him about my—'

'Jess, don't tell him yet,' she said, suddenly urgent.

'Why not?'

'Because if we're to have some sort of future together I want him wanting us, warts and all.'

'Then push him further. You could give up medicine and come surfing. The way he's looking, he might even come, too. I shouldn't say this about my own mother, but you're still hot. He's tempted. Anyone can see it, and you're tempted right back. There's waves of temptation all over the place. Why resist, people? Go for it.'

'Oh, Jess.' Where had this funny, wise, grown-up kid come from?

'So what are you going to do about it?' Jess demanded.

'Maybe I could invite him in for pancakes,' she conceded.

'Why not?' Jess said amiably. 'But don't stop there. Why not knock a hole in the wall and be done with it?'

He had everything he wanted, here, now. Kelly was living in his house. She was part of his life. It was like he'd been missing a part of himself and the part had fitted back together, making him complete.

'Jess says I look like the cat that got the canary,' she told him, lying in his arms on Sunday morning. 'I think you do, too.'

'You're an extraordinarily beautiful canary.'

'I'm a happy canary,' she said, and snuggled down against him. 'Did you know you have the most beautiful body I've ever seen? They should freeze you and use you in anatomy lessons. Perfect male specimen. Plastic surgeons, eat your hearts out.'

'They can have me in fifty years.'

'Okay,' she said. 'I expect you'll still be perfect in fifty years. Goodness, though, think of all the things we'll have done in the interim. You might have a few life scars.'

'We both might,' he said, tugging her closer still. 'But they can't make you less than beautiful. They'll be shared scars.'

'I want to visit the Amazon,' she said, running her

fingers down his chest in a way that made his whole
body feel alive. 'You want to risk a few mosquito bites?'

'The Amazon?'

'One day. It's just...single mom, medicine, there's
never been time or money for anything else. You want
a few adventures with me?'

'I'm pretty happy where I am, right now,' he said,
and she drew away slightly.

'That sounds like the man who loves his house.'

'I'll take you to the Amazon.'

'You'll want to come to the Amazon? It's different.'

'I guess it is.'

'Matt...'

'Mmm?'

'Will we be all right?'

'We'll be all right,' he said, and kissed her and knew
he'd do whatever it took to keep this woman in his arms.

For ever.

They loved, they slept, things were perfect, but there
was this niggle. This faint unease.

She was slotting into his perfect life. Jess had suggested she throw in medicine and go surfing to test him,
but he didn't need testing.

He was her gorgeous Matt, and she'd love him for
ever. She'd do whatever it took.

Would he?

It was a tiny niggle. She should put it aside. It was
nothing, not when he held her, not when he loved her,
not when his loving swept all aside in its wonder.

And then his parents came.

It was late Sunday morning. They'd surfed, dressed,
breakfasted, and were sitting on the veranda, feeling
smug.

'We need two rockers,' Kelly said, pushing away that

stupid, worrying niggle. 'It's not just Pa Kettle. It's Ma and Pa and the whole domestic set-up.'

'Sounds pretty perfect,' Matt said, but then the helicopter hovered into view, and to their mutual astonishment it came down to land on their beach.

'What the…?' Matt said, and rose and stared down the cliff track. And then he swore. 'Dad!'

Dad. Henry Eveldene.

Kelly was wearing shorts, T-shirt and bare feet. Her hair was still damp from their swim.

She wanted to be in hospital whites, she thought. She wanted to be professional, in charge of her world, in a position to face this man on her own terms.

But this was her own terms, she told herself. It had to be.

Jess had limped out of the house with the dogs to see what was happening. She reached behind her and grabbed his hand.

This wasn't threatening, she told herself. This was an elderly couple. How scary could they be?

The woman didn't look scary. She was tiny, seemingly frail, dressed in a plain blue skirt and white shirt, with pearls around her neck, and her white hair caught up into a soft bun with curls escaping. This must be Rose, Jess's mother.

Henry was almost her polar opposite, stout and business-suited. Bald, red faced and already looking angry, he was striding up the path to the house as if he was wielding a battering ram. Rose was struggling behind.

Matt strode down to meet them, heading straight past his father to gather his mother into a hug. 'Mum!'

'Matt,' Rose whispered, and put a hand to his hair as

if assuring herself he was real. But she was ignored by her husband. Henry was obviously here on a mission.

'Who the hell is she?' Henry demanded, booming loudly enough to be heard on the next beach. He shaded his eyes and stared up at the house at Kelly. 'Is that her?'

'Is that who?'

'Kelly Eveldene.' He hauled a newspaper clipping from his breast pocket and waved it angrily at Matt. 'You know I have shares in half the country's local papers and I have a notify order if the name Eveldene ever comes up. Dr Kelly Eveldene was named as treating doctor for a kid who suicided. Based in the hospital you're working at. I called the hospital. It took three calls and a bribe and then I found out she was living with you. With you!' He stared up at the veranda again, at Kelly.

And then he saw the boy beside her.

'Jess.'

The word came out as a strangled gasp but it wasn't from Henry. It was from Rose.

Kelly had seen this woman's picture. It had been in Jess's wallet when he'd died. Sometimes she still looked at it, and Rose's face still smiled out.

Rose wasn't smiling now. Her face was bleached white. 'Jess,' she said again, and possibly she would have crumpled if Matt wasn't holding her.

'Mum,' Matt said, and the way he said it was like a caress. 'I was wondering when this should happen, and I'm so glad it finally has. Mum, this is Jessie's son. He's called Jessie, too, and he's your grandson. And this is Kelly. Kelly was Jessie's wife. They're family.'

And he said 'family' so strongly, so surely, that Kelly's world settled. It was an all-encompassing statement, a word that included her for ever.

But it seemed that Henry Eveldene didn't think so. His breath drew in in a hiss of shock and fury. 'What nonsense is this?'

'It's not nonsense,' Matt said evenly. 'Jess married Kelly eighteen years ago. You knew that, Dad.'

'My Jess…married?' Rose gasped, and Matt's grip on her tightened.

'Dad made a decision not to tell you,' Matt said. 'He thought you were shocked enough. It was the wrong decision. We made a lot of wrong decisions back then.'

'Jess's son…' She sounded dazed beyond belief.

'Hey, Grandma.' Jess was a typical teenager, ignoring undercurrents, listening to everything with his typical insouciance. 'I've always wanted a grandma. Cool. And…Grandpa?'

'I am not your grandfather.' It was a roar of rage that made even Jess blink. 'If you're after money…'

'What are you on about?' Jess asked, astounded, and Rose gave a moan of pain.

'No one's after money,' Matt snapped.

'I paid you off,' Henry roared, directing his fury straight at Kelly. 'You cashed that cheque and the deal was that you kept out of our lives for ever.'

'But Jess's insurance policy belonged to his wife.' Still Matt spoke evenly, and Kelly recognised that he'd faced down his father's fury before. Matt went on, his voice stern. 'That money belonged to Kelly, no matter what we decided. We had no right to claim otherwise. We had no right to put conditions on it.'

But Henry wasn't listening. He couldn't hear past his fury. 'So now you've come crawling back, wanting more—'

'That's enough, Dad,' Matt snapped. 'Kelly and Jess want nothing.'

'You're giving them a place to stay.'

'Yes, but—'

'And what does the boy do? Nothing, like his father?'

'He surfs,' Matt said through gritted teeth.

And Kelly thought she should say something and then she thought, No. She could walk away. This fury was between Matt and his father.

'Surfs…' The word came out like the worst of oaths.

'Dad, leave this. You're shocked,' Matt said. 'Don't say anything you might regret. Come up and meet them.'

'You have no right to be here,' the man snapped at Kelly.

'She has every right.'

'And you're calling yourself a doctor,' Henry spat at Kelly. 'You're not even qualified to practise in Australia. I did a fast check before I came. *Dr* Eveldene. Qualified in Hawaii. Do you intend practising in Australia? Ha! I have influence. If you think I can't get you kicked out of this country, you're dead wrong.'

'Dad, what's Kelly ever done to hurt you?' Matt demanded.

'What she's done is immaterial. I have no idea what her game is but I want no part of it. Jess married her when he was a drug-addicted nut case. The marriage should never have been allowed and we owe her nothing. Whatever story she's conned you with, it's to end. She can get out of this country, now.'

But there was another player in this drama. Rose. The elderly woman's eyes hadn't left Jess.

'Henry, stop yelling,' she said, in a strange, wandering voice that somehow cut across her husband's anger. 'Matt, you're saying Jess had a son?'

'This is nothing to do with us,' Henry snapped.

'But it has!' Rose was stumbling over her words. 'Of course it has. My son had a son? Oh, Matt, why didn't you tell us?'

'I didn't know,' Matt said.

'But you knew about Kelly?'

'I... Yes.'

'But you didn't tell us about her either.'

'Dad knew. He thought the truth would break your heart.'

'But my heart had already broken,' Rose whispered. 'When Jess died.'

And Kelly's heart twisted, just like that. Anger was forgotten. No matter what had gone before, this was a woman who'd lost her son.

'Your Jess carried your photograph in his wallet for all the time I knew him,' she said, speaking directly to Rose and ignoring the crimson-faced bully beside her. 'He had it with him when he died. He spoke of you often, with love. I honoured your husband's wishes not to contact you but now it's happened, I'm glad.' She gripped Jess's hand. 'This is your grandson. No matter what's gone on before, surely that's all that matters.'

'It is,' Matt said strongly. 'Dad, our family has treated Kelly appallingly. It's time for it to stop.'

But Henry Eveldene wasn't done. He'd obviously had twenty-four hours knowing who Kelly must be. Twenty-four hours to work himself into a rage. It'd be part guilt induced, Kelly thought, trying hard to be compassionate. He'd rejected his son. To now embrace his son's wife and his grandson would be acknowledging something that was possibly unbearable.

'There's not one reason for it to stop,' he snapped.

'There's a hundred reasons,' Matt snapped back.

'And not one reason why it has to continue. What is it, Dad? Why can't you accept Jess's family?'

'Jess has no family.' The words were a blast that rang over the cliffs and out to the sea beyond. Down on the beach the helicopter pilot stood by his machine, waiting.

Kelly thought idly, I wonder what he thinks of this family reunion?

Not much, probably. After all, it wasn't much of a family.

'You've broken your pledge. I'll drum you out of the country,' Henry snarled.

But still Kelly was calm. How much self-hatred must lie behind his bluster? She was feeling weird, almost analytical. This man had no power to hurt her.

But Rose... She looked at the elderly woman's distressed face and she thought she couldn't distress her further.

'You won't need to drum me out of the country,' she said. 'We're only here because my Jess broke his leg, surfing.'

'Surfing...' Henry spat, as if the word was foul.

'Surfing,' Kelly continued, cutting over his rage. 'We're stuck here for another few weeks. Matt has been kind and we'll always be grateful, but we acknowledge how you feel. I don't want Jess to have any part of your anger. We'll leave as soon as he's healed, and we won't come back.'

'Kelly...' Matt released his mother, and in a few long strides he was on the veranda. 'No!'

'I want no part of this.'

'Yeah, we don't have to cop this,' Jessie said.

'Leave it, Matt,' Kelly said. 'We want no part of a family feud.'

'It's bullshit,' Jess said.

And Matt stood beside these two who had come to mean so much to him, he looked down at his parents, and he thought that's exactly what this was. Bullshit. He might not have used the teenager's expression but right now it seemed to fit.

But there was no way he could stop this viciousness. His father was powerful. He had contacts in every media outlet in the land. If there was anything in Kelly's past to be dragged up, he'd find it.

Kelly had spent her childhood in a strange, unconventional environment. There'd be things his father could use and he would use them. He'd twist them, he'd spit them out in any form that suited him. He could do real damage.

And he looked again at Kelly, at the tilt of her chin, at her defiance, and he thought of all the other ogres she'd had to face beside his father. He'd been one of them.

No more, he thought, right there and then. This woman was no longer alone. His father was attacking her and it was personal. She was family.

She was his family.

His love.

'If Kelly goes, I go,' he said, into the sun-washed day, and the world seemed to pause at his words. 'I'll leave the country to be with her.'

Kelly gasped. She opened her mouth to speak and nothing came out.

Nothing, nothing and nothing.

Inevitably, it Jess who was first to recover. He had teenage resilience. Teenage enthusiasm.

'You want to come back to Hawaii with us? Cool.' Ignoring the tension around them, he launched himself straight into the future. 'I can show you the best surf spots. The Pipeline's awesome but there are even better places. Matt, it'll be great.'

But Kelly was staring at him as if he'd slapped her.

'You can't…you can't be serious?'

But he looked into her eyes and he'd never been so serious in his life. Everything else faded but his need to say it like it was.

By his side, Bess and Spike were standing very still, as if they, too, knew this moment was life-changing. What were the requirements for taking dogs abroad? He'd need to find out. No matter, that was detail. What mattered now was taking that look of disbelief from Kelly's face.

He fought for the right words and he found them, maybe not word perfect but close enough. He said them now, with all the love that shone through the centuries since the vow had first been made.

'"Whither thou goest, I will go,"' he said softly. '"Thy home will be my home and thy people shall be my people."'

'Matt…' She could hardly breathe. 'Matt, you can't.'

'Why can't I?'

'This is your home.' She gestured around, to the house he'd built with such love and such pride. This house that had been so important to him but now seemed nothing compared to what he felt for this woman.

'I think…' he said softly. 'I hope that my home is you.'

'But you love this house,' she breathed.

'I love you more.'

'You can't.'

'I can't think of a single reason why I can't. I can think of a hundred reasons why I can.'

'You and your hundred reasons,' she said, her eyes

misting with tears, her voice cracked with emotion. 'I bet you can't.'

'Shall I start? Number one, you make excellent pancakes. And hamburgers. We'll forget about cakes. Two, anyone who sees you in a bathing suit will be in love in an instant. Three, your chuckle does something to my insides that leaves me breathless. Four...'

'This could get boring,' Jess said, grinning.

'Not...it's not boring,' Kelly managed. 'I like it.'

'Are you out of your mind?' The baffled roar from beneath the veranda made them all pause. Henry looked as if he was about to explode. 'What nonsense is this? This woman's leaving.'

'With me,' Matt said evenly, and then, because it seemed the right thing to do, the only thing to do, because Kelly's eyes were still confused, because their whole future seemed to hang on this moment, he did what any sane man would do.

He caught her hands and tugged her round to face him. And he dropped to one knee.

'Kelly Eveldene,' he said, strongly and surely, 'will you marry me?'

'Wow,' Jess whooped. 'Wow and wow and wow. Mom, say yes.'

'If she says yes I won't have a son,' Henry roared.

'If she says yes I'll have my own son,' Matt said evenly, his eyes not leaving Kelly's face. 'If Jess will have me.'

'Only if you increase my allowance,' Jess said, and grinned.

'Done,' Matt said grandly, and then looked a bit uneasy. 'Hang on. By how much?'

'We'll negotiate,' Jess said. 'What do they call it? A marriage settlement.'

'Have your lawyers speak to my lawyers,' Matt said, and he was smiling, but he didn't take his eyes from Kelly. 'Love?'

'You can't,' she whispered, and she knelt to join him. 'To leave everything…your career, your gorgeous house, your place in life…'

'People are what's important,' he said, knowing that finally he had it. Kelly held everything important to him, in her smile, in her courage, in her life.

A hundred reasons? There must be a thousand, he thought, and more to come. He had a lifetime of learning how to love this woman. A lifetime of being loved in return.

'Kelly, if you can…'

'You mean it?'

'More than anything else in the world.'

'Then of course I can,' she said, caught between laughter and tears. 'Oh, Matt, I love you. I love you and love you and love you. Do I need to make that a hundred times, too?'

'Three will do,' he said grandly. 'We have all the time in the world to make it up to a hundred. Or a thousand or a million or whatever comes next.'

'We're not making sense.'

'I guess we're not. But you will be my wife?'

'Yes.'

'Then that's all the sense I need. Everything else will follow.'

And finally she was being kissed, deeply, soundly, possessively, and she was kissing back with every single emotion returned in full.

How did she love this man?

For a while she'd thought it was to do with her old love, but it wasn't that. When she'd first married she'd been a child. Her husband had been her saviour and her hero. What she felt for this man was far, far different. It was an adult's love and acceptance.

This man was flawed. He'd been hurt, he'd retired to solitude, he'd built walls around himself. She thought of his failed marriage and knew that he'd probably hurt people himself.

He wouldn't now. She knew that with the same surety she knew her love for him wouldn't fail. He'd shed his armour, he'd opened himself to her, and he was hers. He was her gorgeous wounded warrior, as scarred by life as she was, but ready now to step forward. With her.

He loved her and she loved him. All the love in the world was in this kiss. The years ahead stretched gloriously and she thought, I can love, I can love, I can love.

She did love. She was being kissed until her toes curled and nothing else mattered. Nothing, nothing, nothing.

Except…there was the odd spectator or two. Two dogs, Jess, her…parents-in-law? The helicopter pilot down on the beach?

The world.

Somehow they broke apart but not far. Matt's arms still held her. They rose and she looked down at the couple below and felt sad for the pair of them.

'I'm sorry,' she whispered. 'I didn't mean this to happen.'

'Hey, but it's great.' Jess was practically bouncing. 'But I'm not being a pageboy. Think again, people.'

'But I can see you as a ring bearer in pantaloons,' Kelly said. Matt choked and Jess grabbed a cushion from the settee and tossed it at her. But there were still things to be said. Matt fielded the cushion before it reached his beloved and tossed it back. Then he turned to his parents.

'That's it,' he said, in a voice he hadn't known he possessed until now. He'd never known he could feel so sure. 'It's settled so take it or leave it. I'm sorry, Mum,' he said, gentling as he addressed his mother. 'I know this is a huge amount to toss at you in one hit, but Dad's lied to you for years.

'To my shame, I haven't told you about Kelly either. But no more lies. I loved my big brother and I lost him, as you did, but Kelly lost her husband, and her loss matched yours. She was left with a baby to care for on her own. That she's brought him here now, into my life, is a gift beyond price, and that I've fallen in love with her makes things perfect. Kelly and I are family now, and so is Jess. Mum, I still love you, but my way is with Kelly.'

Once more there was silence. But it was okay, Kelly thought, dazed beyond belief.

She wasn't sure what had just happened. She needed space. She needed to go and lock herself in her room and think it all out.

She'd quite like to take Matt to her room with her.

No. Now was not the appropriate time to jump her man. But he *was* her man. Her fiancé. Her soon-to-be husband. Soon she could jump him whenever she wanted—for the rest of her life?

The thought was so overpowering that she felt herself gasp. Matt glanced sharply at her and then he grinned. Could he read her mind? She hoped not, but she met his glinting laughter and she knew...

Happy ever after was right here by her side.

'We're leaving.' Henry's words cut across the intimacy between them. He had no way of hurting them,

Kelly thought, but then she glanced at Matt and saw him look at his mother and flinch.

Rose was losing another son.

But maybe not. Henry had grasped Rose's arm, hauling her round to march her down the cliff path, but Rose was balking. Her sensible shoes dug into the track, and when he gave her another, harder tug she wrenched away. She dug her toes in further, as if creating a wedge that would keep her here.

'I have my own money.'

'What are you talking about?' Henry demanded, making to grab her again, but she thrust him off.

'I can do this,' she said. Her faltering words were growing stronger. 'I will. Matt, if you don't mind... If I was to get a little apartment in Hawaii...would you mind if I visited?' She glanced at Jess and her longing was naked for all to see. 'Would it be possible for me to get to know my grandson?'

'What a wonderful idea,' Kelly said, before Matt could answer. Matt was so astounded that he hadn't found his voice. His mother had been a doormat for years, a downtrodden mouse. Suddenly the mouse was squeaking. More, she was laying down ultimatums.

'Don't be ridiculous,' Henry gasped. 'You wouldn't dare.'

'I would dare,' the mouse said, and turned and faced him head on. 'I would dare because Matt and Kelly and Jessie...' Her voice trembled as she said Jessie's name but she made herself continue. 'Matt and Kelly and Jess will be a family, and I want to be part of it.'

CHAPTER ELEVEN

TWO MONTHS LATER they left for Hawaii. Not, in the end, to stay, but to visit. Kelly and Jess needed to pack up their apartment and say their goodbyes, and they had another task to do, too.

They carried an urn with them. Matt stood with Jess and his mother and they watched together as Kelly scattered his brother's ashes into the sea at Diamond Head.

This was where Jess had wanted his ashes scattered. Eighteen years later, his ashes had come home.

But this was no longer home for them. They were here to say farewell to a brother, husband, son and father. They were here to let Rose take her fledgling steps as a grandma. Then they were going back to Australia. They were facing Henry's threats down.

'Four against one,' Jess had said. 'We're a family. What threats can possibly mess with us?'

There might be trouble, Matt conceded, but if it came they'd face it together. And Kelly loved his house. His home.

'Let's try,' she'd said. 'The Gold Coast is a perfect place to live. I'm sure I can get full Australian accreditation. Matt, you love it.'

'Not as much as I love you,' he'd growled, but she'd kissed him and held him and smiled.

'Then let's see if we can put it all together as a package,' she'd said. 'Our careers, your house, your dogs, our family. Us. And the university in Brisbane seems great. Jess is already excited about the courses there. It's worth a try.'

And that had been the next shaking of his foundations. His last judgement call shattered. A week after Henry had thrown them his ultimatum, Jess had woken the house with his whooping. It seemed he'd been studying for years, in Hawaii and online when he and his mother were travelling. His exam results—the International Baccalaureate— were through, and meant almost any university course in the world would now be open to him.

'But not until I've surfed for another eighteen months,' Jess told him. 'That's the deal Mum and I made. If I get decent uni entrance exams, Dad's money will fund me for two years on the international surfing tour. She thinks that's what Dad would have wanted.' He'd looked ruefully at his leg. 'I might not make it back to the top,' he conceded, 'but I'll have fun trying. And then, maybe medicine? Maybe architecture? I'm not sure yet, but I have time to plan.'

It had taken Matt's breath away. The pair of them took his breath away. Jess and Kelly. Two astonishing people.

He never ceased to be astonished. And the most astonishing thing was that Kelly loved him. Kelly wanted to be his wife.

And so it was.

Living the dream was what she was doing right now, Kelly thought as she stood by her brand-new husband's side and heard the words that sealed their union for ever.

'I now pronounce you man and wife.'

They were standing on the beach below Matt's house, but this wedding wasn't all about Matt's place in the world. Her world was here, too. They'd timed the wedding so the surfing circuit was back in town, and to her joy a bunch of surfing and doctor friends had made the trip from Hawaii.

Everyone they loved was here, Kelly thought with deep satisfaction. Everyone important.

Even Matt's ex-wife, Jenny, was here with her husband and four kids. She'd flown to the Gold Coast as soon as she'd heard Matt was engaged, and five minutes after meeting Kelly she was beaming.

'I never thought it would happen,' she told Kelly. 'I found it with my Peter but I've always felt sad for Matt. But now... He's smitten. Anyone can see the transformation. Kelly, you're a wonder woman.'

She wasn't a wonder woman, Kelly thought as she and Matt turned to face their friends, hand in hand, man and wife. She was just Kelly. Doctor. Surfer. Mother of Jess. Wife to Matt.

And one extraordinarily happy woman.

'If my chest swells any further I'll bust my tux,' Matt said, and she smiled and smiled.

'Just as well you have your swimming trunks on underneath.'

'I don't. Do you?' he asked, startled.

'Yep. A white bikini.' She spun and showed him the back of her wedding gown. The gown dipped to below her waist, exposing her beautiful bare back, plus the fine cord of a white bikini top, enticingly tied with a bow.

Their audience was cheering, but for this moment

they had eyes for only each other. Man and wife, from this day forward.

'Do you think…?' Matt said longingly, touching the bow.

'I do not think,' she said serenely. 'We have two hours' surfing in front of us and photographs, then dinner, the odd speech, then a bit of dancing. There's a hundred reasons why you can't carry me off to your lair right now.'

'There's a thousand reasons why I should.'

'You have time to tell me,' she said, and she couldn't resist. Her new husband had already kissed her, but she was kissing him again. 'You have a lifetime to tell me.'

'It's not long enough,' Matt growled, kissing her back with a passion that brought gasps and laughter from their friends and family. 'All those reasons…I need to start now.'

* * * * *

MILLS & BOON®

Why shop at millsandboon.co.uk?

Each year, thousands of romance readers
find their perfect read at millsandboon.co.uk.
That's because we're passionate about
bringing you the very best romantic fiction.
Here are some of the advantages of
shopping at www.millsandboon.co.uk:

* **Get new books first**—you'll be able to buy
  your favourite books one month before they
  hit the shops

* **Get exclusive discounts**—you'll also be
  able to buy our specially created monthly
  collections, with up to 50% off the RRP

* **Find your favourite authors**—latest news,
  interviews and new releases for all your
  favourite authors and series on our website,
  plus ideas for what to try next

* **Join in**—once you've bought your favourite
  books, don't forget to register with us to rate,
  review and join in the discussions

Visit **www.millsandboon.co.uk**
for all this and more today!

Join Britain's BIGGEST Romance Book Club

- **EXCLUSIVE** offers every month

- **FREE** delivery direct to your door

- **NEVER MISS** a title

- **EARN** Bonus Book points

Call Customer Services
0844 844 1358*

or visit
millsandboon.co.uk/subscription

RKCB2